18/92

GU01033894

HIRANA'S WAR

THE SEQUEL TO ELOIA BORN

BRITTA JENSEN

Murasaki Press · Est. 2011 · 紫

ALSO BY BRITTA JENSEN

Novels

Eloia Born

Short Stories

Three Fingers

First Noel

The Coral Ring

First published in the United States in 2020 by Murasaki Press LLC

Copyright © 2020 by Britta Jensen
Cover design by Stuart Bache

All characters and events in this publication, other than those clearly in the public domain, are fictitious and any resemblance to real persons, living or dead, is purely coincidental.

All rights reserved, including the right of reproduction in whole or in part in any form. No part of this publication may be reproduced, stored in a retrieval system, or transmitted, in any form or by any means, without the prior permission in writing of the publisher.

ISBN 978-1-7328995-5-1 (hardback)—ISBN 978-1-7328995-4-4 (paperback)—ISBN 978-1-7328995-6-8 (e-book)

First Edition—2020/Designed by Murasaki, Maps by Milo Jens, Editors: Bradley P. Wilson, Dave Aretha, and Rachel Carter with Yellowbird Editors LLC

School and bulk sales of this title may be purchased for business or promotional use. For more information e-mail murasakipress@gmail.com.

Murasaki Press LLC
PO Box 152313
Austin, TX 78715
U.S.A.

Enjoy bonus content and join the author's mailing list at www.britta-jensen.com

For my family

PROLOGUE

The water is the surface
of my drown-ed heart,
flowing where my blood cannot.
For it does not exist,
until you do return,
until you return to me.

Ai, Xele ut sobish-yara
ule mo tufan xele si'djen,
anyak voshe paar mo So'djuul.
Ai, anyak, anzeb forshaime,
na'seri ye Urajde a mo,
na'seri ye urajdu a mo.

—traditional Kardush folk tune, sung in a round

1

GULNAZ

M y one defining trait: I knew what I was before anyone else told me. This unspoken power petrified me. We weren't allowed to be afraid. Fear was supposed to have been drummed out of us by age seven. Had I been the only one terrified of being discovered?

My heart echoed in my ears before I was shaken from my cot and dumped onto the floor. The rocking motion of the ground and horrible growling couldn't be another test from our teachers. I was frozen in place, unable to move. I knew I had to, but my body was immobilized on the floor. A sickening thud, thud, thud, beat outside of me.

Think, Gulnaz.

Don't be a scared girl. Dissect what's happening, break it apart in your mind.

Was it a sea creature, or a prank from horrible housemates? It was still too dark to see. The booming was closer, underneath me, then stirring my insides. Buzzing through my skull before it stopped.

Must find Yelina. Now.

No, must wait to be calm. I'll be punished if they see me like this.

Nearby groaning was drowned out by another boom, boom, whoomppbb.

Thunder?

No. Thunder you hear but don't feel. Another blast ricocheted inside my chest, my heart speeding up, sweat pouring down my face. Bad to be alone.

Go, go go!

I clutched at Yelina, who usually slept beside me. She wasn't there. Everything was crooked. Sideways. I reached around me but only felt the stiffness of blankets and bodies gone cold. So dark. The horrible booming thudded through me again and again, a beast tearing at me.

I pushed myself off the floor, adjusting to the darkness. Narrow slits of light flickered through cracks in the ceiling.

Find the others, I reminded myself. *Keep going. Block the current of fear.*

The ground shook as I walked. *Wipe your face,* I reminded myself. *They will beat you if they see.*

I trembled, stepping over debris scattered across the floor. Slabs of stone blocked me, so I crawled through the kitchen. Another boom knocked me to the ground, and I stayed until the shaking stopped. The moment of silence gave me a second to catch my breath, to listen for others through the thudding of my heartbeat in my ears. An acrid smell wafted in.

Drash. Yelina. Find them.

I pressed forward. Someone moaned and I crawled to them, over a body that made no sound when I landed on it. The rocking started again, the pain in my chest worse as the boom, boom, whommpp reverberated there.

I am just a toy in this stone box. Must get out.

A horrible dread twisted my stomach as I tried to identify the unknown sound. Bombs?

No, we don't use bombs anymore.

Keep going.

I skirted the rubble, dust floating down from above. There were more shafts of light ahead. The noise was unceasing as everything trembled, all my insides in commotion and still no one to help me. Every step I was afraid I would fall again, my seven-year-old body struggling to stay upright.

A gritty hand grasped mine, holding firm. "We have to go." Drash's voice was husky, his face half lit from the cracks in the floor above us. At nine years old, he knew better than me what to do.

Yelina staggered behind him, a thin trickle of blood running down her temple. Her pale, yellow hair glowed in the dawn light.

"Oh, Yelina." I clutched her hand and a low bass thumped through our bones. My training kicked in and I sang. Drash grasped my upper arm and held Yelina between the two of us. I took her hand, now slick with blood.

Yelina slumped against me, her voice a whimper. "Take us away from here, Gulnaz."

"Sing with me." I was shaking.

"They killed them already," Yelina cried.

"Who?" I asked. The pressure of stiff bodies underfoot came back to me. Those had been my classmates I'd stepped over.

Yelina's breath was ragged against my shoulder. Drash tugged on me, the look in his dark eyes sorrowful, the faint light forming tiny fractures in his irises. How was I the strong one?

I dragged them into the next room to see if we could save others. Our teachers were sprawled over the students. When I brought my bare foot near their bodies, they were already cold. Their blood stank in the summer heat. Smoke billowed into the room as the voices of the attackers sought us. I found a break in the collapsed stone walls.

"Get us out of here," Drash begged. He never asked me for anything.

The voices of the attackers blew off the wall behind us. I held onto Drash and Yelina, singing with all of my might to raise our bodies off the ground and away from the soldiers. My muscles convulsed with the effort.

"If they see we are both Kardush and Yarat..." Drash's face was stained with tears.

"...we're dead," Yelina whispered, her eyes wide with fear.

"Sing with me, I can't. Do. It. Alone." I sang again, the tune one of my earliest traveling songs.

Nazra tiyu mai
Tazra ziyu dai.

Over and over we repeated the same phrase, lifting off the ground tentatively, the heat from the fires scorching our bare feet. I had never done this before: traveling with more than myself. I'd been punished plenty of times for escaping. But I'd never ventured beyond the cluster of Thresil Islands we called home.

We rose through the crack in the stone walls, our shoulders knocking debris to the ground when we collided with the edges of our dilapidated home. Rising above the rubble, the smoke didn't obscure the dead. Classmates who taunted me every day. Teachers who let them.

I still would have saved them, if I could have.

I needed them to be alive to tell us what to do next, while our bodies rose into the sky. Fighters dropped around us—their music ceasing in the air on their dying lips. Those still fighting in the distance could have been dancing if their music wasn't so menacing. I aimed us toward the tall stretches of buildings reaching toward the clouds. We zipped away from Kardush troops singing fireballs into the opposing Yarat force below. Their voices clashed before more fire billowed around them and ignited the surrounding buildings.

The larger government and senate trade buildings were rounded spires reaching for the sky in tall, flaming hands. Troops with water surrounded to douse the flames before being picked off by an opposing fighting force in white uniforms. They had stood for centuries and in minutes it all burned as I took us away from the carnage.

The weight of carrying my friends was harder on the outskirts of our island, Thresil Mira, where residential buildings lined the shore. The rounded backs of these buildings seemed untouched by the conflict at the center of my island. I sang harder, trying to speed us up, but we merely floated in the air.

"Sing louder. Drash! Yelina!" I said.

Yelina hummed weakly in tune with me, Drash harmonizing an octave below. I picked up our pace as we passed over the soldiers below, some of who were even young teenagers. A poorly constructed chorii flew around us, knocking people out of the sky. We had to get away from them. I sped up our song to bring us closer to the clusters of shoreline buildings. More and more people fell from the sky, a dull thud when they smacked with the shore. I felt sick with the continual percussion of their bodies.

I held my friends closer, all of us still trembling, our faces wet as we strained to land atop one of the residential buildings. The rounded roof was singed, but we could all fit on its exposed cross-beams. The thin, mesh bio wall of the roofing had been stripped back and bodies were strewn about below. The early morning sky was so cloudy that neither of our suns was visible. I let go of Yelina's hand, turning her head to make sure her bleeding had stopped. She held me close to her, still shaking. I breathed deeply at intervals to attempt to get my heart to stop racing. It wasn't the same without the teacher counting in front of us. Telling us to be calm, or else.

"Can't stay here," Drash said, craning his neck below. His face turned green and he was sick over the side of the building. The bile wafted over on the breeze, and my stomach turned. I leaned over the opposite side, Yelina holding my hair back.

Once I could breathe again, Yelina took hold of my arm. She peered into the stretch of sea in front of us. "Where do we go?"

Behind us lay the two other Thresil islands, the bridges aflame. The building we stood on shook, shuddered, and then was still again. A loud crack reverberated through the structure, the explosions louder. We clutched each other to stay upright.

"You ready to go?" I asked.

Yelina nodded dully.

"Don't go too far," Drash said, taking my hand and squeezing it. His sleeve was stained with Yelina's blood. I closed my eyes, calling the energy back into my body to sustain me. We'd escaped from our classmates enough times together. How hard would it be to travel away from our archipelago?

"We've never gone beyond the Thresils," Drash warned.

I searched across the ocean to the nearest point I'd touched upon. We had to fly further than that. Heat pricked at our feet and I grabbed both of them. "I need you to sing. Harder than you ever have."

"I'll try..." Yelina's lower lip trembled, a familiar look of shame from being punished for crying. Her grey eyes were blood-shot. "I'm not a binary traveller."

"Pretend you are," I said, and I embraced both of them. Fire singed our hair as we floated back into the air, our voices in perfect unison. We plummeted toward the fighting below, soldiers swirling around us, staring at our small bodies in confusion. A few rushed at our trio clinging to each other.

Yelina and Drash sang louder and we zipped away, the sound

of the fighting slowly tapering off. Within minutes it was only us, the wind and the rushing of the pink ocean below. I took one last look back at the smoke billowing from my island. Once it had been beautiful.

"It'll never look the same," I said.

"Let them all burn," Drash said, his brown hair blowing in the wind.

A flock of birds rushed past us. I picked up our song to match the tempo of their beating wings. We sang until there was only ocean beneath and thick grey sky above. We sang until nothing was familiar but pink ocean below and we became the only creatures in the sky. My heartbeat settled for the first time in hours and my friends' eyes were wet with tears. We flew for so long my body was stiff, my voice garbled. If I went hoarse, we'd have to land in the ocean.

"LOOK!" Yelina called out.

I turned us in the air so they could see a shadow of a mound that stretched across the horizon. I had always been told that our planet, Hirana, was nothing but islands. The land ahead was so large that it couldn't be an island. The suns peaked through the clouds to shine on a long stretch of grey sandbar. Steep hills rose beyond and the closer we came, the cooler the air was. Once land was underneath us, I slowed our song before my voice gave out completely. We dropped onto the wet sand, and I sprawled next to my friends. It felt like we were still moving even though I could feel the pressure of the ground against my spine. Voices called out in the distance, and I was too exhausted to run and hide in the sea grasses blowing above us.

A faint pressure tingled at the back of my neck. Within seconds, an adult woman with warm brown skin and long black hair knelt down next to me and the sensation ceased. Her eyes changed to a bright violet, like Kardush people gifted with multi-hued irises. Her eyes were like mine. That was something. Then, her eyes were yellow again within seconds. She reached out and drew us into the air with one gesture, her voice airy and light.

We landed softly on the dry sand, clinging to each other. Yelina's mottled blood against her yellow hair made her look gruesome.

"Where did you come from?" The woman kept her hands where we could see them. When no answer came, she sighed. "I'm Danis." She gestured toward students floating in the air in formations, a man yelling at them to stop when he spotted us. He soared through the air and alighted next to her. He was several inches shorter than Danis.

I stepped forward, bringing my friends with me. "I'm Gulnaz, this is Yelina and Drash." I struggled to keep Yelina's memories at bay when I touched her bare arm. The sea roared behind us, and I turned to look at it. I was afraid they'd send us back and tears pricked at my eyes. If I looked away they couldn't punish my crying. In the long silence I ventured another look at the couple. The kids were now behind them, so much older than us.

"How'd you get here?" the man asked. The heat coming off his eyes was puzzling. Would he kill us like the Kardush on the Thresils? I tried to block out Yelina's memory of the bodies hitting the ground with a sickening thud. I released myself from her grip. The memories stopped. Folding my arms across my body, I met his gaze. I had to die bravely. I owed the people whose memories I carried that much.

"How did you do it, girl?" he asked me gently.

"I sang us here," I said.

"She's a binary traveler," Yelina said.

"She got in trouble for traveling. A lot," Drash said.

He didn't need to add that part. The man came closer and

knelt by us, the students watching curiously. "I am Xibo. Welcome to Maer-lina training school."

"We can't trust them," Drash whispered, squeezing my hand. "Kardush kill half Yarats like us."

Danis kneeled close to Drash. "We do not kill anyone unless they attack us." She kept a hold on his shoulder. "I'm the head healer here, and we need to check your wounds. Get you cleaned up. We'll talk later about how you came." She smiled at us, her now black eyes kind.

Xibo gestured for us to follow him, but it wasn't until Danis took a step that I followed them up the smooth stone steps that led to a massive white building that reminded me of a whale turned on its side. Drash and Yelina's hands were firmly in mine.

FOR SEVEN YEARS, little skirmishes broke out over the islands, leaving Maer-lina in relative peace until I turned fourteen. All of our training to become part of the chorii had become abruptly relevant. The Yarat troops had completely colonized the Thresils by then and stolen the ancient spaceships to rid Hirana of its original Kardush inhabitants. Our training school couldn't avoid the conflict forever.

The heavy metal gleam of the noisy machines in the sky reminded me of the cacophony of that first day of war. I was ready to pounce on them. And I stood taller than anyone my age, including Drash, who was two years older. Still, a gnawing terror pricked at my heart. I waited for the Yarat chorii, joining the symphony of sounds, voices, and clanging metal before an explosion scattered my Kardush chorii group floating in formation above the ocean.

Yelina was my partner on that first big day on Maer-lina. We sped away from the cluster of chorii that had been blasted by the explosion. Drash joined us as we aimed our harps at the next cluster of ships. Smoke curled out of the busted engines we'd hit. The Yarat chorii swarmed out of their damaged ship. We dove lower to avoid the furnace of their voices hurling fireballs at us. Yelina got too close to the flames and one of the Yarat soldiers clipped her and spun her around, knocking her into me. Both of us plummeted into the icy ocean.

The frigid cold bit at my exposed skin, all the breath sucked out of me. A wave hit and tossed me under. I fought for the surface.

"Yelina!" I cried.

I searched underwater for her yellow hair that she refused to pin up for battle. I surfaced.

There was a clamor of sounds above, bodies hammering at each other with their voices before falling out of the sky. The noise blew out my eardrums. I floated on the ocean like useless carrion, the shuddering of my muscles and chattering of my teeth rattling my skull. Not a single person floating beside me moved. They looked strangely peaceful.

I treaded water, weaving through them to find Yelina, shaking each body I found. After minutes of swimming, my muscles cramped and shuddered from the cold. I had to get back in the air. Maybe then I'd find her.

Inhaling deeply, calling the salt back to my muscles, I restored my body's energies, rose shakily into the air, my water-logged body heavy. Yelina floated below me on the waves, her pale, yellow hair streaming behind her. I dove down to collect her, to breathe some life into her, but her almond shaped eyes were open blankly to the skies. We were too far from the healers. I floated above the surface, yanking on her hand. It was too cold, already stiff. I didn't know how to bring her back.

"Gulnaz, she's gone...there's nothing--" Xibo yelled at me.

"But…" I was still alive. I had to fight to stay that way, even if I didn't want to.

She had been my first friend. I couldn't look away from her blank, grey eyes.

She had convinced Drash I was like them. He wouldn't have been my friend if it weren't for her.

Now there were only two of us left.

The Yarats' metal faces gleamed at me in their body armor and I sang, harnessing everything in me to blast them out of the sky. My voice ripped out of my chest and I brought their weapons to me, knocking them into the ocean they'd consigned my friend to. With each death I was that much closer to bringing Yelina back.

Every time I went into battle thereafter I saw Yelina beside me, holding my hand as we rose in the air. "We'll make it to the next day," she always said. But, if I looked down at the ocean, her voice faded away. Instead, I'd catch her lemon-yellow hair streaming behind her. Her pale body floating on the waves and never waking up.

2

GULNAZ

L eanora didn't know what she was. We had been watching her more closely after the war on Hirana. Looking behind me, to make sure that my comrade Mikosh was following, I soared over the mountains, speeding up my traveling song. The crisp air froze the breath in my nostrils, and I sang harder to keep aloft. We had decided we were done waiting when the first snows drifted across the mountains. We kept at a safe distance in the treetops to watch Leanora and Tarrok's tiny figures making their way to the coastal city of Lepidaia. Mikosh landed beside me, her long braids encrusted with ice. She exhaled steam and pulled her scarf tighter around her, her brown cheeks red.

"Gulnaz, they won't make it without help," she said abruptly, her face a mask of tension since her mom died.

"She's packed Tarrok's wounds. He'll be fine." They weren't moving very quickly, Mikosh was right about that. I had watched the night before when Leanora had traveled to rescue her lover. When the stag rammed him, blood oozing out of his shoulder, I had thought I would have to intervene.

Mikosh put a hand on my shoulder. "He's still bleeding. We have to do something for him." She tugged on my arm, pulling us back toward the ground where Leanora and Tarrok were slowly making their way through the snow with their two ulsos, which looked like oversized dogs, and pack of gwynbees, which resembled small cats with squirrel tails. It was easy to get distracted by their strange animals.

I stopped Mikosh from walking over to them. "It's too soon. We have to know what they can do on their own. Whether she will travel again. If what Saren prophesied is true."

Mikosh scowled, both of us slowly drifting back toward the pine treetops when my song faded.

"We have to know what Leanora's capable of before we report back to Xibo," I said.

"What if Tarrok dies?" There was an accusation in her bright blue eyes as they caught the early morning sunlight. "We've seen enough people destroying each other. We can help them." She had that look on her face that I knew from battle. She wasn't budging about this.

"We can follow more closely." I had been watching Tarrok long enough to know that he had been through worse than this.

Mikosh held out the neiko. It measured the abilities of Hiranians to travel through space and between planets. Its rounded shape fit snugly in her large palm.

Leanora stretched and sang a song, lifting into the air and then back to the ground again. The neiko lit up so brightly we had to sing ourselves into the air and away from the forest to the edges of Lepidaia, so we wouldn't be found. The neiko died down once we were a kilometer away from them.

"I've never seen anything like it," Mikosh said in wonder. It was the first time since her mother's death I had seen her smile genuinely. Her blue eyes sparkled with interest. "Do you think she'll come to Hirana?"

When I lightly brushed her shoulder, I made certain not to touch any exposed skin. "If it's as Saren prophesies." I narrowed my eyes back in the direction that we'd last seen them. "We'll have to figure out a way to keep Tarrok behind."

"I'll ask Saren." Mikosh folded her arms and soared away toward Lepidaia, leaving me behind, her voice soon morphing into the stillness of the cold wind blowing over me.

I was glad to have a rare moment alone without her brooding. It had been over a year since I'd seen Drash. Every day I hoped I'd receive word about his whereabouts. Or, that I'd get a chance to kill the Yarats who had taken him. I wasn't supposed to pine for Drash, but he was all I had left. I didn't know what I would do without him.

I floated over the trees toward Bejah and Dex, who were moving so slowly they would die without my help. I wasn't certain I felt like intervening. The snow fell faster as the wind whistled through the lovely, tall trees, shaking the shaggy tree-tops. I wasn't eager to travel back to Asanis and extract answers from Zer. I might as well do something useful, even if it pained me to be kind.

LET ME START AGAIN.

Once we were just like the people of Eloia. But we advanced more quickly. Our music was just as beautiful, but it could do things theirs could not. We sang our way across long distances. Those, like me, gifted with the *haian fusai*, or "singing life force," used the power of our spirits to carry our bodies eventually to other galaxies.

Then the Yarats came and messed everything up.

No, that's not right.

There were the Kardush, half of what I am, the original

people of the planet Hirana in the Wex-Em galaxy. Then the Yarats came and they fought with the Kardush. Eventually the Kardush and Yarats drew up laws for cohabitation on Hirana. The Yarats taught us how to expand our *haian fusai* to travel outside Hirana. We taught them how to abandon their colonizing ships for life on a central planet.

It sounds so dry and simple. It never is when you blend two different cultures.

People like me were occasionally born: half Kardush, half Yarat. Belonging to neither culture fully. Aberrations to be rooted out. Equality of philosophy and law could not be achieved if there were children who were a mix. It made the government unstable, they said. Yet, they loved to make mixed Kardush/Yarat children memory keepers. It was a special form of punishment for couples who indulged in cross-cultural relationships.

Yet, I survived. Memory keeper and soldier, hoping to protect the Eloians from the Yarats coming to destroy this planet, like they had decimated Hirana.

I followed the pattern of the drifting snow, carrying a frost-bitten Dex and Bejah with their animals closer to the valley and out of the blinding white of the approaching blizzard. I hated saving people who were too daft to save themselves, but I knew Mikosh would never forgive me. And perhaps I hoped this act of kindness would bring Drash back to me. I'd missed the way his black eyes held the light.

LEANORA SANG a song that was so bright and fast that I hummed along. The green valley had no evidence of snow while she rode on the enormous hounds that the Eloians called ulsos. She held the hand of her lover, his green skin bright in the golden sunlight. How gentle that sun was compared to our twin red suns on Hirana. I liked the warm, yellow glow of its rays, and I flew over the collection of white stone buildings of Lepidaia. I drifted over their maze-like construction, so unlike our rounded, orderly and large buildings on Hirana. I belted out her song to propel me back toward the mountain range, turning back once more to see if she would travel again.

She did not.

"I'll leave her in Mikosh's capable hands," I said aloud.

I changed the tune to a fast Kardushian song, zipping across the mountain range, past the rainforest, aiming my body for Asanis, curious how long it would take before I saw the pines again.

I WAS LATE.

I grinned, because I liked keeping Zer waiting. The dusty pine trees rose in the distance, seeming to lift out of the sand of the Hagothian desert. The tune slowly dribbled out to a slow lullaby that allowed me to slow my descent and land in Asanis. The village was sleepy and dusty in the morning light. Months prior, Zer had kicked Leanora and Dex out. We had argued about it for days. I had refused to travel across the galaxy to Eloia for months—at least to see him. There was enough rebuilding to do on my planet to keep me busy.

When I didn't see Zer at our usual meeting spot. I sang my way into the air again, floating above the tops of the pines, the aroma of their pitch pleasant. I touched down at the edge of the infirmary where he sat on a bench outside. He startled when he fixed his metallic eyes on me, a familiar grin on his face.

"It has been a long time, Gulnaz." His ebony face was unlined, but his eyebrows and shorn hair were white. He'd gotten rid of his beard, trying to look younger than his sixty years. At nineteen, I had probably killed more people than he'd known in his lifetime. Unlike him, I'd rarely enjoyed it.

I kept my distance, in case he was going to lash out. "I've been watching Leanora every few days, like you asked."

"Good." He folded his arms, finally meeting my gaze with those mirror eyes. I stood up straighter, though my body ached from traveling so far. "She has arrived in Lepidaia by now."

"And..." Impatience was creeping into his voice.

Good. It was easier to manipulate him that way. "Mikosh came." I exhaled noisily, pretending to be bored with him.

Zer stood, his long white jacket flapping behind him as he stormed toward me. "Out with it already."

I held out my hand, my palm glowing blue. A warning. "It was as you said: Leanora is very powerful. She traveled twice."

"Twice?"

"The first time just herself, a short distance after an injury in Nedara. Then an ulso, gwynbee, and herself to her lover who was injured."

"Dex," he grumbled.

"No. Someone else." I folded my arms, gloating.

Zer's dark face beamed. The sun shone off his skin as he turned, almost touching me before stopping himself. He did not want to risk another involuntary memory transfer. Even his impressive control broke down sometimes. Especially when I mentioned Leanora.

"This is the best news I have had in years. My daughter."

"She will find out soon that you were not her father," I reminded him, relaxing my face back into a neutral position.

"I raised her," he insisted.

"And then kicked her out." I looked up at the puffy clouds above us. It was best to avoid eye contact when I was baiting him.

His gaze was fixed on a point beyond me. The trees behind him framed his agitated figure. "Hirana was only the beginning."

He paced, his arms out like he was addressing hundreds. It wasn't the first time he'd mentioned this. "She will bring us back into power. The Kardush will have no chance to settle here." I was waiting for him to issue his commands so I could frustrate his colonization efforts. Could I trust what came next? I liked continuing to pretend I was his Kardushian spy.

I had watched Leanora cross the desert to the rainforests, learning her gifts. She had gone from a weakling to someone worthy of traveling across universes to bring our people to a better home. But she still did not know what she was. Did I have the guts to tell her or would I let Zer steal her destiny?

He sat back on the bench and patted it for me to sit next to him as he crooned a tune that sounded vaguely like something Leanora sang.

"Lua lu lai...."

Was I ready for what she could bring to both our planets? I had been avoiding the time when I had to choose a side and couldn't waver in between as I did now. Zer stared at me, the desire in his eyes so familiar. He held out his hand. "I have a memory that you must keep for me."

I let the shadowed, calm memory flow through me. All was darkness as a soundscape soared around him. He was trying to identify who was speaking, a subtle pain in his head then a terribly bright light that didn't make sense to him. A piercing pain behind his eyes and he was forced into the seeing world.

It was his memory of receiving sight. His digital eyesight sharper and more lurid than natural eyes. The sharpness was painful and I didn't want to experience his memory any longer. I scooted away so he wasn't touching me and the moment ended.

I tucked the memory away deep in the recesses of my body where I stored all the memories I had been gifted with. I crooned the tune Leanora had sung crossing into Lepidaia.

Beware, don't look away,
Lepidaia, my home so fair,
Lepidaia, my dream don't dare,
Sail away without a care.
I'll stay and see you through...

Could I protect Leanora from what he planned next?

"I like that. Where did you learn that song?" Zer asked, his shoulder still close to mine.

"It's hers," I said.

And I recalled an old memory of the Kardush, before the Yarats settled on my home planet. When voices were just voices and music only entertainment. Before half my ancestors said: *"Why not make music do more?"*

I was tired of trying to be more. Without saying a word to Zer, I let the song carry me into the air and soared across the planet again toward Mikosh to bring her back to Hirana.

Now you know the rest.

PART I

"Colonization is a form of love."

—*Yarat-waiya*, Article No. 1

3

LEANORA

Spring burst through the verdant hills surrounding Lepidaia. Tiny yellow flowers crept into the crevices of the white stones of the terraced buildings of the city. I liked tracing my hands across the new life as I made my way home from the hospital in the late afternoon. Every day I scanned the skies in anticipation of more Hiranian refugees, but it had been three months. I wanted to believe we were safe from further arrivals. I stopped on the rounded red bridge that was the last bridge across the channel before the road to my parent's house. Dark clouds were rolling in and the cold sea breeze whistled through the surrounding buildings. I'd forgotten to bring my cloak, the day sunny and cloudless when I'd left home that morning. Tarrok stopped next to me.

"You're cold...come closer," he said, holding out his hand. I didn't move, trying to puzzle out the tension in his face. I had originally thought it had to do with the Kardush refugees and how long I spent at the hospital healing and transporting patients. But after I'd reduced my hours, the tension remained. Vali, my ulso, wove his massive brown body between us every few seconds. His fluffy brown and white fur was shaggier in the winter. I held out a hand for Vali to stop. He barked and sat on his haunches.

Tarrok's green face was stony as he held his hand out. I took it, and he kept staring at me in the lamplight. A light mist turned to rain and still his eyes were hard.

"I have a question." I'd never heard him so tense. "I want us to decide what we are....what our future is." I inhaled the faded scent of lemons off his skin and wrapped my arms around him.

"More ulsos?" I joked with him.

"Stop teasing me." He relaxed in my arms.

"I wish deciding...didn't feel like it would change everything with my parents." I looked up into his now shadowed face. The silence felt like it was communicating more than what I was able to say. The rain whooshed past us in a fine mist, obscuring the hills and darkening the day prematurely. I took hold of his hand, an agitation in his grasp. I didn't want things to change yet, but I could see he didn't feel the same way. I raised my hand to his cheek, but he backed away from me.

"What is it?" I kept my hand outstretched. "What did I do?"

He sandwiched my hand between his large green palms. "You've seen the Wet-al-Wirth light celebrations every month for those who are marrying." He cleared his throat, looking up before meeting my gaze, his dark eyes shining in the dim lamplight. "We can make what we have permanent."

"We can..." But I wasn't certain I was ready right at that moment. "I do want that...you know I do." I squeezed his hand. "It's what we've been waiting for..." How did I tell him I was afraid without hurting his feelings?

"You do not love me enough?" He let go of my hand.

"I'm seventeen, you're eighteen...we live with my parents...so much would need to change to make that happen. Are you ready for us to live on our own?"

"We live in the same house and do not..." His voice trailed off.

"I know." It was a subject we'd discussed enough. It was impossible for us to be fully together in my parents' house. "We've only known each other for nine months," I said. Had it been so short? The trek across Eloia had felt like years. "So much happened to get us here. I want to feel like we're stable before..." Then my mind imagined the possibility of us standing under the brightan tree. Crowns of flowers on our heads, everyone singing under the pink and white blossoms. A distinct peace descended over me when I thought of the two of us there.

He stood up straighter, the outline of his muscles palpable beneath his thin sweater. "In Hagoth I had my own house, my own ulsos, freedom." He leaned into me, his bass voice lower. "I cannot do this for much longer." He tapped his foot against the cobblestones.

If I didn't set a date with him, would I forfeit all the good in our relationship? I wasn't ready to leave my family. "We're too young, Tarrok."

"Last month a couple younger than us was married."

I laughed. "Lexa and Malto are five years older than us."

"What do I have to do to prove this is right for us?" he asked, his lips at my neck. My pulse increased and I brought him closer to me. At that moment I wanted us to be alone and not always stopping because we had no privacy. And maybe I was waiting for something more definite. Now that the moment was here...

"Talk to my parents with me," I said.

Tarrok's lips were on mine and the warmth of his tongue was new. It felt like weeks since we'd really kissed. Both of us had been rushing around to help the Kardush refugees, to save lives. I let all of those frenetic thoughts die under the weight of him against me. I put my hand on his cheek, stopping us before we made fools of ourselves in public. "I want to be with you, but we need to discuss it with them."

"Can't we set a date and tell them without consulting?" He kissed my knuckles. He held me closer to him and I knew what he meant. I let him go and started back toward the house while there was still light. Soon the shadows were too hard to distinguish from the ground and I held tight to Vali's reins for him to guide me.

Tarrok took my hand and we walked in silence, Vali's bushy brown tail slapping at our arms every few seconds. When my father opened the door to welcome us, Tarrok didn't miss a beat.

"Leanora and I want to take on the light...to be married."

Tarrok

MY BACK HURT from sitting against the stone wall of the sitting room. The glow of the lamps cast shadows that danced along the ceiling. The wind howled outside. I hated sitting here. Waiting for them to say something and feeling more awkward than normal. Why couldn't Leanora and I just tell them and have it done? What did we need their permission for?

Saren's black eyes roved between the two of us. Methriel stared at her. His hands resting on his big belly had the same red pattern as Leanora's arms. I looked nothing like any of them. Still, they had become my family since both my parents were dead. Their silence was painful, because I didn't know what combination of words would change the tension I felt.

I had to concentrate on Leanora, her dark hair undone and

grazing my arm. I held her hand tighter, her palm cool in mine. I followed her gaze out the wide windows that overlooked the street. Rows of houses two and three-stories high framed the channel where the river flowed down to the shore. Weeks earlier, couples had walked in a ceremonial procession from this district out to the valley to stand under the brightan trees for their marriages.

I had to be there with her. Everyone singing around us, the white blossoms falling gently. Her eyes changing color when I kissed her.

Leanora let go of my hand and stood up. "I know I want to spend my life with Tarrok, can you try to understand that?" Her voice was so gentle yet powerful.

Saren cleared her throat and brushed her silver hair aside. "It's too soon," she said softly.

My heart fell. "You don't decide that." I looked to Leanora for confirmation, and she sat down next to me on the upholstered bench.

"What is it?" I whispered to Leanora.

"Saren, maybe..." Methriel stopped when she glared at him.

"It cannot happen for several months, I think. Not until we get an understanding of the situation with the Yarats." Saren rubbed her face, exhaustion pouring off her. Outside, Alaric, Leanora's brother, was calling out to the ulsos, his voice already husky and losing its childish pitch.

"Several months is too long," I said.

"Tarrok's right." Leanora smiled and took my hand again.

The first time I saw her in Hagoth, her eyes had changed color rapidly and I had thought the red marks on her arms meant she was dying. Now, the only barrier between us being together was ridiculous. We'd almost died coming to Lepidaia. "I don't see why...we can trek across the planet...almost get ourselves killed multiple times, with very little help from you, and then when we want to be married, you think it's too soon?" I couldn't keep the anger out of my voice. "It's insane."

Leanora looked away from me. I'd done exactly what she'd warned me not to do. *"Don't make a fuss. It's just a discussion. They're still getting used to having me home."*

Methriel lightened his voice, his dark blue eyes artificially cheery. "If you are married, where will you go?"

"We could stay here." Leanora sat up straighter. She avoided my gaze.

I had told her I wanted us to live separate from them.

"You could make the upstairs yours." Some of the darkness dissipated from Saren's face.

"I lived by myself for years..." I stopped when Leanora shook her head. I wasn't going to win this one.

"Don't room with strangers." Methriel tried to cross his legs, but his belly was too large. "Besides, who is going to enforce my daily exercise?" He was always eager to look on the bright side.

I couldn't help smiling a little at his typical Lepidaian cheerfulness. No one in Lepidaia ever went hungry. It was hard to find anyone who wasn't a little bit fat. I stuck out sorely. Too tall, too muscled, and too much one color.

Saren tapped Methriel. "You've gained weight since they arrived." She turned to us, her face softening. "That doesn't mean you need to leave. We like having *both* of you here." She made a point to look at me, her eyes crinkling at the corners. "And you're old enough to make your own decisions."

Leanora was looking out the window. Had she changed her mind? She tucked a strand of her long black hair behind her ear, the lock curling at the end. The red spots had become more pronounced on her arms during the winter and they danced in a pattern across her upper arms, stopping at her neck. I'd loved tracing her spots with my mouth. But we always got to a stopping point, a place where I never got to see all of her. How long did I have to wait?

I stood up, clearing my throat. I wanted to sign, like I would have in Hagoth. It seemed easier in that moment to speak with my hands instead of my mouth. I was a man of action. Not great with words, except when talking to Leanora.

"I had my own house in Hagoth. I gave that up...to come here. To be with Leanora...to see Lepidaia for myself. Living here has been good. But, it doesn't change that this isn't my house. It's yours." I paused, my voice cracking. "I love...Leanora more... than...anyone. We're ready. I can't wait longer than a few weeks." She was grinning at me. "If Leanora wants."

She took my arm. "I agree with Tarrok. At some point we need to have our own place. We can wait a few weeks to get the ceremony details and stay here for the next year." She looked up at me, and I knew that was the final deal.

"What if you change your minds?" Methriel blurted out.

"I won't." Leanora squeezed my hand.

Saren put her hand on Methriel's chest. "Hush and let them be." She stood up. "The oath under the brightan tree, some believe, means you're married forever."

"We know," I said.

The way Leanora looked up at me made me want to jump up and dance a crazy jig. However, Hagothians do not dance crazy jigs in front of their lover's parents. I had to wait until I was outside with Leanora's crazy brother who could sing and dance at any hour of the day. Descending the stairs, I was back inside my head, running around like a maniac dancing to the mozab singing drums from Hagoth.

The ulsos were humming along with me. I waited until we were outside with Alaric, the ulsos jumping around, their tales swishing. They hummed a low ballad that I sang with them, a little off-tune. We were going to be married. Not today, not tomorrow, but soon.

> *Come and sing with me,*
> *My love. The moon is full*
> *and the night is warm.*
> *Come sing with me, my love...*

Alaric crooned to my jaunty tune, speeding up the tempo as the ulsos and gwynbees joined in. His black hair fell into his bright blue eyes, and he smiled that playful smile that meant he was up to mischief.

"Go on, the two of you, work all that noisiness out of his system so we can sleep tonight," Leonora called out to us.

We made several laps around the neighborhood and eventually got yelled at by the neighbors who were trying to sleep. They had to be the only people in Lepidaia who didn't like to party at all hours. I slowed our pace, the feniels lining the street lit up against the black night sky.

"So. You got them to agree?" Alaric asked, one dark eyebrow raised. He tucked his curly hair behind an ear. "When's it happening?"

I ruffled his hair and shoved him ahead of me. "A few weeks."

Alaric put his arms around my waist, his head resting against my chest. "Then we'll really be brothers." His eyes lit up. "Does this mean you can overrule them when they say I have to go to bed early?"

"Probably not," I said, laughing.

He ran on ahead as the ulsos barked and chased him. I let myself walk slowly back to the house, enjoying the feel of the cool rain on my skin. I had to send word to my sister Erena in Hagoth. To tell her the good news.

4

LEANORA

Per, with her feathery white hair and skin like glass, leaned on one of our first patients, Drash. He kept her upright as they wandered the hospital's courtyard slowly. For the past six months, our hospital had been full of Kardush who had escaped Yarat warships where they'd been enslaved and forced to repair the aging vessels. I kept hold of my last patient, Kek, singing us to the top level of the hospital and away from the courtyard, before leaving her to my father's care.

"You need a break." Dad took my green tunic from me so I was officially off duty.

"She never takes a break." I nodded toward where my mother had disappeared.

"You're different." His voice lowered an octave. "Plus, Tarrok's waiting for you." I hugged him and raced down the steps to where Tarrok was stood in the hospital's large outdoor court- yard. I was glad to feel the sunshine on my face after so many hours indoors.

"Methriel says you have an hour to spare." Tarrok grinned, displaying his bright white teeth.

I climbed in front of him onto Vali, and his arms were tight around my waist. I steered him toward the central marketplace in the dragon district of Lepidaia. His massive paws deftly carried both of us up the stone ramp that spiraled up to the market, rising above the white stone apartments to arrive at the highest point of Lepidaia. Vali sniffed the air and I climbed off his furry brown back. Like me, he was probably hungry for roasted pork and borsa nuts from my favorite vendor, Favel.

Faint music played above the din of bartering as we came closer to the marketplace stalls. Lines of laundry hung above us in reds, blues, and yellows amidst the maroon banners of the Dragon district fluttering in the breeze.

Tarrok glanced up. "Looks like Neelan might be right. Those dark clouds could ruin our perfect afternoon."

"No chance," I said, squeezing his hand.

We had to avoid a cart of vegetables led by a team of long-necked, white luoshis. The heavily-lidded eyes of the beasts regarded us coolly from beneath their fuzzy heads. The crowd dispersed, and the aroma of roasted pork turning on spits prickled my nostrils, causing my mouth to water. Guitarists at the farthest edge of the market were more noticeable, crooning loudly while their bandmates struck their handheld drums with wooden mallets. Tarrok took my hand, and I imagined us dancing to a similar ballad in a few weeks at our ceremony. He leaned down and kissed me, his mouth lingering at the edge of my lips. I led him through the crowd before one of my patients saw us.

Everyone milling about kept clear of the scorch marks from the Kardush refugee pod landings six months ago. I moved closer, rubbing my toes in the marks. The twenty refugees, half of whom did not survive, had not changed the upbeat atmosphere in Lepidaia as everyone celebrated the return of spring. No one was more eager to party than Lepidaians.

The song changed to a fast *tula*, and I grinned at Tarrok.

"Dancing?" Tarrok asked, his green face radiant. Gone was the earlier tension of the past weeks. I wanted to hold him tight to me. I took his hand and led him toward the edge of the dancers. We whirled around the square, my eyes unable to keep up with the swirling of people. I closed them to stay in rhythm with him, laughing from the swiftness of his feet, hoping I wouldn't trip him up, but knowing if I did, we'd have a good laugh. He held his forearm firm against my lower back. I loved how it felt to be with him like this. I opened my eyes to catch him grinning down at me. We twirled and twirled and spun, going so fast I was afraid my feet would forget they were attached to my body.

The band's singers burst through the accompaniment of the guitars, drum and violin.

Girl you must say-say,
make your mind straight-straight,
'fore I find another girl
who dances so fast and fine
as you, my love-love,
so fine and fast as you.
My love-love. My love-love.

Someone sang the lyrics off-tune but perfectly in rhythm. Her voice was familiar. I lost my footing and tripped. Tarrok deftly brought me to the edge of the crowd, both of us holding our sides and laughing. I leaned into him, ready to steal a kiss. Then I spotted Bejah sitting with a Kardush refugee, Neelan. She cocked her blue face to the side. The way Neelan looked at her, his face almost healed, I knew that something had changed since his recovery. They had been awfully cozy since he'd left the hospital. Gone were the harsh edges to Bejah; even her accent had begun to fade, except when she was angry.

Neelan waved. "Hi, Tarrok! Leanora! Nice dancing."

Bejah giggled. She knew we weren't Lepidaia's greatest dancers.

"You going to try?" I asked Neelan who looked to Bejah. She jumped up and dragged him across the square. They were a lot worse than Tarrok and me. They didn't care and kept dancing in such an exaggerated way, pumping their arms and running into other couples, I was laughing so hard I was crying. Even Tarrok was doubled over. When we'd calmed down, I brought my hand to his cheek, relishing the feel of his warm skin under my hand.

"I wish we could stay here all day. I need this...with you," I said.

"We *can* stay here all day." He had a mischievous grin, his russet irises shining with anticipation.

"I have patients waiting for me," I said sadly. "We're short a healer today, and I'm the only one who can transport them around the hospital."

He brought his hand to my chin and inhaled deeply. "It's hard to love someone in such demand." He let go and took both my hands. "I'll get you some roasted pork before you go back." He kissed me full on the mouth, and I lost all desire to return to my work. "If we hurry, the other healers won't notice you're gone." His voice fell several octaves. "And then we can both waste a little time?" He bounced his eyebrows at me, and I pulled him away from the crowd, everyone blurring as we rushed past them. A deep warmth spread through my abdomen as I imagined all the ways we could stay occupied.

We wove around the opposite side, behind the vendor's stalls and toward the roasting fires facing the hills of Lepidaia at the back of the market. A loud rumbling started in the distance. Those pesky carts. I looked around for a place where he and I could be alone. The thought was interrupted by a tearing sound increasing above us.

"That isn't..." the clamor was reverberating in my chest, increasing to a deafening level.

"They're back." Tarrok pulled me into him.

The crowd scurried away from the marketplace. Vendors threw their wares into their carts and fled. The center cleared within seconds, the ensuing pandemonium of hundreds escaping caused several luoshis to bolt from their pens. I ran with Tarrok toward the back staging area, trying to keep my distance from the heat of the pods approaching the marketplace. My heart was thudding loudly in my ears; a cold sweat broke out across my back. Vali was again at my side, panting, and I held fast to his reins. I rubbed Vali's enormous brown ears and he tucked his white-flecked snout under my arm, facing away from the melee.

Three pods encased in flame flew toward the marketplace, not hovering like the last group. They were seconds from making impact with the market floor. The halo of flame around the three pods extinguished on impact. A crack reverberated across the ground and threw me against Vali's bulk. The seals on the gray metal vessels cracked open. I tucked my head into my tunic to dampen the rotten stench that wafted through on the breeze. A group of healers rushed past in their green tunics. My parents followed to inspect the vessels. I couldn't stay where I was, frozen in panic. I had to help, even if I didn't want to.

"Get the patients back to the hospital now," my mother instructed the healers.

Alaric, frantic and wild eyed, ran into me. "They've come back?" he asked. "What do they want?"

I tried to be as calm as possible, even though I was quaking inside. "I don't know." I wish they'd stayed away. *So much for my plans with Tarrok.*

I took Alaric's hand and brought him beside the closest surviving pod. It was still smoking, the stench less perceptible.

"What's inside?" my brother asked, his voice wavering

Two healers shone lights over the pod. A man was slumped over, close to my age, his face covered in similar scarring to all the Kardush who had come before. He had huge slash marks across his exposed arms and torso while the lower half of his body was covered in a charred Kardush jumpsuit with their interlocking insignia. Alaric helped me lift him out of the pod and onto a stretcher. The man opened violet eyes. He said something in Hiranian and kept repeating it over and over, the syllables and vowels blurring together.

Ada molrick nyanim. Zurish yuul...zurish yuul.

"What did he say?" I asked.

"This is only the beginning. More will come," Mom repeated softly.

The man kept muttering, and I checked the other two pods, but the women inside them were already gone, their bodies scorched black.

"They never had a chance," Neelan said as he ran his hands through his wispy yellow and pink hair.

"Did you know them?" I asked.

Neelan sucked in the air, his fingers lighting up. "They were prisoners like me: forced to repair Yarat ships. May they rest eternally safe from their suffering." He looked to Bejah, his face softening when she put her blue arms around him.

"They need burial. We not leave them here," Bejah said.

Neelan lifted an entire body by himself despite being short and round. He loaded them onto the luoshi cart. No sign of any energy flowed from them when I touched their scorched skin. Bejah walked with me, her arm through mine while we trudged back to the hospital, the rain beating on our heads. I closed my eyes and sang a mournful song Alaric had taught me, using the song to swiftly lift the carts into the air and transport them back to the hospital grounds for burial.

"It so sad." Bejah exhaled and leaned her head against my arm.

"I hope they went quickly." When the other arrivals had come three months earlier, I had gone home every day bone weary from transporting patients around the hospital. My mother worked around the clock: I didn't understand why I couldn't do the same.

We climbed onto Vali and trudged back slowly on our respective ulsos. Bejah's voice went soft once we reached the hospital. "Neelan say many more come. And we not ready." Her eyes were full of concern as she inspected my face, tension lines around her pink-blue mouth. I took her by the arm, and she stayed by my side as I made my rounds, singing calming songs to the Kardush patients that were agitated after this latest landing.

5

___

TARROK

The next day it was worse. For hours, the slender metal pods kept coming, and they weren't sticking to the marketplace any more. Several crashed into buildings, igniting the wood cross-beams of the older apartments far from where we stood in Leanora's parents' house. We were far enough away that it felt unreal, a distant dream that we could wake from. After a few minutes—that felt much longer—the rush stopped and a fire roared in the Serpent District in the south of the city. Plumes of smoke trailed from the main square and surrounding terraced apartments.

I reached for Leanora, standing so straight and tall next to me in the sitting room. Her calm spread to me as I watched people below running in thin trickles, darting into nearby houses. I had to do something. Hagothians did not give in to shock. At least this one didn't.

"Gwynbees! Carki, Vali, let's go." The gwynbees fluffed their squirrel tails and sped ahead of the barking ulsos. I marched down the stairs, and Neelan chased us out the door.

He raised one pale eyebrow. "Those were Yarats. We need to stay inside until we know more." He held out his glowing hands

42

and gestured for us to follow him back into the house. "We do not know how many might attack."

The gwynbees froze. The ulsos panted and whined, but followed him inside. Alaric was frozen beside Leanora and Bejah in the doorway. His large blue eyes kept darting between the three of us. "What will we do about Mom and Dad?"

"Mom knows what to do," Leanora said.

Neelan shook his head and led us back up the stairs into the sitting room. "Saren was never their prisoner like Drash and me." He pointed to the sky, black with plumes of smoke, but clear of any further vessels. "Those ships that came, you call them the pods, the Talbo-Pii are only the start. Yarats use them to intimidate and get rid of any soldiers killing without brutality."

Leanora came away from the window, her eyes a light blue that told me she was afraid. The minute I took her hand, her eyes morphed to a yellow that told me she was calming down, or pretending to. She squeezed my hand back and there was a steeliness in her face, like her mom.

"We can't stay here and do nothing. There might be people who need rescuing," Leanora said.

"Not the Yarats. I would not save them," Neelan said.

"What if there are Kardush out there too?" I asked.

He turned toward Leanora and me. "Those of us who came, escaped. The rest out there...it is unlikely they want to protect Eloia." His eyes hardened, his voice dropped low but piercing. "The Yarats want Eloia for themselves. They'll do anything to colonize." He held out his arms, which showed jagged red and pink scars that extended the entire length of his hands and arms. "I was treated better than most."

A loud boom shook me to the core, and the whole house pulsed. It was different from the sounds of the Talbo-Pii ships that had plummeted to the earth. The fat vibration drowned out speech, jolting my heartbeat out of sync. I reached for Alaric and Leanora, pulling them to me.

"That's probably a Marwatha," Neelan said. "They are for colonizing." He narrowed his eyes, peering out the window. Bejah put her arm around him.

We all craned to look out the windows.

"Why would all those people let their ships plummet to the ground?" Leanora asked. "Or is it a way of distracting us so invaders..." Her voice trailed off.

A glowing mass of black and gray moved very slowly through the sky. Hovering closer to the northern shore and zipping back around toward the house. "Is that a Marwatha?" I asked.

"Yes," Neelan said.

Like an ancient blue-green jellyfish, the Marwatha floated closer. Rust and grime dulled the hull. Its bulk blocked out the sun. Everyone else ducked as the shadow fell on the house. I was the only one standing when it veered off to the northern shore, near Mesopaikka, with a swiftness that exceeded any bird.

"We must fight." Bejah's green eyes glittered in the lamplight, and she tromped down the stairs and outside. Neelan scurried after her.

"Weapons!" Alaric called out.

I took the kiyo pole that kept Yarat arrivals from using their abilities on me and followed everyone outside. I got onto the back of Carki, smoothing her grey fur. She was shaking with nerves. Vali bucked upward with Leanora on him and bolted ahead, a blur of brown fur. The rest followed on ulsos we had on hand. Alaric was about to pass me when I yelled at him. "Stay by my side!"

I followed Neelan and Bejah to a large clearing close to Mesopaikka. The last rays of sunlight were fading. A large crowd burst through the smoke that still billowed from the burning Talbo-Pii. The Marwatha hovered in the air above them.

"Any survivors from the incoming ships?" a man called out to us.

"Not yet," I grunted. I shook with anticipation. Harnessing my Hagothian training, I hummed very faintly, regulating my inhalations to calm my muscles, to keep my mind clear. I did not want to die like my deceased Hagothian friend, Ori.

I looked to Leanora. I needed to stay strong for her. To keep her out of danger in a way that hadn't been possible when we'd trekked here.

The Marwatha spun and slowly whooshed to a stop on the grassy clearing next to Mesopaikka. A hatch in the ship opened; the cargo door was shaped like a large ulso tongue. It settled in the sand with a creak. I held out my kiyo while others waited in the periphery. Leanora was behind me with two knives out, Bejah and Neelan close behind her.

Three women stepped out of the hatch with their arms raised, no weapons in sight. One of them was a very tall woman, larger than any I'd ever seen, who watched us carefully. Her grey eyes changed to a deep gold and back to grey again as she scanned the distance. A darker woman, her hair in long thin braids stood beside her, a hand-held harp strapped to her back. A third woman hopped off the platform extending to the ground and ran toward the burning Talbo-Pii, her red hair streaming behind her. The tall woman with straight hair was clearly in charge. A ripple went through me when she made eye contact. Neelan ran toward them, and the darker woman's face softened.

"Neelan!" she called out, putting her hand on his shoulder briefly. They were not Yarats at least.

"Mikosh, it has been a long time." Neelan's palm lit up in greeting to her. His face went still when he saw the taller, grey-eyed woman. "Gulnaz. You do not change." He looked over his shoulder. "Drash will be happy to see you."

"I am eager to see Drash— as soon as we speak with Leanora

and Saren." Gulnaz stared at Leanora coldly, a smile plastered to her face.

Leanora stepped forward. "You are here to help, I hope."

"We have come from Hirana to bring you back," Mikosh said. Her dark face was stonier than a Hagothian warrior's.

Bring her back? I thought, but I was distracted by Gulnaz.

Gulnaz raised her palms, a blue light glowed and bounced off all of us before dancing into the distance. Mikosh brought out the metal harp and plucked it lightly, singing with the note she played. Several of the nearby Talbo-Pii vibrated.

"Survivors," Mikosh said and started toward the Talbo-Pii. Within seconds I heard groans as she killed the survivors. She came back, her face drawn.

Gulnaz stepped toward me. "We brought this Marwatha here for the Eloians to fight against the Yarats. It won't be long before Leanora comes back to train with us so we can bring the rest of our fighting force back to help." She reminded me a little of my father. "Questions?" she asked.

Leanora looked confused. "I can't go back with you."

Gulnaz and Mikosh gave each other knowing looks. "Saren has not spoken to you?" they asked in unison.

"She has, but I didn't think...not with everything that's happened..." Leanora's eyes narrowed.

The ulsos crowded in front of Leanora when the women stepped toward her.

Mikosh kept her hand out to them, and Vali hummed at her. "Very intelligent I see. Useful for our battles ahead."

"I need to help with the injured." Leanora took Vali, who was straining to run free.

"Show the way," Mikosh said, while Gulnaz stood there with her arms crossed. I wanted them to pack up their war. Go away, and leave us be.

The smoke was still billowing as we made our way toward the

hospital. I slid behind Leanora on Vali and held her close to me. I was certain they would take her away the first chance they had. Lepidians hauled bodies from smoking houses and apartments. Carts of luoshis and ulsos followed us to the hospital. The silence was broken when Leanora sighed.

"So many injured," she whispered. She met my gaze, "They want me to go to Hirana."

The closer we got to the terraced building of the hospital, the more Lepidaians shuffled around, looking in shock at the hulks of smoking Talbo-Pii. This was not the spring we had imagined.

DAWN CAME before we'd finished at the hospital. My muscles were ready to give out. I needed Leanora all to myself. Not necessarily for me, but to keep her from the incessant demands of transporting patients throughout the understaffed hospital. At one point, she turned to me, her face pale.

"I can't move another patient. I'm done." She leaned against me, falling asleep standing.

The sun peaked above the horizon. I led the two of us out without asking for permission from Methriel. I lifted her up to ride on Vali but took Vali's reins so she could lean against me while I steered.

"My mom has gone to bring more healers...from an enclave in the south shore...Pakopaikka...where Kardush healers live in seclusion," she muttered.

"Let her bring them. You need to rest." I sat behind her on Vali, who ruffed and set off when I shook the reins.

All the fires were out by the time we started back toward the house. The streets were empty, a dusty darkness covering the stone buildings, resisting the shine of the rising sun. Everything was coated with an oily residue that clung to my skin. When I leaned into Leanora, she smelled like disinfectant.

Vali stopped at the stones of the rounded bridge right before the turn toward her house. He was used to us taking a break here to talk. It was cold, and Leanora rested her head against my shoulder.

"Everything feels like it's going to change," she said. "We can't marry with everything happening."

"Why don't we take the oath tomorrow? Before you decide about Hirana." I hopped off Vali.

She looked at me with those dark eyes of hers that I'd gotten lost in the first day we met in Hagoth. Her smile widened, and I leaned down to kiss her gently, savoring the taste of her.

"I'll wait for you, Leanora. I've loved you this long. Nothing will change that." I walked beside her, still sitting atop Vali.

"We always have a reason to be together…even without an oath." She put one hand on my shoulder. "I need you to be prepared for me to go to Hirana." She paused. "Or to come with me."

I did not relish the thought of going to a planet that had caused so many problems for Eloia. "I'll go with you," I heard myself say.

It hit me then as we ambled along, both of us completely depleted, how much she cared for me. The dawn light came up on the red marks on her neck. Here was a woman so powerful that she could transport people across long distances. How could I compare?

"I wish…" I started to say but stopped when I saw Gulnaz and her mother in the distance.

"I know…" Leanora let go of me and stopped Vali, not able to make out the figures in the distance yet.

"What is it?" I watched her narrow her gaze to look out at the sea.

"I need to look at the sea when it's calm. My mother's paintings of the ocean on Hirana look nothing like this. I want to remember how beautiful and blue our sea is. I feel like if I stop looking at it, I'll never see it again." She inhaled deeply and exhaled, the silence blending with the sound of the ocean lapping at the shore. "I dreamt of this very ocean for so long. We suffered so much to be here. I don't want to lose it all again."

I held her to me. I brought my lips to her throat, and she murmured my name.

"Tarrok, I love you almost more than life itself."

"Don't go," I whispered.

Someone cleared their throat, and I let go of her. Saren stood in front of us. "We need to talk with Leanora."

She didn't turn to face them. I wanted to hold her forever, her hair blowing over my face. Leanora didn't let go of me when she finally walked toward her mother, ignoring Gulnaz completely.

"Tarrok is coming with me. If I go."

6

LEANORA

Moisture and heat returned to my skin while I hurtled through clouds. My skin was dry, and my lips were cracking. The tune I sang caused me to levitate over the sands, the light pink ocean lapping at my feet. Gulnaz stopped singing, and my tune faded to a whisper. Tarrok's hand was no longer in mine. I splashed into the warm ocean, sinking up to my chest. He reached for me, now transparent, coughing and sputtering. Gulnaz narrowed her eyes at his vanishing figure. I sang again, but he disappeared.

I tried to move, but I could not work my limbs. Neelan had been right: interplanetary travel took everything out of me. I lifted my arms to swim to shore, but I barely floated.

I had to get Tarrok back.

Tiny beads of water remained on my hands in perfect spheres. When I popped one of the spheres, it squealed.

"Don't kill the water beads." Mikosh levitated and splashed into the water beside me. Her long, black braids dripped with water as she extended a brown arm toward me.

"We have to bring him back. He's supposed...to...be...here..." I was out of breath and Mikosh held me up. Gulnaz lay on her side on the beach.

What had gone wrong? I tried to get a fix on where he was in space. Was he drifting out there between two planets, his body slowly freezing before fracturing apart? I looked back to Mikosh for answers, but she was transfixed, staring at the glowing neiko and what it was telling her, if anything. Then it went dark.

Mikosh reached for me. I shrugged her off. "Help me out here, Leanora."

I looked back toward the deeper water, searching for Tarrok. "Where is he?" I asked.

"Not here." Mikosh snorted. "He'd get in the way." She looked over to Gulnaz, like she was waiting for an explanation.

"He has to be here," I said.

Gulnaz flipped over in the wet sand. She inhaled deeply and murmured a chant. The air around her shifted before she hovered off the ground to stand on the dry sand.

I sunk below the surface of the water, letting the tide carry me away from Mikosh's grasp. It was saltier than the ocean in Eloia. I closed my eyes, channeling for a way to bring Tarrok back. My mind felt like loose noodles floating in a warm ocean. The pink sea surged around me, tumbling me under, bits of seawater and detritus glittering when I opened my eyes.

The feeling of loss without him was so palpable I tried to draw on the energy of his absence. I came up for breath, far enough out now that I couldn't touch the ground. I allowed my body to float on the surface, inhaled, and I closed my eyes. I sung deep within my abdomen the tune we'd heard at the market last week. I reached with everything in me for his energy, the scent of him, anything. I sang again, a wisp of his presence materializing beside me.

"Don't do that!" Mikosh yelled, her neiko glowing again.

"Stop her!" she yelled at Gulnaz, tromping through the water for me.

"Like I could," Gulnaz yelled.

Mikosh dragged me deeper into the water and held me under. The tide surged against my body, and I floated out of her grasp. I struggled to hold onto the idea of Tarrok on Eloia, singing him toward me, a lilting Asanian tune normally played by guitar that was so familiar to me it was a part of my muscle memory.

His green hand lightly grasped mine, fighting against Mikosh, who held fast again. I needed his help to pull him through the galaxy. Was I imagining the scent of lemons? I sang to make more of him materialize, but I saw nothing. The pressure of his hand on mine faded, and a coldness washed through my body. My throat was burning, and I had to stop singing. All my muscles had been injected with venom. The journey from Eloia to Hirana had worn me to the cellular level. Only my mind belonged to me as my sight faded, and I sunk further below the surface.

Mikosh lifted me out, holding me under my arms. She pounded me on the back as I spurted water.

"Don't do that again. Tarrok could have died if you had brought him through and then released him before he'd made his way fully to this side of the planet." Mikosh's voice was gentle. She turned me around, and there was sorrow in her light blue eyes. "I know this isn't what you wanted." She threw her shoulder under my arm and towed me to the soft coral sand.

Gulnaz stood upright on the shore and held her long arms out, the sun picking up the bronze flecks in her skin. "Xibo's waiting."

"She's not moving any faster without your help." Mikosh lifted my arms around their shoulders and helped me limp inland. Mikosh was far gentler than Gulnaz, who was taller than both of us and took longer steps than my jelly legs could handle.

Once we were inland, we passed an orderly configuration of translucent buildings that rose several stories into the air. The cloudless sky allowed me to follow their tops until they were too blurry for me to make out any detail. None of the buildings appeared to be made of solid walls. The closest buildings were burned or singed at the tops. Some of the nearby makeshift lean-to buildings had serrated edges that didn't follow the rest of the rounded modular construction of the larger white, grey, and blue structures around us. When we got closer to the nearest white building, I brushed my hands across the walls. They were made of a loosely woven material that resembled white flax with vines that grew in a lattice-work pattern over a metal frame. When I pushed on the wall, it didn't give way, despite its flimsy, translucent appearance. Several layers had been fused together so that it wasn't possible to see what was on the other side of the walls. I poked my finger into one of the larger holes and the material squeezed my finger. I withdrew it quickly so my hand wouldn't get stuck.

An older man limped over to us. His bald head glistened in the bright twin sunlight. He squinted and leaned against a curved metal staff that glimmered when it struck the ground. His prosthetic wasn't in alignment with his real leg. He kept the staff in his real arm; his prosthetic arm glowed green from where the elbow joint met his skin. His round face stared through me, no warmth coming from him.

"I'm Xibo. Welcome, Leanora." He looked behind me and then met my gaze. "You arrived without Hroth's son, I see." He looked at Gulnaz, one eyebrow raised.

"He has to be here," I said.

Xibo crossed his arms with difficulty, the staff dropping. "Probably not." His wide mouth turned up in a half smile, irking me. He bent down with effort to pick up the staff.

"Then I'm going back." I pulled away from Mikosh and fell

onto the ground, the sand grinding into my skin. I couldn't get up again without her help.

"Try." Xibo's black eyes were piercing. He scratched his chin, looking faintly amused. Then he exhaled noisily. "It doesn't look like you're working very hard on getting him back here."

"She already tried. Let her be," Mikosh said, lifting me back to standing.

Xibo looked like he was relishing in this fact, his eyebrows curved in mock concern.

"The agreement...I would come...to Hirana...with...Tarrok." My mind swam from fatigue. I was ready to vomit, but I breathed back the bile rising in my throat. Mikosh left me where I was and levitated off in the distance. Gulnaz approached but didn't offer to help.

The oppressive humidity made me want to collapse where I was, but I kept inhaling, trying to will myself to not be sick. I swiveled back to watch Mikosh levitating above the pink ocean, swooping in and out of the water. Sound followed her every movement as she drew her hand in again on the next dive and came up with a fistful of wriggling creatures.

"Great. Everyone has decided to do their own thing." Xibo's voice was gravelly and low. "Let me know when you're ready to learn." He winked at Gulnaz, and she laughed, but there was a dullness to her eyes. I fell back to the sandy ground, too exhausted to move. It felt like the will to care had evaporated from me. Then a prickly sensation started at my legs, like something sniffing me. Whatever it was scurried across my face.

"Ah!" I screamed, swiping at it. I rolled in the sand, which stuck to every sweaty bit of exposed skin. A strange chittering started.

"Look what we have here," Gulnaz said.

A familiar brush of tail wound around my neck. I swiped at it nevertheless. There is no way...I opened my eyes, and Inbikh, my white furred gwynbee, was in Gulnaz's grasp.

"Ya-rii...it me," Inbikh spoke.

"It speaks?" Xibo asked.

"Someone didn't want to leave you behind," Gulnaz said, her face softening. She handed Inbikh to me.

Inbikh licked my cheek and purred into my shoulder. "This place strange."

"How...?" My voice was barely a croak. "Why didn't I know she was with us?"

Xibo exhaled in annoyance. Gulnaz reached out to pet Inbikh, who ignored her while she continued to groom me.

"Did you bring her?" I asked.

"You did." Gulnaz gazed at Xibo, her face stiffening. She was lying. Xibo scratched at his unshaved face, suddenly becoming very interested.

"I don't remember her being there with us," I said. Then regretted it. If Gulnaz brought her, why should I care?

"It doesn't mean she wasn't, hmm little one?" Xibo asked, his voice changing as he put out a hand toward Inbikh, who fled away from him. The pink streaks in her white fur were a blur as she jetted around me, coming to rest at my feet.

Xibo called out behind him, "Selchuk!"

A tall young man, closer in age to me than Mikosh or Gulnaz, sauntered toward us. He was darker than Gulnaz, his straight black hair falling in his face. He gathered his hair into a band so it was in a knot at his neck and scowled at Xibo.

"Leanora. I've seen you on the communicator projections." He held out his hand and briefly touched my palm before withdrawing, a half smile playing at the corners of his mouth.

Xibo looked between the two of us, amused by something I had missed. "We're going to the restoration chambers. It's our last chance to use them before leaving." Xibo faced Selchuk and regarded me on the ground. "Get her energy levels where they need to be. See you both inside." Xibo hobbled off, muttering to Gulnaz in Hiranian as they made their way up a ramp to a ramshackle building with only a roof and support beams holding it up.

Selchuk didn't acknowledge Xibo and instead searched my face before kneeling beside me, holding his hands out. They glowed blue before returning to their normal brown color. "I'm the head healer here on Hirana...well, now I am." He didn't seem pleased by this and paused, like he expected me to say something. "Where is the green man?" he asked.

"Hopefully safe on Eloia and not stuck in space," I muttered, trying to sit up but only able to lift my head.

"If he didn't arrive with you, he's definitely on Eloia." He held his hands outside of me, not touching. "Are you ready?"

"I think so." He hummed a rapid tune, his voice harmonizing with itself, the melody thrumming inside of me. I closed my eyes, the burning in my muscles ceasing. A small trickle of energy returned to me before becoming a rush of warmth. I opened my eyes to ascertain how he was doing this. The color had drained out of him. He stopped singing and lowered his hands.

"What happened?" I asked, testing out my legs to try to stand. I was still a little wobbly.

"When I restored some of your energy, you drained my healing reserves," Selchuk said. He whispered softly and the color returned to his face, similar to what had happened with Gulnaz earlier. "Only binary travelers can do that to me."

"What's a binary traveler?"

"People like you and Gulnaz. Who can travel to places you want to, without guarding your attachments. Only a small amount of highly trained individuals can bring themselves and other living creatures across galaxies." He helped me off the ground. "It's no wonder you're exhausted. The trip could have killed you." His jawline hardened, and he narrowed his gaze in the direction Xibo had gone with Gulnaz. "This way."

I walked with him up steps to an open-air building that let the ocean breeze in. At the top of the steps were metal cylinders set into a wooden platform. Steam rose off the cylinders, but I couldn't see what was inside. "Will I be exhausted every time I travel?" I asked.

"Depends on the circumstance," Selchuk said.

In the distance someone sang a soft melody that made it easier to walk up the stairs to the platform. Inbikh came chittering after us and climbed onto my shoulder. When we made it to the top, steam rose from the three vats of water. Vines hung from the ceiling into the water, which had the briny aroma of seawater mixed with sweet herbs that smelled like a mixture of lavender and megula. "Why are we the only people around?" I asked. It had been a long time since I'd been anywhere with so few people.

"Thresil Mira island, where we are, was the worst hit during the war. No one survived from here," Selchuk said. "The Yarats who escaped stole ships we'd had on display for our battle school. Mostly for history lessons." His voice was hard.

"Enough talking, get in." Xibo gestured to the empty steaming vat before jumping in to Gulnaz's pool. "Our launching site was here in the old days, before we learned to travel using our spirits." Xibo raised his arms wide, his smile strained. "No one wanted to stay after the war ended."

"The only useful things that remain are these restoration vats," Gulnaz said. Her stare reached through me in a way that made me want to run.

"Get in so you can fully replenish your energy levels, Leanora. We used these in battles all the time until the Yarats destroyed all of ours." Xibo turned to Gulnaz. "Shame we can't bring them with us?"

"Not a chance I'm going to transport those. Don't ask her, she doesn't need to move your stuff for nothing," she said harshly. Xibo laughed at her with a mirth I didn't understand. Wasn't he their general?

I imagined my mother when she first saw Eloia. Did the deserts and dunes of Hagoth feel anything like this to her?

Inbikh flicked her bushy, white tail in my face. At least I had her. I scratched her fuzzy small head.

Xibo looked up at the afternoon's violet sky visible through the mesh ceiling. "No pets in the chambers." He raised an eyebrow.

"He too growly." Inbikh fluffed her tail at Xibo.

"Says who?" Selchuk jumped into the farthest vat of water from Xibo and Gulnaz. An entire chamber sat unoccupied.

Xibo flushed, and he rose out of the vat, almost hyperventilating. I thought he might be ill until I caught Selchuk rise above him, dripping wet and shaking with anger.

"You're not sending it back," Selchuk said. "Not that you can anyway."

They were fighting without touching each other. A low, atonal melody sounded in my ears. I stepped between them and immediately dropped to the ground from the energy Xibo had been sending Selchuk's way. Inbikh rolled off me unharmed.

"Stop fighting!" I yelled from the ground. They stopped their assault on each other. "I can go back." *I don't need to stay where it's obvious my gwynbee and I are not welcome.*

I stood up, still woozy but not wanting them to know that. "The plan was that Tarrok would come and train with me."

"She's right," Gulnaz said, rising out of the chamber to help me off the ground. "It wasn't fair that Tarrok didn't come. Xibo, can't you do something?" She didn't sound sincere.

Xibo clapped his hands and a ripple went through the room. Inbikh jumped to me and Xibo growled at her.

"No scare me, crazy man," Inbikh said.

"Get in the restorative chambers." He rubbed his bald head and exhaled. "You'll get over your travel sickness faster."

"Not until you give me answers about Tarrok." I crossed my arms.

"We don't need him," Xibo exhaled.

"Why not tell me before I came?"

He looked even more exasperated, water dripping from his cherry red face. "I am the general here, not you."

I stepped toward him. If I didn't stand up to him now, he'd think he could order me around all the time. "Explain why you tricked me."

He looked at Gulnaz and nodded at her. She levitated out of the water vat and soared off to where Mikosh was in the water. "Tarrok does not travel. He would feel lost during our training."

"This is stupid." I crossed my arms.

"Yes, talking like this is—we have work to do. If you were a better traveler and Saren hadn't waited so long, maybe Tarrok would be here."

"I can't be the only Eloian here training."

"See it as an honor and stop complaining." Xibo pointed to the water chamber.

Selchuk floated out of the water to stand next to me. "You'll feel better once you get in." He reached for Inbikh tentatively, and she nuzzled him with her cat-like snout.

"You coming already?" Mikosh asked, racing past us and plopping in the water.

Inbikh dived into the water ahead of me, chittering in pleasure. I took my time getting in, the warmth restoring my limbs but not the aching that still radiated from my heart.

7

LEANORA

The vines surrounding the water chambers were the same cool green as Tarrok's skin. I concentrated on how the water alternated pleasantly between warm and cool. It was easy to float in the briny water. But it also made me excessively thirsty. I reached over to touch the floating fronds and flowers at the rim of my tank. They were as bright pink as the blooms in the rainforests of Nedara.

Selchuk dangled his legs over my tank, playing a flute that trilled several notes at a time. He stopped when he saw Inbikh floating on her back next to me, her paws crossed over her chest.

"It's nice?" Selchuk asked me.

"Better," I said.

Xibo and Gulnaz muttered to each other in Hiranian, their conversation beyond my comprehension.

A blue-winged bird flew into the room with a packet that split into pieces over the tanks. Inbikh clambered out of the water, shaking off. I reached for a piece before it was submerged. Selchuk was quicker and handed it to me. The thin, chewy jerky stilled my rumbling stomach. An unusual calm settled over my weary body, my heartbeat slowing. All the pangs of missing everyone I knew dissipated momentarily.

"Anything to drink?" I asked Selchuk.

Xibo called out to the birds in the rafters above us. "De-laile. Yada." *Refreshment, please.* He was nicer to the animals than to humans, holding out his hand to Inbikh. She wasn't one of his soldiers; she wouldn't be so easy to boss around. I was proud of her when she flicked her bushy white tail, ignoring him and chittering to the birds who brought her a bowl of water.

Another glass descended for me. One large blue bird held it in its clutches, and the other emptied a bag of liquid into the glass. Inbikh watched them with delight.

"They're not for eating," I reminded her.

"Too bad. They pretty." She licked her paws before jumping in the water again.

"It's best to drink out of the water. We don't know how your body will react to the first treatment." Selchuk's dark blue eyes stared through me.

I climbed out to drink, leaving my legs to dangle in the water, a pleasant fizzing at my calves. I immediately thought of my mother and how this had once been her home. Had she been in these same vats of water? The violet skies above us, visible through the dried vegetation on the metal and vine interlaced roof, were darker. I drank the half-liquid, half-solid composition that changed flavors on my tongue.

Selchuk stayed where he was in the tank, his face turned toward me. There was a sharpness to his light brown face with the faint outline of scars on his neck and arms. He watched me very carefully.

I startled to find Xibo leaning next to me. He had been in my non-existent peripheral vision. *That's why Selchuk had been staring.* "I can't see you. I have zero peripheral vision," I said.

"Noted." Xibo cleared his throat. "Get out. We have work to do."

Did he have to be so rude? I climbed out, the tingling in my limbs ceasing. "Once it gets dark I won't be able to see without lamps or some form of light," I said.

"Selchuk can fix all of that," Xibo said dryly.

"I don't need fixing."

My blouse and skirt immediately dried, retaining a stiff chalky appearance against my body. My blousy, layered clothes were very different from the close-fitting, stretchy material that they all wore.

Gulnaz called out from below to us. "She needs more time."

"She'll adjust," Xibo said harshly. He started down the stairs, and when I didn't follow him, he stood there staring at me. There was something in his manner that brought me back to my last day in Lepidaia with my mom. I followed him through the corridor, a melody in the air that was so similar to a song I'd heard before.

THE KARDUSH REFUGEE women sang a lilting tune without words. The walls of the stone enclave, Pakopaikka, were lit by lanterns that cast a yellow glow against the stone and glass walls. The women bustled around us peacefully in long gray and blue cotton dresses. My mother put her arm around me, her black eyes sorrowful. "I was different. I could travel from age seven. It caused a lot of problems. Sadly, I could only travel to places I had seen in books. And it took me a while to control my ability."

"Could you leave the planet?" I was watching her guarded expression.

"No, that took years of training," Mom said, still trying to hide her discomfort.

"What kind of training?"

"It started hundreds of years before—when the Yarats came and helped us develop our process for traveling between planets."

"Why did the Kardush let the Yarats stay on Hirana?" I asked. "Why didn't they kill all of you and take over the planet?"

My mother smoothed back her long silver hair. "We were the first civilization to resist them, despite our lack of technology. We thought they would make our lives better. Maybe we were a little in awe of all the Yarats had accomplished. Imagine your emotions no longer ruling your life?" She gave me a knowing smile. She was talking about Tarrok and me.

"It was revolutionary that experimentation could make our lives better." She folded her pale hands. "Except it didn't." She looked away from me to the women still singing as they wiped down the meal tables. "We stretched our bodies and souls to their limits, and what did we bring ourselves?

"Things, technology, bio-organisms, and architecture that altered itself after only a few tweaks from engineers like myself. We didn't have to spend years building a large structure to house a population burst. We could make rocks grow on their own, like the enclave here in Pakopaikka. We used living things to expand our abilities." She leaned in close. "But in the process of advancing ourselves, we also lost a lot. You have a love inside of you I will never understand, because I didn't grow up like you did. On Hirana—the way they tortured us in the name of personal development—I hate remembering it."

In her eyes was an old pain I remembered from Asanis, when I caught her working on one of her projects late at night or playing her bell organ. Had she been working to expunge everything she'd experienced? Or was it her only way of distancing herself from Zer?

WHY HADN'T she told me it would be like this?

My first instinct was to run.

But I had work to do, people to help. The faster I learned, the swifter my return to Eloia. I continued down the stone corridor, leaving the vats of water behind. We entered a grey building that didn't have the same latticework walls of the other buildings I'd encountered. I touched the cool stone, which was strangely familiar against my palm.

"Up, up." Inbikh clawed at my skirt, and I picked her up before she tore more holes in my hem. Once we were inside an inner corridor, deeper into the building, the light faded.

"There's someone who wants to speak with you," Xibo said, climbing a set of stairs ahead—the corridor poorly lit. I held onto the railing and felt Selchuk behind us, Inbikh purring as I held her close to me.

Our feet made no sound on the steps that spiraled upward. The upper levels had solid white flooring that didn't look like it belonged with the rest of the stone floors below. When we stopped at the top of the stairs, a vast room opened before us that was similar to the stone and glass construction of the enclave at Pakopaikka. The difference was that this room was entirely white with only one source of light. It had rectangular spaces for windows, with vegetation coverings where Eloians always installed glass. A light breeze blew through the room that drew out the stifling heat and humidity.

A projection was on the far-left wall, and Mikosh spoke to it. "She's here now." She stepped away, and my family's faces came into view. My mother stepped forward, her long silver hair hanging limply down, dark shadows under her eyes. She had been crying.

"We're so glad to see you." She moved so my brother and father could see me.

"Come back soon so you can shoot the ship's guns with me,"

Alaric said, his blue eyes so like my father's. My father ruffled his hair and shooed him away before I could say anything.

"We miss you," my dad said and looked behind him to Tarrok.

When I saw Tarrok's russet eyes, his green face filling up the projection, I couldn't help running to the image of him, my eyes welling, my mouth unable to speak for fear of crying in front of everyone in the room.

"Leonora, I wish I were there." His face was so sad. I needed to touch him. "I don't know what happened."

I looked behind me. Xibo and Gulnaz were watching.

"Go," I said.

Mikosh pushed them out before drawing a curtain over the open doorway. I waited before speaking.

"Tarrok, I hate it here." I put one hand close to the screen, imagining his face under my fingers. "I tried to bring you back."

"I know." His eyes were wide with sadness. How I needed him.

"Mikosh stopped me," I muttered.

"I could have died." He sighed and looked up at me. The love behind his emerald chiseled face had gotten me through so much.

Tears coursed down my cheeks. "I feel so different. So weak. I don't understand how I'm supposed to bring a whole army back. What if I can't bring anyone and I'm stuck here?" Worse, what if he stopped loving me while I was gone?

"Mikosh said you had the ability—the neiko showed it was greater than anyone she'd ever tested—to bring hundreds back here with you." He had this hopeful expression on his face when he was trying to encourage me but wasn't entirely certain he believed it himself. I wanted to inhale his calming, natural citrus scent at that moment. But I only smelled the stale window coverings.

I came closer to his projection. "There is a lot I need to learn about traveling in order to bring hundreds back. Especially if I could only bring myself and Inbikh over."

"You *are* strong. You will make it back here soon." He held up a palm like he was ready to touch my face, then stopped when he realized how far away we were.

I wiped away the tears, feeling foolish, wanting to be as strong as he always was for me. "We should have married when we had the chance." I looked up at him, a knowing smile on his face. "I'm sorry."

Tarrok turned behind him. "We only have a little while before the connection will break." There was a shaking in the background, and then it stopped.

"What was that?"

"Another attack," he said. "With the rotational difference between the two planets, it's been three days since I've seen you and already there have been more Yarats arriving. Some just dead ships and one new ship. It took off shortly after arrival, probably scouting out what to destroy and what to keep. Neelan and his team haven't finished completing the armada. We'll evacuate soon."

"How will we talk?" My pulse raced and I tried to calm myself. I couldn't keep losing it in front of him.

He reached out his long green hand toward the projection. "We'll figure out a way. Don't worry, Leanora. We promised each other." His eyes were the last thing I saw before he disappeared from the screen.

XIBO HOBBLED BACK into the room, all business. I wiped off my face and tried to mirror his look of resolve. "Sit. There are things to say," he said.

I remained standing, steeling myself against whatever he said,

66

not flinching from the darkness I saw in his black eyes, reminding myself to breathe and not let my eyes change color.

"If you do not rein in your emotions, it will be hard to save your people from the Yarats."

Obviously my eyes had changed color, despite my best intentions. Xibo stood there, his staff glowing.

"Didn't emotions bring me here?" I asked.

Xibo folded his arms around his staff. "Perhaps, but they can also deceive you." He exhaled and walked over to the window, rolling up the window covering. "We have so little time to train you. I wish you had been here for the war. Then you would understand and wouldn't be so soft."

He stood up and gestured toward the door. "Dinner is downstairs. It won't compare to your Eloian food, but it's better than nothing."

I waited for him to hobble forward before following him, the scent of stale fried fish filling the air around us.

8

TARROK

THREE DAYS EARLIER, MESOPAIKKA, ELOIA

We had been together on that pink shore. Almost. Why wasn't I there now?

The giant minerals in the communications hall still had a pulsing purple glow. It hurt to look up at the crystalline ceiling above. I hadn't been prepared for the cold and nausea when we rushed past star systems, singing to keep our bodies in motion. A throbbing pain hammered at my temples and I had to close my eyes. I had been traveling with her, hadn't I? I opened my eyes again, the light still pulsing inside the meso-paik mineral columns ahead.

Why isn't she here?

Did something happen to her?

Voices echoed off the connecting hallway into Mesopaikka. Vali barked, followed by the grey furred Carki and all-white Dona. They circled around me, taking turns licking my face. I should have been happy to see them, but I knew Vali was going to be a pain without Leanora. Footsteps echoed on the stone floor.

Methriel ran over and groaned when he knelt beside me. "What happened?"

"I thought you would know," I said.

I struggled to peel myself off the floor, Vali nosing my back. I was only able to roll onto my side. Vali started whining. Leanora was his bonded partner, and he was going to be giving me fits for weeks, if I was lucky. I had to keep it together.

"Why am I still here?" I asked Methriel. My voice felt separate from my body, my throat dry.

Saren ran over to us. The look on her face wasn't reassuring. I didn't need her pity.

"I have to go to her," I said, trying to come to a crawling position so I could stand.

Vali nudged me with his snout, his whining more plaintive.

"Vali! Stop," I said. He groaned and settled on his haunches. His ears remained perked up.

Saren and Methriel lifted me to standing. She held a glowing blue finger in front of me, singing as she touched my upper arm, a warm energy making my heart race. She let go. "You'll feel better now."

"Not if I'm still here," I said, finally standing.

"Leanora is the only one who can bring you to Hirana." She searched Methriel's face, turning back to me with her black eyes.

"We need you here, Tarrok," Methriel said.

"I was supposed to go. That was the plan!" I said more loudly than I wanted.

They both took a step back.

"She hasn't been traveling long enough to bring you again. Not without help from Hirana. That does not appear to be forthcoming." Saren gave me her typical concerned healer look. "If I could bring you there I would."

I took Vali's reins. He was eerily quiet.

"I don't know why," she said softly.

"You knew they didn't want me," I said.

Saren became very still. "It might be better for her to learn to travel alone, without feeling distracted…"

"…Because we want to get married?"

"That isn't the reason, Tarrok…"

"My Yarat genes make me inferior to her Kardush ones?" I sauntered away, clicking my tongue for Carki and Dona to follow. I stopped after a few steps, spinning around. "It isn't my fault my father was Yarat. He didn't cause the Mists." I exhaled, thinking of my dead parents. "Don't treat me differently because you think I'm now the enemy." I held on tighter to the ulsos reins. Their tails dragged when they fell in step with me down the corridor.

"Don't go. This has nothing to do with your father being Yarat." Methriel followed me outside the hall and up to the top of the hill. Once we were outside he wheezed, then bent over to catch his breath. "We need you here…your strategies…we can't evacuate Lepidaia without you." He glanced behind him for a moment. "Alaric needs you. Things are going to get worse…"

Methriel never stood up to Saren, not even when she was wrong. "You didn't think I was good enough to marry Leanora. Why believe anything else you say?"

"Tarrok…that isn't true at all…"

I climbed onto Vali's back and rode across the north hills, the ocean a torrent of waves in the moonlight. All five moons were shining. It felt like my future had been ripped away from me by strangers.

I had to regroup, come back, and remember who I was before Leanora.

I am an orphan.

Son of Hroth, a Yarat, and Ygra Jerew, a Hagothian. Both long dead. My sister, Erena, my only surviving relative. Hundreds of miles from here.

But that is not who I am, I reminded myself. I studied the shadowed hills to the west and the white clouds rushing past the moons. This had become my home, more than the desert. Because of Leanora.

All my hopes lay with her. I had to find another way to be the man she loved. I urged Vali on, his brown head rearing up, his mane blowing in the wind as we trotted on, faster and faster. Carki and Dona raced ahead of us down the broken stone streets, their grey and white tales wagging happily.

Even my sister, Erena, had not listened to me the way Leanora did. I loved watching her face change as my words had an impact. Like she lived for everything I said. No matter how awkward my execution.

I turned us back toward the city, avoiding her parents' neighborhood. In the dark, the burning of this district was less obvious. I slowed down, Vali's tail touching my back lightly. He hummed a low ballad that Leanora sang when I was in a foul mood, which wasn't very often. Families in the apartments above were barbecuing fish over spits in their rooftop courtyards. Music spilled over into the streets. Carki and Dona barked ahead, and then circled back to us, their bushy tails wagging. They hummed along with the music, and I wished I could be easy-going like my animals. Trusting things to get better.

Did I belong in Lepidaia without her? Or was I better off traveling back to Hagoth on the first ship? The only thing I was good at was loving her and training animals. Now that she was gone, would part of me disappear?

Leanora, I miss you so much that everything in me hurts.

I rode the rest of the night in silence, watching the waves crash against the shore.

Puzzling out what came after my rage dissolved wasn't easy. I stroked Vali's back and urged him on to the opposite shore where we could catch the sunrise. If I stayed awake long enough.

9

LEANORA

My mother stared at the sea, her face in profile. "I have lost the ability to travel between planets, even the short distances that were once possible for unattached places."

"Why can't I learn everything here?" I asked.

"You need to bring back more Kardush forces to fight with us." She looked at me, a new power behind her eyes. "There are no binary travelers except you and Gulnaz. Think about how easily you transported patients wherever we needed them to go." There was a quiet desperation in her voice. "Or...your trek here to Lepidaia. That journey would have killed someone without your ability." She brought her palms together. "Leanora, I cannot tell you how to proceed. You are no longer a child." She touched my shoulder. "There is a great destiny for you. I don't know everything that entails, because it is yours to create." She looked down at the shale beneath us. "Remember when we lived in Asanis? When I told you that everyone has two hearts?"

I nodded, remembering that day in the woods, before she was taken away. When I thought afterward she was dead.

"Soon you will understand why I said this." Her gaze settled back to the sea.

"I hate when you get like this. There's more you're not saying." I stood there, stewing inside, the salty air no longer soothing.

"You must decide why it is important to go to Hirana." She took my hand and brought me close, our foreheads touching like when I was a child. "If you do not go…"

YOU MUST DECIDE.

It did not yet feel like it had completely been my choice.

Xibo's pipe smoke brought me back to the kitchen where we'd finished dinner. There were only two candles on the table and no other light. "If you doubt your *haian fusai*, we cannot train you," Xibo said. "You have to harness your ability to travel at will in order to carry people long distances. The Yarats crave what you have."

"Isn't it better to train on Eloia?"

"No." Xibo's tone was clipped. "You don't have the ability to bring all of us back yet. Our last ships departed for Eloia already to aid with the evacuation of Lepidaia. Now, we must recruit more Kardush fighters, which isn't easy after the war." He exhaled loudly. "We need you to bring hundreds of recruits to battle and win. But that takes training. If we go back, before your endurance has been built up, before you understand how to use your spirit and music to move people through space, we all die." He took another puff, then exhaled. "We need your eyesight restored."

"My eyes are fine," I said.

"Fine gets people killed." His accent was thicker when he was angry.

I was about to respond when Selchuk came in with two lamps that cast dancing orange light around the room. Xibo's face was more visible. I stared at his thick eyebrows, his forehead criss-crossed with scars.

"How many battles did you fight in?" I asked.

"Too many." He sounded exhausted.

"How long have the Yarats been gone?" I asked, watching Selchuk keep to the shadows of the room.

"A year. It's likely they wandered several galaxies before setting their sights on Eloia." He turned to stare at Selchuk whose hair fell in his face as he perched in the window seat away from us.

I was the only person here who believed that it wasn't a weakness to be soft, to have emotion. Would I lose that part of myself here? My eyes were swollen and itchy from the urge to cry, and I breathed in deep, measured breaths. *Do not show any weakness*, I reminded myself. *You've had enough crying for a day.*

"Your training will be hard. We Kardush have different ways," Xibo said softly.

"Maybe those ways need to change," I said.

"Do not misunderstand your purpose." He snapped his fingers. "We have this much time before the Yarats invade." A projection emitted from his fingers that became a glowing pink planet: Hirana. "That is us."

He produced a blue orbiting image. "This is Eloia. We are only this far apart...." He brought the two glowing orbs closer. "...with your ability to travel." Then the orbs separated to several meters apart. "Without you—" The images drifted until they were tiny pinpricks thousands of leagues apart—"it would take us weeks to bring recruits to Eloia. And in that time...disaster." He stopped the projection and faced me. "The Yarats will decimate a people who don't know how to defend themselves."

He turned back to Selchuk and spoke in Hiranian. "*Mo fela ye.* I need you."

"I don't want to be here," Selchuk said in a thick accent in Eloian. *Nyeh doi mo felash,* he repeated in Hiranian.

Xibo glared at me. "You have excellent company then."

Nevertheless, Selchuk got up and stood between the two of us, forming a triangle.

"The Yarats fight in a way most Eloians are not prepared for," Xibo said, struggling to stand.

He glared at Selchuk. They backed away and both their fingers lit up. Xibo sang a bass melody without words, then his voice quickly divided into three parts, emitting an ancient, guttural sound that hit me in the chest. Selchuk followed several pitches higher, their bodies vibrating until both rose from the ground. The sound waves knocked me back. The flow of the song changed, slamming Xibo into the wall. The song stopped. I vowed to stay away from the receiving end of Xibo's songs.

"Better than usual," Xibo said, rolling over to stand.

"But not as good as Gulnaz," Selchuk said.

"Men are useless in battle, except picking up bodies and doing what the orchester demands," Xibo said.

"Orchester?" I asked.

"That's you," Selchuk said with respect in his voice. "The person who directs the chorii's sound in battle."

"We Kardush believe expanding the capabilities of our minds and spirits is the greatest technology we can create," Gulnaz said. "This made the Yarats want to stay and learn from us when they settled our planet five hundred years ago."

Selchuk nodded. "The Yarats, at first, did not believe women were more capable than men in battle."

Xibo's face became pleasantly animated. "No Kardush

woman would let herself get to the state I'm in." He held out his prosthetic arm and leg stiffly.

Xibo put his hand on Selchuk's shoulder. "Go away."

"No," Selchuk said, moving next to me.

Xibo held out his staff.

"How do I learn in such a short time?" I asked.

"We will train you," Selchuk said. "It won't take you very long."

Xibo came closer to inspect my eyes. "You're already detecting *urijniak,* or individual spiritual energies, without knowing it. Assessing others' emotions, figuring out what our bodies are saying that our mouths aren't."

"Xibo!" Gulnaz called across the room. She remained in the dark, but an acidic energy transmitted from her.

"Busy." Xibo moved between Selchuk and me. "You have the *haian fusai* or singing life force necessary to heal. That same ability, combined with your *urijniak,* allows you to kill."

I saw Zer, the man I had grown up believing was my father, his mirror eyes staring through me the last time I was in Asanis.

Could I kill him?

Wouldn't a person's spirit come screaming for me after they were gone?

"When you see the Yarats slaughtering in such a way that defies the laws of nature and eternity, you will want to annihilate all of them." Xibo drew a last puff of his cigar, exhaling slowly, his eyes burning bright blue before changing back to a deep brown. "You will have to learn to go beyond defending yourself. You must attack first, always. Your *urijniak* and *haian fusai* are why you can travel at will—but your *urijniak* is a liability in battle. You can't afford to let down your guard."

He sat down, blotting at his face. There were bits of blood from where he had fought against Selchuk. "What you saw here was nothing. We were holding back." He leaned toward me, his eyes full of an energy that was piercing. "Your voice, your music, all of it must serve defending Eloia."

"I am only one person," I said, backing away from him.

"That's all it takes to guide hundreds of people's energies," Selchuk said.

"It's time for bed," Gulnaz said, remaining completely cloaked in darkness.

"I don't sleep," Xibo replied, settling back into a wide sprawl in the large chair that reformed, similar to Hagothian terraform.

"She does," Gulnaz said.

"She'll get used to our hours." Xibo let his pipe clank on the ground. Gulnaz came into the light and put a hand on his chest. He kissed her knuckles like a father.

"Stop projecting your nervous energy." Xibo glanced at me, one eyebrow raised.

I drew all my curiosity back to my body.

"Your training starts in the early morning. 'Night." He spoke rapidly with Gulnaz in Hiranian.

Selchuk gestured for me to follow him. "I'll take you to Mikosh's level. She'll have room for you there."

We wound our way up the steps, a single, dim light shining above the stairwell. I held onto the railing to keep from tripping. However, I ran into Selchuk, not noticing he'd stopped. His eyes glowed in the light when he turned to face me. It was frustrating to feel nothing coming from him. So much for my *urijniak*. He gestured for me to follow his glowing fingers and proceeded back up the stairs.

"Sorry, we don't sleep much. The first few days will feel brutal." He continued to the next level where a breeze blew through the rooms that were connected by large corridors without doors. "What doesn't destroy you will serve the battle, Xibo says." His voice was bitter.

Mikosh opened a curtain at the top of the steps and led me

through to an empty room with only two pieces of furniture that I could discern in the lamplight. She wordlessly pointed to an area near the window coverings that fluttered in the wind. There were a few blankets on the ground but no pillow.

So this is what it's like to be a Kardush soldier, I thought. I sank to the ground, a soft melody playing in my ears. I did not remember my head hitting the soft ground. I was asleep within seconds.

THE MORNING LIGHT came up three or four hours later. Two red orbs rose from the magenta and purple streaked sea in the distance. Mikosh pulled down a bamboo-like covering that shaded the glare of the suns on the water.

"Time to eat." Her braids swished as she walked, a fresh aroma of something like sage mixed with laundered linen wafted over me when she drew the long folds of her tunic's sleeves back across her dark brown arms.

"I barely slept." I rubbed my eyes.

"You'll get used to it," she said gently and handed me a bowl full of dry flakes. "Our planet is on an eighteen hour rotation while Eloia is on a twenty-eight hour cycle, so it will feel different for a while." She poured a transparent substance into the bowl that resembled milk, but it had no odor. I bit into the dried flakes soaking up the milk: they had a fishy, fruity taste. If I wasn't so hungry, I might have gagged. After I was finished, I clambered down the stairs, Mikosh following silently after me.

I pulled out the drawers in the kitchen, stuffing extra food packets into my skirt pockets. I unfolded one and devoured it quickly, warmth spreading through my belly.

"Eloia's food is so much better, no?" She grinned and held out an upturned palm. I placed two extra food packets there.

Xibo started bellowing, and Mikosh pushed me outside with her, the humidity of the day causing me to break out in a sweat. We could hear him yelling, but I didn't understand a word he said in Hiranian.

10

LEANORA

I followed Xibo's hobbling figure past a series of collapsed buildings. I couldn't help fixating on the green viney sinews connecting the metal joints of his prosthetic leg and arm. Despite his laborious gait, I struggled to keep up. Mikosh's mint aroma alerted me to her presence behind me. We rounded a row of building ruins with vines climbing the old foundations. The pink sea glistened beyond as it lapped gently against the shore.

"Do you hear them?" Mikosh caught up with me, her bright blue eyes not changing color. She wiped sweat off her dark brow with the sleeve of her white tunic.

"No." The heat felt especially oppressive after so little sleep. My braided hair hung in two rows, my scalp already drenched. We rounded a bend in the shore, and two figures stood facing off. They didn't stop when we approached.

Once we were close enough, I heard Gulnaz. She put her hand on Selchuk's bare shoulder, and he shrugged her off.

"*Nazrim ye...fural ye ti lo ye!* You can't...you remember what happened before!" Gulnaz said.

"*Eskit ye sa. Ye anyak chas do mit zeb.* You're a traitor. You don't get to say what I do." Selchuk pushed her.

"*Anyak ful mit!* Don't touch me," Gulnaz snapped.

They continued shouting incomprehensibly in Hiranian. Xibo inhaled deeply and lifted his good hand up, causing them to levitate in the air. He kept them airborne while he sang softly. They stopped yelling.

"They're always fighting," Mikosh said. "It was like this before the war, but it's worse now." She wiped her brow again.

"Why?" I asked, closing my eyes from the brightness of the early morning dual suns.

Mikosh dropped her voice to a whisper. "Something about someone Selchuk liked. I never quite understood, and then when Xibo's family died..." she paused and I opened my eyes. Xibo turned toward us for a brief moment before going back to Gulnaz and Selchuk. "I wonder if maybe they like each other."

I tried to block the strange energy coming from Selchuk, figuring if I kept Mikosh talking I could get more information than from Selchuk's frenzied *urijniak*. "Have they told you anything?"

"Gulnaz only talks to Xibo. Selchuk and I get along, but he's a healer and I'm a fighter." Mikosh's mouth was set in a thin line. Not a single emotion coming from her.

"What does him being a healer have to do with anything?"

"He hasn't killed as many people as I have," she said quietly, flicking her eyes away. "It was necessary then. But now that the war is over, it feels like a waste. I thought if I kept killing that I'd protect my mom. But she's dead too." Mikosh turned fully toward me, her energy poking and prodding at me before it stopped abruptly. "I shouldn't have said that." She stretched upward. At her full height she was a head taller than me. "Can't take it back now."

She leaned in closer to me, whispering, "There are too many ghosts here." She inclined her chin toward the ocean. "We have to get off this cursed island."

Xibo raised his voice at Selchuk and Gulnaz, still floating in the air.

"We don't have time for your nonsense..." Xibo berated them in Hiranian.

"Won't we get in trouble if we leave now?" I asked Mikosh.

"Not if we're doing something productive." Her grin was scaring me.

First, she tells me she's killed a lot of people...

"We're supposed to leave today anyway." She extended a hand tentatively. "Do you want to see what a battle looked like?"

I nodded, breathing deeply so my anticipation wouldn't show. She touched a finger lightly to my bare shoulder, and I was no longer inside my own mind. I could still feel the ground beneath my feet, a hazy outline of the shore we stood on, but my consciousness was pulled into another time. Silver and black ships zipped overhead, very similar to the ones that had landed on Lepidaia, while a jarring music punctuated inside me. I was going to lose my mind from the scream-singing, mixed with the screeching of violins, and low bass riffs, all firing off a piercing cacophony of sound.

Another, more lyrical song started, and Gulnaz sang beside me in the air. She clutched a hand-held harp when an armada of armored Yarat figures approached.

"Don't hold back!" Gulnaz zipped ahead and slashed through their bodies with a song that shot out a concentrated stream of fire.

They dropped silently to the ground. More Yarats rushed toward me, and a woman attacked, hitting me square in the chest with her song. The eyes of my Yarat female attacker were a bright yellow. She was taking pleasure singing a terrible melody into my brain until my whole body shuddered, my harp floating in front of me, and, with one pluck of its strings, my voice synchronized with its note, a hole blew through the woman, and she disintegrated.

"Good! Now another!" Gulnaz yelled.

The memory stopped. It had been so real, as if I were Mikosh. The tension abated and my mind returned to my body, but my arms and legs still shook with the violence I'd experienced only seconds earlier. The heat was more intense on my skin now that I was inside my own consciousness, but my insides were ice. Mikosh's hand was at her side, her large eyes watching me carefully.

Xibo turned his attention back to us. "Downloading your history already, Mikosh?" He frowned. "I'm not certain she's ready."

Mikosh glared at him. "Then get them to stop fighting." She lifted her hand to cover her face from the sun's glare. "It's too hot here—let's get off Thresil Mira."

"Not until you tell me how you did that," I said.

"Memory transfer," she said tersely. She walked ahead, and I felt like I had to follow her. "We need to go."

"How does it work?" I tried to stop her as she walked past Xibo, still yelling at Selchuk and Gulnaz.

"For most Hiranians, Yarat, and Kardush it's the same—when they touch skin to skin, especially from a hand to someone's bare arms or shoulders, you can project a memory from your mind. But the other person has to be willing to receive it." She stopped for a moment, a quizzical look on her face. "Isn't that normal?"

"That's never happened to me before," I said, crossing my arms.

"Ah..." Mikosh's eyes went wide with realization. I had more questions, but my thoughts were interrupted by Gulnaz and Selchuk arguing again now that they were standing on the shore.

"I'm not going anywhere with you!" Selchuk said in Hiranian before storming away.

"You're not the leader!" Gulnaz bellowed.

Xibo stood there watching them, his arms crossed.

"Won't he do something?" I asked.

"You don't want him to," Mikosh said.

Selchuk pushed Gulnaz into the sand, and she laughed at him. He kicked sand in her face, and a low hum resonated around them. Selchuk flew into the water, a blur in the distance. When he didn't resurface, I dashed into the sea.

"He can swim." Mikosh stopped me from going further. "Don't get involved." She was about to put her hand on my arm, then stopped.

Xibo drew his hands out wide, and Selchuk rose out of the water and landed on him, coughing up seawater.

"Don't use me as your landing pad." Xibo's prosthetic limb came out of joint, and he and Selchuk set it back into place. "Only Gulnaz gets to beat me up."

Selchuk stood and dusted himself off.

"It's no good fighting with Gulnaz. She always gets her way," Xibo said, glancing over at Gulnaz.

She threw back her straight amber hair. Everything about her was more radiant in the sun. She brushed the grains of sand from her tight-fitting trousers and skin-tight cropped top. "Time to go— the wind is just right." There wasn't a single breeze, and she looked straight at me. Like a challenge.

"There isn't any wind." She wasn't going to play games with me.

"Let's go," Mikosh said. Gulnaz came next to us.

"You'll bring us there." Mikosh touched a finger to my shoulder and showed me where we were on Thresil Mira and how far west I needed to go across the ocean to the next island, Maer-lina.

"Your first test." Gulnaz was close enough that I could smell the brine on her skin. Mikosh kept her face completely still while Gulnaz took our hands. She raised her voice upward, and Selchuk and Xibo joined in the melody. I didn't like the song at all. It was too atonal and strange. Mikosh was silent, arms crossed.

I had also never transported this many people at one time. After a few seconds of trying to follow her song, I stopped us. "I need to bring us there using music I know."

"Follow Gulnaz," Xibo said.

"No." I let go of their hands, Gulnaz glaring at me.

"The song doesn't matter—" Gulnaz insisted.

"It does to me." I started a tune that my mother had sung to me when I was very little. It flowed through me with its soft lilts in Hiranian.

Ai, Xele ut sobish-yara
ule mo tufan xele si'djen,
anyak voshe paar mo So'djuul.
Ai, anyak, anzeb forshaime,
na'seri ye Urajde a mo,
na'seri ye urajdu a mo.

WE ALL JOINED HANDS AGAIN. "See Maer-lina's shore in your mind. Take all of us with you," Mikosh said.

As soon as they joined in the song we were airborne, spinning through the sky. Three different versions of Maer-lina projected into my mind. I focused on the shoreline I needed to recognize with its massive green hills that had large patches of exposed, red earth. The ocean glittered below us, tiny islands passing by. My vision changed the faster we traveled. All the color was leaching out the further we got from the Thresil islands.

I closed my eyes, blinking rapidly. But when I opened my eyes, everything was still gray.

We passed through several sets of low-hanging clouds, picking up speed as we approached a new shoreline. The ocean was now gray, like everything in the landscape. I blinked again. The lack of color didn't make sense. I had to slow our pace as we got closer to the clearing in a hillside further inland. We were moving too quickly, our bodies shuddering as we came closer to the shore. They let go of my hands while I crashed, the long grasses only partially cushioning my landing. My legs throbbed where I'd collided with the sandy soil. I took a moment to catch my breath.

Xibo's face poked out from the thick grasses beside me. "Work on the landing."

I had hoped for a few more minutes without him. Could I restore the color back to my vision?

"If you want me to do something well, you'll have to teach me," I said.

"The anger in your voice is very useful." He leaned in too close, reeking of fish. "If it involved talking to that boy of yours, you'd travel anywhere and learn fairly quickly." I felt a crushing in my brain, his voice a series of hisses. "Your insolence is tolerated only if you excel."

I fell back against the itchy long grasses, and my muscles gave out. My field of vision had narrowed further. The pressure on my head stopped, but I couldn't move.

How could I keep traveling between planets if this took everything out of me? I had to...get...up.

No. My body wasn't going anywhere. I could barely move my head from the grass.

My thoughts spun as I kept circling the same point, panic rising in my chest.

Selchuk parted the grasses and leaned over me. "Call the elements to your body. That's how we restore our bodies' essential functions in battle."

"What about those water containers?" I asked weakly.

"They don't exist anywhere else. You'll have to call the energy back to your body." Selchuk knelt beside me.

"How?" It took almost too much effort to speak. I closed my eyes and willed the energy back into my body. I inhaled again, hoping this energy that he spoke of could also make my eyes work properly. After a minute, nothing had changed.

"Try out different elements. For some people it's calling the energy of soil, others water," Selchuk said softly, his voice very close to where I lay.

"For me, it's salt," Gulnaz said.

"I call the material of clouds and weather patterns," Mikosh said, the grasses rustling behind me. "Imagine the place where you feel most like yourself."

"Let her decide," Xibo said gently.

I closed my eyes, and the first thing I thought of was the sapphire ocean of Lepidaia and how it always drew me toward it.

"Do you see it?" Selchuk asked, his voice soothing.

My labored breathing eased. I could feel my arms, though they ached.

"Imagine it giving you its life force, drawing vitality toward your body."

My mind and body merged as I imagined the ocean in Lepidaia, sapphire blue on a warm spring day. Was it just the ocean or the water? When I thought "water," my body sang like a bell ringing at just the right key.

"Let it draw into you from the ground and air around you," Selchuk whispered.

I inhaled and imagined all the water around me siphoning into my body. The liquid filled everything that ached. My pulse increased, my breath easing in my lungs.

"Not too fast," Xibo warned.

I slowed the intake of moisture that came into my stomach first, then radiated outward as the last of the energy rushed back through my limbs. I opened my eyes. Everything was still gray. I had to crane my head side to side to see all of them. I closed my eyes and inhaled again. The ground was dry beneath me, the grass stalks withering and falling over my bare arms and legs. I jumped up to stand, all traces of fatigue gone. A circle of dry grass remained from where I had been lying.

"Water's definitely your restorative substance," Selchuk said.

"Will it work every time like that?" I asked.

"You have to learn to draw the water into you very quickly in battle," Xibo said. "In less than three seconds."

"What if there isn't any water nearby?" I asked.

"Oh, there's always water nearby," Mikosh said with a smile. "You have to be careful that you're not drawing it from the wrong living things." She pointed toward Selchuk.

Why hadn't my sight returned?

"Let's go." Xibo directed us through the grasses until we reached an open field where the vegetation had been mowed. I had to turn entirely around to get a sense of the landscape. In the partial cloud cover, the ocean spread out behind us, a series of hills rose in the distance, but it was hard to get a sense of what lay behind them. I turned again, but the lack of color hurt my ability to see the gradations in the landforms.

"Are you all right?" Selchuk asked.

"I'm good." Then it occurred to me that I had left Inbikh behind. She hadn't been sleeping on me in the morning. "My gwynbee." How had I forgotten her so easily? "I have to get her."

Xibo held out his hand to stop me when I started back toward the shore. "We left her behind on purpose. We have an exercise for you."

Gulnaz gestured toward a series of objects that were placed at intervals. I came closer to inspect what they were. In one pile sat large sheets of metal that were misshapen by fire. Another pile was rocks of various sizes.

"What am I doing?" I was impatient for Inbikh.

"Demonstrate you can safely move objects not just long distances, but also through space and back." Gulnaz crossed her arms. "Then, you can transport Inbikh here."

I looked at them incredulously. "I'm not moving anything off planet today." I put my hands on my hips. I'd seen what it had taken out of me to bring them to another island.

"If you can bring us here, then it will be very simple to send one of these objects through space," Gulnaz said.

I wanted to smack the look off her perfect face. "All by myself?"

She looked to Xibo. He spoke rapidly to Selchuk and Mikosh who moved to the opposite side of the field where they became indistinguishable blurs.

"Where do I start?"

"Always with a song. Remember that living things require something different than objects without spirits," Xibo said. "Watch."

He started a low song and made two of the rocks soar through the air, then he changed the pace of the song and they alternated, dancing before he changed the tempo again and his voice went into a reedy falsetto. The rocks caught fire before exploding.

"Now you try. Make the rocks move past Selchuk and Mikosh."

I started a Lepidaian tula, singing in my middle register. The rock barely rolled along the ground. I increased the pace, and it levitated then fell, but the song hadn't changed.

"Try the metal next," Xibo said. He whispered something in Gulnaz's ear and she nodded.

It was marginally easier to lift into the air with my voice and make it spin, but it fell when I tried to move it past its origin point. Gulnaz sang the metal over to Selchuk.

It was embarrassing how hard this was for me. I tried to stand up straight, to look like this didn't bother me.

"Try something living," Xibo said. I turned to locate where he was, but it took me a few seconds. "Is something wrong?" he asked.

Should I tell him about my eyes and slow down this whole process?

No, I had to keep going.

"Not Inbikh. I'm not ready yet," I said. If I couldn't move rocks, how could I bring her here?

"We don't have time for you to decide what you're ready for. Just try. I'm here and I can help if something goes wrong." Gulnaz's smooth voice grated on me.

"Like you helped me the last two times?" I countered.

"Find Inbikh with your mind. You know her. Use your *urij-niak*. It will feel like a familiar pinprick in your mind," Xibo commanded.

I closed my now semi-useless eyes, better able to place where people were by the energy their bodies gave off. Gulnaz's body shimmered in undulating waves while Xibo had a radiant bursting energy that came off in spurts. Selchuk was a cool spring. Mikosh had a metallic steadiness.

I searched further, coming up with nothing at first. Then, after several seconds, I felt the airiness and light that Inbikh always had. She wasn't too far away.

"Do you feel her?" Gulnaz asked.

"Yes," I said.

"Now bring her here. Imagine closing that space with your song. Your song is folding the distance between the two of you."

I pulled on the energy coming from Inbikh, picturing her spirit folding her body through the air and soaring toward us, increasing the pace once I felt her closer. Within a few minutes, the air whistled with the movement of her.

"Slow her down, Leonora!" Xibo called out.

I slowed the song, but Inbikh smacked right into my chest, knocking me over and we tumbled into the grass. She chittered at me loudly, jumping off and fluffing her tail in annoyance.

"You not tell me, Ya-rii." She dusted off her paws. "No leave wit-out me, nex' time."

"Sorry, Inbikh." I stroked her soft fur, and she jumped onto my shoulder, purring loudly. "I won't leave you again, I promise."

"At least there were no deaths," Xibo said drily. "Always slow the song before you see the ground. Too many bad landings ruin bones. There's a limit to what Selchuk can heal."

I followed Xibo's voice until I found him. "What is going on?" he asked.

I glanced up at two flares radiating from the gray sky. Wasn't it enough that I was weaker than all of them? Inbikh shifted on my shoulder, climbing down to scamper off.

"Don't wander too far," I said to her.

"I fine, fine," she said, fluffing her tail at me while she stalked off through the grass, soon disappearing from the field.

"Go too far and I'll leave you again." I wanted to follow her. Anything was better than training with super perfect Gulnaz.

Xibo had his hands on his hips. "We aren't done."

I closed my eyes and called the elements to me, imagining the water filling up my eyes so the color could return. When I opened them, there was no difference. I didn't know how much longer I could go on like this without asking for help.

I spun around to find Selchuk, seeking out his cool energy, but I couldn't feel him. If Vali were here, he would have shown me where everyone was. It was too dangerous to try and bring Vali this far. I followed Xibo's voice up the hill, the scent of grass strong in the cool air. I couldn't ignore the empty feeling in my belly and heart as I imagined how much better it would be if Vali and Tarrok were here.

Or if I had never come at all.

11

GULNAZ

"I expected you days ago. Where have you been?" Zer demanded, looking imposing in his maroon robes, surrounded by his favorite henchmen. Mila, the murderer, her large eyes bloodshot. Parmit, his head negotiator, glared at me and cracked his knuckles. Only Sofros, his head engineer—still wearing his magnifying spectacles on his head—was peaceful. A hot blast blew through the forest, and my pulse thudded in my ears. The last time I'd been around all three of them had been right before they'd murdered Xibo's family. My hands itched to kill them slowly.

"Gulnaz operates on her own schedule," Mila said, the others cackling. Her shaved head had metallic modifications she'd recently installed.

Would their deaths take away my nightmares?

Zer's hand was outstretched in the midday sun, casting a glow through the forest clearing. "Sofros, you and Parmit continue with the recruits." They rose in the air and barely cleared the treetops, breaking branches as they attempted to stay airborne. I couldn't help smirking until I saw Mila.

One of her eyes was now a digital eye. Too bad her attacker didn't succeed in taking her out.

"Well, Mila, here we are again." My voice sounded lazy and bored. I gazed up at the tall pines, planning my escape, fear pumping icy blood through my veins. I couldn't slit her throat right now. Zer would intercept. That was the problem with healers. Very sensitive urijniaks. I stretched upward lazily and floated in the air, ready to jet away.

"Shame I didn't get Xibo when I had the chance." Mila grinned, her mouth crowded with teeth.

Kundit mazra ha, I cursed in my head. "Your chance is coming..." I landed back on the ground. "...Unless I do it for you."

Mila charged, a fireball launching at me. Zer intercepted and smoke curled from his fingers.

"Leave us. There's still work I left for you, Mila," Zer said cooly.

She spun away, her song barely keeping her in the air.

"Don't bait her. She enjoys killing more than you," Zer said, looking a little guilty as he said it.

"Why keep her around?" I asked.

"You don't decide who I keep around." He crossed his arms, coming closer, like he was inspecting me for flaws. "You...are... always...late. Maybe I'll let Mila do what she wants."

"I can't come whenever I want. Xibo will notice." I kept my voice even, the desire to strangle him rising.

"I need reports every two days." He leaned in, his dull, metallic eyes too close.

"Not possible," I said. "Too much happening on Hirana."

I sent an energy spiral out, and then recalled it before it could hit his face and shortcut his eyes. No need to be nasty...yet. "If your daughter wasn't there..." I said. He backed away, glancing up at the pine trees. The smell of his sweat was nauseating. Could I kill them all so I could go back to making love to Drash?

But without his battle plans, the Yarats would take over Eloia. And it would be my fault. I owed Xibo.

I could sing one of the trees down on Zer. But his troops wouldn't obey me. No. Better to wait. Till we killed all of them. Properly in battle.

"How is Leanora?" Zer's face softened, and he gestured for me to follow him through the forest. We walked by the graveyard. There were new grave sticks.

"Not well." I liked lying to him. "Not as strong as Mikosh predicted."

"They waited too long." He sat on an overturned log and fixed his gaze back on the treetops. "Will she be able to bring the hundreds you predicted?" He touched the low hanging bows of a sapling and rubbed his fingers across the pine needles.

I steepled my fingers and waited.

"Tell me," Zer demanded. He let the branch snap back and patted the log for me to sit with him.

I didn't want to be anywhere near him. "She tires easily from traveling. Landings are bad." I stopped, his expression eager. "She's good at directing the music and pulling from others' energies."

"Will she survive it?" His unguarded emotions drifted toward me.

"Of course—she's your daughter." I hated giving into his delusion.

"She doesn't have my blood." There was a sadness in his expression that I remembered from the first time I'd met him. When I was too young to know his nastier side. "It would have ruined everything here if she knew. She would have told Dex. Thank the planets he's dead."

I stepped away from him. "You killed him?"

He waved a gnat away from his face. "Mila."

My body buzzed with rage.

"You know how she acts quickly." Zer's smile took on a different look. He was with Mila.

I couldn't wait to incinerate them both in battle.

"When does the fleet come?" I kept my tone casual. When he didn't answer, I brought my head forward, taking my hair out of its ponytail. I let my long hair trail down my back.

Zer stared at me with that same expression he'd had when I told him I'd spy for him all those years ago. He walked over and touched my brown hair, running it through his fingers before letting go. He wasn't looking through me like he normally did.

I played up the moment, taking the time to draw my hair back to the top of my head, pulling it into a ponytail again, to where it hung to the middle of my back. It was my stick straight hair that had made Yarats assume I was one of them.

"We need you here," Zer said. His hand was outstretched like he was still holding my hair. I didn't need him sizing me up. I had Drash.

One man's anatomy was enough to deal with. I had a millennium of memories stored inside of me; too many sad romances to want to live more of that.

Zer put out his arm. He wanted to deposit a memory. Not yet. I wanted information.

The dusty air blew past us. I kept myself out of his reach. "When is the fleet coming?" I listened for movement in the woods.

"A few weeks. We have ten more ships that need repairs." He put out his hand again.

"You haven't told me anything." I looked up at the tops of the pines rising above us, birds scurrying from branch to branch.

"Since when do you care?" He paused, turning his head as a sudden breaking of branches in the distance increased. "Does Xibo suspect?"

This was fun. "Xibo suspects everyone. Except Leanora." I lowered my gaze, and Zer scratched his jaw.

"Give me something that I could have found out on my own," I said.

"I need you to keep this for me." He didn't wait for me to say yes and clamped his meaty hand around my forearm. A younger Saren stood in front of him, singing as she rose in the air. He stood on the ground looking at her pale face, her curly black hair whipping around her. Something in her voice and movement through the Hiranian skies reminded me of Leanora. When Saren landed again beside him, she kissed his cheek. The memory sped up, and then he let go of me.

He had loved her.

He shivered, his silver eyes gleaming and wet. "I want Leanora to know."

I put my hand on his wide back as he bent over and tears spilled in the dirt. After a few seconds he stood up, wiping his face, his eyes never changing from their dull gleam.

When I killed him, maybe I could take those eyes and have them implanted on me.

"I'll leave you, for now," I said

"When the time is right, gift her that memory." He put his hand on my arm. "When the battle is over..." For the first time, terror poured off in waves from his dark skin. Was it the fear that he might be wrong? I hoped so.

"I will," I lied.

I lifted off, using the song from Zer's memory, enjoying the fast pace of the melody. I was definitely using the tune for future training sessions with Leanora.

WHEN I SAW the maze-like districts of Lepidaia, I slowed my

descent. I liked the uneven, white stone buildings and canals threading under buildings and bridges. Circling around the shore, I dipped into the deep blue water before soaring to the market square. Drash stood atop a half-constructed ship. He picked up pieces of scrap to fit to the frame the others were bending into shape. It looked like a total pain. I liked destroying things a lot more than building them.

When I looked at Drash's damaged face, I saw someone who had never left me. He was like a younger version of Xibo I was allowed to love. When I was fourteen, I thought it was just the relief of his body in mine. He was the only person who didn't transmit memories. After his escape from the Yarats, it became more than that. I wish I knew why this longing for him was never satisfied.

Drash stopped when I landed a few feet away, a small smile on his swarthy face. He wasn't looking at my face or my boobs. No, he was staring at my legs—his favorite part of me. Then he met my eyes. His face flickered between several very subtle emotions in a way only a Hiranian could. I loved his scarred face, even the metal bits of him that the Yarats had added.

"Why you staring?" Drash blushed.

He was the only person in the universe I cared about like this.

"I like what I see."

"Don't lie, Gulnaz. I've never been much to look at."

"I still like what I see." I wanted to run my fingers over his damaged face, the place where his eye sagged just a bit, despite Leanora's attempts. Selchuk would have done a better job. I came close to him, and he trembled under me. After all this time. To think we could do that to each other.

"You're late," he said without a smile. His brown eyes were warm.

"What's new?" I crossed my arms, grinning at him in a way I didn't with anyone else. "I'm worth it, aren't I?" I glanced about to make sure Tarrok wasn't nearby, so he couldn't question me about Leanora.

"The longer you're away, the more I miss you." He put his hands around my waist and lowered his voice. "You have to tell Xibo."

"Isn't it better to let them destroy each other?" I said.

Drash was about to answer when Neelan waved, then turned back to yell above the din of workers banging into the ships. "Everyone take a break."

"You turned the Yarat rubble into something workable again, eh?" I said to Drash, gesturing to the panel he had been working on.

"Don't avoid my question," he said.

"I can't stay long." I touched my toe to his leg, stroking upward before stopping at the knee.

He knew what my look meant. He had to come now, or I was going back.

"Always too busy, eh, Naz?" He was the only person I let call me that.

"We can't talk here," I whispered.

He gave me his hand, and together we soared over to the north cliffs, near the Mesopaikka communication hall. Once we were at the top, I called the salt into my body. There was so much brine in their sea that it came to me in a rush, speeding up my pulse.

Drash kissed my neck before reaching my lips. I closed my eyes in pleasure.

"Any new memories for me today?" he teased.

"I can't share other people's memories."

"Not on purpose." He took my hand. Not even a flicker. I wondered if his being half Yarat-Kardush, like me, had somehow worked more fully in his favour.

"I saw Zer."

Drash looked up at the clear sky. "What did the all-knowing Zer say?"

I imitated Zer's low voice. "How is Leanora progressing. Would she join him." I pulled Drash closer to me, my voice back to normal. "The usual."

He let go of my hand and searched my face. "What aren't you telling me?"

"He gifted me one of his old memories. I'd like to off-load it on someone."

"To who?" he asked.

"Selchuk's the best candidate." I exhaled. "If we didn't fight all the time."

Drash gave me a look. He knew that if I had killed Mila instead of trying to bargain with her, Selchuk wouldn't be a problem. And maybe Xibo's family would still be alive.

"I'm glad you're here." He was too in love with me to dig into the past. He knelt in front of me. "Don't go back." His arms circled my waist. "Can't Leanora bring all of you here?" He got a funny smile on his face. "Not even you can do that."

"I brought you this far."

"A few miles," he teased, kissing my stomach.

"So ungrateful." I knelt down and let our mouths touch. Zer's memory flowed through me, and I pulled away, trying to keep it from interrupting this moment with Drash.

"What is it?" he asked, holding tighter to me.

"Wishing things were different."

"Is she even progressing?" Drash asked.

"Not as fast as we need. Her body isn't used to battle training and scarcity."

"Didn't she trek across the main continent here?" He planted a kiss on my neck and another on my chest.

"It's hard to adjust to traveling and fighting."

Drash stroked my hair, bringing me down with him to lay

side by side on the grass. "When can we get rid of Zer and have our own way?" he murmured in my ear, reaching into my tight trousers.

For the first time, I didn't want him touching me. I rolled away.

"Have you changed your mind?" I asked.

Drash groaned. "We never wanted to follow him. Not Xibo either. We wanted to live here in Eloia without the Yarats and Kardush."

I pushed him. "No, that isn't what we wanted. At the beginning Zer had the right vision: Eloia for Yarat exploration."

"Then he brought the Mists."

"Didn't that make it easier for us to live here? To do things the way we wanted?"

Drash's expression was incredulous. "He really has changed you. Don't you see what you've become? Zer and Mila will kill everyone who doesn't want the Yarat way."

"Mila won't live. "

"And if she does?" Doubt shadowed his face. He looked out to the sea, the sun reflecting on the ocean. This was our dream. To rule Eloia. A planet for everyone. Even people like us.

"Zer and all his cronies have to go. I haven't changed my mind about that," I said.

"Does that mean you kill Xibo and the others to have your way?" His gaze was so hard I could not lie.

"I don't kill people to have my own way."

Drash was looking at mc like I was a specimen. "You have before." His dark gaze was piercing. "You killed two Kardush students after Yelina died in battle."

"I was too young." I tried to keep the desperation out of my voice. "I didn't mean to."

He threw his hands up. "Of course. You're *never* wrong." He spun around. "I don't know how you can live with yourself. Do you really love or care about anyone?" He stalked off down the cliff, his body rising in the air and floating to the beach.

I watched him walk on the shale below. Usually he came back. Once he had a glimpse of me. But this time he kept walking.

"You are the only person, besides Xibo, that I care about," I whispered.

I watched the waves ahead, hating Mila and the others who had killed Danis even more. *Why hadn't I protected you, Danis?*

I felt a comforting warm breeze on my back, and when I turned around there was nothing but the short grasses swaying on the cliff. Waves broke against the rocks below. I soared into the air toward Hirana, my song a fast-moving angry tune.

12

LEANORA

The afternoon suns were dipping below the hillside and my body temperature dropped, the wind picking up. I'd eaten the last of what I'd stolen from the kitchen, and Xibo didn't seem to believe in breaks.

"Transport yourself to the hill where Selchuk is," Xibo ordered from the center of the field. I narrowed my eyes to find Selchuk. Everything in front of me was grainy. My rumbling stomach was not helping. Calling water back to my body did nothing.

"Anytime now!" Xibo yelled. "Preferably before the sun sets and we're working in the dark."

I closed my eyes and searched for Selchuk's energy. Nothing. *Swaz.* I opened my eyes and couldn't find anyone, turning my head this way and that.

"Go! Now!" Xibo growled.

I started a slow tune...

Two stones,
lay in a bare wood...

Beware, don't look away

I was mixing up the lyrics, but I couldn't remember what they were supposed to be. I barely raised off the ground. I lost the thread of the song and fell. My whole body was shuddering before everything went comfortably black.

"CAN you start at the beginning? Tell me what is easy to remember?"

Mom drew her mouth into a thin line, her dark eyebrows a stark contrast to her silver hair. "I was born on the furthest of the Flax Kardush islands, where it is mostly giant purple flax fields and we have the only natural living trees on Hirana." She smiled then, like it might have been a pleasant place.

"Was that why you liked the trees in Asanis?" I asked.

"Trees feel like people." She paused and looked at her lap. "People I miss and know I'll never see again." There was a new sorrow in her black eyes.

"Who do you miss?"

"In Hirana we are taken from our families early." She held my hand and we walked along the shale outside Pakopaikka's stone and glass walls. "I only remember my mother's songs. I spent my first seven years with her, which is much longer than most Kardush and definitely much longer than any Yarats who are taken from their birth mothers at three-years-old. Only those in the government or military are allowed to have their children live with them until training age."

"Where do the children go?"

"Communal living. Kardush children go to Kardush common homes usually from ages three to ten, then mixed group homes with Yarats from ten to fifteen when our professions are decided."

Shadows formed in her eyes, and she looked away from me. "I was punished severely for having 'too much emotion' and 'love that destroys.'" She threaded her arm through mine. "Music was my only solace. When I didn't do what they wanted, they took that away. My years in the Yarat commons would have been worse, if not for Zer. He grew up in the outer provinces and had been forced to have digital eyes. We would spend hours together talking about what we remembered about our families, which wasn't allowed. He never told anyone I was breaking the rules." She smiled weakly. "He changed when the war started."

We walked toward the lower windows of Pakopaikka where the sea crashed against the glass. "What did they do to you?"

"Physical pain, of course. Any desire to be too emotional, too loving, and you were pushed to your limits. I could not get too attached to anyone or anything, because it meant I wasn't useful." She let go of my hand and sighed, looking out to the ocean where the sun was sinking below the horizon. "I was very good at traveling long distances, especially to other planets. I took large equipment and vegetation with me. But I could not travel if I had an emotional attachment."

"What changed when you came here?" I asked.

"Methriel made everything different." She smiled widely, the light now dancing in her eyes. "Zer was irate. Methriel's and my relationship was nothing more than talking and smiling. What did I know about love? My whole life had been work. I barely needed to sleep." She squeezed my hand. "A life you would see as torture had come to an end. I wasn't going back. The more attachments I had to Eloia the better. If I couldn't travel anymore, I couldn't be used by the Yarats."

We continued hand-in-hand through the shale, the sea roaring louder the further we journeyed from Pakopaikka.

～

"PESHARA," Xibo spat. "You're too weak." The aroma of his unwashed clothes was pungent.

Half of me was still with my mother in Pakopaikka. I would have given my left leg in that moment to go back to her.

"Be patient," Mikosh said, and Xibo's scent faded.

"The Yarats will not be," Xibo said. "Call the water to you and keep going. I don't care if you don't sleep tonight."

"She needs rest, Xibo. It's only her second day," Selchuk said, the calm scent of him wafting over me.

I opened my eyes, and they were all shadows, hardly indistinguishable.

Xibo crouched close to me. "She has to master traveling between two points."

The tense silence was punctuated by the sound of the breeze moving the grasses. My stomach growled loudly, and I rolled over to search for a point of light to guide me back to the training house. "I can barely see," I said. I closed my eyes and reopened them. Nothing had changed.

"Call the elements to you, and let's do it again, this time trying to move one of us while you stay stationary," Xibo insisted.

"I. Can't. See," I said. "My eyesight...it's worse." A burning shame flooded my face and chest. I was afraid Xibo felt it. "I need Selchuk." I tried to keep my voice from quivering. Why couldn't I be stronger?

"Selchuk, get her eyes fixed." He slapped the ground next to me. "See you with the rest of the students in a few minutes."

"Is he gone?" I asked, pulling my knees into my chest and closing my eyes. I tried to calm the growing panic that I was stuck permanently in this state. I stretched my limbs, breathing deeply, counting the inhalations and exhalations.

"He's gone," Mikosh said, her mint scent now faded. "Selchuk is the best."

"Are you ready?" Selchuk asked, his pulsing, cool energy now noticeable beside me.

"What do I need to do?"

"Lay back, and I'll seek out what's affecting your eyesight." My *urijniak* surged with the warmth of him beside me. "May I put my hand on your arm?" Selchuk asked.

"Yes."

When he touched my forearm, a thin line of energy whooshed out of me, the memories of the last few days surging into him. My stomach settled, and the strange fluttering in my limbs stopped. Another hand took my other arm, and the pressure of both their hands on my arms increased as Selchuk sang.

Salmo ya, yurai wi, miishii mashuh
Salmo, ya, yurai zi, miishii mashoh

Mikosh's voice harmonized with him. I inhaled the depth and color of their gentle song, a circulating tension moving from my hands and feet toward my core, pain intensifying behind my eyes. The pressure was so strong that my face felt like it was going to explode with the intense heat. The song changed key, and the pressure spiraled out of my extremities, moving down to my hands before I felt at ease. An earthy scent of pitch accompanied someone grasping my hands as warmth spread through my face. They sang gently, my forehead warm with their song. The melody soared up and down, Mikosh's harmony circling Selchuk's melody. Then her voice faded as he sang onward, keeping hold of my hands.

"Sing with him, Leanora," Mikosh whispered.

Salmo ya, yurai wi, miishii mashuh
Salmo, ya, yurai zi, miishii mashoh

I joined in the melody, my vocal chords dry. It became a song without words as we hummed in unison until the last note. In the accompanying silence, I felt lighter in my body.

"Blink your eyes rapidly at first, then open them very slowly," he instructed. "Mikosh, can you get some of the yiri ash from the training house?"

I blinked, and the blaze of an orange sunset broke from behind the hills. I could see color again! The oranges and pinks were so vibrant I wanted to open my eyes completely, but I stopped. I followed his instructions. When I opened my eyes again, slowly, Selchuk was in front of me, and the intensity of his closeness made me lean backward. There was black beard growth on his chin. His face had more scarring on his cheeks than I'd noticed before. He looked toward Mikosh, who floated beside us, bringing a cannister to my lips.

The liquid was horribly sweet.

"Drink it fast," Mikosh said.

She let go, and I stood on my own. Where there had originally been a grey, narrow field of vision was now stunning dimensionality. Below us was the white training house, an oval shaped building with lanterns burning around it. Behind us, the abrupt chain of shadowed hills glowed red at the top. The blue grasses I had originally imagined green whispered in the wind.

"Is it better?" Selchuk asked.

"There's so much color. It's astonishing." I walked about, the sapphire sky above with such dimensions, so much sight that it was almost overwhelming to no longer see from inside a cavern. I could place where Mikosh and Selchuk were even when I turned my head slightly. Why had I waited so long?

"Thank you. So very much." I wasn't sure if I was allowed to embrace him. Selchuk grinned widely, his teeth perfectly white. "I haven't seen like this since before the Mists."

I could see hundreds of feet in all directions. I embraced him, kissing his cheek, startling him. I held him close, the feeling of joy so overwhelming as tears coursed down my cheeks. He was stiff under my arms. I needed to let go.

"How are you feeling, besides your eyes?" Selchuk asked, stepping away.

"I think I need food," I said.

It felt like he was going to ask me another question. I took a step toward him, my heart racing.

"We should get back to Xibo," Mikosh said.

That was the farthest thing from my mind.

"We can wait a little longer if you like?" Selchuk gazed at the hills that were quickly turning to looming dark shadows where the last rays of the suns danced. We stood there like that for a while. I wished Tarrok were standing with us.

A buzzing started in the distance, and within a few minutes, Xibo and several other students had arrived. "Can she see?" Xibo asked.

"I can," I responded over Mikosh and Selchuk.

"Good." He clapped his hands. "I chose a few bad travelers for you to help out. They've been training all day with Gulnaz and need transporting back to the training house."

"I don't think—" Selchuk started.

Xibo held up a hand to silence him.

"Start with me," Mikosh said, nodding. "Just straight into the air a few feet and back down again."

I lifted her using a simple woodsy melody, something I could sing in my sleep. Before she had touched the ground, Xibo growled in my ear and Mikosh fell onto the grass. "The song has to be crafted around movement, not pretty sounds," Xibo said.

I tried to imitate a sound I'd heard Mikosh make. My voice went low and scratchy and she soared above our heads. I slowed her pace and directed my energy around hers to make a gentle landing. It was marvelous how good eyesight helped to gauge those distances.

"Better," Xibo said, his eyes now shining in the dusk light. "On to Selchuk."

I tried to get a fix on Selchuk in my mind to lift him and felt a heaviness instead. As much as I raised my voice, sang harder, increased the pace, played with the key, I couldn't get him to leave the ground.

I tried again, but he wouldn't move, a strange grin playing on his face.

"Why can't I?" I asked him.

"Don't know."

"Stop playing tricks!" Xibo yelled at Selchuk.

"She needs rest," Selchuk said.

Xibo pulled a pipe out of his pocket but said nothing.

"She isn't like us," Selchuk said. "Her body needs time to adjust."

"Hardship produces results," Xibo growled. Then Gulnaz hovered in the air above him, coming to settle next to me. Her silky hair blew in my face.

"If you don't have patience with what her body can handle, we won't get anywhere," Selchuk said.

"Listen to the best healer you have." Gulnaz's face was somber.

A wave of exhaustion swept over me, and it was hard to stay on my feet. My knees buckled before I called the water back to my body.

Xibo came close to me. "In battle there is no rest, unless you want to die. Right now, you'd already be dead if the Yarats were here." He lit his pipe. "Again, transport everyone except me back to the training house."

My stomach dropped. I couldn't do it, and I knew it. I was too tired. And I needed food.

"Now!" Xibo roared, making me flinch.

I closed my eyes, hooking onto all the disparate energies. I sang the same woodsy melody, and when I opened my eyes, no one had left the ground.

"Again!" Xibo raised his body in the air and came down hard on the ground next to me. "Again, and again and again!" he screamed.

"No!" I yelled back. A new heat coursed through me.

Everyone went very silent. A student holding a lantern put it down on the ground, the glow making Xibo's face even more menacing.

Xibo rose off the ground above me.

Gulnaz looked up at Xibo. "I told you."

"You told him what?" My voice was too loud. I was really losing it. I shook with a terrible rage mixed with exhaustion.

Maybe I wasn't good enough.

But I knew my limits. Pushing them farther today would get me nowhere. Obviously Xibo didn't respect these limits, so I had to do something. The landscape undulated as nausea set in. Inbikh chittered on the ground beneath me.

It felt like I was back in the forest with Tarrok and couldn't find him. *I have to get away, find Tarrok. I can't stay here while they all stare at me with their steely faces.*

A better person would continue, call the water to her body, do everything Xibo said without question, like Mikosh.

The broken towers of Thresil Mira glowed in my memory. If I got away I wouldn't disappoint them anymore.

"Leanora! Don't!" Mikosh called out in the distance, her neiko lighting up around her neck.

"She won't get anywhere," Gulnaz purred.

"Watch me." I turned to Gulnaz, the smile still thin on her lips.

Let it go, Lea... Tarrok's voice said in my head.

I couldn't think, my thoughts fragmenting. I scooped up Inbikh, and in one motion, we were airborne, both singing with all the anger left in my bones.

"Stop!" Selchuk reached for me and missed. A voice called after me. It was a soft voice, but I didn't want to follow it. Inbikh's fur was soft against my face, her claws digging in my shoulder. Reminding me I was still conscious, in control of where we went.

I directed us around the hills of Maer-lina and circled us back toward the ocean, my voice raspy with the effort of keeping both of us in the air. The only other place I'd gone on this wretched planet was the Thresils. Why not go back?

The dark ocean was silent beneath us, its motion languid from where we flew. I knew we were closer to the Thresil islands when the heat pressed against us, dropping us closer to the ocean. My song sputtered out, and we plummeted into the water, several kilometers out from the shore. My skin smacked on impact. All went black.

Again.

At least I was somewhere familiar.

13

LEANORA

THRESIL MIRA

My skin was shriveled and salty when we washed up on the shore. I didn't know how long we'd been in the water. Twilight lit the sky a pale green that caused the towers in the distance to glow. Inbikh was so soaked that she looked like a drowned muskrat. I couldn't help laughing.

It was a relief to be away from all of them.

"Ya-rii, time for breakfast." Inbikh sniffed and jumped back in the water.

"Where're you going?" My stomach was sore from the lack of food.

Inbikh surfaced again. "Fish."

"Get some for me?" I asked.

"Maybe." She dove under.

I had forgotten that leaving Maer-lina meant we had zero food source. It had been almost a day since I'd eaten solid food. I dragged myself upright on the wet sand. Two broken moons in the violet sky shined above the tall fingers of the modular buildings reaching upward. "Maybe it was once beautiful."

Inbikh hummed as she dragged two fish onto shore. "One for me, one for you."

This wasn't the moment to admit I didn't eat raw fish. She neatly drew her claw across the flesh and dug in. I followed suit, trying to keep my gag reflex at bay. The flesh was rich and salty. Inbikh crunched on the bones and I threw her mine.

"Let's find some water," I said. It hit me then that perhaps I had been a bit rash in leaving. I had to keep moving. Escape wasn't the only reason I was here. I had to find answers on my own terms. Inbikh climbed on my shoulder, reeking of salty wet fur and fish. I trudged through the alleyway of rotted smaller buildings toward the tallest cluster of skyscrapers ahead.

WITH MOST OF the debris behind us, a large, circular clearing of colorful tiles spread out for kilometers in all directions, more than double the size of Lepidaia. Cerulean, salmon, and white stones had been placed at intervals in a wave shape that curved around the cluster of five tall buildings that followed the same rounded, modular pattern of the surrounding shorter buildings that were still intact. There were no sharp lines. The tallest building's top was obscured by clouds rolling by. All five buildings had the same semi-transparent look and sparkled in the rising morning suns.

Across the giant tile-way was an older, stone building that rose three-stories tall. It must have been built hundreds of years before the towers across from it. And unlike all of the other structures on Thresil Mira, it had no signs of damage from the war. Long spikes stuck out of its curved, stone roof. Each of the spikes had metal bracings between them, making the building look artificially higher, but it also meant no one could land on its roof.

"What that?" Inbikh asked.

"Let's find out," I said. I put her on the ground, and she sped ahead toward the building with a lot more energy than I could muster. Every few meters I kept looking for a place to drink water. I would hear something that sounded like a spring but would then realize it was just the breeze or other sounds I was unaccustomed to. Occasionally a bird would swoop overhead.

"Water!" Inbikh screeched. She was a tiny white and pink dot weaving in and out of the archways of the grey stone building. Once I caught up, I put my hand on the metal grates of one of the archways and backed away. They were warm to the touch, a vibration radiating inside of me until I let go. I inspected the outside stone wall for another entrance. The grey stones showed no blemishes. Why was this building so pristine when everything around it had been marked by the war?

Inbikh slipped through the grating and cocked her head to the side. "Come, come Yarii. Thing to see!" She swished her tail back and forth but didn't move forward without me.

"How do I get inside?" I asked.

I moved toward the metal grating again to see if I could lift it up, but the bars were too heavy—it was impossible to lift them. The pulsating when I touched them was stronger. A whispering began, a cool wind blowing from the cave-like building.

"Leanora Tela, approach," it said in Hiranian.

The gates lifted the moment my hands touched the grating. A deep peace settled over me, like being lifted effortlessly above the clouds. Water flowed from a fountain in the center of the tiled floor. The whispering and wind stopped when the gate closed again. All was silent and cool inside of the building. I ran with Inbikh to the fountain, drank and washed my face.

I walked through the stone entranceway, glow lamps dotting the far walls. Small porthole windows adorned the top, letting in the dawn light. The floor was covered with a mosaic painted scene that was chipped and had faded with time into swirls of sapphire, crimson, and yellow.

"Come, we look," Inbikh called out to me and trotted up one of the stone ramps from the first level where I stood. The ceiling formed a dome above us that had a skylight that revealed a light blue morning sky. For the first time in my days on Hirana, I felt tranquil and as though I had been here before, even though that was impossible.

I wondered if my mother knew this place. As we rounded the mezzanine, rows and rows of scrolls were carefully stacked in tall stone shelves that seemed to go on endlessly. Inbikh sniffed at them, then sneezed.

"Old stuff," she said and climbed up my skirt and onto my shoulder. I held her close to me, feeling that we were truly in this together. I strolled down the rows, drawing my fingertips across the top, until I touched scrolls that were pristine compared to the older, yellowed ones. There was a carving of letters above each set, but the script looked like a series of shapes and figures instead of the script that we used in the Eloian language. I didn't know how to decipher it, because the Hiranians—both Yarat and Kardush—had stopped using a written language for three hundred years.

"What it say?" Inbikh asked.

"I don't know." I pulled out one of the scrolls and unfolded it, laying it on the tiled floor, the cold pressing on us through the thick paper. The scene depicted on the page was a night battle scene but appeared to come from an earlier time on Thresil Mira, perhaps at the start of the war. All the buildings in the center were still intact. Individuals were fighting and being thrown from buildings. Several on the ground had severed limbs, their faces twisted in agony. The chaos became so real that I began to see myself as part of the scene, and I had to close the scroll to stop the sounds of explosions I wondered if I was imagining.

"It's from the war, Inbikh," I said.

"The fighting, the killing?" she asked.

"Yes. Let's look at another." I reached for a different scroll, and Inbikh scampered along the rows to a case of small scrolls and brought it back. The scenes seemed to depict similar scenes of carnage but in different settings. The Yarats were figured as the aggressors with their metal studded faces, dark uniforms, and metal or algae bracings on their limbs and heads. There was an inhumanity to the depiction of their faces that reminded me of Gulnaz, a coldness that I didn't understand. It frightened me to see the Yarats' pleasure in the work of death.

And to what end?

I left the scroll open and pondered why I was there...how a civilization could spend so much time trying to kill their own people—

"I thought I'd find you here."

I startled and dropped the scroll, scurrying for a place to hide. Standing a few feet away was Mikosh staring down at me. Her hands were on her hips, her face still. She seemed neither annoyed nor pleased. When I made eye contact she exhaled and crouched down so our faces were level. I picked up the scroll, watching for any sudden movement on her part or if she'd brought reinforcements.

"I'm not here to make things worse," she said, her face still unreadable.

"That depends on your perspective." I stood up so she was below me, still crouched.

She rose up to stand, arms crossed. "Usually only memory keepers can get in here," she said.

"Why?" I asked.

"A person who stores people's memories. Usually you have to be half Kardush, half Yarat, like Gulnaz, to be a memory keeper. So, they're pretty rare."

"I don't understand," I said.

"It started as a punishment for people who mixed the two cultural groups. But there are a few full Kardush memory keepers." Mikosh gestured toward me. "Thankfully, I don't have the necessary emotional sensitivity to be one." She rolled her eyes. "As if Gulnaz does."

I held out the scrolls, not wanting to comment on Gulnaz. "Who did these?"

"Memory keepers, their apprentices. There weren't many left in the end, so some scenes haven't been finished." Mikosh gingerly pulled out a scroll, unrolling it, then quickly shelving it. "We should go. It doesn't make sense to stay in here."

I wasn't in any hurry and slowly rolled up the scrolls I'd been looking at. Mikosh took the last scroll and put it back in the shelf. Inbikh held up her paws for Mikosh to pick her up. She bent down, and Inbikh climbed onto her, disappearing under the curtain of her thick braids to emerge on her other shoulder.

"Those scenes were horrible," I finally said.

"I didn't have time to think about it when I was in the middle of it. I just had to survive." Mikosh's accent got thick. "Everyone seems to have forgotten you weren't there. We're still wading through how it was, but you don't know what it was like, except from our memories." She traced a finger along the shelves. "There's more I can show you."

She stood up, and I followed her out of the warm Memory Keeper's Hall. I took one last glance behind at the old mosaic before walking with Mikosh to a field that stretched out behind the massive building. The field was filled with brilliant red grasses that looked like they had been dyed. After several minutes of walking across, there were lumps of debris littering the entire field. Stumps of living matter mixed with the remains of people. When the breeze blew through a stink rose up from the ground, and I buried my face in my tunic, which didn't help very much.

"This is where the fighting first began. Outside our Congress Hall, over there." Mikosh pointed to the shortest round building in the cluster of skyscrapers. The Congress Hall had sustained more burn marks than any of the other buildings. A massive pile of rocks was in front of where the entrance should be, and further up, all the walls had blast holes in them.

"Why didn't they bury these people?" I asked, still covering my nose.

"They started the war." She gestured across the field. "Most of the people here are Yarats and high government officials. All wanting more from us: more experimentation, more colonization, and less of the Kardush ways. After the Mists of Eloia, my mother and Xibo had enough. The first war began. Then things died down for a little bit...so we thought." She put Inbikh down. "But the Yarats were never interested in peace. Now they want your planet."

The grasses blew and hissed, noisy for something so insubstantial. The stench of the remains was strong: they had to have altered the biochemistry to make a statement. It was a sick thought and I left Mikosh where she stood, this type of remembrance a step too far. I kept seeing the bodies superimposed over the landscape, even after I left the crimson field. I was glad I had so little in my stomach.

Mikosh walked with me back toward the shore, the only sound the warm breeze blowing past us and whistling through the remains of what must have once been a great city.

"What was it like before the war?" I asked.

"I can't remember anything before the war," Mikosh said. Her face was so strained, her eyes almost dead in how they looked through me. "Because my life before that seems like a dream. And the war was the reality. Even now, everything I do every day, it feels like I'm waiting for the war to come back and claim me." She looked away and up at the sky. "Like it did my mother."

I put out my hand to comfort Mikosh, and then remembered that she didn't know me that way. Touch here wasn't like it was on Eloia.

She placed a hand to my shoulder, and Inbikh peeked out from her hair. "I'm not Gulnaz. Say what you need to." She let go and crossed her arms. "I won't tell your secrets to Xibo." She smiled a little, but there was a deep sadness to it. "Besides, whatever you think you're hiding, isn't working very well." She laughed a short snort that then made me laugh, and we stood there laughing for a while in the blazing suns.

"I wish Tarrok could see all of this," I said. "It would make it easier for me."

"But then how would Selchuk ever improve his fighting here without you alone as an incentive?" Her voice changed when she said it, and she was holding back the beginnings of a wry smile. "I had to lie to Xibo so Selchuk wouldn't come with me to find you." She exhaled noisily. "I thought you should know, so it didn't come as a surprise when you're training. But it might be nothing, so don't worry."

She held up her hands, like she was testing the wind. "You ready to bring us back?"

"No." I shaded the sun's glare with my hands, looking out at the placid sea. "But I'll do it." I took her hands, and no memories flowed into me. I started singing.

Lua lu lai, I caught you with my eye... and once I'd made one round of the song, Mikosh joined with her deep, low voice on the harmony. We rose in the air, and after several minutes, made a very bumpy landing on the sandy hills rimming the north side of the white training house on Maer-lina.

I was glad to come back to a place that was far more peaceful than the Thresils. This time it felt like it was my choice to train. I could have left, I reminded myself, if I wanted to.

When we were a few steps from the training house I caught her sleeve and then made contact with her forearm, a memory flicking into her as it drained out of me. It was the night after the sandstorm when Tarrok was afraid I was dead. I had returned to his house and he looked more relieved than Dex. Tarrok's green face was dusty from watching for me from his porch during the storm. I remember Dex walking away from the two of us once he was certain I was alive. Tarrok searched my face, and I felt whole in his presence. I had to get away from him and pretended it was because I had to wash all the sand off my body. I sat in the cold shower, letting the water wash over me, not wanting to admit the strength of his pull on me. The feeling of loving him terrified me. My fear then was equal to the surging warmth from seeing him again the next morning in Hagoth.

The memory merged with him asking me to marry him. I let go, and like a puff of smoke, the memory vanished back into my consciousness.

Mikosh held my forearm for a second, watching the light pink sea pound against the beach. She exhaled and looked at me. "You can never lose him." We stood there on the steps outside the training house for awhile—each digesting what we were mourning. The clouds had rolled in to block out the suns' glare.

"You have so much to live for," she said after awhile. "And now I think I may have found a better way to survive."

I searched her face, her blue eyes shining. "There is more to life than survival— there are dreams you must hold onto. And if you do not have them yet, you will," I said.

"I am afraid to dream. That is what war does to you. It makes you feel foolish for having ever been happy." She turned back to look toward the hills, her whole body in profile while the wind picked up her braids and blew them about. The silence was comfortable between us. The steady beating of the ocean roared on the sand below, picking up as a breeze caused the window shades above us to tap back and forth against the window frames. The voices inside had hushed for a moment.

She walked onward into the training house, her gait stiff and powerful. I stood outside, wondering what I could do to help her. The sea crashed louder against the shore. I did not see it, but I could feel its fury nonetheless.

14

LEANORA

MAER-LINA, HIRANA

Xibo was yelling at the students in the training house when I came in. Everyone was standing around him in the common room, chairs and tables scattered at the edges of the airy room. The minute he caught sight of me, everyone hushed. With one sweep of his arm, they silently filed out faster than I'd ever seen any of them move on foot. Only Selchuk remained, standing very straight, his face trained on Zibo.

"You can go too," Xibo said in Hiranian.

"I'd rather stay," Selchuk said in Eloian. "I need to check her eyes."

I thought back to what Mikosh had said and I stepped away from Selchuk's approach. "My eyesight is fine—"

"—Where were you?" Xibo interrupted. In that moment, I was glad Selchuk moved next to me. Mikosh had vanished.

"Thresil Mira," I said.

"That's it? Not off planet?" Xibo asked.

I had to fight to not lose my cool with him again. It was a waste of energy. "No." I kept my gaze even with his. "I saw the

Field of Carnage, Memory Keeper's Hall, Congress. That was enough."

He sucked his teeth and circled around Selchuk and me. I stepped out of his pathway so that he understood I wasn't cowering to him. "I understand why I'm here. But I need incremental increases in my daily training. So there's time for my body to adjust, and I won't keep blacking out when I've traveled too far."

Xibo stared us both down. Selchuk smirked, his blue eyes softening. "She's right."

"Get out Selchuk," Xibo said softly.

Selchuk ambled away, then ran when Xibo lurched toward him.

Xibo turned back to me, crossing both his arms and leaning against his staff. "You have two allies already." He lifted an eyebrow, his scarred forehead wrinkling. "Good. Battle training is the real test. Can you move a lot of people *and* fight?"

"I can now that I understand what happened here," I said more confidently than I felt, Xibo's gaze boring into me.

I resisted the pull of his *urijniak*. He stopped and the tug on my chest ceased. "Good. Rest. Eat. We start at first light tomorrow."

I TOOK my meal outside and sat with Inbikh in the grass, anticipating that this might be my last peaceful moment for perhaps weeks or longer.

"The days are much shorter here," I said to Inbikh.

"Short hunting nights. No fish in dark," Inbikh said, swiping another piece of dried fish from my plate.

I laid back in the grasses, letting the long strands blow above me, the sky almost black. I startled when I heard footsteps beside me, and Inbikh scampered off. Selchuk stood above me.

"The weather is turning." He held out a hand to help me to my feet. I ignored him and rolled over to stand.

"Inbikh, come on!" I called out to her, but I couldn't find her white body scurrying through the grasses.

I followed Selchuk down the dirt path from the green hillsides back to the training house, which was only a few feet from the shore. Several groups of students were walking beside the beach.

"*Arsha ye*," they called out.

"*Arsha ye*," Selchuk answered.

Lanterns lit the pathway up to the training house that wound away from the sea. The combined music of the various people walking to and fro made me want to stay and listen to them. Hardly anyone played instruments, and it was interesting how many of their voices sometimes reminded me of the instruments I missed: flutes, guitars, and drums.

"Will it get easier?" I asked Selchuk.

"It depends on how much you want it to." He chuckled a little. "The first years I was learning how to travel, I was terrible. I can only move myself and small objects. If I want to attack something, it takes a lot out of me. I'm a healer. Not a warrior." He stopped at the steps to the training house. "The war made us all into something that we wished we weren't." He looked back out to the dark sea. "It will do the same to you, if you're not careful."

The white stairs had a warm sheen in the dark, glowing in the lamplight. Rain started as a hush in the distance before it pelted us. I wanted to stand under the showers to wash away the grime I'd acquired from days without bathing.

"It will get too cold for you to do that," Selchuk said, running for cover inside the open-air awning of the main entrance. The glow light cast shadows on his face, and his black hair slid over his eyes. He brushed it out of his face and leaned against one of the pillars, crossing his arms and laughing at me.

I stayed where I was, relishing the cool of the rain and the warmth of his laughter.

"You don't like being told what to do," he said.

I closed my eyes, the rain pelting my face softly. My clothes soaked through and stuck to my skin. Then I felt Selchuk's *urijniak* nearer. His presence reminded me of something familiar. In an instant, I knew why he'd been hiding his energy from me. When I opened my eyes, meeting his gaze, I didn't want to believe what was stirring in my chest.

Everyone has two hearts, Leanora.

He slipped inside without a word.

I stood under the eaves, the rain painfully pelting my skin. I thought back to what I'd felt coming from him. I had to be wrong. If I'd been right, he'd still be here.

A stream ran from the center of the building down to the ocean. The entire building was constructed out of fossilized trees that had grown together to form the house, their trunks curving into the plaster of the walls and stretching out over the round ceilings. As I walked through the building there were other people lounging in groups on the ground level's interconnected rooms. There were no doors anywhere in the building that I could find, except at the main entrances. Standing next to one of the columns in the lounge, Selchuk waited for me. Like nothing had happened.

"Who are the others training here?" I asked, trying to maintain a sense of normalcy.

"Mostly Kardush who moved away from populous centers. We opened up the center to any former soldiers and healers," Selchuk said.

"Will they join us on Eloia?"

"Many don't want to be reminded of what happened." He turned his attention back to the house. "This place used to house over five hundred Kardush students. Gulnaz was one of the

126

youngest teachers. Mikosh and I trained under her." He gestured out to the other rooms, his voice hushed. "Those of us involved in preparing to leave for Eloia are still scattered around Hirana. Xibo and Gulnaz are trying to gather them. Without Mikosh's mother, General Bezma, it is hard."

Selchuk's luminous eyes glowed in the evening light. Mikosh and Gulnaz came to a nearby table with food, and he lingered until I joined them at the table. Selchuk brought over drinks.

They all ate so fast that they were staring at me while I struggled to finish without getting crumbs all over me. I wasn't about to admit I'd eaten earlier.

"Are you all planning on settling on Eloia?" I asked.

Gulnaz's expression brightened. "Since I'm half Yarat, half Kardush, Eloia is the only choice for me."

Selchuk and Mikosh rolled their eyes. "She knows," they said.

"Are you the only one?" I asked.

"No, Drash is too. You know him?" Gulnaz's face lit up.

"He was one of my patients." There was something in her expression that was challenging me. "He almost didn't make it after arriving on Eloia."

"The healing on your planet is more primitive." Gulnaz walked over to one of the cool boxes set in the wall, then popped a piece of food in her mouth and sauntered off.

"She gets touchy about Drash," Mikosh said dryly, her gaze still on the corridor Gulnaz exited through.

"Is there a communicator here?" I needed to talk to Tarrok.

Selchuk gestured for me to follow him through a glass corridor, down a set of stairs into a room with a loamy odor and minerals set around the periphery, much like Mesopaikka. In the center of the back wall was a sheet that had been tacked to the corners with string. It looked so different from our structure back home.

"Close your eyes, filter everything you're thinking out of your mind, and concentrate on who you want to speak to. Use all your thoughts to see them." Selchuk hummed and I kept my eyes closed, trying to channel my energies, as worry over Tarrok and my family coursed through my brain.

"Leanora? Is it you?" Tarrok said.

His face was blurry and indistinct at first, then he appeared. Bejah was behind him. I was so overjoyed I started to cry. Selchuk pulled the doorway curtain behind him.

"It's me, Tarrok. I can see you so clearly!" I exclaimed.

"What happened?" Tarrok asked, his voice sleepy.

"Oh, Lea-nora! We miss you." Bejah's accent was thick. "What it like there? You good? When you come home?"

Tarrok came closer to the screen. I touched his face, forgetting he was just a projection.

"Selchuk healed my eyes. They're normal again!" I said.

Tarrok grinned at me. Even though he was tired, I could feel the pleasure coming from him. I needed to hold him.

Tarrok brought Bejah closer to the screen. "She waited here with me for you. Most of the city has evacuated—Alaric is staying with Bejah, Neelan, and me. Your mom and dad thought it was safer. In case…" He looked at Bejah who nodded to him. "…Something happened to them, because Zer will be looking for her."

"How is Alaric? How are my parents?" I asked, trying to keep from tearing up. I needed to stay strong for them.

Tarrok exhaled. "It's hard for them. Especially Alaric. More Yarats came, and we have retreated into the hills on the outskirts. Alaric wants to go back to the house to rescue things, but it isn't safe."

"You come back to us, you hear?" Neelan came next to Bejah and waved one of his glowing fingers before departing with her.

Tarrok's face filled the projection, his skin a pale, unhealthy green.

"I miss you so much," I said.

"It's getting worse." Tarrok's face fell.

"My first days have been a disaster." I inhaled deeply to keep from tearing up, my throat swollen with the strain. I couldn't pretend with Tarrok. He saw through that, even several galaxies away.

"Leanora, there's a reason you're there. But if you need to come back, you can." His eyes were large and hopeful.

It made me ache even more, my throat dry and sore. "Every time I move through the air or make another living thing move, I'm so exhausted I can barely move. Or I black out."

Tarrok frowned. "There has to be a way for you to get energy back."

"Water helps."

He looked at me. "Make the water come to you. I've seen how the Yarats fight. The ships we're building, they're not going to be enough. We need the Kardush forces. Be ready for a real fight."

"I don't know how to access the killing part of myself."

"What about the deer?" he asked, his eyes shining.

He was right. I had done that, even with poor vision on a moonlit night. "That was with help from our animals."

"No, that was you. You transported yourself and Vali there and Dona and I back with you to the mountainside. That was all you."

He came close to the screen. I saw that incredible light in his eyes, that knowledge that was even more than love. An intense belonging resided in him. My eyes welled up, and I couldn't speak. I turned away to catch my breath before facing him again.

"Tell my mother, Methriel, Alaric—" I heard a movement behind me and wiped my eyes—"that I'll be back soon, that I'm going to fight to make sure Eloia stays ours."

"We won't let this war divide us." His face faded from the projection. "Leanora, remember...I believe..." Then he was gone.

I sank to the floor, trying to will myself to get up and go to bed, walk outside, anything other than sit here and feel sorry about missing everyone I loved.

I turned toward the doorframe. Selchuk stood there with water and some dried bits on a plate. "Do you want to eat more, in case you can talk to him when you wake?" He set the tray down on the floor. I noticed then how thin he was, how the bones along his collar and neck stood out in the lamplight.

"Thank you." I took a few bites and blew my nose into the napkin he'd brought with him.

"The buildings here are not designed for comfort," Selchuk said. "Even our food is the same."

Everything tasted like variations on fish paste, but it was better than what I'd had for dinner. Selchuk looked toward the windows that had been shut with oil fabric flaps that vibrated in the wind, the rain pelting against them.

"How long will the storm last, do you think?" I asked.

Selchuk faced me with an energy behind his eyes that I didn't understand. "It depends on which storm you're talking about."

PART II

———————

"The greatest inventions are not made with one's hands but instead through the development of living biology, stretched to the limits of its natural capabilities."

—*Kardush-waiya Chronicles of Living No. 1*

15

TARROK

I had to keep busy. I leaned against a stubborn ribbon of steel that needed extra bolts to stay in place. I still couldn't stop thinking about Leanora, and we had to evacuate soon.

The Kardush refugees, like Drash and Neelan, were counting on me. They'd seen worse. Been tortured.

My heartache was nothing compared to what they were going through.

I knocked the rubber hammer against the bottom edge of the steel. The last bolt on my side of the Marwatha was in place. I wiped the sweat from my face. The uneven bracings we'd replaced in the previously rusty hull looked like they'd hold. Neelan came around my side, tugged at the bolts with his crank-tool, then gave me a satisfied nod. "Good work, Tarrok."

He pointed at the Yelti-Duri we'd finished repairing the day before making its way westward to Hagoth. He knocked on the Marwatha then smoothed it with his palm.

"It will hold up in battle," Neelan whistled then yelled, "Drash! Seams. Now!" He bustled off when Drash took a giant leap into the air, the charred remnants of the city blocks behind him when he sang his way softly to where I was. He moved quickly with a torch, binding the metal, turning the seams into a smooth surface. He looked at me for a second, his dark brown eyes pained.

"She'll be back, you know," Drash said. "Xibo and Gulnaz won't keep her for long."

There was so much swirling inside of me when he said that. I had to look away. If I named all the sadness it would be real. Consuming. The waves broke in the afternoon sun, white foam swallowing the shore. I inhaled before saying anything.

"What news from Gulnaz?" I asked.

Drash was eerily still in a way only Hiranians were able to be. Even Hagothian warriors were not so rigid.

"Gulnaz tells me little. The training is hard. Leanora tires easily. Nothing more." Drash's stare was unsettling. I turned to the last of the ship repairs, thinking the conversation was over.

"It is hard to be without Gulnaz. Especially after my capture." Drash looked out to the ocean, away from me. "If we kill all the Yarats we may be free, then." He walked away before I could answer him.

"Tarrok!" Alaric called out. "Over here." He held four ulsos by their reins, and he was straining to keep them from entering the Talbo-Pii that the gwynbees were getting ready to pilot.

I ran over to him and took all but one set of reins. Alaric exhaled. "Thanks, Tarrok." Something about the crinkling at his eyes reminded me of Leanora, but when he frowned the resemblance was gone. "Are we ready to leave?" he asked.

"I think so. Not not much left to do except a test flight."

I was ready to leave Lepidaia. No longer fluttering with bright colors of laundry and flags, it was a miserable song repeating forever in my mind. No more fast-paced music and sweet ballads. Every district I passed through was empty without her. I had to keep going, though, for Alaric. Saren and Methriel expected as much.

It felt worse because usually I had Leanora to talk to about everything that was going wrong. Now I couldn't burden anyone else with the tempest inside me. It would be too much.

"My ship will leave soon. Can I bring a few more gwynbees?" Drash asked, wiping his stained hands on his shorts.

"Just keep them in multiples of two." I smiled a little, remembering traveling across to Lepidaia with forty of them.

"Gwynbees!" he called out. A group of blue-grey and green striped gwynbees stood on their haunches at attention when he directed them toward his ship. They didn't move until Alaric intervened and trilled his tongue at them.

"Come on little ones, we're going with Drashi. Come on, come on," Alaric cooed and they followed behind.

The look on Drash's face was incredulous. "Drashi?" He folded his arms. "No one has called me that."

Bejah hopped down from the top of his ship. "Maybe it time for new names."

Leave it up to Bejah to lighten things up.

A dark mood resumed as soon as she stopped laughing. Had Lepidaia's beauty lulled me into an easy way of living that now made me miserable? Maybe Leanora's love spoiled me.

I gathered my tools, calling out to Vali so I could load them into his saddlebags.

"We're leaving as soon as I've made a test run," Neelan called out. He was watching me more carefully today. Bejah came around and kissed him on the cheek. Her dark hair was tied up away from her cobalt face.

"Don't go without me." She stroked his cheek, and he blushed.

Alaric cleared his throat. He was staring at us. That quiet look on his face so like Leanora.

"Let's get the luoshis and ulsos ready," I said to him. The luoshis fuzzy faces were pressed into each other. We had to move their terrified bodies slowly onto the ship.

"Unleash Vali and Dona, but keep Carki with you to corral the luoshis," I said.

"On it," he called out, eager to be of assistance.

The luoshis were not accustomed to being trapped inside of a chunk of metal flying through the air. The ulsos, on the other hand, were excited to go wherever we were. Vali's brown tail swished back and forth, and he herded the luoshis into the ship, barking and growling when they tried to bolt, Carki and Dona pulling up the rear.

Alaric had created the rope pens for the luoshis. They snorted and bleated until they were onboard.

"Leash the ulsos, Alaric."

"I'm not stupid," he said.

When I glared at him, his shoulders sunk. "I'm sorry."

I put out a hand on his arm. "You're doing a great job. Don't worry."

"I don't want anything to happen to you." His blue eyes were dark with worry.

I laid a hand on his head and pulled him into an embrace.

"She'll be back before we know it." I released him. "It will feel like she never left."

"What if something happens to my parents?" he asked.

"Let's fight for that not to happen," I replied.

I pushed the thought down inside of me, turning my attention to the ulsos and harnessing them together so that Vali couldn't try to take off like he did the day before. His ears perked up when music sounded on the breeze. It was very faint. I stopped tying his restraints and waited for the tune to start again. It was a mournful song played on a flute.

Bejah took over. "Take a break. We will finish." Her green eyes were playful. "Out! We see you soon, soon."

Alaric ran to me, his hand on my sleeve. "Come back soon. I don't want to lose you too." I held him to me, inhaling the dusty smell that we all had after days of no bathing.

"Just getting fresh air," I said.

Alaric pursed his lips. "You've been outside all day."

"I'll be back." I smoothed down his hair. When his expression didn't change, I hugged him. He held onto me until Bejah called him. "Come on, you best at this, Alaric."

I whistled for Vali. We trudged up the hill leading to the north shore cliffs of Mesopaikka. The breeze was warm. It would have been soothing if I hadn't been frantic to hear her voice. Even a glimpse of her alive was enough.

Had being apart changed her mind? The dark thoughts were swirling further inside of my brain, churning a terrible, sinking feeling in my stomach and throat. To my right, the dark sea was streaked with gold from the setting sun. I held onto my kiyo but kept the bulb off to surprise anyone who might attack. Foolish to have come all this way with only Vali. I trudged up the stone steps carved into the mossy hillside. I couldn't turn back now.

THE HAIR on the back of my head tingled, and I turned slowly but spotted nothing.

I kept walking up the cliffside of Mesopaikka, Vali humming a melody Alaric had sung earlier that day. It was a strange tune that followed a chromatic pattern. It sounded a lot like the songs the Kardush sang when they were traveling through the air.

Vali stopped in front of me and ruffed. I looked behind us. Only the breeze and ocean's roar. No one there. I pulled him ahead of me, entering the communication hall. Then I stopped and heard it. Very faintly, the breath of someone behind me.

They were following at a distance, the footsteps soft. Vali growled, and I clicked my tongue to hush him. I was more afraid of him getting hurt. A high-pitched voice whispered, "Why you no talk?" Gwynbee.

"Hush."

I flicked the kiyo on, and Bejah stood below me—her black hair whipping around her face.

"You not walk alone in the dark, Tarrok. It bad idea." Her voice was raspy.

"What about Alaric?"

"Neelan need him, so I come." Bejah folded her arm in mine and walked with me into Mesopaikka.

"I can't go back to the ship without talking to her," I said.

Radjek jumped on me and purred, his cat-like ears perking up as his whiskers touched my face. "I need my Inbikh. You need Ya-rii."

My heart raced the closer we got. I remembered how pale Leanora's face had looked the last time we'd spoken.

"You stop taking care yourself." Bejah looked me over, and I felt strange. "She not like this. You no shave, no wash."

I sniffed myself. "I don't stink."

Bejah cackled. "Everyone stink." I liked how much she'd changed since we came from Nedara. All of the harsh bits of her had subsided into a very pleasant person to be around. I didn't want to think it was only because of her relationship with Neelan. Since Leanora had been gone, Bejah had reminded me of Erena: trying to keep me from being too serious.

"You miss her. Bad." Bejah rested her head on my arm, like my sister used to. "Me too." I turned the light so it showed the path before us. "She peaceful and nice. I wish she come back now." She turned behind us as an explosion fired into the sky above Pakopaikka on the opposite shore.

Another burst of light illuminated the hills in the distance.

Sirens wailed as more projectiles rained through the dark sky in plumes of yellow and red. I snuffed out the kiyo, grabbed Vali's reins, and hopped on, Bejah and Radjek sliding in behind me. We sped down the hill, and I tried to quash the disappointment. I ached from no sleep without her around.

I need to hear your voice to keep me going.

Ships zipped back and forth along the hillsides, more than I could count. Half the city was in flames. Bejah's hair blew into my face, and I brushed it away, every thought of hurrying back to the Marwatha.

The wind stirred up the flames, and the plumes of smoke blew in our direction, infecting my breathing with a chemical smell. Everyone choked from the smoke. There was nothing to do but hop off and make a run for it. I bolted, holding Vali's reins and Bejah's hand. I looked at the ocean one last time before sprinting onto the levitating Marwatha, the last of our ships already airborne.

Her engines were already fired up. A blue gas emitted from the back of the gigantic Marwatha. Alaric ran out to grab Carki who had broken from her restraints to find us. "We're going!" he shouted.

We climbed up the landing platform, and it closed with us still clambering into the ship. It sealed us inside with a thunk. We jumped down to the main circular passenger area. All the luoshis huddled silently against each other. I tied up Carki and Vali, who didn't buck against their restraints for the first time.

"We're taking off in a few seconds," Ncclan shouted from the cockpit above us, putting one ear device in. "No chance for a test flight."

"Will she stay together?" I asked.

"I hope," Neelan said, flicking switches while Bejah climbed up the metal ladder, flipping her copilot controls up. She had become an extremely adept pilot of the Marwatha—even training gwynbees to help her.

The engines revved, and Alaric tugged on my sleeve. "We're up there." Neelan waved us away, the ground under us groaning and shaking.

"Take lead on guns, Tarrok," Alaric commanded and started climbing up to one of the gun mounts.

Another explosion sounded, and a pounding music beat through us. With the Yarat music, we had to get everyone's ear protection in place. It didn't completely keep their music out, but it muffled it so we could still operate the guns.

The music tore into my brain. I hummed with the animals, like Neelan had instructed me, but it wasn't working. Invisible daggers stabbed at my skull, turning my thoughts to an angry, disjointed static. I slipped my headgear on, and the world was muffled. Sign language was our only method of communication.

I ran up the metal ladder to the first gunner's deck and took a position at one of the empty long guns. The pain in my head subdued. Someone hung onto the outside of the gunner's deck. I glanced down to see if it was an errant Lepidaian. A half metal face stared back at me with eyes that glowed an angry yellow.

A Yarat.

It was my first time seeing them up close. He slithered closer to the gun mount, his mouth open wide, trying to tear me apart with his song.

I unlocked the gun's mount so I could rotate it, pointed the barrel and fired, not prepared for the recoil to my gut. He didn't make a sound when he dropped to the ground. We lifted into the air, the ship vibrating as we spun away from the city.

I had killed my first person.

My insides had been sucked out of me and hung out to dry.

Death was on my hands.

I imagined Leanora's sad face in the distance. A single tear tracked down my face. I concentrated on what was ahead, humming with the frantic ulsos and gwynbees below me, trying to imagine her beside me.

I strapped in when the ship lurched sideways, knocking me against the bulkhead. Radjek straddled the top of the gun barrel. I kept my finger on the trigger. Yarat ships zipped around us, silver streaks in the night playing tricks with my eyes.

"Alaric, shoot the second they appear in sight."

"I will," he squeaked.

I squeezed the trigger the moment metal appeared in my sights. I hit the sides of one ship and the hull of another. Two others zipped away. The sea and land merged as we rotated to lose the ships headed for us. Two Yelti-Duri swarmed, and I kept firing until there was nothing but blackness. We lifted higher into the air, gaining speed. I kept my finger at the trigger, expecting them to return any moment.

A brisk wind picked up as we passed through the dark shadows of the Traske Mountain's first range. I wiped off the tears that fell. There was still a way through this.

I'm coming back, I heard a faint voice say in my head. I had to believe it was her. I looked back at Alaric who was staring at me, his eyes wide with fear. He didn't move from his mount. He stared through the gun sight, and I wished she could see how brave he was. How I wanted to keep him from having to grow up so fast. But we needed him.

I swiveled back to shoot more ships out of the skies, imagining her beside me.

We will be together soon.

Her voice didn't stop the tears from dripping onto the floor. I hoped Alaric wouldn't see.

16

LEANORA

"Channel what you know," Tarrok whispered in my ear. I sat across from him on the lower level of the hospital in Lepidaia. Through the large glass windows, the sea crashed against the rocks and the sun was peach-hued, the ocean purple. I leaned against Tarrok, and his body felt foreign against mine.

"How am I here?" I asked him.

"You are here whenever you want." His large green hands were holding mine before he let them go, leaping up as he twirled, the Yarat patients looking at him like he was deranged. He never acted this silly in public.

"You dancing today, Tarrok-wana?" Drash asked. The metal bracings in Drash's skull looked less severe than when he'd first arrived in the Talbo-Pii. His expression fell as he directed his gaze away from us. I held out a draft for Drash to drink.

"You will not be here long," Drash said to me, his eyes an unchanging dark brown as he downed the medicine in one gulp. "She will teach you many things." His face relaxed when the medicine kicked in.

"Who?" I asked.

"My Gulnaz. The Yarats separated us...we will kill them all in the end." His face took on a sinister look, and he pointed upward. The ceiling of the hospital cracked, and the earth beneath us rocked back and forth violently. I rushed to transport the patients, singing their bodies out the main entrance, running out of breath faster than usual. After several transportations, only Tarrok, Drash, and I were left. I wiped the sweat from my clammy forehead.

"Get us out," Drash demanded.

Tarrok held onto me. Chunks of stone fell in rhythm with the clashing Yarat music piercing my brain. I modified my song, harmonizing off what they sung, but it hurt to counter their music. Darkness fell on us, a pressure squeezing all around me. All was quiet. I couldn't even hear myself breathing. I sang into the quiet, pushing with everything in me as I sang us out of the darkness.

Seconds later, I stood above the hospital clutching a bleeding Tarrok. He was so heavy, it was hard to keep him upright. Everyone else we knew were sprawled out on the square of Lepidaia, the entire city aflame above us. Oily smoke filled my nostrils, choking me. I coughed into my tunic, dragging Tarrok away from the inferno.

"Could you not save them?" Tarrok's voice echoed off the rubble. Someone moaned in the distance, their shouts mixing with the half singing behind us.

I WOKE with a start in a dark room. I tried to control my ragged breath and still my heart, which beat loudly in my chest. I didn't realize I had fallen asleep, a sticky pool of drool beside me.

"No...please...you can't take them," a young man's voice moaned behind me.

I couldn't tell where I was, and I patted the ground around me. It was soft to the touch, but when I crawled to the end of where I had been lying, the flooring was solid.

"No! Mila! You trained with us. How can you...no! Not Danis!...The children..." He was going to wake up the whole house if I didn't get to him.

I jumped to my feet, throwing off the blanket. He was near the large window ledges where cushions were inset. Occasionally Selchuk or Mikosh would fall asleep there. No one had tied down the window coverings, which flapped in the breeze. I crawled along the ledge and flipped up the coverings. Selchuk thrashed, tipping to the edge of the window.

I ran to him and rolled him back toward me. My pulse was deafening. I shook him awake.

"Selchuk. It's me, Leanora." I shook him again. "Wake up."

He groaned and rubbed his eyes. "Don't tell me...Xibo wants us to train at night again." He turned away from me and closed his eyes.

"No." I kept my hands on his shoulders, afraid he might roll off again and hurt himself. I shook him awake again. He sat up, removing his blanket. He had slept in the clothes he'd worn the day before, despite stains on his trousers from my botched landings in the dirty surrounding hillsides.

A brisk wind blew across, and I folded the window coverings up. Two broken moons shone on the calm ocean. The sky wasn't as dark as Eloia's. Instead of seeing bits of stars, there was a multitude of color and light, mostly greens, purples, and blues streaking the sky in a cosmic gas that was glorious, almost as if the sky were translucent, revealing the star systems beyond.

"Unbelievable." It was a relief to see such beauty after my terrible nightmare.

I searched the sky, unable to tear my eyes away from the various orbs and streaks of purple light shining in the sky. Such a multitude of galaxies were contained there. It was the most beautiful thing I had ever seen.

"You've finally beheld our night sky," he whispered and crawled along the wide ledge to sit closer me.

"I've never seen anything like it before," I said. "So many dimensions, it's like there's a thin covering between us and the rest of space."

Heat radiated off of him. I expected someone so thin and tall to be cold. I pulled the blanket closer around myself. Selchuk's face was shadowed except for where the moonlight hit. His profile was soft in shadow, his nose a little large for his face. When he turned to look at me, he grinned.

"You stare at people for too long they can't help notice it," Selchuk said. "Be careful doing this with other Kardush."

I turned away from him, embarrassed. "You all stared at me when I first came."

He put his hand out, then withdrew it quickly. It was strange how physically restrained they were, yet had no problem destroying each other with their voices.

No wonder their planet was in disarray.

"We had to stare at you so we could train you." His voice was teasing me while his face remained serious. His shoulder only a few centimeters from mine. Warmth curled up around me from him. Our legs dangled outside the window, making small circles in the air and then coming back to the wall.

"What's wrong with your moons?" I asked.

"They were broken in earlier wars."

"Which war?" I was trying not to stare at him.

"When the Yarats came, around four or five hundred years ago, they wanted to prove how powerful they were. So they blew up the sides of both our moons. One is like half of its size, and the other has a nice chunk bitten out of it. We let them come after we saw that. Maybe we should have put up more of a fuss and let them destroy both of them." He laughed and looked at me, his gaze inquisitive. "You know, take the moons, leave the planet as it is."

"I wonder how different things would have been if the Kardush had decided that." I looked at the shadows of the hills, barely perceptible in the moonlight. A burning question was on my tongue, but the silence felt so comfortable. Still, I couldn't let it rest. "Why couldn't I find you last week when Xibo wanted me to transport myself to you?" I asked.

"*Urijniak,*" he said, his face losing all its mirth.

"What?" I asked.

"Sensing tracks. You draw people's energies, the life force of their spirit, toward you when you're trying to figure out where they are...both physically and mentally." His face became very serious as he swiveled around to face me.

"Is that bad?"

"It is for me." He looked up at the sky. "I should have let you find me, but my training was so intense that my default is to keep my guard very high to protect from someone's *urijniak* finding me. I have few other defenses. I'm not a great traveler."

"But you are a great healer," I said.

He stiffened, drawing his legs into his chest. "I still couldn't save the right people. I lost everyone I knew in the war except Xibo, Mikosh, and a few other fighters on my team who probably won't fight on Eloia." He rubbed his hands together and blew into them. "It is hard not to blame myself..." His jaw tensed. "Or others."

I offered him the blanket around me, and he scooted closer, tucking the ends around both of us while still keeping a proper distance. "You couldn't have prevented their deaths."

"I was lucky I didn't see my family die. Xibo and Mikosh were not so lucky." His voice broke a little, dropping his gaze to his hands. "We're raised to watch our emotions, to be these almost perfect people." His voice got smaller.

"If you delete your emotions, you take away your will to live," I said.

"I lost so much," he whispered.

"Can you tell me?"

He spun to the right, like he heard something. He waited a few moments, then turned back to me. "I knew many of the people we were fighting. They were soldiers Xibo had trained, even healers his wife had taught."

"That's horrible."

"I wasn't fully trained when the war started. Mikosh and Gulnaz are a few years older than me."

"How old are you?" I asked.

"Probably nineteen, but I don't know for sure because on Spirthen, where I was born, they don't care about birthdates. Here, twenty is considered very young, almost a child. You aren't fully grown until you're forty." He drew the blanket closer to him.

I thought back to when my mother came to Eloia, when she was almost fifty, and it made sense that she could still have kids at a time when most Eloians had gray hair and counted their grandchildren.

"I'll be eighteen in a few months," I said.

"Still a child." He grinned then looked up at the sky. "Like me."

"Definitely not a child." I sat up straighter. Our bare shoulders touched, and for a moment he didn't move. I was no longer in my body but displaced. Half of me sat in the windowsill, while my consciousness lived in his memory. He was running through the grasses, two small children holding hands with him. The girl was a few years older than the boy. Selchuk was already out of breath, the children stopping every few minutes. He lifted the boy, explosions breaking up mounds of earth around them, the ground quaking.

"*Uraj noi. Ani. Anyak doi!* Over there. No. Not here!" Xibo yelled.

A flame roared overhead. Selchuk grabbed the kids, pushing them down into the tall grasses. They kept standing to listen to Xibo's voice. Two shadows swooped in and materialized as Yarat soldiers. While Selchuk sang a counter-melody, flames curled around him and the children. He belted louder, shielding the children with his body while they screamed, the flames engulfing them. Selchuk reached for them, but they were gone, turned to ash by the time his fingers touched them.

He pulled away from me, and the memory stopped. I was sick to my stomach, bile rising in my throat.

Selchuk was shaking. "It's my...fault...they're...gone," he muttered in Hiranian.

"You could not prevent that," I said.

"But I had to," he whispered.

I put my arms around him while he trembled, tears running down his face and onto my shoulder. I sang one of Agda's lullabies, imagining the tendrils of my song soothing him. I rocked him back and forth, lifting the poisonous pain out of his body and releasing it to the sky with my song.

After three rounds of the lullaby, Selchuk's head rose from my shoulder. There was so much darkness in him yet to release, but he resisted so I let go of him. He wiped his eyes, separating from me and resting his back against the frame of the window. "Xibo doesn't know everything."

"What doesn't he know?" I asked.

"His wife, Danis...she..." He wiped his eyes again. "She was killed. Those were his kids I was trying to rescue. She and I..." His voice trailed off.

"What?" I asked softly.

"It doesn't matter...she's gone." He looked back at me, his eyes puffy. "That's why I'm like this. Because of her, because they're all gone." He looked away from me. "They were all I had left to live for."

Selchuk went silent and laid back down in the wide windowsill, his breath steadying until he was asleep again. I was too worried to leave him alone. I let him fall against me, stroking his shoulder-length hair. I closed my eyes and hummed Agda's melody again until it became an entirely different song.

MY MOTHER TOOK MY HAND, and we found a passageway out to the shale outside Pakopaikka. We strolled along the beach as the tide went out. I liked the steady sound of our feet crunching on the sand and shale. The seabirds above us, called to each other. A few luoshis were being chased by ulsos on the cliff above us.

A tune soared on the waves that reminded me of the wordless songs Mom used to sing in the forest. A cluster of women walked along the stone steps that led along the cliff face below. They crooned in Hiranian,

The water is the surface
of my drown-ed heart,
flowing where my blood cannot.
For it does not exist,
until you do return.

"It is not so happy now that you know the words," Mom said.

"There is a feeling of uplift in it though, like a release from something terrible," I said.

She kissed my hand and led me back up the steps. "You

understand already the deeper meanings behind our songs. Let's go inside and meet the Kardush women who came here during the war." She gestured toward stone steps that curved around the glass and stone building without a rail. We climbed steadily up the side of the cliff that the Pakopaikka enclave had been built into. She gestured toward the glass front on the building. "When my eyesight came back after the forabera treatment, I wanted to create something that felt like it was from both Eloia and Hirana. I wanted to bring you here. So I called this Pakopaikka—or 'the retreat from strife' in Hiranian."

She held me to her. "It will be yours when I am gone."

WHEN XIBO FOUND us at first light, Selchuk was lying across my legs while I watched the twin suns come up across the magenta water.

"I did not expect this so soon." Xibo's face settled into a wry grin, his thick eyebrows drawn up in a question.

I slipped out from under Selchuk. He woke with a start, his face calm compared to the night before. He walked away, ignoring Xibo.

"It's not..." I watched Selchuk disappear into the next room.

Xibo's face was steely, all mirth gone. "I'm not stupid. I know how it is." He leaned against the window ledge, balancing on his good leg. "He has not slept since the war ended. A whole year of wandering or thrashing every night." He folded up the window shades and squinted into the sunrise. "The question is: can you kill as well as you heal, Leanora?"

I wanted to push him out the window. Even if he could levitate off the ground, I stepped away, folding my arms across my body. "I will do what is necessary to protect Eloia." I had to get away from him.

I started toward the kitchens below, but Xibo blocked my exit. "It is dangerous to get too close to that one. Shadows follow him." He held up a finger in warning. "If you are not careful, you will be caught." His lined face softened, and he rubbed the top of his bald head.

The white floor below reflected Xibo and me facing off. I needed an ally. Someone who wasn't afraid to feel. I pushed the pained expression of Selchuk's blue eyes out of my mind, trying to replace them with the warm concern in Tarrok's face.

Xibo tipped his staff toward me. "What you have with Tarrok must carry you to the other side."

"What do you mean?"

A mixture of emotions he fought against flickered across his face. He exhaled noisily. "You have something still to fight for." He held his hands out wide. "My whole family: gone. Mikosh's family also gone. Selchuk and Gulnaz are all I have left."

"Do you blame Selchuk?" I asked.

Xibo looked away from me. "No." He spoke more softly than I'd ever heard him before. He glanced up at the white ceiling, fixating on a point there. "Don't confuse issues. I'm here to talk about you. Stop being afraid. Harness the power you already have." He backed away, crossing his arms. "You will want to hate me soon. Compared to the creatures you are about to face, I will be like a puff of smoke, a bit of ocean bead. Nothing."

I started toward the staircase, but Xibo held out a hand. A warning. "Touch is dangerous here. You do not need to learn so much about a person."

"There is a better way," I said.

"Not from where I stand." He indicated for me to continue down the stairwell and hobbled after me. After descending one floor, I didn't want his energy anywhere near me.

"Eat fast people. The battle is waiting for us," Xibo yelled to students scurrying about.

How much of me would change? And would Tarrok recognize me after it was all done?

I sang a quick song that transported me from the stairwell to the kitchen three levels down, surprising the trainees gathered around the large common table.

"Show off," Gulnaz sneered and threw a pile of clothes at me.

I looked down at my blouse and skirt, which were on their last legs. The stretchy fabric she gave me would hide very little. I left them on the floor to get food before Xibo started barking orders. Selchuk had a wry smile on his face, and Mikosh pushed him off his chair. I retreated to the bathroom to change.

MY MOTHER HAD tears in her eyes. "Oh, my daughter." She held me close then, and she was shaking. I did not know why.

"What is it? Please tell me."

The women's voices coming from Pakopaikka were low and comforting as they passed by us, their song a calming tide. I threaded my mother's arm in mine while we walked back inside, following the trail their hand lanterns created in the sunset.

"It will be dark soon, and I want you to be able to see the way," my mother said. "Soon everything will depend on trusting your instincts to guide all of us."

I watched the firelight from the lanterns play across her pale face, her dark eyes reflecting the light. She had never looked like she loved me more than in that moment. The lanterns swayed as the women sang. We joined our voices with theirs, the heavy outside door closing securely behind us.

WHEN I EMERGED in the most comfortable of the set of

clothes Gulnaz had thrown at me, my stomach and back were still exposed to the air. There were no sleeves on the stretchy top that had crisscrossing fabric at the back that covered nothing but kept my chest well protected, at least. The pants were high-waisted and covered my ankles, but every muscle was visible. I wanted to put my old clothes back on, but they weren't practical.

Mikosh stood before me, arms crossed, head cocked to the side. "You'll get used to it, come on. Xibo's waiting for us."

"I feel ridiculous," I said.

"It could be worse."

17

LEANORA

rust your instincts to guide all of us.
I struggled to climb the hillsides in the stretchy
trousers and close-fitting cropped top. Maybe that was the point,
to increase my discomfort. Gulnaz nodded at me from the hilltop.
I'd love to have wiped that smug expression from her face.

We'd spent the previous week making certain I could sustain
myself in the air, even with projectiles thrown at me. Now I
could dart from location to location quickly: up the green hillsides of Maer-lina, over to the dwarf forest on the opposite shore,
up to the peak of the mountain in the southern tip of the island
and back to the training house.

"People! Time for battle simulations traveling," Xibo yelled.
Thirty students were assembled, and Xibo divided us in half.
One group went with Gulnaz. The other went with Mikosh and
me. Selchuk unwillingly joined Gulnaz's group.

"Stay together when you're attacking. No fireballs, no crazy
elements or weapons to attack. Simple hand-to-hand, when
appropriate, but mostly sing to distract and destabilize. If your
feet touch the ground, you're dead. The last group with the

most people in the air wins and gets first pick at dinner," Xibo said.

Inbikh let out a cheer, and a few students groaned.

"Ya-rii! Go!" Inbikh yelped, before she realized how many people were watching her. She froze in place for a moment, then scampered off to fish. She was learning it was better to avoid us when we had combat rounds.

Gulnaz's group didn't wait for Xibo to leave the hillside. She sang them into a formation, and they attacked before my people were in the air.

Mikosh glared at me. "Do something!"

I sang one of the popular market stall songs to whisk our group up the opposite hillside where there were dwarf trees we could hide in and discuss our battle plan.

"No hiding. Fight..." Xibo's voice faded away the further we traveled from Gulnaz's group.

We sailed over the dwarf trees and into a corner where two hilltops met, full of tall sapphire grasses to hide us. I stopped the song, and we abruptly sunk to the ground, several dropping abruptly.

"Landings." A blonde-haired male student reminded me.

Mikosh glanced behind us. "We have a few minutes. Luka, Malvo, Yew, Vi, stay with me and keep a rotating circuit around Leanora. She'll keep us in the air, but she isn't a good enough fighter to break out on her own. The rest of you rotate on offense."

"I thought Leanora decided tactics," a sour-faced redhead boy said.

"I'm choosing which of you to keep in the air and which to let plummet to the ground because you're not fighting," I said with a sneer.

He snorted but didn't say anything else.

A tunnel of noise barreled toward us, and I was knocked off

my feet. Half of our team rose in the air, and Mikosh reached down to pick me up. "Come on, you have to get the rest of us into the air."

I sang again, but the song faltered in my mouth. We needed something angrier. I crafted a new melody completely from scratch: a simple three chord minor tune. Easy to harmonize. The rest of us rose out of the grasses, but the minute we were airborne, bodies slammed us. It was a good thing Xibo didn't see me tumbling to the ground. I kept up the pace of the tune before levitating upward. I pulled our group with me back toward the field where we had originally been training, forcing Gulnaz's group to chase us while we zipped away on a fast loop.

Several of the outside ranks swirled around each other, making students fall to the field floor where they were grounded under Xibo's watchful eye.

Gulnaz flew toward me, and I narrowly missed getting knocked back to the ground. Mikosh and the redhead chased her, and Gulnaz was pushed toward the field, her face almost touching the ground before heading them off. Mikosh and the redhead tumbled backwards to the ground. There were only three of my group left against Gulnaz and Selchuk. He pushed Gulnaz, and she lost her song, falling with a shout. Xibo spread his arms.

"Enough."

Gulnaz didn't stop. She sang toward me, and I plummeted to the ground, the wind knocked out of me. I struggled to breathe and forgot to call the water back to my body. Selchuk was immediately at my side.

Gulnaz cackled. "She isn't a fighter. It was pure luck, along with Mikosh and Vi who defended her." She flicked her hair off her shoulder. "More sparring and less traveling, that's the only way she's going to learn."

"Take a break, Gulnaz," Xibo growled.

"She'll get us all killed."

"No, your arrogance will," I countered.

Her face was red with fury. When I met her gaze and didn't back down—floating to my feet and dusting off my hands, though my back was throbbing—she backed off. She sang loudly, flying into the air and back toward the hillside. I was fighting the feeling that my brain was melting. I closed my eyes and breathed the water back into my limbs and extremities, staving off the lingering fatigue from lack of sleep. Once I'd had enough, I opened my eyes. A dry patch gathered from the ground around me, and the students who had been standing there inched away.

Xibo hovered in front of me. An incremental burning spread from my face across to the rest of my exposed skin, which—thanks to Gulnaz's wardrobe 'fix'—was half my body. A low bass thrumming, interspersed with a vibration pulsing through me, pulled me back to the ground.

"What...are...you...?" I had to counterattack.

I sang my counter-melody, an octave above him, rooting it deep in my core. Xibo's nostrils flared, and the burning aroma increased, choking me. With the next inhalation I harmonized with his melody, interrupting his song's pattern. I focused my sound to morph into a shield that siphoned off the energy he was blasting my way. I hunched down to concentrate the sound, using my body to launch it forward.

Fight with everything you have, a familiar voice said in my ear.

My skin flaked off and I was distracted by how much floated through the air. I closed my eyes, belting out everything within me. Then I dropped to the grass.

Xibo plummeted to the ground a few seconds after.

"Not good," he said, coughing and sputtering. He hummed a series of arpeggios. Then he rose, hobbling over to me. The rest of the students were watching from a distance.

"I'm the enemy right now; if you stay on the ground you're dead," Xibo commanded.

I called the water back into my body. Spit flew from my face, my first Hiranian curse spewing out. "*Kundit mazra ha!*"

"Make me feel it. Attack! Again!" Xibo shouted. His voice turned into a low growl that shook me. "I have the power to banish you to places you'll never come back from."

A new energy surged through me, and I pushed him back into the grass. I stood over him, ready to punch him in the face.

"Do it!" he yelled.

Instead, I sang a scratch across his face. His cheeks tore in a thin line. His smile disappeared. I lifted his body through the air, spinning it before letting him slam into the dirt.

A hand rested on my shoulder. I collapsed. When I opened my eyes, Selchuk stood over me.

"Don't! She has to learn how to restore herself," Xibo said.

"She's too depleted." Selchuk's voice was calm but powerful. He touched a finger lightly to my arm and trilled a soft melody, my skin no longer burning with pain. Xibo crouched next to him, and when Selchuk saw him, he kept one finger on my arm and held out his other hand. "Leave us." Xibo's body flew away from us, and it was just Selchuk and me. The grass blew in the salty ocean air, and I relaxed for the first time that day.

"If you don't remember to keep drawing water into yourself or siphoning energy off the Yarats, you'll die quickly," Selchuk said. "We are lucky—our bodies are already inclined to heal. But, as healers, we are in additional danger, because we're used to caring for others before ourselves." His cobalt eyes were hard. "Get yourself healed first. Always. Otherwise you are of no use."

I nodded. The sky was darkening already. "I need sleep and food," I whispered.

He tapped his finger on my bare shoulder, making sure to not make contact for too long. "You need to call the water to yourself more quickly, efficiently. Perhaps it would help to seek the closest water source, though miniscule, and imagine it refilling and doubling itself."

I brought my mind back to the ocean here, its churning, and willed its energy to be mine. Its waves now my waves, its water replacing whatever in me needed that water, and the roar of its sound now a part of my body. I opened my eyes, and the waves were closer to us, crashing just inches away from where we stood. I was able to stand on my own, but there was still a gnawing in my stomach. I couldn't operate on the paltry amount of food and water they ate every day. "I'm finished."

Selchuk's face fell. "Only Xibo decides when we're done."

Xibo floated above us like a misshapen eagle. The puffy clouds above him made him look especially ominous in his black clothes. He touched down a few steps from us.

"I'm taking her inside," Selchuk said, surprising me.

"You know the rules," Xibo said.

Gulnaz landed next to him, her face still twisted in fury. "Push her limits. Otherwise, she's a liability in battle."

Selchuk's eyes flashed. He put his hands on his hips and sang. I joined him: it was a lilting, jaunty tune. Xibo narrowed his dark eyes; his counter-melody blew us against the hillside. Gulnaz backed away.

I pictured our song creating a ball of fire to scorch him. My voice lowered, harmonizing with Selchuk. A light burst out of us and surrounded Xibo. He tumbled to the ground, his forehead bleeding where we burned him. His whole face had already taken a battering. I ran to him but stopped when I realized he was still conscious and could attack. When he didn't move, I ventured closer.

"Why does he let us hurt him?" I asked, but Selchuk took my hand, Gulnaz waving us away.

"Go. Before he wakes," she said.

"Doesn't he need healing?" I asked.

"Not from you," she snapped.

I took Selchuk's hand, and we ran off the hilltop. I sang our bodies into the air, and within seconds we touched down, albeit fairly shakily, at the grounds of the training house. I let go of him.

"Not bad." Selchuk grinned at me.

I ignored his smile, searching for Inbikh without finding her. When I turned around, Selchuk was still smiling and Xibo had landed next to him.

"No more fireballs from you two." He nodded at me. "You're finally making progress." He looked between us, like he was deciding something. "Five hours of rest. Then we start again." He walked up the steps to the building, humming a short tune that made my head hurt until he was inside.

Inbikh sped out of the house to greet me. It made me miss Vali. When I was tired I could ride on him wherever I needed to go. No chance of that with Inbikh.

"I missed you. What did you do?" I asked her.

"Best fish." I lifted her onto my shoulder, where she purred and fussed with my hair. "Bath time!"

I didn't look back at Selchuk, ignoring his searching energy as we made our way up the stairs to find a place to wash and exchange clothing. When I found an empty washing chamber at the end of the corridor, the tiles gleaming a soft white, I locked the door and filled up the large tub while Inbikh danced around the rim. I pushed her in.

"What do dat for?" she squealed.

"You need a bath too!" I said. Inbikh fluffed herself and shook off the water beads. Steam rose off her small body.

"No fish for you," she said. I laughed at her, hoping she wasn't serious.

Someone rattled the door.

"I'm in here," I said.

"Hurry up, we all need to wash," Gulnaz called through the door. She'd never cared before.

"There are plenty more washing chambers to choose from." I had no intention of hurrying up. I waited for a few minutes to see if she was going to break down the door, but she went silent.

I floated in the enormous bath, soaking in the warm water for the first time in weeks. "Inbikh, can you go bring me food?" I pleaded.

"From Eloia?" She perked up.

"I wish." I glanced up at the ceiling, where a series of tiles formed a mosaic scene that swirled like the ocean around Maerlina. It reminded me of how divided I felt. The blue tiles were the same hue as Selchuk's eyes. Would avoiding him in my spare time make it easier to train with him?

18

TARROK

The smell of the engine grease from the cantankerous Marwatha made all of our noses run while the ulso's whining continued. They weren't used to being indoors for so long. Vali and Carki tucked their noses under my arms. White-furred Dona slept on the floor next to peach-furred Possum. We'd landed in the rainforests of Nedara, hoping to hide at the bottom of the forest canopy.

The pounding of the Yarat music was a mere vibration at first. I could have dismissed it for engine noise if I hadn't felt it pulsing through my limbs. Their music was seeking us out. I regretted not paying more attention to my warrior training in Hagoth. There we were trained as warriors first. Men of flesh and blood second. I knew, at an early age, that I was different from other warriors. More sensitive. More prone to action than conversation. When we did our apprenticeship rounds, I often snuck away to be with the animals. Or to listen to my sister while she healed others.

I knew, by age ten, when I was apprenticed to the master ulso trainer, that my life would be spent outside like other warriors, just not grappling with men. I preferred the calm and patient training of the furry, large-bodied ulsos. Each ulso had to cultivate their humms for their bonded partner and learn to bear the weight of Hagothians without bolting ahead at the sight of prey.

The Yarat music stopped. A stillness came for a few minutes. I felt like we could finally catch our breath before artillery hit our hull. Two more blasts and Neelan shouted, "Peshara! Get ready!"

The music boomed, then came a screeching that alternated between eerie flutes and scream-singing. The animals were terrified. All my muscles seized up and the interior of the ship flashed neon. I ran about with Alaric, putting ear protection over the animals again. Alaric slid his protection on, and we climbed up to the gun mounts.

Neelan had turned over the controls to Bejah, and he joined us at the third gun mount. We were battered by the sonorous beating of their percussion against our bodies. The ear protection kept the sound from infiltrating my brain, but not much else.

A shot glanced off our bow, and the engines sputtered.

I closed my eyes, the song outside intensifying as pockets of jarring noise interspersed with the soft flowing music you'd hear from a multi-stringed guitar. Bejah cut out the engines, and Neelan yelled down to her. "Why did you do that?"

"They hit one," Bejah said. "Go fix it." She climbed up the gun mount to change places with him.

"Gwynbees, to the consoles," Alaric yelled at them, and they swarmed to the deck.

"Don't touch anything until Bejah says," I added. I looked to Alaric. "Keep shooting."

Yarat ships darted above us, and I kept the gun at the ready. The minute metal appeared in front of me, I fired.

Neelan came back from the engine console, his skin black with grease. Something in his expression reminded me of my best friend, Ori, right before his last battle. I remembered thinking,

Say something to him that he'll remember, if you never see him again. He was bitten fatally by a sand eel, because he hadn't listened to his trainer. A stupid death.

"You'll regret not being a warrior," Ori had said that last time. His emerald skin shone in the sunlight, his braggadocios voice echoing in my memories after he was gone. I had missed him even more after my father died. There was no one to give me that humorous balance I had needed once I became a master ulso trainer.

The music stopped, and Neelan shook his head. "Don't move. No sound, nothing." His whole hand lit up, and he moved slowly, an arc of light surrounding him. He crawled up the service ladder between Alaric and me to an upper hatch. The ulsos watched him noiselessly before slumping down when he didn't return. Bejah leaned out of her seat but didn't move. It was raining, the liquid pelting the cockpit's glass and the end of the gun mounts. I would have pulled them in, but I heeded Neelan's warning.

Then there was a banging on the ship. The thumping increasing to a deafening vibration. Wild-eyed faces mangled from battle and laced with metal hung from the gun mount. Their thin, long limbs pulled on the barrel, reaching for me. There were too many of them.

"Shoot them, Alaric. Bejah, we need you at the third gun. Now!" No matter how many I shot, they kept coming. There were so many of them darting in and out. I didn't know if I had hit any of them, if I was doing anything, searing panic choking me.

Don't worry. I heard Leanora's voice. *Keep going.* My heart settled for half a second before more of them banged on the cockpit windows. Their voices cracked the cockpit glass, until the ulsos hummed louder with a countermelody. We continued to shoot.

Then the banging stopped. The rain had produced a wall of muddy water. Several Yarats were swept below the gun mounts when the flooding started. Our landing gear wasn't very high. If we didn't leave soon, we would be swept away.

Neelan swung down, landing with a thud. "Let's use the rain to get to Hagoth!"

Bejah swung down to join him at the controls. "Destuba," she cursed.

I felt a lurch as the ship started and then choked to a stop. Neelan looked to me. "Help me get it going!" I followed him into the upper panels that were better suited to someone his size.

"Snake cable now!" Neelan yelled, and I found a blue cable he seemed to be referring to. "No, the black one." I let the blue one drop and snatched the black one, throwing it up to him.

The entire ship was powered by a combination of algae fuel that reacted to the sunlight and air of our planet, which had a slightly different chemical combination than what they had on Hirana. It looked like we were hotwiring the circuitry.

"Blue one!" he yelled again, and once he had it, he stuck it into the socket and spread out the surrounding wires, reaffixing them while I handed him tools.

"We have to outrun them while we have the chance." Neelan put the last plug into the massive circuit board, closed the panel, and indicated with his head that we should go down. "They want me. I'm the only one who can fix their stupid ships."

The engines started up again, and the Gwynbees strapped the ulsos in, chittering to each other.

"Let's get out of here. Don't wait to shoot," Neelan yelled.

"Lift-off!" Bejah yelled and pulled back on the controls.

"5...4...3...2..1," Neelan counted down as the launch gear folded up. The ship groaned and wheezed until we were off the ground, spinning away from the canopy and back toward the mountains.

"Watch that peak, Bejah."

"I see it," she growled at Neelan.

The terrain below us was a bright green blur. Two Yarat Yelti-Duri darted in and out, shooting at us while Neelan sang a protective song. I got the ulsos started on the same melody.

"Two more coming to my side!" Alaric yelled.

The ships moved so quickly it was hard to hit them. Then one floated close by, teasing us. "Be ready, hand on trigger." I had detected a pattern with the ship where it would dart out, wait, and then swoop in again. If we timed it right, we could knock it out of the sky.

I shot at the right wing, making it spin. Bejah shifted us to the other side so that Alaric could shoot.

"I missed. Turn her again," Alaric called out.

"I'll get her," I said.

"There's another," Neelan said.

"Stay on controls. I take it out." Bejah climbed up to the gun mount.

We took two more hits, one of the engines faltering. We sunk lower, and Neelan cursed.

"We have to get rid of all of them. Now!" Bejah yelled from the top gun mount.

The two following us dodged in and out, firing directly at us, one shot coming through the gun mount and disabling my gun. I jumped up to where Bejah was. "Go help, Neelan—I've got this."

"You better." Bejah clambered down to the cockpit.

"Tarrok, another at my right flank, coming at you," Alaric shouted.

I wasn't strapped in yet. I shot a succession of rounds and blew the Yarat ship out of the sky. Bodies flew out with the busted ship.

"One more," Alaric said.

166

I kept shooting and released the trigger, sighing. "Not anymore."

Within seconds we were far enough away to witness the smoking hulk of ship wreckage on the outskirts of Nedara. I kept watching for more ships, scanning the borderlands for any sign of them, my body unable to relax from a tension that felt permanent. My mind reached out for Leanora, clinging to the hope that I would see her again. *I need you here by my side.* I imagined us sitting on the dunes again, racing our ulsos like the war wasn't here. Then I fixed my eyes through the gun sight, watching the intersecting spheres that showed me a target was within sight. Three more Yarat ships zipped across the horizon.

"Alaric, more coming our way."

"We'll get them, Tarrok," he said.

I looked across at him, his blue eyes wide with fright. I wished he didn't have to do this.

"We do it for her, so we can all see each other another day," I said.

19

LEANORA

W e stood on the dusty hilltop behind the training house while the wind rushed around us. I turned my back on the late afternoon suns, letting the last of their warmth spread across my exposed back. Inbikh perched on my shoulder, her fur still damp. A mist crept in, obscuring the view of the ocean. I had to try to send Inbikh back to Eloia, to take initiative in expanding the range of my traveling ability. But I was afraid. Old voices from Asanis crowded my thoughts.

Such a loser, Leanora.

Good for nothing.

They didn't decide my future. I had to do that myself.

I watched Inbikh, her round yellow eyes wide with anticipation, and I held her to me.

Soon everything will depend on trusting your instincts to guide all of us.

My mother's voice, so warm and soothing, made me want to transport myself back. I let go of Inbikh and set her on the ground. I couldn't get carried away by my emotions. There too much at stake. The mist crept further, obscuring the shore below. I had to send Inbikh to Eloia quickly, to put all my powers of concentration into taking her there.

"I go to Tarrok?" she asked.

"I don't know if you'll find him." I closed my eyes and felt for the trajectory I'd take her on through the galaxies. "You ready?"

"Be quick, quick," she chirped, and I sang a fast traveling song. It had a Lepidaian lilt to the key, and as I wove the song into Inbikh, she disappeared from my hands. I opened my eyes. I felt her spirit hurtling toward Eloia, past the twin suns, away from the Wex-Em galaxy and through four more star systems until the last of Inbikh's presence left me. Was she with Tarrok and my family now?

I sang a traveling song to float myself back to the training house. I felt a sharp turn in my stomach as my body left the hill.

I arrived dizzy but intact. I drew all the water toward me and had overestimated the draw of my song when rain pelted me, droplets settling on my arms from calling the elements too suddenly to restore me. The muscles in my neck relaxed, and I managed a step without wobbling. I gingerly walked in the house, students sprawled everywhere from our midday training. I took off my shoes so as not to wake anyone, least of all Xibo.

Maybe if I had some sustenance I'd feel better. I followed the scent of fried fish and ate the last of the crackers and fish that were left out on a platter. A few grey birds roosted in the corners of the kitchen.

I tried to recall how Xibo had called to them. "De...le...la... yada..." I said softly.

They woke from their roosting, and a few swooped down to the white counter, their claws clicking against the stone surface. Their heads moved a little like pigeons, except they were enormous. So much larger than I'd expected. One pecked at the counter and eyed me, its eyes rimmed in white and blue rings.

"De...le....la...yada," I said again. The one pecking flew away, but the other perched beside my hand and uttered a soft "cooo." I obviously wasn't saying "refreshment, please" correctly. The bird became bored and flew back up to its perch.

I found a pitcher of liquid from the previous night, sniffed it, and opted for water instead.

How long did I wait before transporting Inbikh back? Would she remember to bring me some food from home, if there was any?

It was selfish to want something from home at a time like this. What if Inbikh didn't make it and I'd killed her?

And if I couldn't transport her safely, how could I bring Tarrok here?

I needed to hear his voice again, not inside my head but in real time. Panic seized me, and I clamored up the stairs, two at a time, to the room where I had last spoken to him. I didn't check to see if anyone was around. I stood in front of the cloth screen and centered all my thoughts on where he might be. I hummed a low song that he would know. Nothing happened, not even a projection of light on the screen.

"Please be there." I tried again. I needed some confirmation that Inbikh may have reached him. Or that he was as lost without me as I was without him. I was tired of imagining his hands in mine, replaying faded memories of his voice. I had to hear it. I closed my eyes, seeking out his energy again. I waited in the thick silence for anything, even a slight murmur to suggest he was alive on the other end of the galaxy.

I closed my eyes, pinpointing my *urijniak* again on Tarrok, searching out where he might be. There was a connection at the back of my mind. I opened my eyes, a flicker of light on the screen, and then it was gone. Running toward the spot where the flicker had appeared, I waited. But nothing came from the projection minerals. I tried again, my brain drowning with the effort.

It didn't make sense, unless they had evacuated Lepidaia. I

sunk to the floor, rubbing my eyes, overexertion overwhelming me. I lay back on the floor, trying to steady my beating heart. What if something terrible happened...what if...?

A sharp, flowery scent filled the room. "It's no use if he isn't near a communication hall." Gulnaz's voice was soft. She sat next to me, her strong perfume waking me up.

"How do you know?"

Gulnaz held out a canister of water to me. "Xibo spoke to Saren last night. She was on a transport out of Lepidaia with the rest of those evacuating."

"I have to go back." I bolted out to the staircase, and Gulnaz leapt over me, blocking my exit.

"Don't give into it. Not a good idea, Leanora." Gulnaz's accent was thicker than usual.

Xibo could have told me he was speaking to my mother. A terrible homesickness swelled inside of me, and I couldn't suppress the dark, snarling anger that engulfed my gnawing sadness. I took the water from her and gulped it down. It wasn't enough. I called the water outside to the glass, and when it was filled I marched down the stairs toward Xibo, seeking out his throbbing energy in the room, walking around the hushed building, Gulnaz following on my heels.

"It isn't Xibo's fault," she said.

"You would say that."

"This is just what happens in war."

"Leave me alone," I said through gritted teeth.

Humming a sinister song, I ignored the warning in Gulnaz's voice and jumped from the top floor balcony in the large breezeway to the ground-floor kitchen where Xibo's energy was most prominent. I knocked him over when I landed, wind rushing past my ears, blowing my hair back.

"Still working on the landing, I see," Xibo said.

"Where are they?" I demanded.

"Gulnaz told you." He was too slow scuttling away.

The water in the cannister was boiling, and I dumped it in his face. "Why. Didn't. You. TELL ME?" The entire building shook as a symphony of sound rushed behind my eyes. Rain pelted the window frames and wind rushed through, knocking plates off the shelves and onto the floor where they shattered. If he was going to turn me into one of his creatures...I saw pain, a little fear, but mostly pride in Xibo's scarred face. He grinned widely and stood up, arms raised like he'd won some victory. The rest of the students kept a safe distance. The shock in their eyes was unmistakable, but they wanted front row seats to the show. I had become what Xibo said I would.

Must stop. To continue would be wrong. The wind died down.

I stepped away from him, trying to get my breath under control. Searching for the nearest exit that would preclude anyone following me toward the hillside and into the tallest patch of the grasses. Students crowded the closest open windows and doorways I could have flown out of.

I bent over and rubbed my face to dislodge the feeling of destruction coursing through me. When I looked up, everyone, including Xibo, had taken several steps away from me. Rain still dripped from the awning beyond the common room.

"You're coming along nicely. You are as Mikosh predicted," Xibo said, crossing his arms, his gaze prying into me.

Mikosh came down the steps with a glow lamp. She stood with us, her expression softer than usual. "I didn't predict this."

I whipped around to face Xibo. "Why didn't you tell me Lepidaia was evacuated?" I asked. I felt like my emotions had left me and I was barren. There was something I had to do, but I couldn't remember what it was.

"Where's your Gwynbee?" Mikosh asked.

Then I remembered Inbikh. "Hopefully on Eloia."

"That would be helpful," Xibo said, wiping his face with a dishrag.

"You disgust me," I said and charged out of the training house. Someone was following me, and I hoped it wasn't him, because at that moment I felt like I could kill him. I hated him that much. And it was probably what he wanted. This was his process for turning me into the killer he thought I needed to be against the Yarats.

I sang my body wearily back up the hill, touching down in a patch of waist-length grasses that itched my exposed skin.

"Leanora, stop," Mikosh said, sounding tired. "Please."

She stood there, the lantern still in her hands. "I know you're angry with Xibo, and you have every right to be. But, don't...hold onto it...longer than necessary."

"What would you know about it?" I was not in the mood for her advice.

"Love is a trap. A terrible affliction that changes how we feel about everything..." She paused, looking above us at the low cloud cover obscuring the setting suns. "And yet...I wish my mother was still here. I'd give anything for her not to have died." She set the lantern down and took a step closer to me. "So I understand, more than Xibo, that the way we've seen love is wrong. Those bonds count for something. And maybe if we'd recognized that, we wouldn't be in this state." She exhaled and sat down on the steps. She drew her hair into a fat bun of braids at the top of her head. "There's no chance I'll ever see her again."

I sat next to her, the cool wind icy against my still hot skin.

"What happened to your mom?"

Mikosh kept her gaze trained upward, like she was afraid she would cry. "She was the general over all the Kardush armies. Your mom was her best friend during their training when they were young. They went down to Eloia at the same time, and for a long time I lived without her. Most of our relationship here surrounded making sure I didn't get killed, after she returned. She was always giving me tactical advice, using my ability to train the young soldiers." She looked at me, scooting closer. "Many of them were too young to fight. And she knew that, but the Kardush were desperate near the end. We'd lost so many people, and the Yarats wanted us all gone."

I put a hand on her shoulder. "I'm sorry." Mikosh took both my hands; she was trembling and trying to keep her memories from flowing into me. I let go and kept my hand on her shoulder, which was covered by her thick tunic. Mikosh was the only one who had never asked anything from me.

"The war will take away everything that is good, if you let it." She smiled at me, looking so exhausted. "Just concentrate on getting Inbikh back and finding a way to your family." She rose up, and we both stood there in the quiet of the hushed grasses blowing about us, the sea barely audible over the wind.

"I'll bring Inbikh back before I get too tired." I closed my eyes, gauging her energy's location and felt a connection immediately with my consciousness. I hooked onto that and sang her back. She appeared in my lap within a few seconds, purring and turning in circles.

"I back...I back! Tank you, Ya-rii!"

"Why does she call you Ya-rii?" Mikosh asked, laughing as Inbikh purred and climbed all over both of us in excitement.

"Long story," I said. I wasn't in the mood to talk about Nedara. "Let's call it my nickname.

"Inbikh, where's the food?" I asked.

Inbikh turned her cat face to me, her yellow eyes bright in the sunset. "No food, Ya-rii. Just burned out Lepee-daii-aa." She hopped back in my lap before bouncing off again. Singing as she made her way to the shore.

Mikosh walked a little way after Inbikh and stopped. I was

about to follow them through the mist down to the shore until I felt a calm sensation at my back. I turned around.

"Looks like Xibo's in a good mood," Selchuk said. "I haven't seen him that happy since the war ended." He smiled at me and then turned to Mikosh, his face serious. "So, what happened?"

"It's not worth repeating. Come on, let's get away from there for a bit," Mikosh said, continuing toward Inbikh's barely visible white tail. We followed her down to the shore, the noise of soldiers sparring in the distance mixed with the pounding of the ocean against the shoreline.

"How long before we leave for the Flax Islands?" I asked Mikosh.

She put the lantern down in the sand. "Whenever you're ready." She kept her arms outstretched, her long-sleeved blouse blowing in the breeze, then sat in the sand, crossing the legs of her cropped pants.

"Why is it that you can wear clothes that cover you up, but the rest of us are stuck with these stupid crop tops?" I asked her.

Selchuk started laughing. "You...are...fun-nnyyy." He looked behind him and waited a few seconds. "It's because of Gulnaz," he said in a hushed voice, imitating her way of speaking and over-emphasizing her consonants. "It's important for ventilation."

"More like titillation," Mikosh said in Hiranian.

"As if she's giving out anything to anyone other than Drash," Selchuk said dryly.

Mikosh leaned into him. "Oh, and you're sad?" She poked him, teasing.

Selchuk got very serious. "She's been with so many men I would not want to be next. I'd catch something."

A redhaired female student approached, and they both went stiff. I made certain to keep my expression neutral. She joined the sparring in the distance that now seemed lackluster. They weren't even rising in the air.

"Good thing she didn't hear you," I said.

"We don't care." Mikosh snorted. "Gulnaz is an arrogant pain. Xibo's the only one who likes her." She brushed off her pants. "You can raid my tunics if you want better clothes." She leaned in. "But Gulnaz'll give you a hard time about it. Watch."

I narrowed my eyes. "Why doesn't she bother you about it?"

Mikosh's face went horribly serious. "I've killed more people than her." She looked back up to the training house. "She's never forgotten that."

I exhaled the discomfort I felt in Mikosh revealing that. I drew my knees up to my chest, the cloud cover sweeping away to give us a momentary glimpse of the green stardust above and millions of clusters of multicolored stars.

"I could never get sick of that view," I said.

"You say that now..." Mikosh laughed.

Selchuk softly sang a tune I'd heard him humming earlier. He sang in Hiranian, the ballad soft and flowing.

The water may rush
and lap at us:
a source of restoration,
it is not enough.

His voice modulated upward, Mikosh harmonizing softly with him.

When you are near
even a whisper
can carry me away
from a past of ashes
and blood
never to be erased.

I hummed along with them as their voices crescendoed, Selchuk's voice mournful. He looked straight at me on this last verse.

> *Yet a look from you*
> *Yes, those very eyes*
> *gentle and unknowing*
> *what beats within for you.*

Gulnaz appeared behind me, her amber hair loose and glossy in the lamplight. Selchuk started the song again, and we joined in with him, the joy of the tune arcing between all of us while we harmonized. The rest of the students stopped their manoeuvers, and Xibo floated over to stand by us.

Selchuk stopped mid-round and glanced up at Xibo. "What?" he asked, his tone defensive.

"It has been a long time since that was sung." Xibo stalked off. The rest of the students stood there, stiff and still, afraid to make a move.

Gulnaz took one of the lamps. "Selchuk, come with me."

He got up reluctantly, and Mikosh watched him go, her eyes wide with fear. "He's in trouble."

"Why? We were just singing," I said.

"We don't just sing here. It is almost always for a purpose. Something happens when we sing. Emotions get exchanged, maybe in ways we don't want them to?" Mikosh raised an eyebrow.

"Isn't that why we sing?" I watched Selchuk's retreating figure and thought of Tarrok.

"Maybe," she said, looking behind us before continuing. "That's not how things work here, at least they haven't since the war. We might sing to ourselves, when no one else is around...or when we like someone, and we want them to know." She stared at me, inviting me to say something about the attention Selchuk had been paying to me. I had been trying to ignore it, pretending that when he looked at me it meant nothing.

"He knows I belong to Tarrok." I held her steady gaze, the lamplight dancing shadows across her soft face.

"Maybe." She brought her palms together. "That was one of Danis' old songs. No one has sung it since she died. At least not within earshot of Xibo." She was very still, the silence thick between us. After several minutes, it was broken by birds calling above us, then the soft chirping of lizards in the grass before they scurried away, long thin shadows moving through the sands. She gave me a warning look and left me to ponder what came next.

I hummed the tune, imagining my family here with me, instead of the cold sand pressing into my sore legs. I would give anything for the familiarity of their embraces, and Vali humming in the evenings before I settled in to sleep. I tried to recall one of his tunes as I slowly made my way up the stone steps leading back to the training house's glowing white entranceway. The only song in my head was Selchuk's. I whistled his tune the entire way back and stopped when I thought I was within earshot. I stood there at the entranceway, all the lanterns lit to guide my way toward a house full of strangers.

20

GULNAZ

THE SAME DAY

"*Zoldit*, Selchuk! You cannot sing that song to her!" I tossed Selchuk against the wall. He crashed against it, protecting his head. I wanted it to crack. His face was too beautiful, even more than Drash's. Selchuk's defiance hadn't waned since the end of the war. All that arrogance behind his blue eyes. I wanted to burn him blind.

But we needed him.

"First Danis and now her? Do you know what you're doing?" I lowered my voice and stood over where he was slumped. He hated when I invaded his space. "You'll ruin everything, break her focus, and then—" I snapped my fingers—"she'll never get us there. The Yarats destroy another planet.

"*Kundit mazra ha*," I cursed, exhaustion making my head buzz. I didn't normally feel so tired. Selchuk was siphoning energy off me to heal himself. I held out a palm to stop him draining me with his *urijniak*. When the buzzing got louder, I pounded the wall above his head. I wanted to beat all the resistance out of his handsome face.

"You lost the right to tell me what to do. When she died," he

179

whisper-spoke, meeting my gaze. He lunged toward me and put his hand on my arm, the memory of Danis and the children searing through me. They turned to ash in front of me again and again as he replayed the memory.

I had been too late. Trying to appease Mila, like an idiot. I should have fought harder, not been distracted and worried about being caught for spying.

Selchuk withdrew the memory. I knocked his hand off my bare shoulder.

"Leanora isn't like Danis," he said wearily.

"Oh, she doesn't worship everything you heal?" I said. "Danis spoiled you." I turned away from him, completely disgusted from the memories of him and Xibo's wife flicking through my mind.

He stood up, arms folded over his chest. "I need her—"

"She can't. She has Tarrok—" I cut him off.

"Because I only deserve to love a ghost?" Selchuk's eyes were burning, and I had to turn away from him.

"Love has nothing to do with this." I didn't know if I believed my words in that moment, but I had to. I had to drive the point home that he couldn't do this. "If you really love her, leave her alone. Wait until she's ready to know what she needs." I wiped sweat from my forehead. "Once we're finally done."

A deep silence ate up the space between us. The glowing light above was harsh and bright. I was too tired to reach for it and dim it. "How stupid can you be to sing Danis's song to a girl you barely know? Make up your own song. Don't borrow from your dead lover."

He backed away from me, his head hanging low. Good, I was getting through.

"How do you know that my song will change anything?" Selchuk finally asked. He rubbed the back of his head, humming a soft healing song. He winced when he walked toward me.

I was so exhausted by the constant friction between us. But

hadn't I made decisions that meant our fighting might never end? Rain started outside, and the window flaps were still rolled up, the drops splattering on the glossy flooring, reminding me of blood.

"I kept Tarrok from coming here." I exhaled, trying to remain calm, in control. But if Selchuk knew the plan, he'd stop this ridiculous quest for Leanora. "I won't be the orchester on Eloia. She will be." I waited for him to gloat.

I walked over to the window, keeping my distance in case he attacked again.

"Not powerful enough to bring the soldiers, eh, Gulnaz? That must be a blow." Selchuk kept to the shadows of the room.

"It's nothing to do with me." I leaned against the window ledge. "She can transport more people than me...theoretically." I watched the droplets outside turn to a surge of water tumbling down the window ledge.

"I was just singing." He reached for the window coverings to stop the water. "You read too much into these things." He tied them down.

I swung him around to face me, making sure to only touch the cloth-covered parts of his arm. "I know too much about these things. You could jeopardize our whole mission." I let go of his tunic. "I miss Danis as much as anyone." My voice caught, and I backed away from him, so he couldn't see how hard it was to talk about her. "She was the best person I ever met besides Yelina. If I could change things and die instead, I would."

He stood there, arrogantly looking up at me. His blue eyes turned black, and I let go of him. Selchuk saw me for who I was. No matter how I tried to prove otherwise. He refused to see past my veneer. I could hate him for it, or I could let go and appeal to him. But it was hard to try to convince him that some part of me still remained good, when I wasn't sure I believed it anymore.

His voice was low, so soft it was barely audible. "You...are...a traitor...The only thing that keeps you here is Xibo's goodwill," he spat and pushed the song he'd been singing with Danis back at me. He sang it down the corridors, grabbed a lamp, and continued up the stairs. Like a singing firebug, he didn't stop. I wanted to hate him, but I couldn't. I was too wracked with guilt and shame and the desire to take back the alliance I'd made with Zer so long ago.

I wanted the Yarats gone, but if I pulled out now, Zer would attack early. I couldn't let all my work go to waste. And Xibo's final wish would go unfulfilled. I owed him that much, to finish things the way he wanted them to be done.

Xibo clanked down the stairs on his prosthetic. "It's time to go." I followed him through the corridor. "We'll assess how she travels with full vision at night. Four hours before daylight." He'd heard Selchuk and me fighting. But he was all business. No discussion of the songs.

"I'll find her," I said.

Xibo paused then, his eyes narrowing. "Let Selchuk."

Like always, I followed his lead. He clanked down the hallway on his prosthetic leg, and I kept my pace behind him. He was my last ally. I sang the large stone door shut behind us as I left the training house for the last time. Neither of us would ever be coming back to this place of too many memories. The sea sang in the distance as a new song started on the beach. It was Leanora singing in Hiranian. From this far away, the tides were turning without me knowing what to do.

21

LEANORA

We'd left the lanterns in the sand, the glow from their surrounding light illuminating everyone. With Inbikh safely nestled inside my sweater, all thirty of us students stood in a giant cluster with me at the center while they looked on expectantly. Maybe it was nerves, or the fact that my mind was completely consumed in the process of bringing them to the Flax Islands, a place I'd never been to before, but it was hard to pick a song to take us away from Maer-lina. Maybe I wasn't ready to leave.

I craned my head to marvel at the forest green night sky glowing with stars, nebulas, and half-moons. The motion of the sky was calling me toward Eloia, a sensation ran through me like a swelling river, mixed with the hope of my family and Tarrok beyond those stars. I was certain that an embrace from one of them could sustain me for another month here. But without it...

Maybe that's why I'm here alone. The students beside me took my hands, the pressure to transport us building.

"I'll start the song." I looked into the faces of the students around me, Mikosh at my right.

"We've got all night," Xibo said. "You're the one who needs sleep. We can go on for days." Groans issued from around us. Gulnaz nodded once. It was time.

I sang in Hiranian:

> *The water flows like the surface of my drowned heart.*
> *flowing where my heart cannot,*
> *for it does not exist,*
> *in the wake of the dream of what was.*

A rush of energy from everyone's haian fusai funneled through my body when their voices joined me, building into harmonies that lifted us into the air. Mikosh tugged on my sweater's sleeve. I picked up the pace, the cold air spiraling around us. I aimed to keep us low, the black ocean reflecting the broken moons in the waves' ripples.

"We'll be in the air for awhile," Gulnaz remarked before continuing to sing with us.

WE'D BEEN in the air for a half hour before I caught sight of a landform and slowed our song. From this height, there were several dark, long islands in the distance. I brought us closer to the first island.

"Not yet, the next one, with the lights." Mikosh spoke as the others continued to sing with me. "Keep the pace steady for our landing."

The next island had yellow lights along its western shore. They flickered as I brought us closer, our pace quickening while the wind resisted our descent. I slowed our melody, but not everyone was in sync. I sang louder to retune us. We picked up velocity, hurtling downward. Another counter-melody started with Gulnaz, and everyone followed her. We abruptly halted a few feet in the air before falling to the ground again. A soft fiber brushed across my face, and Inbikh leaped out of my sweater. I spun around to find Gulnaz. She wasn't going to get away with sabotaging my landing. I rose to my feet, searching through the long stalks of vegetation to find her. They were hard to navigate through, tickling my face. Students were already complaining; I stopped to see if she was amongst them.

"Seriously terrible landing."

"Why is she even taking us there, if Gulnaz can?"

"Gulnaz can't—only Leanora can."

"You're stupid. She's only half Kardush and has been here what, a few weeks?"

"Get me out of here."

Once the group saw me they retreated sullenly through the long stalks of flax. Behind us loomed a dark shadow of forest. The night sky glowed behind the tall trees that were almost as tall as the pines in Asanis. I walked toward the trees, figuring Gulnaz may have gone in that direction.

I called the water to my body, inhaling deeply as my muscles stopped aching. I sang myself into the air and found her at the edge of the forest, looking lost. I almost didn't say anything. She turned around to look at me, her face blank.

"I could have handled the landing," I said.

"You didn't. I don't have time for you to break everyone's bones," she said and stalked off through the forest before I could say anything else.

"This way, Leanora," Mikosh called to me, waving her arm. I took one last look at where Gulnaz had disappeared into the forest before following Mikosh past the field to a dirt clearing filled with mud houses that rose four stories above us. There was more artificial light in the town than I'd seen on any of the other islands. Hundreds milled about on the dusty streets. They watched us with curiosity. Most wore padded jackets and billowy pants that tied closely at the ankles. Mikosh pointed toward the opposite rim of the large circular township area. "We have a hut we usually stay in when we train here. You can follow me, if you want." She gestured to a lane through several taller mud houses that had large wooden beams across the tops of the taller buildings. Selchuk strolled ahead of us, not looking back but seeming to, like Gulnaz, be on a mission.

Xibo rose through the crowd, barking commands. I was hoping he didn't see me and I might be able to rest until daylight.

"Not so fast," Xibo said.

I held Inbikh at my side, and she scampered up to my shoulder.

"A word, Leanora." He turned to Mikosh. "See you at the command hut at first light."

So much for an early night.

He led us through a narrow alleyway to one of the taller mud huts that was surrounded by ivy and blooming flowers. "Where are we going?" I asked.

"Command hut." He held a glow cube that threw white light across his face.

"Why?"

"Only a few minutes, then I'll let you sleep," he said.

At least I had Inbikh, who ran from my shoulder to my head and back again watching all the people with delight. I wished I had her energy.

THE COMMAND HUT reminded me of an oversized version of the rainforest huts in Nedara. The walls were thick, keeping in the heat of the occupants. On the first floor, a few women sat at wooden desks talking with one another. They stopped when we came in through the leather door opening. I followed Xibo up the wooden stairs to the second level, which was unoccupied. I sat down on one of the wooden benches as far from Xibo as possible. He lit his pipe, and I was glad I was on the opposite side of the room. I glanced up at the ceiling, which had leaves woven into the plaster.

"You make decent progress..." he took a puff of his pipe, "... but we have to dial things up. Get ready for battle," Xibo said. He exhaled sweet smoke.

"When do I have to bring us to Eloia?" I asked. Inbikh leapt off me. "Don't go too far," I said to her. She fluffed her tail and took off.

He stared at me, his eyes trying to probe at me, I was certain. I glanced up at the dark green leaves suspended in the grey plaster ceiling.

"We may need to go back to Eloia earlier than planned." He exhaled smoke, puffing on his pipe again. "The next few days will push your limits. Prepare yourself for battle conditions." He placed his pipe on the armrest of his chair. "Gulnaz knows what tests are necessary."

"Like sabotaging my landings?"

He took another puff of his pipe. "Harness your will to fight for everything you care about.." He exhaled smoke, his face so drawn I felt uncomfortable with the pain reflected in his normally flint eyes. "I fight for that life force flowing through us." He paused, his face going soft in the glow of the lamps. "We need you. I'm an old man, and I only have so long." He coughed and put the pipe to the side, leaning closer. "Everything you're learning must integrate your muscles and spirit—so you don't have to think about it."

"Your training methods don't always produce the best results," I said, thinking of the pain Selchuk still carried around with him.

He stared into the lamplight, halfway somewhere else. "Danis, my dead wife, thought the same thing." He sat back on the wooden bench and crossed his prosthetic arm, bending his metal leg across his living one. "If I had listened to her and changed my training, how many more would have survived?" He looked up at the ceiling. "We'll never know."

I stared at his scarred face, his misaligned body after losing a leg and an arm. And yet here he was still fighting. If I didn't do my best, we could lose our planet because we wouldn't have enough experienced fighters on Eloia. "I will give everything I have." I met his gaze with confidence. "I know I will have to kill people." I recalled all the dead I'd seen on Thresil Mira.

"You're not killing; you're defending. There's a difference." He went silent, and I felt like I had been dismissed. He crossed and uncrossed his legs, then picked up the pipe and stood. "I'm glad you came. To remind us that there is something better. Love doesn't necessarily last, but something else can." He had his hand outstretched toward me.

I rose and took his calloused hand. "Thank you for training me, Xibo." I descended the stairs, my legs feeling heavy.

Inbikh waited for me outside and climbed up my thick trousers to settle on my shoulder, wrapping her tail around my neck.

"I know way. We cross at middle, three lamp down, four over," Inbikh chittered.

I followed her, taking in the brown huts with actual glass-paned windows and brightly colored wooden shutters. When we came to our hut, Gulnaz and Mikosh were whispering in Hiranian.

"Let me know next time you decide to sabotage a landing," I said to Gulnaz.

"Don't let me do it so it doesn't happen." Gulnaz took our only lantern and sauntered off.

"That's it?" I asked, our hut completely dark. Inbikh stepped on something and it glowed. Mikosh took the glow rock from her and hung it from the hook where the lantern originally was.

"Something is going on with her." Mikosh threw a bedroll my way. "Night."

I drew the heavy cloth over the entrance door to the hut and laid down. Inbikh climbed under the covers with me, but I couldn't get comfortable on the hard ground. I tossed and turned throughout the night. The faces of my family, Tarrok, and Gulnaz kept flashing in front of me.

AT DAWN I woke and scooped up a yawning Inbikh who was sleeping on my side. "Too early. Need more..." She drifted off.

I moved the curtain of the hut's front entrance aside, the sky still dark with edges of light illuminating the forest.

I sought out Gulnaz's energy and followed her *urijniak* into the air, singing myself above the perimeter of the brown huts, much more numerous than I had noticed the previous night. Surrounding the egg-shaped town were tall stalks of purple flax with narrow trails winding through them to the forest beyond. I flew above the tall purple fields to touch down at the entrance of a trail leading to the forest. The nearby trees had turquoise pine needles gathered in bunches at their upper branches. A few silvery and purple pine cones hung down from the pine stalks.

Gulnaz stood at the entrance of the red dirt trail. She wore all white, her clothes from the previous day bunched under her arm. Her hair was wet and plastered against her head. "What do you want?"

"Why did you ruin my landing yesterday?" I asked, folding my arms in front of me.

"This again?" She rubbed her wet hair and flipped her head over.

"We haven't resolved whatever happened yesterday." I stepped closer. "And if we're going to train together some resolution is needed."

She exhaled noisily. "When you're in battle, you'll have counter melodies like the one yesterday. Get used to it."

She took off, and I followed her through the tall stalks, their whispery purple heads rubbing against my face. They reminded me of riverweeds clinging to my legs when I went swimming in the lake in Asanis.

She sat on a log. The sky was a light purple with gray and white clouds flitting by above us. The moons were already fading into the morning sky.

"Why do you dislike me?" I asked.

Her face remained stony.

"Don't hold back now."

She laughed, some of her facade fading. "Everyone here holds back." She glared at me. "Except you." Her expression softened out of obligation, her dark eyes still burning.

"There's nothing wrong with me," I said.

"You don't push yourself hard enough." She folded her arms and watched me carefully.

"I don't believe in self-annihilation."

"Be thankful you weren't born here then. We've had plenty of that and lucky me..." Her accent was thick, and her voice cracked as she looked at the ground.

"What is it?" I asked.

She picked up her clothes from the ground, folding them. "Nothing to concern you."

"Why do you keep leaving during our training?" I asked.

Her face changed, like I'd caught her. She stared at me for awhile, saying nothing. When she was done folding, she put the clothes on the log.

"I'm a memory keeper, or Fernais, in our language. When I

was younger, I had to keep people's memories and now there are only a few of us left. Often I'm sent away to recruit new fighters and to preserve the memories of those who won't fight."

"Isn't there a better way of preserving memories?" I asked.

"Sometimes my knowledge of people's memories can help. We stopped using written language several hundred years ago, with a few exceptions of certain Fernais preserving the scroll tradition, as you saw in the Fernais House. All Kardush and Yarat can transmit memories from brain-to-brain using touch. But Yarats cannot store other's memories. Only mixed Yarat/Kardush children can." She looked away from me.

"What is it?"

"You know so little, how do I tell you..." She shifted uncomfortably and stood, gazing at the morning sky. "My parents did not claim me. So I was forced to carry memories against my will, at first." She looked at my face, searching it for something before continuing to speak. "If I die, all those memories stop with me."

"Who else can be a memory keeper?" I asked.

She shrugged. "None of Xibo's existing students."

"Why?" I asked.

"None of them have the ability, even the full Kardush ones." She held out her large palm. "It's important for you to know what it was like to be half Kardush-Yarat."

I put a finger to her palm, unsure if this was the best way to learn her history. She closed her eyes, and I was sucked into the body of a young child, the memory more vivid and in brighter hues than what I'd seen from Mikosh's memory. Gulnaz was very young, waiting outside a cluster of small children in a concrete house. They were younger than my brother, Alaric.

"Stay away from the other children," one of the adults said, looming over her. He had a metal implant over his left eye and beckoned the other children to follow him. Two children remained staring at Gulnaz. One had pale yellow hair and her arms outstretched until the adult yelled at her and she put her arms down. The little boy's eyes were large and brown, and he took the yellow-haired girl's hand but didn't move toward Gulnaz.

Gulnaz wailed, and no one comforted her. The two children watched her without moving, their eyes sorrowful while they wept silently. The walls seemed to close in on her cries. These cries turned into a song, and the memory merged with one of her much older.

She was singing for hundreds of students who banged their feet on the ground, and her song lifted them airborne before they fell to their seats in an enormous hall. Laughing ensued. I recognized the training house at Maer-lina. Students disbursed, and a younger version of Selchuk with short hair waved to her. His face fell when she didn't acknowledge him. Instead, she threw her arms around Drash. His long, dark hair was streaked with green and yellow. She ran her fingers through it before kissing him. He wrapped his hands around her waist as they rose into the air and flew out of the hall.

The memory stopped. I was back in my own head while I felt a strange disentangling from her memories.

"There's more for you to learn, because you will be the orchester, not me." She looked down at me, her face serious. "You are not ready to be orchester yet."

"What do you think will make me ready?"

"You need to take all of our stories, the energies of this place, its sorrows, so you can bring us back to Eloia." She held her hands out wide. "Sing us to a better place."

I held out my hand to her forearm and pushed a memory into her. I felt her relax as she saw my entire journey across Eloia, from when I caught Zer blinding babies to my reunion with my mother. I stopped there, withdrawing the memory.

"Perhaps we are not so different." She came close to me then, her eyes a deep, dark brown. "The fact that none of your memories previously transferred to me means you are stronger." She paused for a few seconds, the stalks whispering in the breeze. "You must overcome what the Yarats plan." She put a hand on my shoulder. "At some point my memories will need to pass on to someone else." She released her hand. "Maybe you will be the next Fernais."

She put her clothes down on a log. "Enough history. Let's do something that will help you travel better." Gulnaz held her palms flat, like she was testing the wind. "When we travel in groups, we always touch. It makes it easier to keep the *haian fusai* running through us. Memory transfer is held at bay by the fact that we're using a different energy to move ourselves through space."

"Where will I bring you?" I asked.

"Good question." She squinted, the corners of her mouth turning up. "Somewhere far but familiar. Not off planet."

"Thresils." I sang a few measures before she joined me, the tempo of my song picking up as we soared through clouds.

"Closer to the ocean to expend less energy," she yelled.

I slowed the tempo as we touched down on shore with only a small bump.

"Call the water to you immediately," she said.

I sang the water back inside of me, and my muscles stopped burning.

"Now, back to the Flax islands," Gulnaz said.

I brought us back swiftly, an ease to the movement, until I saw Xibo looking up at us from the field. I lost the thread of the song, and we tumbled into the stalks of flax, which luckily cushioned our landing. I immediately brought the water back to restore my energy and stopped when I felt a pressure in my stomach that told me I had enough.

"Landings! Peshara, Leonora!" Xibo cursed.

"She's doing better," Gulnaz said.

A crowd of a hundred strangers from the Flax Islands, their tired faces streaked with dirt, gathered around. A few were as young as Alaric. I turned to Gulnaz, who gave me a nod.

"This is Leanora Tela from Eloia," Xibo explained, and a hush went over the crowd. "She'll transport herself to Eloia today and back while we train."

Great stars, I wish he would have told me that earlier.

If I ask for
the tree we're under to be more
than it is,
Will you see all its leaves,
how they spread
like an embrace between
the two of us?
The forbidden boundary we tread
never voiced aloud,
sticking to safe
blades of grass,
hummed secret melodies.
The lines at your
mouth turning
down so lovely and sad.
Do you mourn me,
as I do you,
every time we part?
Wanting more and never knowing,
when next the roots will appear.

"Leaves Ungrown," by Selchuk Quoresriun for Danis
(translated from Hiranian)

22

LEANORA

I didn't want this many people watching me mess up. The purple stalks of flax billowed around us like a whispering ocean. We formed a loose semicircle around Xibo in the open field. I stamped my feet in the loose dirt to keep my legs warm. More field workers approached, whether out of curiosity or interest in joining forces, I didn't know.

"Am I going alone...or?" My voice trailed off when I saw Xibo searching the crowd and stopping when he came to Gulnaz.

"Not alone." Xibo narrowed his eyes, scratching his chin. "I need a witness to tell me how the journey was." His mouth turned up in amusement.

I couldn't sneak in a visit to Tarrok unless I bribed the other person. I hadn't yet gleaned what was valuable to bribe a Kardush with.

"Gulnaz—" I started.

"No," he interrupted. "She'll be too tempted to help you."

Like she 'helped' me with my landing yesterday night?

Xibo held out his prosthetic hand toward the crowd. I tried to calm my rising nerves.

"You need someone who isn't a binary traveler. But who can help you recover quickly." He pointed a lighted fingertip at Selchuk, who walked through the group. Several let out sighs of relief.

Great, they think I'm going to kill them. I intentionally slowed my breathing, gazing at the puffy clouds sailing by. In a few moments I would travel through those clouds...

"Sure you don't need me here...?" Selchuk asked.

"Thanks." I kept my gaze on the sky.

"It's not that..." Selchuk paused. "If they get seriously injured sparring..."

"You'll be back in five hours or less." Xibo said. He swiftly turned back to dividing the soldiers into diamond-shaped configurations that rose and lowered in the air as he yelled at them.

"Where do we go?" I asked. Gulnaz materialized at my side.

"Aim for the middle of the main continent. Move swiftly. You're on your own this time." Gulnaz's face was pale, her eyes a calm black I'd never seen before. "Inhale deeply before leaving the atmosphere so you don't run out of air." She paused, searching my face. "You'll do fine." There was no warmth in her voice. She walked back to the sparring groups.

"I hope I don't kill you," I said to Selchuk and Inbikh.

"You won't. I've traveled with Gulnaz before." His jaw tightened. "I hate her, and she didn't kill me." He turned back to where she'd gone. "Not yet." When his gaze met mine again, I took his hand like I was supposed to. The weight of his warm palm in mine felt too comfortable. Taking up space where Tarrok's wasn't.

In a few minutes, I could see Tarrok. I tried to still the rising anticipation that caused my stomach to flutter.

"We need to go." Selchuk gripped my hand tighter.

"I know." I couldn't say how afraid I was, my heart thudding in my ears, the ease of his hand distracting me from finding a melody.

One of the workers faintly whistled the start of a song. Not a good one, but it would help me create the traveling song with the necessary lift off. The melody had a lilting quality, similar to lullabies my mother use to sing to me when I was very little.

I started the song, imagining my voice like one of the bells on my mother's organ in Asanis.

The branches of the trees
Reach into the depths
Singing for you...
All the way to the seas...

Selchuk joined in. Inbikh harmonized several octaves above, her body wound around my neck. We shot into the air. I opened my eyes and aimed us through the clouds, toward Eloia, the song a staccato pulsation of my voice with Selchuk's and Inbikh's. We jetted upward, the air frozen. We cut through thin clouds, and I took a deep breath before leaving the atmosphere and bursting into the frigid black of space.

We soared past the nebulas, leaving the warmth of Hirana's twin suns to the outer reaches, and past asteroid belts. Our song's pace increased, and I was assaulted with a memory of Asanis, of Zer singing and rising slowly into the air in the forest and touching back down on the ground. The memory morphed with Agda and me picking berries, singing a song very similar to the one that was slowly dying on my tongue.

Singing for you...
All the way to the seas...

We were already in the outer rim of the Derian galaxy, the sun a yellow pinprick. My lungs heaved with the effort of singing.

Keep singing, Leanora. You can't stop now—we'll all run out of air, Selchuk said in my head and gripped my hand tighter.

I mustered my remaining strength and sang louder, soaring through another star system, past asteroid clusters and a few dead planets, onward to the Derian galaxy. It was a struggle to keep pace as my energy flagged. Something inside me was going to burst. I was running out of air. I looked over to Selchuk who was encased, like I was, in a bubble of air that was running out.

Selchuk picked up the threads of the song, and I sang louder, inside and outside of my body, but we were barely moving. Then I saw a bright blue pinprick in the distance.

Eloia.

I gathered whatever was left in my lungs and sang with every cell inside of me. My voice was hoarse and dry, heat licking at us when we came into orbit. Our linked bodies picked up massive speed. I aimed us for the long brown main continent and we re-entered the atmosphere, warmth returning to my limbs. I could feel Selchuk's hand in mine again and Inbikh panting. We were gravitating westward, toward Hagoth and Asanis. The further we fell, I tried to sing us eastward, but we kept drifting closer to the forests of Asanis. Selchuk's grip on me slipped. I couldn't stop us hurtling toward the forest, the treetops only a few meters from our feet. I decreased our pace, but we were falling. I pressed with all the power within me, syncing our voices, but we were moving too fast. I was out of energy.

We crashed through pine branches that scratched at my exposed arms and neck. I found my voice again, too late, before I landed with a thump on hard ground. Pain radiated from my lower back. I opened my eyes in the familiar deep green forests of Asanis. The smell of pitch made me cough, and I rolled over. I remembered too late to call water to my body and blacked out.

When I opened my eyes, it took me a while to remember where I was. My exposed back was itchy and sticky. But I was warm and dry. Forest hens flitted by. There was a tapping of wood above me, the calling of birds a familiar, beautiful sound. But I wasn't here to stay. I had to call the water to me, restore my energy levels before I blacked out again.

All went dark.

When I inhaled upon waking again, I immediately called the water into my aching limbs. Some of the pain subsided, and my labored breath eased as I drained all the liquid from the living creatures beneath me. I rolled away from where I had been lying, dead insects shriveled up in the cracked earth and dry grasses. I could move again, but my back was stiff. It was hard to bend to get up.

"Selchuk?" I whispered.

Only the call of birds and taps of wood peckers. "Selchuk?" I called out again.

What if Zer found us?

I stood up, my legs stiff, and looked around for Inbikh and Selchuk. I softly walked through saplings, turning to listen for anyone in the vicinity. After a few minutes, I couldn't find anyone. Had I killed them with my terrible landing? Were their bodies hanging lifelessly in one of the giant pines around us? My body trembled with the possibility, and I frantically circled the perimeter, a faint prickling at the back of my head.

"Selchuk, Inbikh, where are you?" I whispered, not wanting to be noticed by anyone in Asanis. We had to get out of here.

I searched for something familiar in the landscape: the tall trees crowding out a good portion of the sunlight. How often, since escaping Asanis, had I imagined coming back? I trudged around in a circle, looking for Selchuk and Inbikh, scanning the trees above.

There was no one around, I concluded after several minutes

of scaring forest birds who flew from their hiding places behind ferns.

Where could they be?

This wasn't like the last time I had brought Dex back to Hagoth so he could trek to Asanis—those brief moments when the forest in the distance was a fuzzy haze. I could see everything now. Why couldn't I find them?

I tried to identify anything in the forest that would give me an indication, a landmark to tell me how far I'd gone in case I was walking in a circle. The giant tree behind me, with its reddish-brown thick bark, was the largest of any within the vicinity. I paced with it at my back, holding up my hand to keep the low-hanging branches from scratching my face. I kept at this pace for some time before I had to stop and rest. Several trees had recently been felled nearby, and I walked over to a small clearing where a mound of dirt had fresh flowers and branches thrown across it. I leaned into it to find something that would indicate what it was.

A wooden marker had been stuck haphazardly. A raised surface appeared when I ran my fingers across the marker at the head of the mound. It took several tries before I made out the name.

A-g-d-a R-u-s-o-r-i-a-n.

My Agda. Our old housekeeper. My closest friend beside Dex. There was a loadstone in my stomach. I hadn't saved her after all. I almost sank to the ground, but then remembered there wasn't time for me to mourn her.

There was another mound, and I walked over to this marker. When I reached out to touch the marker and read D-e-x, my body was hurled through the air away from the grave.

I whipped around, and Zer stood there in his white tunic. I sang myself to the ground. Nothing about him had changed. His glassy, metallic eyes stared through me. I hummed, lifting off the ground, but then something seized my brain, keeping me from singing, and I sank into the dirt, out of breath.

"You've come back." His face was morose and drawn.

"Leave me alone," I said. I was certain he was responsible for that gravemarker indicating my best friend was gone too.

"How is Xibo?" he asked. His facial expression looked so much like the memories of the Yarats. The deadness in his eyes. He was a stranger to me. Never my father.

I didn't know how to answer, a pressure on my head increasing. If I let this go on much longer...My training came back to me. *Sing against whatever he is doing; create a song that will counter it. Quickly.*

I vocalized the first song that came to mind. It came out sounding crooked and broken, but it was better than letting him kill every brain cell. The pressure released, but I didn't let up on the tune. I kept humming it, moving away from Zer and planning my escape trajectory. But I couldn't leave without Inbikh and Selchuk. Zer would happily kill them. Then the pressure on my mind let up, and he stepped closer to the gravemarker.

"You did everything you could to save her." Zer pointed at Agda's grave. Then he walked over to where Dex's marker was. "Dex didn't have a chance, even with his new eyesight." He wasn't at all remorseful. "He was a liability to everything this planet could become. I don't know why he came back."

Dex wanted to stop Zer. "You killed him," I said. Some small part of me had hoped that Dex had stayed in Hagoth, that he hadn't confronted Zer. My heart sank with the fact that he was gone. So much potential wasted.

"He chose poorly. There he remains." Zer turned with a wave of his hand, and the trees swayed with the movement of his arms, like our lives were nothing to him. "Your training will be complete, if you stay here." He stopped moving the trees. "No more destruction, no more death or suffering. Just peace and advancement of Eloia. One continent united in purpose."

"You killed my childhood friend."

"If you stay, all the killing is over," he said.

I heard a rustling behind me, and within seconds Selchuk was behind Zer, knocking him to the ground. Inbikh landed on Zer's face, scratching and biting at his nose.

"Get it off, get it—" Zer screamed.

I ripped off his tunic, wrapped it around his torso, and knotted it, immobilizing him. We had seconds to get away.

I grabbed Selchuk's hands, called Inbikh to me. She clung to my neck, her claws scratching at my tender flesh.

Vu-shuul xal yus walid,
yus walid vu-shuul xal.

I sang and we rose swiftly into the air, our bodies above the treetops, then we were falling downward again as Zer's counter-melody pulled us back to the ground.

Selchuk and Inbikh's voices rose with mine, but we were still sinking, the treetops at our feet again. I threw everything inside of me into the song, but nothing was working. We were sinking below the treeline and back into the branches. I tried to block him with my brain, and instead a clawing tore from inside my head, crushing my thoughts where he, the father I had grown up with, knew how to keep me tethered to him. Even if it killed me.

His hands were outstretched below, only a few meters from grabbing our feet.

"No!" I shouted and sang with all my soul, everything I held in reserve, to lift us away from him, imagining Lepidaia and the ocean's song channelling into us. Our bodies shot into the sky as our song swelled. Our voices blended into one, singing of Lepidaia's sky, its oceans, and flew through the sky toward it. We soared swiftly over the deserts, faster than I had ever traveled before, our song trilling quickly on our tongues. The mountains passed below us, and beyond was the ocean and Lepidaia. As soon as the white stones of the city were within view, I slowed our pace, keeping the song a soft fluttering of sound in my mouth and willing us to slow down as we landed softly on the top mezzanine of the scorched city market. The three districts of the city were still recognizeable, though so much was crumbling and in ruins.

"That was too close," Selchuk said, out of breath. He murmured, calling the energy back into his body. "You did good." He dusted himself off and held his arms outstretched, embracing me. "I thought we were done for." His azure eyes were warm as he looked up at the single sun in the sky and at the sapphire ocean ahead. His face softened, and he met my gaze. "It is so beautiful."

"It so sad." Inbikh jumped down from my shoulder.

I called the water back into my body, a fizzing sensation spreading through my limbs. I was going to need food very soon. I craned my neck to look behind me at the apartments built into the hillside littered with debris on their balconies. It was strange to see Lepidaia without any inhabitants. The silence was pierced by the beating of metal and shouting. They were not speaking a familiar language. The syllables were wrong and clashing.

"Yarats." Selchuk took my hand. "Let's hide and recover our strength before going back."

As soon as I took a step, I saw what he meant. I was completely drained. Inbikh was even dragging. Selchuk was pale and put his other hand on my back, guiding me toward the back of the marketplace.

A small ship rose in the air above us.

"Quick, in here." I was barely able to keep upright when we bolted to the staging area where vendors stowed their stalls. A singed curtain was rolled up and I pulled it down to conceal us within the stone facade. "How long do we wait?" I asked.

"I get food," Inbikh offered. Her large eyes gleamed in the dim light.

"Stay here. We have to leave as soon as we've recovered our energy."

"Food give us energy," Inbikh said.

I held her close to me. "Stay here."

Selchuk murmured as he restored his energy levels, and I followed suit, the water saltier in my system. I had to call more of it to me than usual. A group of people shouted and argued with one another in the distance. I needed more time to recover my strength.

"A few more minutes," I said.

"If they find us..." Selchuk said.

We were very still. He scooted closer to me, his hand on my forearm. He murmured as he restored my energy levels.

"My stomach is completely empty right now," I said.

He stared at my lips, and the space was too small to move away. Selchuk continued to murmur in Hiranian, the song increasing as energy returned to me. I tried to let go, but he held on.

"Leonora, while we're here. I must tell you..."

The shouts mixed with the stomping of boots echoing in the square.

Selchuk's face was close to mine...and then I thought of Tarrok, how disappointed I would be if I took the easy way with someone I barely knew. I put my hand on his chest, keeping a distance.

The curtain was drawn across, and three faces peered in. The metal embedded into their temples shined in the sunlight above them. The tallest one grinned, his teeth made entirely of steel. He grabbed me and flung me into the square, where I sung myself to a soft landing. Xibo would have been proud. But if I didn't get us away, there would be nothing to report back. I crouched low and sang Selchuk and Inbikh beside me and out of the grasp of the other two.

"*Kardush-waiya fil fos,*" he said in Hiranian. His voice was low and gravely, his dark, straight hair hanging in greasy braids from his half-bald head.

"*Kundit mazra ha!*" I said and sang a fireball at him, which he dodged.

The other one grabbed me from behind and spun me around. Selchuk was fighting with the third one, a woman.

I had to kill both of them, or we were done.

I swung my head back to hit the man who held me. His nose crunched from the blow of my head and blood spurted over me. He let me go, and I sang into his brain, causing his eyes to bleed, and he passed out. The other one backed away from me and ran.

The woman was still choking Selchuk. I kicked her from behind and put my hand on the back of her head, singing one of Xibo's songs. Her head cracked, and she fell backward, blood pouring from where I'd killed her.

I'd killed someone. I felt a deep darkness enter my stomach.

"Leanora, we have go!" Selchuk tugged on my arm. "Now!" He started a song and grabbed Inbikh, folding his arms around me. I sang with him, operating on instinct entirely, the face of the dead woman swimming before me. I held Selchuk tighter, and we rose into the sky on a fast tula song, Selchuk's voice supporting the melody the entire way back to Hirana.

I HAD NEVER BEEN SO glad to see Xibo.

"So?" he asked when we landed without a hitch.

"We saw Zer." I leaned over, drawing the water into me. Everything went eerily silent. Even the stalks of flax appeared to have their own song as the lack of noise gnawed at me. He was going to lose it, but I couldn't lie to him. "Lepidaia has been destroyed by the Yarats, especially the inner city," I said quietly.

Xibo scratched his chin. "Asanis *and* Lepidaia?" His mouth pursed. "Trying to kill yourself?" He came closer to where we stood, crowding us together. The students stopped their training to watch. "I told you to go to the middle of the continent! What part of that didn't you understand?" he yelled and stalked off toward where Gulnaz was working with a group of students.

Selchuk looked between the two of us. "What just happened? He never lets anyone get off that easy."

Xibo was laying into Gulnaz, their voices rising in Hiranian. I didn't have the energy to translate.

I saw the Yarat woman's face again, her dead eyes. I had killed someone. I couldn't get past the sound of her head hitting the stone. The dull thud that I felt at the bottom of my stomach.

"Leanora, are you..." Selchuk called after me, but I was already in the air, racing toward the closest place where I could get something edible. When I touched down on the opposite side of the village square, facing a large roasting pit where fish lay in long rows of skewers, I took two off the rack without asking, gobbling them down within seconds. Then my stomach turned, and I fought against the queasiness, inhaling deeply to keep the food down. My stomach won, and I had to bend in the dirt until my stomach was empty again. I spit out the last of the half-digested food.

I stood there in the square, trying to forget the feeling of death that loomed over me. Would I ever get rid of it, or was this just the beginning?

23

TARROK

The red-brown of the desert landscape was wonderfully familiar. The thin silver ribbon of the river wound through Hagoth's dusty hills. I could draw my home in my sleep. I sat back against my chair at the gunner's mount inside the Marwatha. The last time I'd been in Hagoth had been with Leanora, over a year ago. Her black, curly hair had fallen across my face when she sat in front of me on Vali.

The first thing I had loved about her was that she listened more fully than anyone else I knew. Her face took in all I said. I kept asking myself—in those early days— did her attentiveness mean anything? Or was I imagining it all, because I was an alien in my own village? When her black eyes changed to a cool, deep green after I told her about Hirana, I saw a kindness that meant I was hers. Now, galaxies away, I craved her voice.

I need you here.

Vali ran around me in circles, like he expected something. Like he too, was waiting for her. After I clicked my tongue, he settled at my feet, humming a melody Alaric had taught him, atonal and strange.

Suns, I'm fading without the light that is you, Leanora.

My mouth was parched. I had been strapped in for hours, waiting for the signal that it was safe to approach Metria, where the evacuee Eloians were stowed away underground with the rest of Hagoth. The ulsos thrummed with nervous energy. Neelan edged the ship toward the center of Hagoth, and the engines roared and sputtered when we swooped over the C-shaped collections of houses, slowing at the ridges of the eastern dunes. A hatch opened up in the ground that was double our ship's width, dozens of warriors riding out on large ulsos. Instead of spears, they held kiyo poles.

"We're the good guys," Alaric yelled at them through the gun mount.

"They know," Neelan said. "They wouldn't open the hatch if Saren hadn't told them to watch for us."

"Oh." Alaric jumped down from the guns, stretching his muscles as the animals watched his descent to the cargo hold.

Our engines sputtered as we pulled into Metria, smoke billowing behind us. The ulsos shook out their bodies while the luoshis whined. The underground training facility we landed in had been converted from an extensive inactive mine.

When we landed, I looked above me at the familiar skies: cloudless and cobalt blue in the afternoon heat. Ahead of me was a familiar, light green face. Erena, my sister. I grinned from ear-to-ear while Vali, Dona, and Carki ran ahead to her. Her shaved head glistened as she rushed to greet me. A kiss for each cheek.

"It's really you!" She put both hands on the sides of my face. I had missed Erena's bubbly energy. I held her close to me and cherished her natural cinnamon scent.

"You need to eat more," she signed. "Come. Saren and Methriel wait for you."

Radjek, his brown fur rippling, climbed up my trousers and

perched on my shoulder. "I need...my...Inbikh," he chittered, his front paws cold on my neck.

"You're not the only one," I replied.

There was a rumbling, very faint, along the western horizon. I narrowed my eyes while the defensive metal grating lowered over us and locked into place. A second metal shield whined above it. A whooshing started that sounded like sand being scooped overhead, and the temperature dropped. I followed Erena through the massive underground corridors, everything ringed in amber light. There had to be a way for them to see what was above ground. When I passed small shafts of daylight leaking below to the corridor, I scrambled to one of the underground spy mounts. A deep shaking continued beneath, dust flying in my face.

Warning drums rolled, and warriors ran to stations with their ulsos. I looked through the scope. Five ships were coming for us: we'd been followed after all. The warrior music crescendoed, and I drew our ulsos and gwynbees close to Alaric and me. Neelan yelled incomprehensibly over the din.

"I'm going to warn Saren and Methriel," Erena signed.

"Earphones in! Moons keep us protected from the Yarat noise!" Neelan clamped a hand on my shoulder. It was funny to hear him using our exclamatory words.

"We need extra spears and gunners." The warriors signed for us to join them.

Bejah ran on ahead while Neelan puffed behind Alaric.

"I wish she were fighting with us," Alaric said.

I put my arm around Alaric, drawing his small body into mine. "You don't have to fight, you can rest." I searched for the direction Erena had gone, so Alaric could follow her to his parents.

"Fighting is better than being scared," Alaric said. He ran to the nearest circular mount of a Hagothian spear gun. "How does this work?"

"We're not touching that thing, my friend." I hurried him along with me, Vali barking while the rest of the ulsos followed. We ran down the earthen corridor, orange lights flickering. Explosions and guns fired outside.

I stopped and looked at the closest warrior, his face tense. "We have four open gun stations. You know how to use a tracking gun. It recoils badly, so be careful." He left Alaric, Neelan, Bejah, and me to scramble to our stations.

"Alaric, beside me," I said. He climbed to the mount next to me, swiveling in the seat to bring it up high enough that he could see through the scope.

I climbed onto a rickety seat, switched on the level, and the mount warmed up. A separate spear function was attached to a second trigger. I unlocked the separate guns and aligned their sights. There was a wide 360 view scope that allowed me to rotate the gun on the mount. I showed Alaric how to operate it. We trained our sights on anything that moved. I test fired; a red stream followed the spear, which whistled ahead.

"What if they try to come down the gun mount?" Alaric asked. It was a good question; the area around the mount was wide enough.

"The ulsos will help us." They hummed in agreement. I called out to Alaric. "Keep your ear protection on."

A screaming sang in my ears, and Alaric put his earcoverings back in. He hummed with the ulsos, his feet tapping the rhythm. I followed and signaled Vali next to me. Carki stood at attention next to Alaric's mount.

The zipping of the lighter Yarat craft flew over us. The glare from the metal was blinding. I shot anyway. Then I tripled the shots every time I thought I caught a glimpse, since there was a second delay until impact because they were moving so fast.

"Clipped a side," Neelan called out.

"Got the starboard," Bejah followed up.

"A hole to the cockpit!" Alaric shouted.

"This one's for Ori." I blew another hole in a smaller vessel coming our way. "This one's for my father." I shot the side of a Talbo-Pii zooming close to the gun mount. Another Talbo-Pii came toward the cockpit, and I swiveled to blast it out of the sky. "That's for Leanora."

A cheer went out among all the crew. Neelan and I were silent. This was only the beginning. He was still swiveling the sight, watching the skies. Bejah grunted, shot her gun, then screamed. She leapt off her seat, knives drawn. Vali and Carki barked, then tore halfway up her gun mount opening.

"Watch my sight," I said and went over to where a Yarat woman had slithered down the gun bay and was lodged in the shaft. I took out my knife and slit her throat. She shuddered and fell down the shaft, followed by a live Yarat man. His half metal face crinkled in disgust at me. When my knife sunk into his thigh, he reached for my throat. I yanked back, used a deadweight drop, and he let go. I swiveled and cracked his head on the stone ground. A pair of Hagothian warriors slit his throat.

Alaric looked on in shock, so pale and still I was afraid he'd pass out. I couldn't protect him from this. Another Yarat slithered down, and we were in full fight mode. Alaric was frozen in front of me.

"Get on the guns. You have to cover us. Shoot to keep them from coming down," I yelled at him.

Alaric climbed back on his mount. I followed him and used battle breaths to keep my heart steady as I squeezed the trigger, checking Alaric every chance I got. Vali patrolled with the other ulsos. The clanking of metal and shouting above us continued throughout the night. Alaric kept shooting, swiveling in the chair, sometimes standing and looking over at me. Checking that I was okay too.

"Got another one. Two more coming down the shaft," he yelled. All the youth gone from his voice. He'd rapidly learned the signs to call the nearby warriors who electrocuted the Yarats with their spears when they came below.

I needed Leanora here. Now more than ever.

"When are you coming?" I yelled. Everyone turned to look at me, all going quiet for a moment.

"You need rest," Bejah said, dark circles prominent under her tired green eyes.

"No, let's finish," I said, nodding to Alaric who kept his hands on the trigger.

"There's nothing out there," Bejah said.

"For now," Neelan answered, his pudgy hand heavy on my shoulder.

I was terrified to stop. Afraid that when I did, it would all start again.

When I saw Alaric's face, I knew I had to take him away so he could rest. He was too young. Leanora would never forgive me if I didn't protect him.

"Alaric, let's find your parents. Time to eat."

He collapsed into my arms, and I carried him the entire way, Vali humming at my side.

PART III

"The more advanced a civilization is, the more right it has to inform and enlighten the developmentally delayed civilization. Integration can be abided for mutual benefit only."—*Yarat-waiya*, Article No. 2

Your eyes ringed in amber
finally saying—
My hand close enough
for you to grasp.
But we are not allowed.
What I imagine is inside,
a spring steadily trickling,
has the possibility
of flooding
when you rain,
the premonition you're near
and this orbit of never touching
or saying
what lies below the
soil of our feet.

—Selchuk Quoresriun, "Our Spirthen" (translated from Hiranian)

24

LEANORA

The small storm inside of me that had started when I set off for Eloia was now a hurricane I had to contain. The bonfire crackled, and I couldn't help looking into it and seeing the woman's face that I'd killed. What if someone similarly killed my brother? Or, what if Tarrok was dead before I saw him or my parents again? The thought tormented me and Zer's face floated back into my memory. I pushed his menacing expression out of my mind.

I turned away from the flames, the heat leaving my face. I had escaped Zer. I had done that. No one had helped me. Then why hadn't I been able to bring myself to Tarrok and my family? Xibo held out his hands to the fire. The night wind whipped around us on the periphery of the village, everyone seated on logs around the firepit.

Our original group of thirty from the Maer-lina training house were the only ones gathered around; the rest of the locals had gone back to their huts. Some of the students stared at me, a few of their hands glowing from time to time as they passed around skewers of barbecued fish and insects they'd collected at sunset. Only Gulnaz was missing.

Xibo finished his food first, staring at where Mikosh, Selchuk, and I sat. "How was Zer?"

"He tried to kill us." I explained the rest, with Selchuk filling in details for several minutes.

"But you got away." Xibo narrowed his gaze into the fire. "That's something, my young ones." He glanced at the rest of the group, beaming with his rare toothy grin. "I trained with Zer before he became a healer. Typical Yarat, but good fighter." He rubbed the sides of his face. "Most couldn't have escaped from him."

"I'm waiting for him to say what we did wrong," I whispered to Selchuk.

"It's coming." He took another bite of fish and watched me.

My face felt flushed, and I put my cool hands on it.

Xibo leaned in, his large eyes in a certain rapture.

"Here it comes..." Selchuk whispered.

"You've successfully sent Inbikh solo and then yourself with Selchuk to not one, but two locations in Eloia—despite my orders." He coughed into his hand, the fire casting an ominous glow over his face. "When I say one place, I mean it. You could have lost all your energy reserves and died in space."

"I didn't." I had to hold my own against him if I was going to fight an entire army.

He finished off the last of his fish, throwing the skewers into the fire. "That doesn't mean it can't happen. There's no more time for mistakes. We have three days, maybe less, until I get reinforcements from the other islands. Then we go to Eloia." He sniffed the air, looking at the dark skies. "You two are off for final battle training tonight."

"No." The wind died down, the air stale with Selchuk's refusal.

"Why can't we stay here?" I asked, trying to get a sense from Selchuk's expression what this meant.

Xibo glanced over his shoulder. "Have you seen Gulnaz?"

I felt for her energy. She was nowhere in the vicinity. "She isn't nearby."

"What is final training?" I whispered to Mikosh, seated on the other side of me.

"It sucks. Like bad." Mikosh was trying to imitate our Eloian inflection.

"What do I have to do?" I asked.

"Survive," Mikosh said dryly, watching Xibo.

"Mikosh isn't going with you two yet," Xibo said.

She stood up abruptly, her usually calm voice trembling. "Why can't I go? I'm one of the best fighters."

"We'll talk in the morning." He raised his prosthetic hand. "When you see Gulnaz, tell her I need to speak to her. Tonight."

Xibo rose into the air and flew back to the village.

I watched his retreating figure. "What is that about?"

"He's a mess right now. We're down to the wire, and Gulnaz keeps taking off and not telling him where she's going," Mikosh said.

A whooshing sound started, and Gulnaz touched down lightly in the clearing. She sat down across from us, clearly winded. Damn her perfect landings. She murmured energy back to her body.

"Where were you?" I asked.

"Thresil islands first, then Pyor-ish. Trying to recruit a few more and gather supplies we may have overlooked." She pointed to a sack on her shoulder. "There are a few harps we can use— some we'll have to re-string." She searched the firepit. "Any food?" She was avoiding something.

"You wouldn't be so winded after such a short trip," Mikosh observed.

"We've been training nonstop," Gulnaz said thinly. "Food anyone?"

I handed her three of the skewers, and she looked at me for the first time, her eyes wild in the firelight.

"We saw Zer," I said.

Her whole body tensed, and she didn't settle down until Mikosh put her hand on her shoulder. "Go get rest."

Gulnaz grabbed the bag and was off. Selchuk waited until she disappeared behind the collection of huts in the distance. "She went to Eloia."

"Why?" Mikosh asked, still looking in the direction Gulnaz had gone, before turning back. "She's got too much going on to go that far. And for what?"

"Drash," I said, remembering the way they'd looked at each other in her memory.

Selchuk threw his arms in the air. "She's up to no good, as usual. Why are we surprised?"

Mikosh looked at the two of us. "I forgot to tell her Xibo was looking for her. I'd better go." She stopped for a second and turned back. "You'll need this." She took off her shawl and wrapped it around me. "See you in Spirthen."

"Thanks, Mikosh." I watched her rise into the air after Gulnaz.

Selchuk put a hand lightly on my shoulder. "Spirthen will test your endurance, everything you have. Xibo wants you to be prepared to both transport people and fight them off so you can transport the chorii at a moments notice."

"What about the harps?"

"Harps are only used in dire circumstances. Instant incineration. They'll turn a body to ash and a ship to almost nothing. But most have three shots in them before you have to restring them. It's a huge energy sump." Selchuk dusted off his pants and stood up. He held out his hand. "We'd better go."

"Now?" I asked. I was dirty and had barely eaten enough for all the missed meals of the last two days.

"You'll get used to it." He took my hand, and his warmth suffused through my arm, a pang starting in my heart. I let go of his hand, and the pain in my chest increased.

"Is Inbikh coming?" I walked away from him to find her and give myself a moment of distance.

"He didn't say she couldn't."

I found her asleep next to the fire and scooped her up, tucking her into my sweater, her white, bushy tail sticking out of the top. "Show me the way," I said and took his hand. An image of a small island came up in my mind when our palms touched.

"We're going to the southernmost island: Spirthen." He sounded stressed.

"What's wrong?" I asked.

"Get ready to freeze," he said, and I was inside of his memory, following the best route in moonlight. I inhaled and began a traveling tune while we soared into the air. Selchuk brought his arms gently around my shoulders while we headed south, the moons lighting our way across the ocean and through a thick mist. I knew we were close to the main island when I spotted thick tree trunks, or towers like enormous trees raised to the heavens.

I changed the tempo of our song to slow our descent, when a cold draft blew us toward the towers. I lost the song and fell into a bottomless, dark mist. Panic kept me from controlling our descent; Selchuk's hand slipped from mine. Inbikh still clutched at my neck. My breath was erratic.

I had to find the song again. Ice crystals exploded in my nostrils. It was hard to breathe. More crystals formed every time I opened my mouth. I recovered my voice, but it came out as a croak. I hit the side of a frozen trunk and slid to the bottom of a small clearing between the thick-trunked towers. Mist and greenish gray columns rose everywhere. It was hard to see where the tree's limbs began.

I was so sore I crawled along the frozen ground, clouds of mists clearing only a few feet in front of me, even with my perfect vision. We'd been separated again in our descent, and it was my fault.

"Selchuk? Inbikh?"

My bare hands stuck to the frozen earth. Pins-and-needles shot through my palms every time I pushed off the ground to look for my companions. I sat back against one of the trunks and exhaled a long, loud sigh. I couldn't sit here. My legs were sticking to the ice.

"I wished I had stayed on Eloia." I looked up at the curling mists above me. "If Tarrok were here, instead..."

Selchuk appeared through the mist with Inbikh chittering on his shoulder, her fluffy white tail flipping in his face. "There you are." He pulled me up to standing. "Since you did better than Xibo expected..." He exhaled a stream of mist. "Now I'm your loyal companion in his last form of torture." He was shivering, though heat radiated off him. "Welcome to Spirthen. Home of my ancestors." He held out his hand for me to take.

I ignored it and called the water back into my body. The water flowed very slowly into my limbs, a cold seep that restored my energy but dropped my body temperature significantly once the water hit my core. I was shivering within seconds.

"We need shelter for the night," I said.

Selchuk was searching above us, his black hair hanging away from his face.

Inbikh jumped onto me and crawled to the top of my head. At least she provided some warmth there.

"Are those trees?" I asked. Their trunks were as wide around as the largest mud huts in the Flax islands, but there was something artificial about how they reflected the moonlight.

"We call them spire trees, or spires for short." His face was drawn as he surveyed the area above us.

The ground was barely visible in the changing mists. Birds circled above us in ghostly clusters. The evidence of their life coated the rocks that grew out of the green-gray spires surrounding us.

"Any ideas on shelter and food, since you come from here?" I looked around to assess where to get warm, tying the shawl Mikosh had given me tighter around my shoulders. "Why didn't Xibo let us get jackets?"

"He likes to torture us." He imitated Xibo's voice. "Hardship is good for the soul."

Selchuk was worse off in a long-woven shirt with only a thin undergarment beneath. We walked along the uneven frozen ground. Above us, when the mist alternated, were bridges and walkways that connected between the spires. During daylight we could have found a way up there.

"Why aren't there any branches or living things on the trees? Or are they not visible at night?"

Selchuk's eyes shone in the moonlight. "You're seeing what's left of the giant sea trees after the Yarats first came."

Frozen trees that looked like weapons. When I touched the spires, they were icy and slick. Birds called out to us, the mist rising up to greet them. I moved closer to Selchuk.

"Do you want my shawl?" I asked.

"Keep it, we'll need to stay close to keep warm," he replied. When he put his arm around me, I was too cold to care about propriety. The cedar scent of his skin didn't hurt either.

"It's been a long time since I was here." He sighed and slowed our pace. "I hope this time is better than the last…" He offered me his hand. I let him help me up a set of stairs that led to connecting woven bridges between two nearby spires. "There should be several alcoves for us to get warm in until the mist clears at dawn." His voice echoed in the hollow of the spire we walked through.

We climbed up onto a platform in an open alcove that was carved out of a wide tree trunk. Inside it wasn't frozen, which allowed us to sit side by side on a curved shelf that blocked the wind. He scooted next to me, my back to the hard wood wall. We lay side by side in the cold, rubbing our hands together for warmth.

"Did you grow up here?" I asked.

"For a very short time," he said. He blew into his hands before taking my palms in his, rubbing them together. We kept rearranging how we sat together until we found an ideal corner of the alcove, our legs pressed together, arms around each other. It felt like too much energy to talk, and I started to drift off.

"Does Tarrok sing?" he asked abruptly, waking me up.

"A little bit, mostly with the ulsos." I felt a change in him, his face entirely in shadow. "Why?"

"What good is a man who can't sing? How can he help you?"

I laughed, and Inbikh climbed between the two of us, snuggling between our chests. "Do I need so much help?"

"No...I just...I figured...because you have *haian fusai*...it doesn't matter..." He looked down before scooting closer.

There was a moment of awkward silence when his breath was closer. Inbikh was already asleep but still purring. He reached for an errant strand of hair that hung in front of my face and curled it around his finger. "It's so soft." He reached for another strand, and his fingers lightly brushed my cheek. An energy seared from him that drove out all the cold.

I watched the frozen mists curling outside the alcove. It was dangerous to feel this way. Hunger, fatigue, absence were talking here, not something more.

Yes.

"We need to sleep," I said.

He released the tendril and took both my hands in his. "We need to stay warm tonight." I moved so that my knees touched his, our foreheads closer. Was I justifying the need for us to stay warm?

The wind whipped up, and my hands and feet tingled. I brought his hands to my mouth and blew on them. My head eventually leaned on his shoulder. I drifted off but kept waking, one side of my body frozen. Then I would turn to make certain that Selchuk was still breathing. His arms were wrapped tight around me, his breathing shallow.

If I died of hypothermia, would Tarrok know my last thought was of him?

Or would my heart betray me?

It all depends on you, a voice whispered in my head.

25

GULNAZ

This had to be my last time in Asanis. The tops of the giant pines swayed with the Yarat ships circling overhead. Probably heading for Hagoth when Zer gave them the signal. I hoped the Hagothians would blow the Yarat ships out of the sky. An unexpected grin came over me. I'd always enjoyed watching things blow up. Destruction is so final. Once something's gone it can't come back.

A shame feelings don't work in the same way. My emotions constantly churned over, under, and inside, sometimes choking me.

If there was a way to make the war stop, I would've done it. Gladly sacrificed myself to make that happen.

I pulled the clasp on my ponytail tighter and descended toward the trees. My song stopped a few measures into Danis' song, the sorrow in the melody overpowering. I wish I'd chosen something else. I was losing my grip on all I cared about, even power.

I landed on the lower branch of one of the birches, wishing I could sit and rest my head against the bark. The dry thickness of it melding with my skin. If only I could lay here and not think about war or destruction. Just be.

"Gulnaz!" Zer called out to me.

"*Peshara*," I cursed and let go of the tree before floating to the ground, sealing in any traces of the emotions I'd been battling with.

He stood with Mila and Parmit. They peered at me suspiciously, Mila's newly scarred face looking worse than last time.

"Still here? Not off at battle?" I asked Mila. Better to goad her before she attacked me with her *urijniak* and wore me out. It was how she'd been able to kill Danis so quickly.

"We're waiting on the last of our ship repairs." Mila crossed her arms grumpily.

"Maybe you can help us?" Parmit sneered and hit Mila's sleeve, but Mila's expression didn't change, her eyes narrowing further.

"Of course," I said graciously.

Zer put out his hand to stop Mila. "She's not here for that. Update?"

"Leonora's still in training. Probably another month before she's ready, because of a recent injury." I kept my gaze even with his.

"Good, good. We should have possession of the whole planet by then." He brought the palms of his hands together and touched them to his chin. "Hagoth is better defended than we estimated."

"Nedara?" I asked.

"Not worth attacking," Parmit said. "The tribes are too fractured—very easy to subdue."

"Leave us," Zer said. Parmit took off in a flash, but Mila remained. "There are a few prisoners for you." He had a short smile on his face.

Mila smiled like she was eating a squished bug and nodded curtly to me. "Till the final battle...if you make it there, Gulnaz."

Kundit mazra ha, I hated her. I struggled to appear at ease.

"She killed Xibo's family, didn't she?" Zer asked.

"Oh?" I feigned.

"You didn't know?" he asked.

"No." I hummed Danis' song under my breath.

"That's a nice tune. Is it one of Leanora's?" he asked.

"Yes, it has a nice ring to it, I think."

"It will be good to see her again." He gestured for me to follow him to a thick copse of trees.

I stayed put.

"Will she be agreeable?" he asked.

I folded my arms, deciding that half-truths were more enjoyable. "After everything Xibo and I have put her through, she will be most agreeable." I paused, my expression serious. "But, if there are too many deaths, it will be harder to recruit her."

Zer's eyes narrowed. "For progress to occur, some must fall by the wayside."

Said like a true Yarat.

"At some point, you must accept what she is. And what you can't change," I said, waiting for him to explode, but instead he remained thoughtful. I looked up at the tops of the trees. "I need to get back."

Zer took a hold of my arm before I could rise into the sky. "Can she carry people across galaxies?" Such hunger in his voice, like a small animal examining its prey.

I wriggled out of his grasp, rising in the air. "Remember that she operates from a place of love, a desire to do good. If you take that away from her, you'll destroy her."

His metal eyes were sad. I was glad he had no hold over me anymore. I knew what I needed to do.

Even if it meant that in a few days I would join Danis and her children.

WHILE I SOARED over the deserts, the dry heat dragged on me, and I sank to the sand, watching the sky for ships. I thought back to Leanora and how her songs were so pure.

I sang because I had to, not because I loved it. She sang with everything inside of her. Not to conquer or possess power. She cared so little about power it was frightening to someone as degenerate as me.

But wasn't I just a tool in my designer's hands?

"GULNAZ, WHAT HAVE YOU DONE NOW?" Drash asked, absently stroking my thighs. He wanted more. I was sore and swiveled around, flicking the harsh light in his underground bunker on.

I am what I am. Not what other's will, I reminded myself.

"Think about my new plan." I removed his hand from the inside of my bare thigh.

"What about *this* plan? Right now?" He rose to hover over me before pressing his lips into mine. I struggled to keep my hands on his bare chest. I wanted more, but I couldn't afford to let go. Could I? He'd taken off all his clothes. It wouldn't be difficult to start again.

I laid back and curled into him. "I wish it was all over."

"We can leave. Explore the other continent..." He dragged his fingertips over my hips. "Let them figure it out." Drash's brown eyes grew sorrowful. "Haven't we given enough of ourselves to this mess?"

"We have to see this through in order to be free." I pushed him off me.

"We'll never be free. Not you and me." Drash brought his arms around me, folding himself into me. "We will either be subject to a Yarat ruler or a Kardush one. There's no one like us making the big decisions regardless of who wins here."

A new thought occurred to me. "Or we ask Leanora to send us away when it's all done."

Drash snorted. "When she finds out you were a double agent?" Then he was serious. He saw my face, how wretched I must have looked. "If I could change things, I'd be fully Kardush. I would have never been captured by the Yarats to work on their stupid ships. And I would've taken you away from Zer and Xibo. Made sure you didn't work for both of them." He put a hand on my bare thigh again. "When Xibo asked you, I wish I had convinced you to say no all those years ago. So you wouldn't be like this now."

He took my hands in his, kissed them. So many years between the two of us, and I still couldn't say no when he wanted me. I folded my legs around his back.

"Something has changed in you," I said, kissing his neck.

"I'm ready to be done with all of it, Naz." He held me tighter to him.

"We need lots of luck in the coming battles." I brought my hips closer to his. "Let's go back to the old days."

"I hate the old days." He grinned at me. Not touching me. Yet.

"I need one more good memory, to help me in the days ahead." I slid beneath him. My bare skin against his. He started the familiar dance we'd been doing since we were kids.

When we were finished, sweating and exhausted, I held onto him. Not eager to leave.

"When it gets down to the wire, I want to be with you," I said to him.

"If I go first that won't be possible," he murmured in my ear.

"I can't live here without you." I knew that now.

"Then I'll go first, and you do something to make sure that you follow close behind," he said.

Drash held me, and I cried. Then he wept, and we turned out the light. It was my first time staying the night since the Yarats had taken him over a year ago.

It was fitting to let the darkness close over us. Preparation for things to come.

26

LEANORA

I had never been happier to see Hirana's twin suns rise. Unfortunately, the glowing orbs brought little warmth to where I was huddled inside the alcove with Selchuk. The mist had cleared, and the light shone in our faces, illuminating a turquoise, sparkling sea. Inbikh was no longer nestled between us. I couldn't feel my fingers and toes. Stretching brought excruciating pain.

"*Zoldit*," I cursed in Hiranian.

I slipped down from the shelf we'd slept on, careful to leave Selchuk undisturbed, feeling slowly returning to my tingly feet. When I stepped onto the pathway we'd followed the previous night, six levels of bridges and walkways rose above me between the surrounding spires. The birds soared overhead, but there were no other living creatures or signs of food. I walked back into the shadow of the hollowed-out alcove to wake up Selchuk, who turned over on the shelf.

"I heard you cursing," he said, rubbing his eyes.

"Let's get food." I was dizzy with hunger. I called the water to me, but it didn't stop the gnawing in my stomach.

"There must be villagers somewhere," Selchuk said.

"I don't understand why we're here," I said. "We're going to freeze to death."

"We'll find something or someone to help us," he said absently, still rubbing his eyes as he followed me into the morning sunlight.

He glanced at the outcropping of spires and connecting bridges and platforms. The sky was a cornflower blue with only a scattering of thin clouds. Nothing grew from the branchless trees. "Is starvation and sleep deprivation supposed to make me better in battle?" I asked.

Selchuk stopped searching and looked at me with an expression I didn't understand. "We could be fighting for months. You have to be ready for that." His gaze was on my mouth. "I wish I could make this easier." His eyes slowly traced my face, something new reflected in them that I was afraid of.

I couldn't look at him. *Think of Tarrok*, I reminded myself. Nothing came to mind.

"The last time I had battle training here was with Gulnaz," he said.

"She's certainly more beautiful to look at," I said.

He scowled, the dark circles under his eyes more prominent. "There are many people far more beautiful than Gulnaz. What she is fades quickly to the eyes."

"The question is: does she know that?" I stepped away from him, not wanting to talk about my appearance. "How I look doesn't matter here anyway."

"I like how you look, especially those red...um...what do you call them?" he asked.

"Splotches, dots? Marks?" This was definitely getting awkward quickly. I flushed. *Think of Tarrok, not Selchuk*, I reminded myself. I had to change the subject, get him back into survival mode. "If we don't find food, I'm going to pass out," I said.

He took my arm and whisper-sang a few words of a healing song. My stomach stopped gnawing on itself. A warm glow suffused through me. There was that draw to him again. I couldn't ignore it.

"I'm not supposed to...but you look miserable." Selchuk had risked his wellbeing to partially heal me. He was several shades paler as a result.

"Let's find Inbikh. She might know where the best fish is," I said.

"Take this pathway. There are more stones, but we can avoid the rotten ladders leading down to the shore," Selchuk said.

"How do you know?"

"My family came from here." He led the way down the steps. "What little I remember of them." His face was tranquil as he held out a hand to help me, but I ignored it and let my hands ache as I grabbed onto the cold spires for balance while I descended.

"Why were the two of us sent here, instead of Mikosh and me?" I asked.

"Healers are the 'lesser' of the Kardush fighters."

"Yet I'm supposed to bring us back to Eloia. We can't be second-class forever," I replied. "No one recovers from their injuries without us." I stopped where the stairs ended at a long land-bridge I hadn't remembered crossing the night before.

"It really gets on Gulnaz's case how powerful you are." He grinned, his gleaming white teeth showing. "Being half from Eloia gives you an advantage. You are bound to two planets that you can harness energy from." He peered at me from under his hair, which had flopped in his face. "If you wanted."

I started across the bridge, testing the planks first. "What do you mean, if I wanted?"

He followed closely behind me, arms outstretched like he

expected me to fall. "Healers take people's energies, the broken parts of their spirits, their bodies, and give them back to people whole. Music is a vehicle for doing that, like traveling." He paused, surprised by my reaction. "Didn't you already know that?"

"On some level I suppose I knew I was using people's energies, but that wasn't clear to me until you said it."

He flushed with pleasure, and we kept walking. "I can't travel well, because I never wanted to develop the emotional distance necessary to leave Hirana. Maybe I want too badly to be on Eloia and never come back here."

He stopped and gazed at me. "I've always had trouble with emotional distances. It makes me a great healer, but perhaps not the best at other things. The more distance there is, emotionally, between myself and a patient, the less I'm able to heal them."

There was a deep fizzing in my chest, my pulse increasing. I moved involuntarily closer to him. The sea was a deep green behind him, making his eyes a deeper blue.

Leanora, don't.

I turned around to see who spoke, but there was only the frigid air between me and twenty feet below the bridge. I stepped away from Selchuk and walked to the other side.

"What is it?" Selchuk asked. In the bright sunlight he was paler than before.

"I'm dying of hunger."

"You were walking earlier—you can't be dying." A small smile played on his lips. Some of the hauntedness to his face lifted, heat shimmering off his body when he came closer. It was harder to avoid the energy pouring off him.

"We need to find food. Now," I said and pointed at the series of connecting bridges that ran through the spires leading to the other side of the island.

"Be careful, I don't know how well they've maintained the bridges in that direction."

I led the way as we walked through hollowed-out spires that groaned in the wind.

The next bridge sloped downward and blew about, listing with each gust of wind. I held onto the rope sides, but one of them was frayed and coming loose. When one section broke, the bridge sagged and I dropped to the rotted planks.

"Don't move, Leanora." Selchuk shimmied past me and tripped, his legs hanging loose. "Zoldit!" he cursed.

If I didn't pull him up, he'd fall through. I didn't have enough energy to transport him to the ground safely. The bridge sagged further.

"I've got you, hold on." I tugged him closer to me.

"I weigh too much. Let go. I'll travel down," he said.

He was too depleted to travel. If I had more sustenance I could have helped both of us make it to the bottom, but it was too dangerous. The ground below was uneven with too many objects that could impale us if we traveled too quickly.

"Keep holding on," I insisted.

"I'm slipping," Selchuk groaned.

I inhaled and threw my weight against the bridge, lifting him halfway towards me. He started to slip again, clawing to find purchase, and I clenched my teeth, pulling him across me. Once his torso was on mine, he pulled himself the rest of the way, the wind swaying us about on the flimsy bridge, more planks clattering below. There was so little between us and the points of the next spire.

"Thanks," he said, out of breath, holding tight to my arms, our bodies pressed against each other.

"Let's get off here."

"It might be better to crawl," he suggested.

I led the way on all fours as the bridge kept listing to and fro in the wind. Once we'd reached the other side, it twisted completely upside down.

"You okay?" he asked. "I felt like I was crushing you."

"We're safe, that's all that matters."

"There used to be ladders attached to the spires, because the bridges were made originally in a spiral pattern around the outskirts of the island. The ladders helped people descend faster." I looked below for anything that would give a decent foothold, but there was nothing.

"I'll take us to the bottom; I don't want to deal with any more bridges," I said.

I took his hand, and he let go, grabbing my forearm. "Don't. There are too many objects in the way. It's better to climb down, especially in the state we're in."

"Aren't we supposed to test our endurance?" I asked, stepping onto the next bridge, which felt much more solid than the last, until my foot went through one of the planks and I had trouble extracting it. He was immediately by my side, and I swiftly put my arms around him so he couldn't let go. I inhaled and sang a very short tune that elevated us into the air and down to the ground below.

"Nicely done." Selchuk kept hold on me, though we were on solid ground. His eyes reminded me of shining river stones. I stepped away from him, and the earth below sunk several centimeters. Selchuk rose in the air a half meter above me as I kept sinking into the slow-moving mud.

"We're in a bog. I'll help you out," he said.

I spoke a fast chant, and I traveled back to stand beside him.

"Let's see if Inbikh has found any good spots for fish." He held out his hand, and I ignored it.

"Why don't you people eat?" I asked while we walked forward, careful to avoid the tangled roots of the trees.

"Xibo trained us to go at least three weeks without solid food, and seven days without water. Gulnaz and Mikosh can go even longer than I can."

"How?" We avoided small boulders that were interspersed the closer we got to the shore.

"If you couldn't survive, you weren't allowed to fight in battle, except when we were desperate." Selchuk looked ahead, the sound of water crashing against rocks somewhere behind us. "That desperation cost a lot of lives."

"How do you fight without things your bodies need?"

He turned to look at me in a way I could remember Tarrok gazing at me, his face relaxed and open, his eyes reflecting the ocean's blue. "Some things you can delay in your body. Like solid food, by drawing the element your body craves into your energy stores. Other things, you need more rapidly. Each person is different."

We walked the rest of the way to the rocky shore with no beach. Green water with a faint pink tint stretched out in front of us. No other land formations were in sight. He sat down on the rocks, clearly spent.

"The Yarats created the training regimen, and the Kardush refined it. Made it more biologically compatible. Too many soldiers in the very early days, hundreds of years before we were born, were dying because the Yarats thought they had to push all living things to their limit."

"And now the Kardush still follow this tradition." I sat on the rocks to catch my breath. "Is it possible you almost lost because you pushed people too far?"

Selchuk was shivering, and I scooted next to him, wrapping my shawl around him and entwining my arm with his. The warmth of him radiated against me while his teeth chattered. "We did lose. If we'd won there would be no Yarats, not even ones like Gulnaz." He bowed his head. "I shouldn't have said that."

The wind blew harder against us. "What makes you hate Gulnaz?"

"If I tell you, it will change how you feel about me." Selchuk took my hand again. He visibly strained to hold back the memory.

"Isn't it better for me to know?" I put my shawl around him, letting go of his hand to get a fix for what was in the water. "I'll search for food while you tell me." I spotted bushes along the shore ahead and walked slowly toward them, taking him with me.

"During the tail end of the war, a group of Yarats came: Mila and Parmit. Gulnaz was supposed to stay with Mikosh and me, because I couldn't protect Xibo's family alone..." He glanced at me and continued. "Gulnaz left us when Mikosh and I were ambushed. Mikosh thought she could handle them herself and chased them off but didn't have a second soldier to pair with. I was left alone with Danis and the children." His memory then surged and overlaid where we were walking.

Danis stood in front of Selchuk, and he gently kissed her. She looked behind him before kissing him back. She let him go, murmuring, "Xibo will kill us."

Gulnaz appeared, causing them to separate. "Danis, he's fifteen years your junior." Gulnaz threw Selchuk across the wall in a short burst of sound. He was sprawled on the ground, laughing hoarsely. Danis put out her hand to heal him then waved her other arm and Gulnaz hit the wall.

"I'm not covering for you," Gulnaz said.

"Because you love Xibo," Danis said.

Gulnaz hissed. "This is the problem with...you can't see what's around you. You assume everyone is as stupid about love as you are." She came closer to where Danis stood in front of Selchuk, her voice low. "What will your children think?"

Danis smiled, tears streaming down her face. "I'd rather they die knowing love from someone who is here for them. What good is a shadowy hero they never see?"

Gulnaz's face was flushed with rage. She soared out the front entrance.

Danis clutched Selchuk. "If I die today in battle, know that I loved you best of all." She stroked the sides of his cheek, her face coming closer...

The memory stopped. Selchuk held my hand gently. "I lost everything: Danis, the children, and Xibo's respect when I couldn't protect his family. At least Gulnaz made certain that the secret died with Danis and the kids. If Xibo knew..." His voice trailed off and a single tear tracked down his face. "He'd destroy me." He released my hand, inhaling deeply as he tried to control the surge of emotions I could feel rippling through him.

"Gulnaz didn't intentionally let them die."

"She doesn't care about anyone except Xibo," Selchuk whispered.

"I saw her memory of that day," I said quietly, unsure if I was supposed to tell anyone.

"She could have manipulated the memory—she's a Fernais." He ran his hands through his hair, looking away from me, anger pouring off him. "You haven't trained with her as long as I have. I have known Gulnaz for twelve years. I was the family healer. She was the family pet. With them gone, she had Xibo all to herself and no one to question her loyalty." He was shaking.

I put my hands on his trembling shoulders and brought him close to me, singing a soothing tune into the black lines of grief he held onto like it was all he had.

"I tried to kill myself so many times afterward, but Gulnaz always found me before it was too late," he whispered softly and swiveled around facing me so I had to let go of him. "When I saw you on the screen of the communicator months ago, I thought..." His voice cracked, heavy with emotion. "There's hope...I will hold on longer...Not for her...but for what she might bring."

He took my other hand. A memory of him watching me

began, then he let go. We were outside his mind, the air colder without him touching me. "I know you are with Tarrok, but I have to tell you..."

"Don't make this harder..." I started, but couldn't find the right combination of words.

"But if you don't know..."

His voice faded, and he sprinted over to bushes that were behind us. "Food!" He grabbed at a cluster of branches.

I ran to where he was crouched next to a small crop of dwarf trees growing out of the rocks. Small globes grew from their green and purple branches. I picked the ones that were the softest.

"They're edible, go ahead." Selchuk spoke with his mouth full.

I had to remind myself to slow down and chew.

"Musk nuts. Not tasty, but something," he said.

My mouth burned from the taste, but my stomach wasn't empty. That was the important part, I reminded myself. I searched for something else that could wash down the taste. A spring coursed down the side of a crop of spires that grew out of a steep ravine of rocks. I leaned down to drink from the stream, and Selchuk followed, his eyes locked on me every time I glanced at him.

I concentrated on the spring water trickling down the rocks. What he'd said earlier must have been influenced by hunger: I remembered how my trek across Eloia to find my mother had changed my perceptions. There was something in Selchuk's blue eyes that reminded me of...*No, don't think of him.*

He paused there, close enough to feel the heat radiating off of him. His blue eyes were now so calm. He brushed his black hair off his face and reached out, his brown hand against my red blotched skin.

If I let him, what would happen? Would touching him change everything?

A pleasurable warmth surged through my body. I needed the feeling of his hand in mine. I felt I could not live if he didn't touch me. For a few seconds he hovered there, waiting for me to bridge the distance.

I took a step back, a pain searing across my chest. I had to be responsible, remember my promise to Tarrok. He was waiting for me when I returned. I walked over to the water lapping against the large boulders lining the shore. I hated feeling this way. That if I returned to Selchuk, all the longing I was feeling would finally settle into some measure of peace.

"Why is the sea green here and not pink?" I asked

"We're really far south, close to the poles where the water is cooler. Stick your hand in—you'll see."

I put my hand in and retracted it immediately, the sting of the cold seizing my muscles. Fish moved under the clear water. It was too cold to catch fish bare-handed. I dried my hands on my thin sweater and searched the perimeter.

"What are you looking for?" Selchuk asked.

"Something to make a net."

"Waste of time."

His bass voice sang a deep, resonant melody. It felt ancient in its simple construction, none of the adornments of most Kardush music. Fish swam close to the surface. He sang from a deep place I hadn't heard anyone yet sing from on Hirana, the swarm of fish increasing.

> *Letye, letye, moir bon fas,* Fish so strong and beautiful,
> *hale mosh ze.* sing your way to me.
> *Utka, grolve, klarsi, bos,* Scales and throats and eyes and tails,
> *file a yus mot.* find your way to me.
> *Mos halen zir klaru,* My voice to guide,
> *mos haiane zir ale,* my spirit to lift,
> *rusyun o le tal,* out of the ocean,

tallenye, ut fassenye. come and be swift.

It sounded so plain in my language, but in Hiranian it was beautiful with the trills of the tongue. The melody moved the way I imagined fish swimming. The song carried me closer to him as I sang the harmony with him on the last repeating verse.

Mos halen zir klaru,
mos haiane zir ale,
rusyun o le tal,
tallenye, ut fassenye.

The fish leapt out and plopped on the rocks. I scurried about to beat all of them until they were still.

"How will we cook them?"

"There is no firewood here. Everything is eaten raw. What-ever we don't eat, we'll leave to dry in the sun."

He took three of the fishes and left the other three for me. I ignored their slippery bodies on my tongue. Their bones crunched unpleasantly, but I kept eating because I needed the energy. Maybe I was changing, becoming something better than I was before. More self-sufficient and strong. How changed would I be when Tarrok saw me again? Would he love what I'd become? Or was I better suited with someone else?

I looked back at Selchuk. His eyes a sparkling cobalt in the sunlight, his lips full. I needed something from him. A gentle tug at my navel warned me.

The wind was picking up, and I needed to find somewhere warmer for us or a place that had supplies. I stood, jumping to warm up. Selchuk came next to me, hesitant at first, one hand on my shoulder. He was staring at my lips again. I closed my eyes, singing the same song he had just taught me, but using it to make him float above me. As soon as the song ended he was back by my side, his hand in mine.

"Please, Leanora."

I brought one hand to his cheek. It was rough, and he turned like he was going to kiss my hand. I stepped away. "I can't, it isn't right."

"We decide what is right, not other people."

It was painful to behold him, because I wanted him. But I was certain this feeling would fade. I had to keep my distance. One of the spire trees above was thicker around the middle than the others. I closed my eyes and transported myself to the bridge at its highest point.

It was only a matter of time before he found me again.

27

LEANORA

The air smelled like rain. In the late afternoon suns' glare, the bridges and spires cast shadows over where I stood on one of the lowest level bridges. I scanned the area above me before transporting myself rapidly to the highest bridge to look for Selchuk. It had become a game between the two of us: first him trying to find me—and being far too good at locating me.

Then he'd disappeared. I was on my own to keep searching for food and any supplies that might be hidden on this desolate island. I was afraid of finding him, even if that was inevitable. At least I had some measure of freedom. The clouds were rolling in and I felt the desire to wander. To enjoy a moment to think without being forced to act.

I shot into the sky, flying into the air and flipping over the highest spire before slowing my song to land on the tallest bridge. I could see half the tiny island from up this high, the suns lowering behind the spires' trunks. We had an hour or more of daylight, at the most. Though there were lanterns in some of the alcoves that had been carved in the spires, I hadn't found anything to ignite them with.

"Whoever finds the other first makes dinner." I turned around and there was only wind and the creaking of the bridge I stood on.

Better be quick. It's hard to find fish in the dark. He spoke inside my mind. It sounded like Selchuk, but I wasn't certain if I was imagining it, the temperature dropping when the wind picked up. The sea was white capped, crashing against the boulders rimming the shore below.

I searched the bridges and walkways between the tree spires, darting onto the bridges below, calling the water to my body so I didn't run out of energy. I landed on the topmost bridge of a spire on the opposite end of the island. Large, gray seabirds swooped overhead, their white wings spanning several feet, their caws comforting.

One of the largest of the flock perched on the handrails and stared me down with its orange beak and opalescent blue-black eyes.

"Hello there, big one," I said.

It was half my size, even larger than I had estimated.

"Have you seen my comrade?" I moved closer, and the bird flew away as soon as I took another step on the bridge. I scanned below for Inbikh and Selchuk. There was nothing moving below except birds swooping down. The first few hours on my own had been exhilerating. Now the ache of only hearing my own voice gnawed at me. A cold wind gusted across the bridge, knocking me into the railing. The seabirds flocked into the holes and caverns in the rocks and spires. Another gust of wind arrived, and the mist crept in, the bases of the spires soon occluded from view.

The next gust of wind pushed me through the rope supports holding the wood bridge planks in place. I tore my nails gripping the planks to keep from slipping off into nothingness. I was kicking at thin air. One minute I was on the bridge, and the next nothing was below me.

"*Peshara*. Please don't let me fall," I yelled. Half of me dangled over the edge, my legs unable to kick back up onto the bridge. I fought to bring my legs up, my abdomen cramping with the effort. I kicked upward, my arms burning. My hands were slipping from the rope supports. I thrashed, swinging my body like a pendulum.

"*Kundit...mazra...ha!*" I cursed again, trying to propel myself upward. In my panic, all instincts to sing my way out of this mess were suspended. I didn't feel like I had enough clearance to travel out of this, after so many hours of exertion. I was operating from pure panic, my heart racing, sweat dripping down my back. Nausea kicked in, and I knew I had to do something.

My entire body shook with the effort, and panic took over. Out of breath, my legs hung limp. Had it come to this, my body dangling into the swirling fog and wind? Would I never have my chance to conquer the Yarats? To see Tarrok again?

"No!" I yelled, my voice echoing.

I closed my eyes, pulling with my arms to try and swing my legs over, but it wasn't possible. I didn't have the strength, and my hands slipped. I was falling fast, crashing through bridges, the rotten wood splintering on impact with my back.

You have to travel, if you want to survive this.

I spotted the nearest spire tree and sang quick and low. I closed my eyes, and a pressure started in my core, like I was being turned inside out. I kept dropping. I sang louder, opening my eyes in time to soar upward through the stone bark of the closest spire. I didn't have time to scream or turn back. I was inside the enormous stone tree. I thumped to the floor, landing painfully on my side, my ribs sore. I was safe indoors.

When I rolled over, everything felt tender. I checked the solidity of the ground before assessing my surroundings. The temperature was significantly warmer, the wind no longer blowing across my skin. The place looked like a sparse version of a Lepidaian apartment, with smaller circular windows all along the walls. There were steps that led down in front of me, and when I turned around another set let up to a platform area above me. Large flat pillows were shoved in the corner. A small table and two chairs sat against a wall, collecting dust. The floor was gleaming, which made me wonder if whoever lived here was coming back.

It was annoying that Selchuk probably knew this place existed and hadn't told me. It was a good thing he wasn't here so I wouldn't tell him off.

The porthole windows in the tree's massive trunk were placed at intervals and constructed of a thick resin. I peered out to face a turbulent, grey ocean, the wind gusting white caps. It was such a pleasure to be where it was warm and insulated from the cold. The fog rolled in, the suns creating a spectacular sunset with ribbons of golds and pinks that rippled on the stormy sea. I was even higher, it seemed, than the bridge I had fallen from.

As I walked around, searching for Selchuk, I couldn't find a proper entrance other than traveling in through the walls. Xibo and Gulnaz had never mentioned that was possible. I knocked at the walls, the stone feeling different, more maleable than I had ever recalled stone feeling in Lepidaia. I ventured up the stairs to the platform overlooking the main level of the kitchen. The platform room was cozier than the alcove Selchuk and I had stayed in the night before. Someone had taken care to live here in some measure of comfort. I set about to explore and find food or clothing. The lower level was mostly empty with a few chairs and tables. No sign of food.

The main level housed a kitchen and adjoining living room, but once again, no food. I climbed the upper stairs again to the platform room where mats had been rolled in addition to blankets and scarves. I rummaged through the neat piles and found several thin sweaters with pockets in odd places along the sides and collar.

I put on the thickest sweater, which was an unfortunate drab grey, and was instantly warmer. The lack of sleep from the night before weighed on me, and the sudden warmth made my eyelids heavy. I unrolled one of the mat bundles, calling the water to energize me. I was asleep within minutes, the sound of wind rushing in my ears.

I STOOD in the kitchen with Danis. When I looked around, it was obvious I wasn't in my body, nor was I completely dreaming. The kitchen was identical to the configuration of the training house on Maer-lina, except happier, more complete. Danis stared at me like she knew me. She took my hand and sat down next to me. Such power flowed through her, her voice in my head. *Selchuk is pure love.*

She let go and flitted to the double windowed door. Her movement was light and fast as she waved to her children playing outside. "You might ask, how can I love someone so much younger than me?"

"Do you know what you're saying, Danis?" a familiar female voice asked.

Selchuk was outside playing with the children. His hair was longer and drawn into a ponytail, with a few black tendrils falling into his face.

"He is beautiful because of his kindness," Danis said.

A roaring sound came from outside, and she stood up then relaxed when the sound ceased. "It is dangerous. Xibo will kill either him or me." Danis' large eyes grew darker, a few tears streaking down her cheeks while she smiled, bringing her hands to her chest. "I can't let this secret devour me," she whispered, wiping her face.

How could someone who was so lovely stay with Xibo? I thought.

She put her arm around me, her head on my shoulder. "Our lives have changed since he came as my apprentice. Selchuk is so good with the children." Her hands lit up a soft violet and she folded them under her arms, glancing up at me. "You must know why I tell you this." She took my hand again. *I am inadequate in the presence of his kindness. He has healed so many and yet there's so much turmoil inside.* She kept a hold on my hand, like I could save her.

Selchuk called out to the children as someone approached with a delivery. He waved to them as they departed, and the children opened the parcel.

When I am with him, I am neither mother nor wife. He sees me as myself.

I didn't know what to say to Danis. In her golden-brown face was a mixture of pain and joy. Her whole body lit up when she turned toward him. She glanced back to me, her voice inside my head now, her arms and hands glowing violet. *We have not done anything wrong. But, I caused him to miss a healing appointment by making him travel to me in Spirthen. Such a remote and desolate place, surrounded by strangers; I knew I could not leave him.* She let go of me and stood by the door, her hands stretched toward him. He did not notice us watching him with the children. *Our days are limited.*

She let go of my hand, speaking so softly I had to lean into her. "Now I cannot look at Xibo except to fight with him. With Selchuk there is only possibility. Even when we do not touch."

She embraced me, the weight of her tall body emitting a sense of calm that only healers could give.

She put her hands to her lips. "Gulnaz, I've talked for too long. Please keep this memory for me. Whatever happens."

"Whatever happens, I will," Gulnaz said, her voice tentative in a way I'd never heard.

A SHIVER TRAVELED through my skin when I woke, the pressure of someone's hand leaving mine. Her perfumed scent was in the air, and then with a whoosh, she was gone. I rose to the window, and she disappeared into the mist. Gulnaz had been here.

I'm freezing—where are you? a voice called to me. I turned around in the dark room, the faint moonlight coming through the portholes.

Leanora, the voice called again.

Selchuk? I croaked.

Who else? He sounded miserable. How was he talking inside my head?

Where are you? I asked.

Can you bring me to you? It's too cold for me to keep wandering.

I sought him out with my mind, drawing his tranquil energy toward me while I sung rapidly. I didn't want him stuck between those walls. A bright light flashed, and Selchuk appeared and collapsed on the floor.

I was so pleased to see him that I immediately embraced him, holding him close. Then I remembered the memory, and I abruptly let him go. This was where he and Danis had been before. They had been in love and now...

He kept one hand on my arm, like a question. "Thank you for...bringing me here..." He was still catching his breath. "I was freezing." He tried to draw me closer to him, and I took a step back. "I know, I owe you dinner."

I needed to keep him from touching me. "How did you speak inside my mind?" I asked.

"Easy." He held a glowing stone in his hand. "Healers can speak in each other's minds." He put the stone in my hand and folded my fingers around it. "Certain materials, like this stone, help amplify communication over long distances."

"Did you run into anyone else or find more food?" I asked.

"Just more fish and musk nuts." He walked over to the kitchen and placed what he had left from his pockets on the counter.

"There are sweaters and blankets up there." I placed the stone into one of the darkest corners, away from the windows.

"Oh." Selchuk's face filled with recognition and a certain terror. He'd been here before. He leaned against the counter then bent over, exhaling. "Of all the places for you to find."

"You knew about this place?"

He nodded his head, looking toward the windows. I didn't like the way part of him seemed to collapse. His face fell, the sorrow dripping off him like a slow poison. I rushed up the stairs to grab the pile of sweaters and blankets. I scrambled back, trying to change the atmosphere.

He took the second sweater in the pile and put it on before switching it for another. "Too warm," he said. I saw a flash of his sinewy chest, and I fixed my gaze out the windows instead.

"How does speaking into another person's mind work?" I asked.

"I'm not supposed to be here." He ran his hands through his hair then let it fall across one of his eyes. "Xibo said to leave you on your own for the whole day." His guilty expression turned darker, and he looked away from me. "I wasn't supposed to cheat and speak inside your mind."

"Well, you are here, so are you going to tell me how it works?" I asked, watching him carefully, his discomfort growing as he sank to the floor.

I sat next to him, our shoulders touching. "All healers can talk with each other through their minds." He spoke distractedly, like he was somewhere else. "We share a similar brain make-up that allows us...to communicate with each other. Sometimes we can do this with non-healers." He looked up, his expression darkening.

"What's wrong?" I asked. Gulnaz's memory was still on my mind, but I wanted him to tell me. So much about Gulnaz was suspect.

He didn't answer me, the gap between us widening, even though our shoulders still touched. All the energy in the room felt like it had been sucked out. He abruptly stood and walked to the window, his black hair falling into his eyes. It was dark outside, and I doubted there was anything he could see.

"This was my ancestor's home. Seventeen generations born here.... I brought Danis here...before and during the war." He stayed staring at the window, his body rigid. "I wish I'd kept her here for the duration, hid her and the kids away." He exhaled, bringing his hand to the glasspane. "Then maybe she'd still be alive." He wiped his eyes before he walked back to me.

"I don't want to be reminded of her, but here we are." He slumped down next to me. "Usually when I dream about her, I see her holding the children, Moki and Simun. I knew them since they were born. I sometimes dream they're alive, and we are a real family...then Xibo crashes through the dream. I cannot heal his burning hatred, his lust for war. I want to destroy him, obliterate him—but I cannot, because to kill him would be to kill the last bit of her that is alive."

I put my hand on his shoulder, and he took my palm, turned

it upward to face him, and kissed it. His lips traced my fingers, the sensation bringing a needed equilibrium.

"I wish you hadn't found this place." Selchuk leaned in, but I backed away from him, withdrawing my hand.

He watched me carefully in the glow light. When I looked away, I could still feel his gaze burning into the side of my face. His warm hand caressed my cheek. "I have to remember she is dead. She is not here. But you are." He brought his arms around me, and I held him close to me.

My face so close to his. It would be so easy to...the memories were destroying him, I could feel it. I took both his hands. "There is something that belongs to you." I embraced him, and he relaxed in my arms. He was light against my body and his gentle embrace unleashed a new energy. My hands moved to his face, where I let my mind unlock the memory of Danis and it flowed into him. His breathing evened out as he relived the memory.

When it finished, he relaxed, bringing his face close to mine. His eyes flooded, and he turned away, catching his breath. I rubbed his back while we sat on the floor. I sang into his pain, attempting to untether all the shattered pieces of him.

"It will get better, Selchuk. Gulnaz didn't kill them."

"She gave you the memory." He wiped his nose on his sleeve.

We sat there for a while until his breathing settled. Then he exhaled and nodded his head. I released my hold on him. A new energy arced from him toward me. "You remind me of her."

"Danis?" I asked.

"Except with so much more energy. It was overpowering the first time I met you. You didn't have Xibo to live with and clip your wings." He brought me closer to him, and it was hard to not want to heal him further, to deceive myself.

Was it compassion or something more?

His long fingers caressed my neck, and he closed his eyes, his hands gently at my face. A flood of memories surged and abated.

"But you are not her. You are alive, and she is gone." He brought his hands back to both sides of my face. "There is so much about you that is impossible to say, only to..." His voice trailed off as he brought his lips to mine.

He gently touched my top lip, then bottom. Asking. His lips so soft. Too comfortable...

"I can't," I whispered, pulling away. If I let him continue...No, I had to stop while I had the strength. He was confusing me with his dead lover.

"I'm sorry..." He stepped away, running his hands through his hair and pacing, a faint shadow following him. The silence between us was terrible. Not even the wind was audible. I was frozen on the floor, Selchuk at the windows. Then he shoved his hands in his pockets and exhaled.

I stood up, keeping a safe distance from him. "I feel something for you, Selchuk. But I cannot do this and stay true to Tarrok."

"We could die on Eloia, and then what? Will you have been glad you stayed loyal?"

"I don't know." I came closer to where he stood. "Would you ask the same of Danis if she were here instead of me?"

"I know how I feel," he said, his voice catching.

"Because I remind you of her?" I had to be careful, he was still grieving. "What if, after you've had years..." I was afraid to say it.

"...Of loving you?"

"No, of letting go of Danis, and you realize that what you feel for me was confused, mixed up with the terrible loss of her?"

He came closer, heat shimmering off his body. "I know how this feels different. I'm aware that you are your own person, Leanora. I see you as you are. How could I not love you?"

My throat went dry, my eyes filling. I folded my arms, taking a step back. "This can't be, Selchuk."

"Not now, maybe." He took one step forward, and I had to walk away while I still had the strength. So he couldn't see how much it hurt to part from him. As soon as we were several feet away, I wanted Selchuk back beside me.

But wasn't that loneliness talking? Because he was here where Tarrok wasn't? Tarrok's face burned in my mind, so bright it was painful. I wiped the moisture of Selchuk from my lips.

"If you feel what I did for Danis, then you have the power to bring Tarrok wherever you wish." His voice hardened. "We'll soon be back on Eloia anyhow, if Xibo's plan goes as he wills it." He leaned against the wall, his face now in profile. "Be careful bringing anyone from Eloia. The physical toll it takes on you is greater than any of us, because your ability for traveling is greater." He gave me a half smile. "Soon your training won't matter, only survival will."

"I'm sorry, Selchuk." And I meant it. I didn't want to make him suffer.

"That's why we're here. In this miserable place that used to be the loveliest of almost all the islands of Hirana."

"What happened?" I asked, drawing my legs into my chest.

"The trees we are sitting inside of used to look like normal trees that you have on Eloia. Leaves, bark, trunks, and they changed with seasons. Even fruit." He laughed. "Now that's something I haven't tasted for a while."

He turned to face me, his hands glowing violet. "When the Yarats came, they wanted to eradicate seasons and make the growing cycle longer. All the trees died here except bushes and ones that were genetically altered to become slow-growing rock. The tallest trees here had large leafy branches that the Yarats cut down for their massive ugly buildings on the Thresils. The trees could not thrive without all their branches and leaves, and they altered their lifecycle so they became the fossilized giants you see now. Hovering between life and death, and never quite existing in either plane."

"You can feel their mournfulness," I said.

"You can," he replied after a time. The wind blew around the tree we sat inside, but it was a distant noise not touching us.

"It will get better," I said, laying a hand lightly on his shoulder.

"I'm fighting and living for that hope I feel inside of you, Leanora." He paused. "Maybe that's what I'm most scared of: losing that hope."

"You will always have it." I took his palms in mine and brought them gently to my lips.

"I wish I had your heart too," he whispered. I released his hands.

He dragged one of the sleep mats some distance from where I sat. I tried to close my eyes, to sleep and not think about both Danis and Selchuk's memories. I concentrated the last of my energies on Tarrok, guilt heating my face.

Tarrok? Hello. Do you hear me? I called out to him with my mind, trying to open the same corridor of communication Selchuk had earlier.

I had betrayed Tarrok; would he want to speak to me now?

I waited, counting the seconds. The silence was eating away at me, making my stomach churn.

Tarrok? Please say something.

I imagined his green face turned toward me, his deep russet eyes and what lay behind the depths of them. I desperately needed to see his face with my newly healed eyes. There was a rightness to his touch that Selchuk didn't have. I focused my whole energy on calling out to him.

Tarrok, please. Are you there?

There was no answer.

Only silence and darkness.

28

LEANORA

The morning light shone through the porthole windows, circular light patterns illuminating the smooth flooring. My back was still sore from the previous day's fall. I rolled onto my side and padded over to where Selchuk lay fast asleep on the floor. His face was completely peaceful, his dark lashes framing his prominent cheeks. I thought about his lips touching mine the night before, and a flush crept up to my face.

My muscles tensed. That wasn't going to happen again.

I walked gingerly away and scratched my wild hair that was sorely in need of washing, braiding it hurriedly back while looking through the windows at the early morning mist blanketing the ground from view. I needed to get outside. I had to either travel out or break the thick resin windows. Half of the bridges were obscured by mist, and I was dizzy with hunger and thirst.

I imagined myself on the rocks by the shore, the fish coming up to greet me. I inhaled and sang low, then sped up the pace to quicken my descent through the spire's walls. The last thing I wanted was to get stuck in the tree because I wasn't moving fast enough. The centrifugal pull started in my abdomen, and within seconds I was whisked outside. I whirled past the bridges and rope walkways, the freezing air assaulting me. Rapidly approaching the ground, I slowed the song, successfully keeping myself from slamming into the rocks.

Finally, a decent landing.

I almost touched the water and grabbed the rocks to keep from slipping into the freezing sea.

Leanora. A familiar bass voice resonated in my head.

Leanora, come home, he said.

"Tarrok!"

The waves lapped against the shore, and there was a long silence. A large wave in the distance was headed for the rocks I stood on, and I jumped down. I waited for it to break, spray hitting my face and dampening my hair. Was hunger making me hear things?

Tarrok, please. If you're there, say something.

I hear you! Is it really you, Leanora? His voice breaking.

I sat on the cold rocks. *I'm coming. I promise.*

I closed my eyes, ignoring my gnawing hunger, pulling my energy toward where I imagined he was.

Tarrok, I'm coming. Tell me where you are.

I'm home. In Hagoth. The battle has already started.

I saw us in the desert and directed myself toward his house, the dunes in the distance and a fresh batch of cacti growing in the surrounding village gardens. I focused my melody there. Inhaling with the song, I directed my body upward into the air, until a tug on my feet brought me back toward the rocks.

"You're not leaving without me," Selchuk said. He floated down to stand beside me.

"You can't stop me."

"I can, but I don't want to. I'm here to help train you." His face was more relaxed than I'd ever seen. It was difficult to be so close to him, everything in me wracked with guilt.

"I'll come right back."

"They'll be here soon to do battle training, to make sure you can transport all of us." His mouth was in a taut line. He reached for me, and I stepped back.

"Last night can't happen again," I said.

He plopped on the rocks beside me, and I made sure to stay standing.

"I woke up, and for the first time, I felt free of everything that happened." He watched me carefully.

"I'm glad you feel better, but I don't," I said, scanning the island for any trace of Inbikh.

"It was just a moment, nothing more." Nothing in his expression made me want to believe him.

"Inbikh!" I called out. "Inbikh!" She chittered and came out of a hole in one of the spires nearby.

"Yes?" she said lazily, stretching.

"Where have you been?" I asked.

"Sleep. Fish. Sleep. So cold here." She climbed up my trousers and found her favorite place inside my sweater. Little beast. I drew her fluffy body out of my sweater.

"Help me get more fish," I said. She chittered but complied.

Selchuk stood by as I called the fish out of the water with his tune, and we all gave them a quick death. We ate in silence for a while, the morning sun warm on our skin as the cold air blew around us. I missed my family. I needed to see all of them, even my pesky younger brother and his strange atonal songs. I was ready to fight for my home.

"When we arrive in Eloia, could battle begin straight away?" I asked.

Selchuk took another bite and turned away from the suns. "You will be one of the Yarats primary targets when they figure out what you can do. They will want to go for the outside lines of battle before attacking the orchester. Xibo will be at the front with a few others. But you are the only one who can make our positions change rapidly."

"Can anyone else do this?"

"Gulnaz and Mikosh can move individuals but only one person at a time. You can transport whole groups of people. No Yarat can do that. We'll rely on you to help keep the chorii moving and following Xibo's instructions if he doesn't get taken out this time."

"How many battles has he been through?" I asked.

"Too many. I don't think he knows how to live anymore, just fight. Gulnaz isn't much better." He said her name without bitterness for the first time. He seemed much older than before, less like the teenagers we both were. He stood up, washing his hands rapidly in the ocean before drying them on his stained trousers. "You'll have to stay close to Mikosh and away from Zer."

My eyes widened. "You know Zer?"

"He trained me when I was starting the healer branch. Xibo is an angel next to Zer."

I tried to keep my face neutral about the man I'd grown up thinking was my father.

"He'll use your anger, Leanora. Let *us* destroy the armada. Don't go solo. You haven't had enough time to train. Know your weakness so that you aren't a liability."

He stood a safe distance from me. "I don't want to lose you. Whatever happens..." His voice wavered, and a single tear streaked down his face. He exhaled and turned away, wiping his face and lifting Inbikh onto his shoulder. I was surprised she let him.

"Let's have some fun before Xibo comes back to torture us." We transported ourselves up to the bridges again, and I liked the feeling of my body in the air, an ease to traveling as my voice sang against the pressure of the wind.

MIKOSH AND GULNAZ materialized on either side of us, the late afternoon suns hazy behind the cloud cover. They weren't eager to be back on Spirthen.

"Remember we're fighting on the same side," Mikosh warned, her black eyebrows raised in concern.

"It won't feel like it." Gulnaz smirked. She closed her eyes and sang, a group of thirty soldiers materializing in the air before touching down on the shoreline, a few perching on the boulders. There was no other clearing of space that could hold all of them. "Half of you with her, and the rest of you with me."

"With *us*." Mikosh's voice was steel as she gestured her group over to her and away from Gulnaz.

Xibo landed in a gust of wind and stood on one of the bridges a few feet above us. "No, that isn't going to work: half of you with Leanora, the rest with Mikosh and Gulnaz." Gulnaz folded her arms, the smirk wiped from her face.

Selchuk nodded at me once and joined them. It was painful to be apart from him, his eyes not leaving my face, their imprint searing me when I looked away.

Xibo floated in the air above all of us. "We're going to create battle conditions as real as we can. But..." He raised a finger to all of us. "No killing, no maiming. Some of you might get injured, and that's why we have Selchuk here. But he'll be fighting too. No fireballs or ice winds. Nothing that will take days to heal."

My group ranged in ages—from a little older than my brother, Alaric, to as old as my father. They beheld me with respect. I shook hands with all of them and was surprised to find only four women in my group of fifteen. Some looked downright scared, especially the younger men. The women, a few years older than me, were fierce looking as they held their hands out, fingers glowing.

I closed my eyes, cataloging their different energies so it would be easier to transport them. Inbikh climbed off me and sat on the rocks closest to the ocean. "I fight too. I on you side." Her white, cat-like body tensed for battle, while her bushy tail flicked back and forth.

"You ready?" I asked them. They all nodded tersely.

I raised our whole group in the air, and they looked at me in wonder as we zoomed off to the opposite side of the island, with Inbikh hanging off an unsuspecting student's shoulder.

"But I didn't give you—" Xibo's voice faded away.

He wasn't going to keep telling us how to fight. We needed an element of surprise. "Stay close by. If you get picked off, always come back to the group. Don't try to go solo unless you have a good chance of disabling another soldier."

"We're going to the highest bridges where we can see best. You ready?" I asked, and they all lifted their hands in the air, fists lighting up. I sang us over to the tops of the spires so we occupied the highest bridges in groups of threes and fours. Immediately a counter-song began, and the other group was rushing at us, knocking my group's members off the bridges or through them. I picked them up, unless they were strong enough to keep themselves afloat in the air.

I had to remember to keep calling the water back into my body at intervals when we started to sink toward the ground. Gulnaz dove through us, Mikosh blasting us with a low energy blast that divided us apart and scattered all of us away from each other. I sang our group to the lower bridges. When our numbers dwindled to half of what we'd started with, I called out to all who remained and transported them down to the ground. We hid in one of the ground-level alcove spires so it would be easier to pick off anyone floating overhead.

"No cheating, Leanora," Xibo yelled from the distance. I sang a gust of wind into him, and he toppled off the bridge.

"I'll cheat if I have to," I whispered to my group. I couldn't imagine the Yarats were following any rules.

Gulnaz and Mikosh spotted us and rushed at me. I brought us up over the ocean, but the crushing weight of their song tether separated me from my group. We collected ourselves and circled around them before two young guys were knocked to the ground. I put my hand out, and it glowed for the first time while I sang a counter-song that my remaining female companions picked up, and Gulnaz and Mikosh disappeared. Selchuk appeared on the bridge above us, jumped down to where I was, and for a moment I forgot whose side he was on.

"Get away from him!" a silver-haired girl yelled.

Selchuk darted at me before I was airborne and shoved me off the bridge. There wasn't a warning, a moment where he hesitated. He'd simply pushed me, his face perfectly relaxed. I was plummeting, heading for a spike below. I remembered in that moment of terror to slow my descent with a soft song, all of us touching down on the ground and rushing into the alcoves.

"*Zoldit.*" I leaned over and called the water into my body. I couldn't believe him.

Not even Gulnaz had tried to push me off the tallest bridge in Spirthen. What if I had been depleted and hadn't been able to stop my fall like the day before, when panic temporarily prevented me from transporting myself?

I looked up to see Selchuk still on the bridge. *Destuba.* Tarrok would have never done that. Not in a million years. Not for a training. Not for any bribe in this world.

I wanted to smash Selchuk's face in, destroy him. I had to turn away before I did something horrid.

I focused back on the two remaining women. "When they come, attack. Don't hold back," I said, keeping very still.

Xibo and his group appeared, and we blasted them with song, acting as one group. He held up one hand. "Enough." He clapped his hands and whistled for the others above to stop fighting. Xibo nodded to Gulnaz, who settled next to me.

"Keep your memories to yourself," I said to her, still seething.

Xibo cleared his throat, inspecting everyone who had gathered into a group of thirty. He nodded at Selchuk, who transported himself down from the bridge. Xibo leaned into me, his face much calmer and less severe. "You have to communicate more with the chorii. But, you're ready. We're leaving tonight for Eloia."

Gulnaz turned to face me, terror reflected in her brown eyes. This was something new.

Selchuk shuffled forward, head bent, looking very guilty.

"I'll push you off a cliff the next chance I get," I said before turning to the whole group. "Let's get out of here." Inbikh jumped into my arms and settled inside my sweater. I didn't wait for Xibo and transported my group back to the Flax islands, leaving the others to rely upon Gulnaz, which gave me a small amount of satisfaction.

Xibo appeared within a few minutes. "You have to bring the rest back." He crossed his arms, waiting for me to bring them back. When I had sung them all over to join us, I avoided Selchuk's gaze.

AT SUNSET on the Flax Islands, we were back in the harvest clearing. Hundreds waited for us in various states of dress. It seemed like Gulnaz had gathered people from all over the planet.

"Are you Leanora?" a woman with a bright red scarf asked. I stood up straighter, ready for what was to come.

"I am. We're leaving soon for Eloia," I said.

Xibo, Selchuk, and Gulnaz appeared on my right.

Mikosh nodded her head. "Let's go."

I paused, taking in the whole group. There were over a hundred people. I had never transported this many. I closed my eyes, calling the water into me. There was no time to worry about the fear of failure looming on the periphery of my mind. No, I had to let go. We needed all hundred or so of us. Or my planet didn't have a chance.

"Hagoth," I said. I closed my eyes and saw my family, Tarrok, our animals. I let them stay in my mind while I started the song that would bring us there. I sang an old Hagothian tune:

> *Dark desert sands,*
> *The drums call to us,*
> *And we answer...*

Woven in the song were the faces of those I loved. Mikosh took my hand, and Gulnaz held the other. Selchuk kept next to Xibo. The whole group became a honeycomb of interconnected people via hands and arms. I stopped singing.

"Tell us when," Mikosh said.

"It is time for us to drive the Yarats out of our galaxies for good. Make sure that you sing with everything you have so we travel quickly!" I sang the water back into my body, leaching every bit of moisture from the soil around us. "I am counting on you. Sing well, my friends. Before you leave the atmosphere, remember, deep breaths!"

I started the song again, six-part harmonies joined with my melody, an immense chorus of sound. The chorii, ordinary men and women who had worked all of their lives, raised their rough voices in response. We rose slowly at first into the air. My hair billowed out behind me. I increased our tempo, and we shot through the skies. A deep weight in my abdomen again, all of us shaking as we spiraled in the air and through the atmosphere. The cold of the outer galaxies pushed on us as we whirled past nebulae.

WITHIN MINUTES of speeding through the galaxies, a tunnel of energy funneled us toward Eloia. I saw the outside of the Trench Wave Galaxy, the single yellow sun guiding me back home. We were almost there, moving much faster than before. I sped up our melody, lowering my voice to the basement tones, several notes sounding at once throughout my body to keep us moving forward. Stars rushed past, and I slowed our tempo when the blue-green surface of Eloia loomed before us. We came into orbit and rushed into the atmosphere. Once we were through, everything I saw was granulated, eventually going black as I plummeted downward.

I remembered to call the water to me, the voices around me faltering without me leading. My energies were back, at least halfway, and I sang louder, now dizzy and disoriented. My mouth was so dry I wasn't certain I could go on much longer. I belted out the song, our voices syncing up again, and I slowed our descent. I tried to ignore the panic in their strained voices. Our melody slowed to a flutter until the earth was warm and soft beneath me. My body gave in to the accumulation of fatigue, and I blacked out.

I AWOKE to the unwelcome sound of Selchuk singing. There were too many people standing over me. His face was too close, and I pushed him away while he was still singing, his hands raised over me. I didn't care if he had restored my energy levels so I could wake up. I didn't want him anywhere near me.

"Are we in Hagoth?" I asked Mikosh, whose eyes were wide, her mouth twitching as she took in the sand stretching out for miles around us.

29

LEANORA

HAGOTH, ELOIA

I closed my eyes, calling the water to me again, the ground beneath me cracking. People nearby gasped and moved back. The single sun was an inferno on my face, and I turned over, my cheek cushioned by the hot sand. I peeled off my sweater to get relief from the burning heat and spit out the grit in my mouth before standing. Mikosh and Selchuk were looking at me like they expected some instruction. Some were still collecting themselves from where we landed, a strange silence cast over all of us. The younger members of our group had eyes wide with fear. I tried to find the source of their terror in the dunes in front of us, shimmering from the heat. Instead, I felt at peace for the first time in weeks.

We were finally in Hagoth.

Gulnaz's face was tense and alert, eyes a pale yellow. "Where do we go?"

We were too far from any of the human settlements, and beyond us were the blue-grey dusty hills that led on to Nedara. A thin sliver in the distance was one of the river tributaries. A pounding started, and dust clouds obscured my view. When the dust settled, a ring of emerald skinned warriors stood around us with their spears. I scanned the skies for ships, but the cloudless sky remained cornflower blue.

The warriors on brown and white ulsos lowered their spears, and one warrior signed to me. "Who are you?"

"Leanora Tela. We're here from Hirana, to help," I said.

They conferred with each other and signed for us to follow. I looked behind us, and all felt calm in the desert. Then it hit me, and I trembled with anticipation. I could see my family. Tarrok. Hold him in my arms.

I needed a moment to collect myself. I inhaled the dusty warmth of Hagoth and followed the warriors, trying to keep from stepping on their heels. Inbikh jumped down from my shoulder, and I stopped when I realized no one else was following.

"Come, let's go," I said. Did they expect me to transport them down below?

For several minutes, I had to keep checking on the steely faces of the Kardush students behind me, Xibo occasionally floating into the air with a short tune before descending back down again. This was a different silence than what we'd had on Hirana. Their worry was palpable.

The warriors led us to a slight depression in the sand. Their ulsos pawed at a spot where a long metal door moved upward and then slid to the side, leading to terraform steps going down. Everyone filed downward quickly, but I lingered on the surface, searching for something familiar in the landscape. A few white dots, Hagothians houses, shimmered in the distance. A peachy-white male ulso hummed to me, making me miss Vali. I followed him down the stairs, keeping my eyes on that unbelievably familiar blue sky. The grate groaned back overhead, a terraform tarp sliding across the top to block out the sun.

Selchuk's face lit up when the ulso sniffed him then licked

his hands. The ulso followed us down the corridor, and my heart sped up. Tarrok. Alaric. My parents. Their faces flashed in my mind, worried expressions from each of them, and I pushed through the group to follow the warriors in the lead.

Each turn we made in the cavern's massive network of tunnels, I expected to find a familiar face. I tried to slow my breaths, but it wasn't working. The deeper we went, the less natural light came through ventilation shafts spaced at intervals. We rounded a circular, small atrium before descending down earthen stairs to another level where amber artificial light cast an orange glow across the tunnels we passed through. Green skinned warriors would occasionally stop to stare at us, but no one remotely familiar.

A swelling started in me as I thought about my family. The further we travelled, the more people were milling about. There were a few brown and red hued Lepidaians—with their characteristic multi-coloured spots—lingering and eating bread in the corridor. I searched the growing crowd of Hagothians for Tarrok, more people streaming down the corridors to peer at us. I couldn't find him, even though my eyes were so perfect they could see every movement. I looked for anyone familiar, and after several sweeps, caught sight of Erena in the sea of green faces.

"Lea-nora!" she yelled.

I ran, throwing my arms around her. Her familiar cinnamon scent was muted but felt like coming back to some resemblance of home.

"Is Tarrok here?" I asked.

"Come, I'll show you where to go." She led me by the hand, swiftly down the next tunnel. There was no mention of how he was. We threaded our way through tunnel after tunnel as people pushed themselves against the walls to let us speed by. She was moving too quickly to have a conversation, the corridors loud with so many people. Every time I turned a corner I was certain this was going to be the moment when I saw him or my family. When I didn't, my heart fell a little. There was a movement at my shoulder when we passed into a less populous area. Mikosh, Gulnaz, Selchuk, and Xibo were tailing me. That was the last thing I needed. But I was too anxious to slow our descent.

We went through three different caverns, ulsos rushed by, and the corridor ended as it opened into an enormous, underground, ring-shaped arena where ulsos were practicing with their trainers around ship repairs. I spotted a Tarrok-shaped man, and I ran toward him. He threw an object for his ulso to catch. The giant animal leapt into the air, catching the ring. When I got close enough, halfway across the arena, I realized I was disturbing their training. The height was right, his face a similar shape. When he turned around, he had a puzzled look. It wasn't Tarrok. His face had none of his warmth.

He wasn't here. I'd waited too long. I hadn't tried hard enough to bring him to me in Hirana. I collapsed inside from the weight of going so long without holding him. I sank to the dirt floor. A terror that I hadn't given voice to spread across my chest and arms, causing me to tremble. *Maybe he is not here.* Why didn't I try to transport him again? *Was he gone, and that's why I heard his voice calling out to me?*

I leaned over to catch my breath. I was weeping as my knees ground into the packed sand. I had let others decide what my life should be instead of choosing for myself. And now he was gone. I had never told him what I needed to. That I really loved him. The swirling black mass of grief was so overwhelming I bent over to stop myself from sobbing. Was all my training and traveling for nothing? I used the sleeves of my blouse to blow my nose. I couldn't stop weeping, and I almost didn't want to. To stop would be to acknowledge that he wasn't here.

I thought it was Selchuk at my side, touching my back

gingerly. The heat of his nearness was comforting. But when I turned, it was not Selchuk.

"Leanora." He lifted me up.

"Oh, Tarrok." His green face was so familiar, beaming at me with such love. I threw my arms around him, and he held me closer than I could ever recall. I felt so foolish but also so relieved that Tarrok was here. I opened my eyes, wrapping myself closer around him to make sure I wasn't hallucinating or imagining this moment. Both our faces were wet. I didn't care that it felt like a thousand people watched us. They faded into a blur, and my tears didn't feel like a weakness, for once. I was whole. All the aches and fatigue had evaporated in that moment. The weight that I had carried with me to Hirana and back was gone.

Tarrok traced my face with his green hands, grinning. "This moment. I must remember forever."

I kissed his dark eyebrows.

"When we take the oath, under the brightan tree, I will sing about this." His russet eyes took me in completely.

But his face was more drawn and angular than I had ever seen. I held him closer to me, afraid to let him go, that he would disappear. I drank in his lemon scent. "I was afraid you'd died."

"I was dying without you," he whispered in my ear. "We all were."

"I missed you horribly," I replied.

He stroked my hair and kissed my forehead again.

A furry muzzle nudged my ear. Vali jumped up to meet me, quickly settling down when he heard Tarrok's voice. "Vali. Down!" He cocked one head to the side, his large, brown ears petal soft.

Inbikh and Radjek clambered over us to give me kisses, and the whole room exploded with well-wishers. I spotted my parents and Alaric. My father had lost weight, and my mother leaned against him, tears running down her pale cheeks. I ran to them, and my father wrapped his arms around all of us.

Alaric was much taller and looked older than his eight years. "I have killed Yarats, you know. I'm a good gunner." He smiled a little, but there was a pain in his deep blue eyes.

"I missed you, little brother." I held him to me.

"You smell like fish," he said.

"Probably," I replied, unsure if I ought to feel embarrassed.

"Don't they bathe on Hirana?" He took a step away from me but didn't let go of my hand.

"Not very often," I said quietly.

A creaking sound came through the cavern, and a ship descended, reeking of oil. The ventilation system whooshed most of the aroma away. Out stepped Bejah and Neelan, with a dozen Gwynbees and two warriors. "They almost had us," Neelan coughed as he stepped down the platform.

Alaric squeezed me close. "Two of our gunners died last night." The sorrow in Alaric's eyes made sense now.

Bejah hugged both of us, her blue face shiny but tired. "I glad you back." She kissed both sides of my face. "We need you here."

I was so happy to hear her voice.

"Those Yarat destuba." Even she was using the Hiranian curse words now. "We must destroy them." Neelan came close in and gave me a light pat on the shoulder before taking Bejah's hand.

The Kardush group formed a perfect clump of stony faces, their eyes all alert.

"We need food. We have to discuss strategy before another attack." Gulnaz was the only one who didn't look worried. She didn't seem confident either. Strangely resigned, leaning against one of the pillars holding up the arena. They were spaced evenly so that the largest ships could still fit into the massive underground space.

Bejah led us out of the arena and up the main arteries toward the dining hall. The chiefs had tables set up with stacks of rolled paper littering the surfaces, where they signed and indicated various points on the charts. Xibo quickly came over to the table, followed by my mother and the rest of our small group.

I studied the charts while they spoke in Hiranian. "How many attacks have we had so far?" I asked in Eloian. Everyone went silent and looked at me.

"Half a dozen. They sometimes fly overhead and nothing happens, or they try to draw us out with their awful music," one of the chiefs said. He looked between Tarrok and me with curiosity.

"How many Yarat ships?" I asked.

"Over twenty," Neelan jumped in.

"We need a plan for the troop formations between ground and air," I said. Tarrok unrolled a map, and everyone gathered around.

"Here the chorii should stand," I said, watching Xibo for objections.

"The ulsos and luoshis need to surround them, to support their sound," Tarrok said.

Xibo stroked his chin and looked to my mom, who was considering it. My mother smiled at me. "It's a good plan, but we have to change our formations frequently."

"The chorii will be in the air, which means that having a set formation won't work," I said.

Gulnaz stepped in. "We have to keep ourselves in four points at all times: you at the head, Mikosh at one point, myself at the other, and that leaves..." She looked between Selchuk and Xibo.

"Selchuk. Saren and I will be at the front lines," Xibo said. His voice brooked no objection.

I didn't like the idea of my mother being in front with Xibo, who took unnecessary risks.

Gulnaz settled next to Drash and curled a finger around his spiky hair. He kissed her cheek, his eyes trained on her face.

"Do we keep anyone back who has healing abilities?" I asked.

My mother broke in. "All of us who are healthy have to be out fighting. Methriel will stay at the hospital with half a dozen healers. Everyone else must go."

"What about Alaric?" I asked.

"He's our best gunner," she said quietly.

"He's too young," I whispered.

"I wish we had the luxury of deciding such things." She sounded so Kardush when she said that. I understood, but I didn't like it.

I considered the map and battle formations, making certain to memorize them, sear them into my brain. "How long have you all been living underground?"

"A few weeks," one of the chiefs said. His face was lined with age.

I drew my hand across the area where the dunes morphed and over to the hills in the east. How long would it take to destroy all the Yarats and their ships? "We have to cover all four corners here, otherwise it's too easy for them to hide in the hills and circle back."

"We can't spread ourselves too far out," Drash countered.

"The Yarats do not care about casualties. Eloians outnumber them troop-wise, but we have fewer ships. You aren't used to this type of fighting," Gulnaz said.

"We can transport our troops more efficiently though. The Yarats don't have an orchester who can do what I can," I said to Gulnaz.

The rest of the room murmured in response. She stayed silent.

"We will be ready," Bejah said. She held up a spear. Mikosh

smiled at me, no doubt happy to see me stand up to Gulnaz in public.

Gulnaz stood, and Drash put his arm around her, rubbing her bare arms, an eerie sensation coming off the two of them. Xibo frowned at them.

"The animals are important, because the Yarats will not expect it," Drash said.

"What if they are hurt?" Mikosh asked.

"We'll heal them." Selchuk said and smiled.

Tarrok cleared his throat. I took his hand.

"The most important thing," my mom said, "is to make sure they don't have access to us here. Avoid going above ground, except when absolutely necessary." She looked around the room. "We meet at first light here tomorrow. Everyone get some rest. If the Yarats should attack tonight, you will hear sirens. Be at the ready."

I looked out at the chorii. "Get something to eat. Check with Methriel and Erena about sleeping places after you've had dinner." The group departed, shuffling out of the room.

Xibo stood in the middle of the room for a while, looking at all of us. "Well, Saren, it is good to see you again." He took her hand and held it for a while, an understanding passing between them as my mother gave Xibo the same icy stare I'd seen him give me when he was disappointed in me.

"I'm glad you brought her back to us." She let go of his hand, glancing back at me. "A little underfed, I see?"

"I have my methods, Saren. And they produce results." He indicated the chorii that was now feasting.

"You are on Eloia now." She kept her gaze on him until he limped off. "Everyone be ready if the alarm goes off tonight, but otherwise you're dismissed until dawn training tomorrow." The rest of the group dispersed, and I was left with a handful of people: the Hiranians not certain where to go, and my family on the other side.

"You look so different." My father hugged me to him. His dark blue eyes were radiant as he smiled at my mother. But there was something else there when he stopped smiling.

"Of course she does." Mom took my hand. "Now let's feed you."

My father threaded his arms through both of ours as we walked out of the room. "It looks like they've been starving you and that will not do for the Eloian side of you."

Alaric and Tarrok followed us out with the ulsos humming behind. Nearby, Gulnaz and Drash's hushed voices were arguing in the corridor to my left.

I let my parents go on and Tarrok stood with me to listen to them. I drew us into the corner where a column kept us from view.

"Go ahead with the plan. It's the only way," Gulnaz whispered.

"We're not destroying Eloia," Drash countered.

"—I don't want to stay if it means—" People walked by, keeping me from hearing them for a few seconds.

"...I'm so tired of fighting.... If Zer doesn't die."

Why would she mention Zer? Goosebumps rose on my skin, and a terror coursed through me. Tarrok took my arm, his eyes wide with concern.

"...If that happens, you know what to do. I can't live with him in charge," Drash said.

Another group of warriors strolled by signing, the ulsos humming, snippets of words coming and going.

"...Whatever happens we have to be together," she said clearly.

"We've been apart too long," Drash said. "Even in death."

I shuddered when they walked toward us. Tarrok leaned in to

kiss me, his lips pausing over mine, asking permission. I kissed him eagerly, making certain there was as little space between us as possible when they passed by. Once they were gone, Tarrok exhaled, bringing me back to standing. "Whatever is going on between them, it isn't good." He kept his hands on my lower back, stroking my ribcage.

"Why mention Zer?" I asked.

"He's a threat?" Tarrok offered.

"What if...she's also in touch with Zer?" I was afraid to say that Gulnaz was a traitor. She'd been treated like one by almost everyone except Xibo.

"Why would she still be here?" Tarrok asked.

"I don't know." I thought about all the times Gulnaz had disappeared. Would she betray us for someone who would destroy her too? It seemed so improbable, with everything she'd been through. I was distracted by a familiar scent in the air.

The aroma of purple Hagothian bread and spicy yams made my stomach prickle with hunger. We followed our noses toward the serving area. Even though I was starving, I ate slowly. I could not get Gulnaz's conversation out of my mind, despite the joy of proper food. When we sat at the communal tables, Drash and Gulnaz were seated far away from anyone else.

There were hundreds seated around tables, ulsos and gwyn-bees running between. My parents joined us, and I tucked into the food, eating six helpings without feeling full. It was the most delicious thing I'd eaten in weeks, even if it was simple Hagothian fare.

"How was it on Hirana?" my brother asked, in between bites of yams.

"Weird," I said.

My parents were stricken.

"No, I mean it was good. It was just really different. The sea is pink there," I said. "And when you touch people's hands some-times their memories play inside you."

"Really?" my father said and stared at my mother. She had definitely not told him about that.

Tarrok indicated with his head that we should go. I looked at my parents and brother. Was this the last time we would sit peacefully like this?

"I'm going to rest for the night," I said. We all embraced, and my mother planted a cool kiss on my cheek.

"I'm glad you're back in one piece." She held onto my fore-arms. "I'm so proud of you. You cannot imagine." She hugged Tarrok and stroked his cheek. That was new. I was guessing there wouldn't be any objections going forward about our marriage.

I followed Tarrok to the outer caverns where it was cooler and up to the next level. Along a stone wall, an entire row of sleeping bunks on the second level were empty. Tarrok lifted me onto the uppermost bunk and climbed in next to me. It was our first time alone in what felt like months. My stomach was a flurry of nerves. And guilt. Did I ruin the moment by telling him about a stupid moment with Selchuk? Or did I let it go because it had been nothing?

Neither of us seemed to know what to do with each other, the yellow lantern backlighting his green face. Every beautiful muscle in his forehead was tensed, and I stroked his face until he relaxed.

I raised my arms, and he held me tight to him. The canvas flaps were closed to allow for some semblance of privacy, while I folded my legs and arms around him. He laughed with pleasure while we peeled off our clothes to our underwear. It wasn't enough.

"Will this do for tonight?" he asked, his eyebrows bouncing in the dim light.

"Only if you're sleeping beside me." He turned, and I moved toward the wall so both of us would fit side by side.

"I missed you more than you could ever know," I said, his head resting on my shoulder while he folded his knees into my legs. I hoped I still didn't reek of fish. I rolled over to face him.

He kissed me full on the lips, a rush of longing suffusing through my entire body. I rose up to meet him, his hips close to mine. He reached into my chest band, and I stopped him.

"Not yet."

He groaned and kissed my neck, folding himself around me, his hands at my chest again.

"Hey!" someone yelled below us. "Some of us are trying to get some sleep. If you can't stop your moaning, go somewhere else."

Tarrok jumped out, ready to kill the person below. I peeked out of the bunk to catch Neelan and Bejah peering up at me. Neelan laughed, and Tarrok soon followed. Only Neelan could get away with talking to Tarrok like that.

"Have a good night, you two," Bejah said, before giggling and pulling Neelan away with her from the bunk suite.

Tarrok and I turned over, facing the earthen wall, his body pressed into mine. There was no chance of a pre-battle tryst. He kept his arms around me, humming a Hagothian lullaby until he snored. I tossed, turned, but couldn't get comfortable once he was asleep.

A dream would start, then stop when I heard his breath rattle. At one point, I was barely dreaming. My arms were being scratched by pine trees, and I couldn't see. Everything went black. We only had my voice guiding us, blindly, through the void. I sang and I felt our bodies rise into the air, but I had no idea where to go, Tarrok's voice muffled in my ear.

. . .

THE SONG MORPHED into a high-pitched wailing. All was dark around us, and Tarrok leapt out of the bunk. My ears were ringing from sirens. All the lights flickered as they blared and everyone hurriedly dressed.

Tarrok held onto me without speaking. He exhaled and pressed his lips to my neck and jaw. "There is never enough time."

"*Kundit mazra ha*, we have to obliterate all the Yarats," I said. I jumped out of the bunk in my underwear. There were piles of clothes next to the bunks. I picked one up, the thick stretchy material similar to what Gulnaz had given me on Hirana, except this shimmered in the dim light. When I expanded it, it formed a solid barrier. I put the top on first, pulling the sleeves over my forearms.

My mother appeared in the doorway in close-fitting battle trousers. I had never seen her wear anything other than dresses. "One ship sighted by patrol. More are coming." She stood there in the yellow lights, not moving, just looking at me like it was the last time she was going to see me. Before she could rush out, I caught her by the sleeve.

"I saw Zer in Asanis."

"I know."

"We have to stop him," I said.

She embraced me, holding me tightly to her. "Everything that you are is greater than his worst crimes. We can be free of him. Much of how this battle goes will depend on you." She kissed my forehead. "Be very brave. Stronger than you have ever been in your short life. More people than you know are counting on you."

The wailing siren was making my hair stand on end, my body now trembling. "I will fight."

"You must do more than that. You must live." She swept my hair off my face and back into its messy braid. "Let the love you feel for all of us fuel you to keep going." She paused there, her hand outstretched, not quite touching me, her black eyes more sorrowful than I had ever seen them. "It is what is in your heart that matters most Leanora." She held me to her again. "I'm proud of the woman you've become. Sing well, my daughter. I will be fighting beside you." She released me and rushed up the corridor and away from where Tarrok and I stood, his arm now around my waist. The room was cold without her in it.

30

TARROK

I t was going to start and end here in the desert.

I reached for the last bit of her long dark hair before she pinned her braids into a crown around her head. The sun had barely inched its way over the horizon, three of our moons glowing beyond the eastern hills leading to Nedara. We couldn't hear the sirens from here. All was eerily quiet, except for the thumping of my heart and the roaring of our ships. Bits of sand blew in my face. It distracted me from the gutting anticipation.

"We need the orchester over here," Xibo said.

"Another minute." Leanora smirked. Her eyes were a deep black, reminding me of her mother. She watched Vali weave between us, the gwynbees standing on the outskirts in a large clump around Radjek and Inbikh, piling into our Talbo-Pii ships. "Vali, stay with Tarrok." She kissed the tip of his brown and white snout, ruffling his mane. I didn't know what to say. How to hold her?

I'm afraid I might lose you.

"Remember to call the water to you at intervals. Even if you're fine," I said instead.

"I'll remember." She was immediately tense. Her eyes changed to a dark green, only briefly, fear pouring off her.

I lifted Leanora into my arms and held her close to me while she wrapped her legs around me. I prayed with all my strength to the moons above that she would come back to me. In her hair was a faint scent of lavender, like when we first met. I was afraid to release her, knowing how painful it would be to let her go. She unwrapped her legs, and I knew if I held her for longer I'd cause a scene.

"This is not the end for all of us," I murmured.

"It's only another fight. We've done this before and we can do it again," she said. The steely set to her mouth made her seem impossibly strong. But in her changing blue-black eyes I saw the same fear I felt. The wind whipped around us, and we pulled our scarves into place.

It was hard to let her go and not know what came next. If this was the end for us, didn't I have something better to say? The wind picked up, and a gust of sand separated us from everyone else momentarily.

"You are everything to me. Please come back alive." I took her hand and kissed it.

She held my face in her hands then kissed both my eyelids. "No crazy bravery. I want to see you under the brightan tree." She held me close to her and kissed me again. "You are the reason I sing," she whispered.

The sand cleared, and everyone was watching us again, Xibo ready to explode. The light crept over the dunes, and the ulsos howled. The last of the fighters piled into ships, and the ulsos and I watched Leanora round up the chorii into the middle of the clearing, the ships taking off around them. The wind kicked up between us, and she rose in the air as the ground swelled with the approach of distant silver Yarat ships gleaming dully in the rising sun.

"Today we fight for our planets, our people, and a future without the Yarats controlling us!" Leanora yelled. "Sing well and fight for what you love!" She sang a new tune I'd never heard, but the others in her group recognized. The chorii harmonized, their varied voices reverberating through my body, making me feel I could lift into the air.

The ships were closer now, artillery firing into the sand.

A team of warriors on ulsos shot exploding harpoons as they darted between the dunes ahead. The chorii's melody, a call and response jaunty tune, was joined by Xibo and Saren rising in the air and soaring toward the Yarat ships. The mozab singing drums bass call and response energized my ulsos' humms.

We were halfway to the dunes when the clashing of weapons and voices distracted the ulsos. I signed to the chiefs and ground warriors. It was time to fight. The bass of the mozab drums rose higher as we pushed forward against the first Yarat chorii darting in and out of our ranks. They were outnumbered, but I had to remember that they had nothing to lose, unlike us.

"Voices raised, keep the ulsos grounded," I signed and yelled.

I roused Vali to humm louder so we supported the melody of the chorii. My spear shot off sparks when it hit a Yarat hovering over me. His face was encased in metal, eyes wild and frenzied. He screamed in his approach, and another warrior joined me to stab him, but his voice continued to press on my skull.

I fell off Vali, who advanced on the singing Yarat. The rest of the warriors raised their voices, and the Yarat jumped on me, knocking me back into the sand. Vali pounced and ripped his throat out, silencing him. A ring of warriors took off, launching exploding sandbags at the approaching Yarat ships before charging off on the ulsos. The ships exploded, and Yarats tumbled out, some on fire, others running at us.

I rolled under them, and Vali heeled next to me so I could jump back on him. We headed back toward the melee.

I yelled with all my might, calling to my fellow warriors. This was our land, our planet. They could not take it from us. I aimed my spears and fired at the Yarats in the air, more bodies littering the sand. A handful of Yarats rose back up after we hit them, in their ragtag armor, fireballs whooshing across at us. Vali stopped and barked loudly. An unseen Yarat jumped behind me, his burning hands closing around my throat.

Leanora

SELCHUK HELD out a harp gun to me. Mikosh strapped it to my back without asking—in her usual fashion. "You only get about three shots before it has to be restrung." She held up her harp, testing the strings before Selchuk strapped it to her back. "It takes a lot of energy out of you when you fire. Only shoot things that can't be destroyed any other way." Mikosh's face took on an excited glow when she tested my harp. "These are way better strings than we had on Hirana."

Selchuk kept his hand out for me to grasp. "I'll be at your side, holding up the song. Sing well, Leanora." He held my hand a little longer, and I pulled him into an embrace, our harp guns making it awkward to reach around each other. He walked away when Gulnaz approached.

Not a single strand of hair was out of place in the high pony-tail that trailed down her back. She still appeared unsettled. "If something happens, all the memories inside me will die." She lowered her voice to a barely perceptible whisper. "Can I transmit them to you? So they are safe?" She was pleading, her eyes a soft brown, her palm outstretched.

"What if we both die?" I asked.

"At least I tried to preserve the history of our people," she said somberly.

I touched my fingertip to her glowing hand, and the memories rushed through and filled me. It was like watching hundreds of pictures scrolling through my mind. They weren't heavy like I had expected; instead they gave me additional energy, while the golden color leached out of her. Gulnaz let go and stared through me, her face peaceful. I'd unburdened her.

"I hope it goes well today. Someday you'll understand..." She looked over her shoulder at Mikosh, who was listening. Her tone changed back to her usual haughtiness. "I am proud to have trained you." She put a hand on my shoulder. "Sing well, Leanora. I will be on your left." She brought her cheek against mine. "Stay close to Mikosh and Selchuk. Do not fight alone." She soared into the air above me, hovering there with her harp strapped to her back.

Mikosh was somber. "Use the harp when it's right. Kill swiftly." She embraced me then held me by the elbows, pain in her dark blue eyes. "You are well defended, my friend. Sing well, Leanora."

"Thank you. Sing well, Mikosh," I replied, relishing that bit of protectiveness from her.

A thrashing melody crashed through my body, quickly morphing into an eerily calm song. It was not our music.

"Start!" Xibo said while rising in the air. "It is our battle now."

I engaged the chorii in the same tune the ulsos hummed in a low bass nearby. Our voices were so strong they made the sand rise in the morning sun.

The moons were fading beyond the hillside, and I changed the melody to a slower-paced tula tune from Lepidaia before nodding to Selchuk to serve counterpart while the body of the chorii rotated with me into the sky. Our volume increased to a swell, our ships zipping overhead, the firing of guns marring the approaching Yarats.

A group of stringy haired Yarat chorii were headed straight for us in dark clothes. Several smashed through our formation. We deftly blasted them away with our voices. The Hagothian singing drums accompanied our melody as we pressed on through the air.

I closed my eyes, hooking into the energy of my chorii, and redirected them upward and away from the three Yarats flying toward us. The Yarat ships' noses were turned back at us, and they darted around us in silver streams, the roaring of their engines deafening. They were shooting at the ground warriors. I brought us higher into the sky, the Yarat chorii rushing at us in dance-like formations that were arranged so quickly I had to throw up counter-songs as they pried at our melody, temporarily breaking the sonic bubble of protection around the nearest Eloian Yelti-Duri. The rust-colored ship circled and flipped back over to scatter the Yarat chorii.

I increased our pace, whisking us away toward the east hills where we were out of the center of action but still close enough to retreat to the dunes if needed. "We need smaller groups to fight them off," I said to the closest cluster of chorii.

I broke us into four groups, reappearing beside a group of Yarats attacking on the ground. We aimed our voices at them.

"Fire!" I yelled, and the chorii sang fireballs into them. A few warriors were still picked off by the Yarats, who incinerated their bodies with their voices.

"No!" I yelled. I took one look at Mikosh, and she nodded to me. I moved us as a complete group toward the western flank where we could continue on the offensive and decoy the Yarats away from the remaining group of warriors.

The Yarat chorii were confused by our disappearance and

descended to the ground, the rest finished off by the Hagothian warriors. Our song's tempo quickened with a new group of Hagothian drummers approaching, their enormous mozab drums resounding throughout the desert. Our combined song grew in intensity until it produced a ball of fire that I aimed at the silver sharp nose of the Yelti-Duri ship that was headed straight toward us.

Upon impact, it continued in its course toward us. The cockpit was cracked, but no other damage was visible.

"*Destuba!*" There wasn't time for me to whisk everyone away again. I aimed my harp and sung a note, sending a green fireball straight to the engine. I transported us swiftly to the ground, while the disemboweled silver ship spun before whirling over us, thick, black smoke trailing behind it before it crashed into a dune. The ground warriors scattered while the ship burned to a crisp on the desert floor.

The Yarat chorii, though smaller than us, took the opportunity to knock my distracted chorii out of the air and to the ground. The ulsos and warriors ran at the Yarats attacking my chorii, but they were too late. I'd forgotten that the harp drained me, and I called the water back into me, the ground cracking beneath me.

I sang us back into the air, flipping and swirling us around so we were harder to hit with artillery while we headed to the outskirts of the battle to take out more ships.

Remember, you only have two shots left.

I looked at Mikosh, who indicated with her head the direction we should go. Gulnaz and Selchuk raised their harps at the approaching ships, which darted away, chasing our ships on the periphery.

I picked up the pace of the song, raising us higher in the sky. Our Talbo-Pii shot at three ships headed straight for us. I split our chorii into four, but the ships were too fast. We had to destroy them now. I pulled back on the harp, the strings biting into my fingers. Gulnaz let the first tone fly, followed by Mikosh with another note in the same chord. I followed up with another tone, and finally Selchuk hit the last ship still standing. The three ships in front of us turned to dust, and the other remaining ships reversed course, firing shots at our two Talbo-Pii, grounding them.

I sunk toward the sand, my energy reserves depleted, spots appearing in my vision. I couldn't be this exhausted so early on. I heard a tune in my ear, coming from Selchuk. *Call the elements to you now!*

I closed my eyes, asking for sustaining energy from the waters deep below the desert's surface, a slow trickle refilling my reserves.

You must do more than fight. I started a new protective tune, Gulnaz picking up first, Mikosh and Selchuk harmonizing while the chorii shifted and joined in. I lifted us higher in the air than any of the ships, and we drilled down on where we were needed most. As we dove down, I'd miscalculated our position.

"*Zoldit!*" I cursed.

Two more of our ships crashed, and the remaining five Yarat ships were headed for our Marwatha. We aimed our song toward protecting the Marwatha and zoomed closer. More Yarat chorii shot forward, picking off four of my young chorii. I struggled to keep my voice going against the harsh metallic tones of the Yarat music. I called the water into my body and felt an uptake in liquid, calling more of it to us, like I had on Maer-lina. Water rushed out of the ground in spouts and broke over the Yarat chorii, felling them while Mikosh whipped up sand to bury them in the dunes beyond. Within seconds it was only us in the air and a pinprick of something coming closer from the horizon.

"Well done," Selchuk called out to us, while Gulnaz remained silent.

A ship was headed straight toward us. I relocated all of us back to the base of the dunes, and the Yarat Yelti-Duri sailed above us, its belly shiny and new as it floated noiselessly by.

"We need another soundwave to tear that ship apart. Two harps!" Mikosh yelled.

Another wave of ships unleashed a new set of musicians more fearsome than the last, and their high-pitched voices pierced my brain. I struggled to keep us in the air. Our chorii was half its original size, and my strength was waning. Then I heard the Hagothian drums, and a fresh idea struck.

"Let's hammer the remaining Yarat ships with our voices," I said.

I extended our protective song, leeching energy from the approaching ships, and synced all our voices, the *haian fusai* channeling through us and speeding up our pace. I narrowed our configuration so that we were all touching shoulders while our voices harmonized.

The ships were so close. We only had one shot; I could hear the smell of their engines.

"Now!" I said, harnessing all that energy into one large shockwave that hit the hulls, metal ripping in angry slashes. Bodies dropped out of the inferno of exploding engines. I wanted them all gone. We had to keep singing to stay airborne and hold back the attackers.

"Keep pushing them back, tearing them apart," I yelled. The chorii sang with me as our voices blew back the last of the Yarats floating in the air, their bodies burning before their charred flesh mixed with the dunes below. We were sinking toward the dunes, a few of the remaining Yarat soldiers weaving in and out of us, picking off my remaining chorii.

They all avoided Gulnaz, and when I turned to her, she held her harp at the ready but didn't sing. I looked out in the distance for Xibo and my mother, but they weren't in the vicinity. I swung around to see if I could locate them.

I was knocked out of the air.

I landed on my back at the top of a dune. I flipped over to face a woman whose cheeks were malleable metal. She zipped in close, her hands around my neck. She was much stronger than me, and the more I resisted, the tighter her grip was. I yanked back and head-butted her, a terrible crack reverberating as our heads made contact. The chorii fell around me, and I sang, struggling against her hands still at my throat, burning my skin. I belted, but no sound came out.

"Give up. You too weak, halfling," she screeched.

I relaxed my body, throwing her off, and punched her in the nose before shoving my fingers in her open eyes. They popped, and she dropped into a heap, writhing. The warriors finished her off. I would have gladly slit her throat myself.

Another Yarat with a shaved head appeared at my side, and I sang a protective layer around us.

"You were supposed to—" The Yarat's voice stopped, a red line across her throat where Gulnaz, now directly above me, had cut it.

A small Yarat ship darted in and out over the dunes. Our Marwatha followed it, smoke trailing from its engines. The Marwatha couldn't stay airborn for long. I raised my voice to collect the handful of our chorii into the air. The Yarats dove at us in a hornet hive of sound. They were hard to anticipate, and I signaled the ulsos to drill down on them with their voices while their warriors shot at them.

It was blazing hot. Waves of heat caused the distant scenery to shimmer: a complete disaster of bodies and smoking rubble. Three more Yarat ships appeared and shot at us. Two more of my chorii fell and were dragged away by ulsos. Xibo shot forward, followed by Gulnaz, and I created a song of cover, whipping up the wind and sand around us to keep our remaining group of five from sight. We rose in the air to higher ground, which didn't stop the hornet of Yarats from following us.

"We need the cover of something," I yelled and started singing again. We whirled past the dunes, where it would be harder to take a direct shot at us if we stayed at the bases. The warriors were circling the remainder of Yarats on the ground, picking them off, while the Yarats barraged us with their screeching treble sound. I whipped up the wind with the chorii to carry the sand that would wipe out the Yarats in front of us.

One Yarat ship was shot down by the grounded Marwatha, smoke still billowing out of its sides. Selchuk plucked his harp while we drilled our song toward the closest Yarat ship. I took out my harp and shot, the Yelti-Duri's entire bulk exploding above us, separating me from the chorii so Selchuk, Mikosh, and I had to take cover.

"That was close," Mikosh said.

The solitary surviving blackYarat Yelti-Duri was moving swiftly toward us. It was rounder and sleeker than any of the ships I'd seen. I kept us on the ground. Gulnaz was nowhere nearby.

"Focus your sound to tear the ship apart," Mikosh yelled, taking out her harp when Selchuk and I shot again.

Our song reverberated, knocking the ship back, but nothing fell apart. We sang harder, our voices barely piercing its hull. Xibo and my mother joined with us, but we were exhausted. The heat pressed on us from all sides, and finally the ship groaned to a stop in front of us. I called the water to me, but there was little in the earth beneath me. Every muscle in my body was aflame.

Three Yarats tumbled out of the black ship, and my mother sprinted through the air to one of the cloaked individuals, their face covered in a metallic material until her song disintegrated it. She paused, and I tried to transport her out of there, but she didn't move. All was quiet except for the wind, the swirling of sand. A small cry broke through. Drash lunged forward and speared a bald Yarat on the left before Gulnaz stabbed him through with her dagger.

Why would she kill her lover? I transported us closer to Gulnaz.

"Remember to join me," Drash yelled before collapsing. Gulnaz held out her knife and it glistened in the sun.

Mikosh pushed me out of the way and blasted Gulnaz with a gust of icy wind.

Xibo ran at Gulnaz. "You cannot—"

"It's over for me," Gulnaz said. "I brought him to you. Now let me go."

"Do what you promised, then," Xibo said, plucking his harp and killing the other cloaked Yarat, leaving one standing. Gulnaz stabbed Xibo, and Mikosh appeared at Gulnaz's side, taking her knife and thrusting it into Gulnaz's ribs. Mikosh held her by the hair, ready to slit her throat.

"Drash, I am coming," Gulnaz said before she died.

Xibo let out a low gurgle and was still. The sand beneath them turned crimson before dust blew over their still bodies. None of it made any sense. Such useless deaths. The ulsos howled, and the last Yarat floated toward us. I ran to Mikosh.

Selchuk was at my back. He grabbed me before I could reach Mikosh. My mother lunged at the last Yarat. She stopped midair and fell in a heap in the sand. I rose in the air toward her, Mikosh immediately beside me. Tarrok screamed in the distance, the ulsos humming a new tune. Then all was silent, the Yarat's metal face familiar as he raised his hands over my mother's still body. I couldn't let him hurt her, but I was frozen in the sand against my will.

His voice was singing to me. *Come home.* The metal on his

face disintegrated. His ebony skin shone in the sun, the light catching his white beard. Zer.

"You finally have the eyesight you always wanted." His face was devoid of any kindness.

"No thanks to you." I tried to sing my mother's body away from him, but Zer was preventing me. I closed my eyes, vocalizing louder, her prone body in front of me after a few seconds.

"Don't, Leanora." Selchuk held me from rising back into the air.

"You truly are my daughter." Zer soared toward me, his hands splayed. "Join me."

I brought my harp up, backing away from the pull of his voice, Selchuk falling down.

Zer's song knocked the harp to the ground. The remaining chorii sang a counter-melody, and he fought against us, my mother stirring at my feet. She was murmuring something. I reached for her, straining to stay by her side on the ground.

"Stay with me—don't go," I pleaded.

"I am always with you. Keep fighting..." she whispered. Then her eyes opened, her gaze somewhere beyond me. "You will go on. And we will be better than what we were."

"Mom—don't." I took her limp hand in mine.

Zer's glowing hand came up, fire shooting from his fingers in a stream of fire toward her. Selchuk rose to intercept...

He was too late.

My mother slowly turned to ash. Her hand crumbling in mine as she disintegrated. Her eyes were the last to go. There was nothing left to hold, her ashes mixing with the sand.

Zer soared through the air, one hand at my throat, the other wrapped around my braids, keeping my head back. "It is only you and me now," he said, making it impossible for me to turn around. Those cold, digital eyes of his bored into me. His voice stabbed at the back of my head as I fought against him with everything in me, dozens whirling around us, unable to pierce Zer's song.

I closed my eyes, calling the harp from its location on the ground to my hands. I yanked my head back from him, a fist of hair still in his grasp. I plucked the harp, singing an inferno of fire through him. Zer's eyes were wide with terror, his entire body engulfed in flame while he screamed. I backed away, his voice reverberating through my head. My eyes burned, a searing at the back of my sockets, black dots filling my vision.

Mikosh held onto me with Selchuk, the remaining chorii and warriors knocking Zer's song out of my head. Tarrok held Zer, my sight slowly darkening as I saw Tarrok raise a spear and stab Zer over and over again until he dropped to the sand.

All was completely still. The gray figures before me morphed into dark shadows that stopped moving.

"Zer's dead now. It's over," Mikosh yelled. "Anyone remaining loyal to the Yarats will be killed!"

The air around me reeked of engine oil, and the hot earth scorched my arms and face. I wondered if this was the point where I could stop fighting? Or would it never end? My head was lifted up, something cool at my lips. I coughed and tried to move, but my body wouldn't cooperate. Hot grains of sand spilled over my burning face. At least that was familiar.

Selchuk sang beside me in the burning sand while ulsos hummed before everything went peacefully black.

I WOKE up to Vali whining and turning me over in the hot sand. I could not see a single pinprick of light, but the sun was killing every nerve fiber in my skin.

A soothing chanting behind me accompanied someone lifting my weary body from the ground while wet material was placed over my eyes. My body pitched from side to side, but it felt like someone else's body. Did anything I'd fought for matter now that Mom and so many were gone?

Zer's wretched song reverberated in my brain, modulating up and down, the bass notes jarring. I had heard it before, when Dex was still alive.

It was the song that had accompanied the Mists that had blinded us the first time. Zer had punished me for not joining him.

For choosing my mother.

Her voice echoed in my mind.

Remember.

She said those words to me the first time I'd lost her in Asanis.

You are always my daughter. No one can take that from us.

Would I let Zer win now that she was dead?

PART IV

"Understanding and peace will always overcome conflict and hatred." —*Kardush-waiya*, Article No. 2.

31

LEANORA

The darkness was drowning me. I rolled over, blinked my eyes, hoping that my sight would come back to me. All the while feeling in a deeper part of myself that it was gone. I should have been thankful I wouldn't have to see another dead body if I didn't want to.

But was this better?

A wailing persisted that I couldn't pinpoint, because there was no depth to the sound, no gradations to get an idea of distance. The aroma of sweat and blood wafted in and out. Another voice joined the song of mourning. They were almost a third of a pitch apart, harmonizing their distress.

My mouth was sandpaper dry, even after all the water they'd given me. Tarrok's lemon scent was the only familiar aroma around me. Someone with a familiar, calm *urijniak* walked into the room. They muttered, and I rolled away from them. I wasn't ready to discuss the murkiness pressing on me. Couldn't I sleep now that it was over?

Stars, didn't I deserve as much?

Their voices moved away, curving like liquid in a barrel.

Sleep became impossible when I kept trying to decipher the hundreds of voices, only to get exhausted with the effort. The last hours were on constant replay in my mind.

My mother in her last moments. She reached for me, turning to ash before I could stop it.

Nothing in this supposedly powerful body of mine could reverse that. Selchuk and I combined could not bring her back. The shame stung.

Zer's blood was on my hands like I'd feared on Hirana. Yet there was no satisfaction in knowing he was gone. By blinding me he had the last word. I was again trapped in the evil that lingered in his wake. Why hadn't I tried to kill him in Asanis?

Because I wasn't a killer.

Did that make this my fault?

I'm so sorry, Mom.

You must live, I heard her whisper next to me. *Let your love fuel you to keep going.*

People rushed by in intermittent moments of mental clarity. The passage of time was no longer delineated for me by light. I was certain we were underground, but I needed a breeze, something to help me believe I wasn't trapped in this oppressive shadowland. I rose and tripped over Vali, who whined. His voice was more piercing than ever before.

"It's okay, boy. You'll be my eyes now." He nuzzled my hand, his snout feeling more enormous than usual. I buried my face in his mane.

"It's me, Mikosh." She put a hand on my bare shoulder, trying to steady me. When a flow of memories came, she let go. "How you feeling?"

"I can't see," I said.

"I know." She helped me to stand. Voices murmured in the corner. I didn't like not knowing who else was there. She must have done something, because the area around us hushed.

"The Yarats are all gone." Mikosh's low voice had a new gentleness to it. She touched a fingertip to my bare shoulder and showed me the desert littered with bodies as people buried the dead, the skies cobalt and clear of ships. The memory ended when she withdrew a hand. "I can't believe I killed Gulnaz."

"I'd have killed her myself, if I'd had the chance," I said. All my emotions were in a vice grip locked inside of me. Gulnaz had watched the Yarats kill almost everyone she knew, why would she have helped them by killing Drash and then Xibo? It didn't make any sense, until I remembered her memories.

She had been ready to die all along.

"I hated her. But for all the wrong reasons." Mikosh laughed bitterly. She put a hand gently on my back. "Selchuk can heal you."

"No one can heal me," I whispered.

"It will feel like that, at first." She dropped her voice to a whisper. "My mom wasn't half as nice as yours, when she died. Be patient with yourself." She put her arm around me. "I wasn't, and it made it worse."

"Xibo wouldn't let you," I said.

"Maybe." She sounded as glum as I felt. "But he's gone too, and you and Selchuk are all I have left." She kept a hand on my back, only withdrawing when a commotion started in the distance. "You're in a bad way, Leanora. Don't give up. We're here for you."

"I'll try," I said without feeling it.

There was a bustle at the door, and after a few exchanges, I recognized Bejah's voice. She sucked in her breath and exhaled noisily, her face close to mine. "Leanora, you need Erena and Selchuk. All the healers will get together and fix this." Her familiar accent lifted me temporarily out of the well of pity I was stuck in.

Selchuk sang some distance away. I wasn't certain I wanted

him to heal me. It would be too painful if there was nothing he could do. Then the image of my mother sailed before me, so helpless. I walked a few steps to shake myself out of it. I needed my eyesight so my mind stopped replaying images from the battle.

Tarrok's scent preceded him standing next to me. He took me in his arms, stroking my back. The room went silent, no more mumbling or shuffling of feet. I was afraid of what I might say. His large hands were heavy at my back.

Would he love me if I was a burden?

I felt nothing in his arms besides the tang of citrus on his breath. My mom was gone. She had been the center of everything I knew. All I had thought about for the last few weeks had been him. I had wasted the few moments she and I had left before she died.

"Zer is dead. I made sure," Tarrok said. His lips were at my brow. "We'll get this right." Him holding me wasn't enough anymore. His large hands awkwardly held mine, and it was my fault. "Leanora? What is it?"

I could not see what his face wanted to tell me. His voice was hollow.

Why did I want to get away from the one person who had always comforted me?

"Leanora, do you hear me?" His voice cracked.

"I hear you," I said, whisper-soft.

"Please say something." He was crying. "I can't believe... this... I'm sorry... For this... For her. I don't know how to make it better." I held him tight to me, his steady inhalations calming me.

He didn't understand that losing my eyesight was nothing compared to missing her. I could never regain all those years without her. It was a loss I didn't comprehend. He couldn't make up for this void eroding everything good inside of me.

He stroked my hair, grabbing a brush and gently running it through the tangles as best as he could. "You need a bath," he said. Normally this would make me laugh. It was strange to turn up the corners of my mouth without knowing how my expression affected him, if at all.

"Come, let's go," he said, taking my outer tunic off.

"I can undress myself." I stopped him, feeling a sudden need for privacy. "Bejah can help me."

He called out for her and guided me toward the water chambers. Vali whined behind him and nuzzled me onto his back. I fell off, too wobbly. I climbed back up and held onto Vali's reins while we shuffled through so many corridors I lost track. Finally, a cool wind blew past us, water echoing in the cavern. I had always felt better immersed in water.

I forgot Tarrok was there or simply didn't care and removed all my clothing.

"You go get clean on the men's side," Bejah said, and Tarrok shuffled off.

Vali jumped in ahead of me, barking and splashing.

"Don't do the same, you'll get hurt." Bejah helped me down the stone ramp into the water. It had a light current that tugged at my calves. Bejah kept one hand outstretched to me, so I knew where she was. The water was perfectly cool and swirled around my body pleasantly. A diverted underground river, it seemed. I let the current wash over me, everything inside me churning. I couldn't wash it all away.

"We've been through a lot, haven't we?" I asked Bejah.

"We have."

Vali shook water droplets all over us. I sunk below the surface, letting my body become buoyant while all sound temporarily muffled before scenes from the battle shuffled across my mind. Vali pushed me back to the surface; I held onto his fur and inhaled the fresh air.

"He wants to play." Bejah had her hand on my upper arm. "I can send him back to Tarrok."

"He can stay. I'm not ready to leave."

"We can stay as long as you like."

"Only a little while longer." A twisty melody, sad but jarring started again in my head. It was so loud I thought Bejah might hear it too. It was the last song Zer sang. I would gladly kill him again if it meant I never had to hear that tune again. I sank below the surface into a deeper blackness, surrounded by liquid where I couldn't get any sense of depth. I came up for air when I couldn't take the silence of the water anymore.

I hummed Selchuk's fish melody, my voice scratchy and painful. It was better than hearing Zer's voice in my head. I stopped when Bejah's shoulder touched mine.

"It's bad, what happened," she whispered. "You see anything now?"

"Nothing."

"Maybe it come back?"

"I like how dark everything is right now. Like I feel inside." I wanted to release the seizure of emotion inside me, to feel something other than the terrible weight that pressed on me whenever I inhaled.

"I sorry." She hugged me then. It was awkward to feel her bare breasts against mine. But she'd grown up in Nedara where that wouldn't have been weird. "I sad too to lose Saren. She so good to me. To everyone. We feel the loss a long, long time." I took her hand, and she guided me out of the water.

There were folded bits of linen to dry off on. I slowly shrugged into a soft jumpsuit that was lighter than what I had been wearing in battle.

"I'll never wear those again," I said and left my battle clothes in a heap on the stone floor.

Vali snuffled my legs and leaned into me, his nose edging me toward him. I fell onto his massive back, and he carried me out of the room, Tarrok calling after us.

"Where are you going?" He caught up to us after a few seconds.

"I have no idea." I settled into a rhythm on Vali's back, afraid to say what I wanted. Afraid that if I said it, then it would really be over. I had been fighting for so long. Now, all the fight had been extinguished.

Can I give up, or at least join everyone who is gone too?

Living like this is worse than dying.

The aroma of roasted yams and curried bread wafted along the corridor. My stomach didn't growl or show any indication that it was empty. I held onto Vali's mane while he steered us onward. I had not a hope in the world that roasted yams would change anything.

32

LEANORA

I held on tighter to Vali while he navigated the sea of people we waded through. The cacophony of voices obscured my ability to pick out a single voice. Spices and roasted vegetables made my stomach flop, and I didn't know if I wanted to eat. Did I wait for help, ask someone in the throng...?

I ran into someone and fell off Vali.

"It's me," Tarrok whispered in my ear, startling me. "Sorry."

"You have to tell me you're there."

"I will."

I hopped off Vali and followed him toward the nearest setting of food, Tarrok's hand on my elbow.

"We can sit here—let me help you." Tarrok directed me toward the bench and table.

I hated being helpless. I knocked my shins on the bench. Halfway through drinking, a clamor of voices was around me.

"Are you okay?"

"Do you need anything?"

"Shouldn't you be in the healing center?"

I couldn't identify anyone. My appetite evaporated. I was about to take a bite of bread, and Vali snatched it away.

"Bejah here." Her voice cut through the clamor. "We go. I have food." She steered me out of the communal kitchen and away from the noise of too many voices and scents I could not identify.

I held onto Vali and his smoky fur aroma, keeping one hand in front to sweep for unseen hazards in the corridor. Bejah handed me a piece of bread.

There is a great destiny for you. I saw my mother again, except we were back at Pakopaikka. I reached for her, but my hands went through her and all was black. Then she appeared again, the memory of her turning to ash in my arms.

I kept rewinding, reviewing what I could have done differently. How I could have shot Zer earlier with the harp. The scene of my shooting Zer then played again and again, until the scent of lemons was nearby.

"Tarrok?" I asked.

"He's coming." It sounded like Mikosh.

"Mikosh?"

She didn't say anything.

"She can't see you," Bejah said. "You have to say."

"You didn't," Mikosh said.

"My voice don't sound like everyone here. So it easy to know," Bejah said calmly.

"Sorry," Mikosh said. "I'll stay here at the back while Bejah continues ahead, okay, Leanora?"

"Thanks for letting me know. Where are we going?"

"We're taking you outside. There's no reason to stay underground, right?" Mikosh's voice was overly cheery. We walked up a ramp and I heard the groaning of the grate above us.

"There are about fifteen steps up. You want to hold onto me and we count them together?" Mikosh asked.

"She be fine," Bejah said.

Vali squeezed closer to me, and I held onto Mikosh's arm, counting with her until I felt the cool breeze. It had to be close to nighttime. We stood there, waiting for something. No one was saying anything, and a sickeningly sweet scent, like rotten fruit mixed with dung, carried on the breeze. There were shouts in the distance. People probably burying the dead.

"Come follow me dis way." Bejah hummed a light and airy tune.

Mikosh stayed at my elbow, Vali still at my left side. He hummed with Bejah, and I heard the familiar chittering of gwynbees.

"Ya-rii! It you!" Inbikh and Radjek yelled as they climbed over me. Their claws scratched at my exposed neck while their fluffy tails waved in my face.

"Calm down, calm down," I said, relieved they were okay. My mood lightened in their noisy chatter as they licked the sides of my neck and face before purring loudly. "We sorry, sorry."

"Very sorry, sorry." Their voices were mournful as their tails flicked back and forth. I thought of my brother and father in that moment, how I hadn't seen them yet. I was dreading that reunion.

Vali yowled when we stopped, and a door slid open, Bejah taking over for Mikosh. "Come dis way, almos' there." Inside it smelled like someone familiar: piney and earthen. It was cooler than outside. I put my palms out, and the walls were cool stone. Tarrok's house. The hope of familiarity lightened my mood. I bumped into furniture before Mikosh steered me toward the back of the room and into a seat. The furniture morphed to my sitting position, and I remembered Dex complaining about it when we first came to Hagoth. He was gone now too.

"I'll stay with Leanora and send the gwynbees if we need anything else." Tarrok's voice was hard to pinpoint in the large room. He put his arm gently around my waist, and one hand soothed a tension knot in my shoulder, gently kneading it, the gwynbees jumping off.

"Bye, Leanora, we'll see you tomorrow," Mikosh said.

Bejah kissed me on the cheek. "See you tomorrow. Yes?"

"Yes." I tried to sound normal.

When the door closed, Tarrok folded me into his arms, his face next to mine. The citrus scent of him was faint, and there was something else I detected. Was it fear?

A palpable void sat in the weird space between us. I was too empty and light in his arms. That had never happened before. I held him closer and still nothing. His hands came to massage my back, but there was none of the usual feelings I had hoped I would feel once the war was over. The only true sensation was his warmth, and Vali panting beside us. He released me, keeping his arm draped around my shoulder.

"She was the loveliest person I'd ever known, besides you. I wish there was a way to turn this around."

"Was I not strong enough?" I asked.

"You are the mightiest person I know." He held me closer to him, rocking me side to side. He hummed a tune that was low and mournful, perfectly fitting the mood. A small spiral of doubt and recrimination combined with the battle scene came flashing back. It dug a wound so deep I didn't know how I was going to climb out of it. Tarrok fell silent.

"I feel so..." All the breath left me. I expected I would cry, but I couldn't. "Please hold me."

He folded me into his large chest. He didn't realize he was holding onto nothing. I was not here. A vital part of me had been taken away with my eyes. I trembled with the terrible knowledge that I would never see my mother again. A rustling started in the distance, and the door creaked when it slid across the floor.

"Leanora!" Alaric called out to me. Vali ran, his nails clicking on the stone floor, humming appreciatively while the gwynbees chittered.

Another familiar scent, of musk and sweet spices, followed Alaric's voice. Tarrok rose, still holding my hand. "She cannot see you."

"Let me tell them," I said.

"I heard," my father said, his bread scent enveloping me as he embraced me.

I wanted to feel glad to not be an orphan. But it was overwhelming to know they were also grieving and I could not comfort them. They had been my family for less than a year. Now we had to find a way forward without her.

"You fought so hard. She was so proud." My father kissed me on the cheek. His face was wet.

Alaric sniffled. I reached out for him clumsily, and he clung to my waist. I still couldn't cry with him. Vali hummed while the gwynbees sang softly. It was one of Alaric's tunes from months ago. After a few minutes, Alaric breathed more deeply, his tears subsiding as he kept one arm around my waist, guiding us to a larger seat.

"I'm sorry about your eyes..." His voice trailed off. The distance from everyone's emotions weighed on me. The healer in me wanted to help them, but I could not heal myself. I had to escape all the swirling emotions that were choking me. Breathing deeply eased it only a little: a new spiral inside me twisting painfully in my chest.

"I don't know what we'll do without Mom," Alaric said, hugging me again. I needed him to stop talking about her, because the image of her dying flickered before me again.

The room hushed for several minutes. The lack of noise was deafening.

Tarrok broke the gnawing silence. "We both saw everything.

This will take time. You are welcome to stay here or with Erena, if that's better. We'll go back to Lepidaia in a few days." Tarrok put his hand on my knee. "I am here for you, please know that."

My father took my hand. "We will have a ceremony for her crossing over when you're ready, Leanora." He cleared his throat before continuing. "Alaric and I are helping Neelan and his crew repair the Marwatha." My father put his arm around me. "You have joined a new fight, I think."

"I am useless now," My voice was barely a whisper.

"Never useless. Just exhausted." My father put his meaty arm around me and kissed the top of my head. "You saved us from the Yarats. You inspired so many people to fight."

My father let go of me, and he and Tarrok went to the back of the room, whispering. Alaric settled against me, singing a wordless song with the animals.

"I'm cold," I said.

He brought a blanket, and the warmth of his weight settled against me, a comfort after being separated. At least I had him, I reminded myself. But my body did not want comfort. It wanted to punish me endlessly. Alaric's head rested on my shoulder, and his breathing eased as I drifted into an uneasy sleep.

I was back in battle, everything flying around me as my vision flickered in and out. I was trying to sing but only dry sobs came, and I couldn't make the music direct anyone where they were supposed to go. Even in my dreams I was powerless.

"SHE'S STILL ASLEEP," Tarrok whispered.

Wet fur was the first thing I smelled when I woke up. My stomach was a heavy rock of pain, my head spinning. I needed water. I stood up too quickly and knocked over the table.

A cedar scent wafted into the room.

Selchuk.

I was not ready for him.

"Morning, Leanora. I'm here...to see what I can do about your...vision." His voice was tired. "Here, let me..."

"I've got her. I'm here, Leanora." Tarrok swiftly guided me through the room. I couldn't hear any of our animals.

Selchuk was in front of me. "Can I try to heal you?"

"You can try," I said to him. The heat of him was close.

He took my hand and inspected my exposed skin. I was wearing thin desert robes and felt colder next to him. He guided me toward one of the chairs, which he forced into a lounging position. "Let's see what's going on." A blanket was thrown around me.

"Tarrok will wrap you in this. I need to check the flow of blood and your energy levels to make sure that Zer didn't transmit a substance he was testing." He took my wrist and tapped at the pulse points, holding them up. He drew his fingers across my palm and stopped, tapping again. I wished I could see what he was doing.

After several minutes he was so quiet I suspected he was avoiding the truth. "We can't tell the extent of the damage. It might be irreversible. I don't know. If it's anything like what he used to...anyway, we won't worry about that now."

Selchuk took both my hands, singing softly. He stopped. "Tarrok, I need your voice." Selchuk started again, singing several rounds of a searching song, the melody simple but piercing.

> *Alar-ye moshe ze ru ke*
> *alar-ye moshe ze ru ke,*
> *sofi selet bosk bet yet,*
> *sofi selet yusk rew yet.*
> *Maiyele maiyele mosh,*

maiyele maiyele mosh ye...

A warmth started from behind my eyes, and then I could move them again. The deep pain was slowly drawn out of the center of my abdomen. A new sensation, like water trickling through my legs and arms flowed forward to my hands and feet. There was a tiny pinprick of light, a subtle change in my vision. My body lighter, my stomach finally calm.

Selchuk finished the song, his voice tying up the last of the melody. He let go of my hands, his warmth retreating.

He leaned in close to me, his breath on my cheek. "Open your eyes."

"Aren't they open?" I asked.

"Only a little."

He kept nearby, a warmth against my eyes, but I couldn't open my lids further; the air outside made me tear up. I closed them again.

"What did you see, if anything?" Selchuk asked.

"A small bit of light."

He put his hand on my arm. "He planted an airborne energy burst in you. I extracted it with Tarrok's help but need to research repairing the blood vessels in your eyes that were damaged. The toxin settles into muscles and works slowly on them. I saw this with a few other fighters I've healed." He patted me on the shoulder. "When you're better, I could use another healer here to help me."

"That's impossible without any vision."

"Maybe that will change," Selchuk said softly.

"Thank you, Sel," I said, taking his hand then letting it go, words failing me.

He walked away, his cedar scent fading.

"Thank you, Selchuk," Tarrok said and closed the door.

I stood up and paced the room, memorizing where everything

was so I didn't keep tripping. Tarrok took my arm, joining me on my circuit around the room.

"I wish I liked him," he said. "He looks at you in that way that makes me want to hit him." We stopped walking.

"Oh, Tarrok." I leaned against him out of habit. "There's nothing between Sel and me."

"There's something coming from him. You can't deny that." He let go of me.

"He did like me on Hirana...but he isn't for me." A small smile played at the corners of my mouth. "He is in love with a woman who is dead. I remind him of her. That's all."

"Oh." Tarrok sounded glum.

My heart was bounding in my chest. I didn't want to have this conversation. "Is this really about me being blind?"

He didn't move, and the whole room was palpably tense.

"Will you stop loving me if I never see again?" I asked, my voice barely above a whisper.

Still nothing from him.

"Because if that's what's upsetting you...tell me. Don't make this about Selchuk."

He instantly softened against me, taking my hand and kissing me. I rose against him.

"I want to be the one to heal you. To bring you back from this...place." Tarrok smoothed back my hair, his lips at my temple before bringing his arms around my waist, kneeling so his head was at my belly, raising my robes to kiss me there.

"The Kardush are so cold, even though they're the good guys." He guided me to a seat next to him that expanded to fit both of us. "I saw how crazy they were when they fought, not flinching when they spilled someone's blood..." His voice trailed off. "I want them all gone so we can have our planet back."

A new thought occurred to me. "What if we're supposed to teach them?" There was a moment of hope that buoyed me, like I felt when I was with my mom at Pakopaikka, the stones beneath us glowing orange from the hearth. The memory faded quickly from my mind. All was inky before me again.

A familiar emptiness, like a river swelling in the midst of a storm, flowed into me. I didn't believe I could teach anyone.

I reached for Tarrok, my body calling for him. His warmth and heat could take away this abyss. I brought him closer, unsure exactly what I was doing as I took my tunic off. He stroked my bare chest, his hands moving lower, asking. A small fire was ignited, and I wanted to lay everything bare with him. I pressed my lips to his, letting the rest of my clothes drop. I was suddenly cold. The fire went out as fast as it had started.

A heaviness pressed on me again, my desire extinguished. I grabbed my tunic and threw it over my head, walking away before I did something stupid that could hurt us both.

I wanted him, but it was to cover my anguish. That wasn't a good reason for giving myself completely over to him. I pushed past him, toward where I thought the door was.

"Where are you going?" he asked.

"Out," I said, gropping for the sliding door.

"You'll get hurt," he said.

"Vali's with me."

He didn't ask to come with me.

I was strangely disappointed. I found the door and slid it swiftly open. I wandered out into the early morning warmth, holding tight to Vali's reins. The tinkling of women's jewelry and ankle bells rang out as people passed by—no one speaking to me.

I might as well have been a ghost.

I wanted Mom back that minute, just to tell her that I loved her, that I was proud she was my mother.

I brought Vali closer so I could hop onto his back. I shook the reins so he would go faster. The faster he went, the less I would feel. We rode on in the full sun, Vali panting beneath me but continuing onward at a steady pace as the battle scenes played before me, ships zooming in and out. For the first time, I didn't try to stop them. I had decided I would ride all day until they stopped playing in my head. Or until Vali had enough. I let the heat of the day burn into my battle-worn skin.

33

LEANORA

The midday sun engulfed me in its dry heat, my mouth acidic and parched. Calling the water back into my body only worked for so long and did nothing for Vali. I couldn't ride endlessly in the desert, trudging up and down dunes, wearing myself out to beat my grief. Nor could I go back to Tarrok's old house. There were too many memories there. I clicked my heels against Vali, ready to change course back to my family. But if I spent time with Alaric and Dad I would dwell on her again.

No, I had to do something to keep the swirl of memories at bay.

Keep riding then.

"To Erena's healing center," I said to Vali.

He barked and changed course. The sun bore down on us, and I was eager to seek shelter indoors, my exposed neck and face blistering. There was no breeze to give me a sense of what was around us. The only sound was his paws trudging through sand and the jangling of his reins. Closer to settlements, I heard various voices talking amongst themselves. Once I approached, they were silent. I dismounted from Vali, holding onto his reins to follow him inside. I detected the faint hint of cinnamon and cedar once we'd slid the door shut behind us.

"Leanora, hello." Erena embraced me. "Sorry, I forgot to say it is Erena." She giggled. "Selchuk, Leanora's here for you." Though her cheerfulness was annoying, I couldn't keep a sour face around her. The sound of her bells departing helped me to orient where she was.

"You've decided to help us after all?" Selchuk asked. He murmured to Vali, and I was glad for the distance that blindness brought between us. I didn't want to see his face and remember Spirthen.

"I'll try," I said.

"We're short-handed. You missed your dad, he was on the nightshift here. You could work on some of the worse cases, if you feel up to it." He paused, clearing his throat. "After I take a look at you." He clicked his teeth at Vali. "Come on, boy, let's bring you both over here."

I sat down, releasing Vali's reins. Selchuk put one hand on my arm. "What's changed?" He held a warm object in front of my face that radiated a comfortable heat across my cheekbones, and my eyes warmed up, the pinpricks of light starting again. When he moved away the sensation stopped.

"What is it?" I asked.

"The eyes aren't changing at all. Your irises remain black, which worries me. There's been so much trauma I have to wait for the swelling to go down."

A wailing started in the back of the room, and the entire center reeked of blood.

"Leanora, we need your help with this woman."

I couldn't even help myself. Vali put his back under my hand, making it easy to find his reins. No chance to mull over my uselessness. Vali brought me to the groaning woman then settled at my feet.

"There's an internal injury I can't find," Selchuk said.

I followed the suffering as it pulsed through the woman's *urij-niak*. I touched her forearm. I was sucked into the moment that a Yarat had planted a bursting injury inside her. Her memories came to me, very faintly. She had been lying in the desert, pinned under her dead comrades, unable to call for help. I exposed the energy, seeking it out through her veins and capillaries. It was a twisting, aggressive energy. I felt it pulling on me, sucking me into its vortex.

I was reminded of Zer, his silver eyes flashing in front of my black vision momentarily. The sounds of the healing center silenced me, and the song I was singing died on my tongue. I couldn't push the pain out of the patient, who writhed under my touch. My torment was drowning me, the darkness within her consuming me to the point where I could not feel the ground under me.

"Leanora, sing what you started. Continue," Selchuk whispered. "Heal her."

Vali hummed, and his muzzle was against my arm, picking up the tune I had lost. I sang again, pushing my diaphragm against its will to sing onward, though my lungs burned. A light flared within me, and I pushed this light toward the patient, singing the damaged energies out of her body.

She stopped wailing, and her inhalations resumed an easy, unlabored rise and fall. A weight within me lifted a little. I wished I could see her face. She relaxed, and I checked her bandages, which were wet and needed changing.

"Bandages, Vali." He trotted off and brought me back clean dressings for her.

"I knew you could do it." Selchuk embraced me. "You are still a great healer." There was such pride and familiarity in his voice. I eased myself out of his grasp. He took the dressings from my hands and started applying them.

When we were finished, my head spun, and the dizziness kept me from being able to orient myself. I had to sit down. Vali led me to the closest cot. The darkness returned like an inky stain on my heart, and it was hard to breathe. I bent over, inhaling deeply, but it wasn't working. My lungs tightened further.

"Are you all right Leanora?" Selchuk asked.

The low, raw voice of Erena broke through, and she helped me to my feet while Selchuk whispered instructions to her. He was busy. There were plenty of injured. I needed to help them, not sit about doing nothing. But it felt like all the oxygen inside me was squeezing out.

Pinpricks started in my vision then faded. Vali hummed a comforting song, his yowls more melodic and happier than usual. Selchuk's song washed over me, my vision flickering with tiny bits of light. My breathing was less labored, my lungs relaxing.

It felt like bright, welcome sunshine was above and around me for several minutes. Then the sensation subsided, and the noise of the busy room surrounded me. It was a relief to feel present again.

"You can't heal in one sitting. It will take time." Selchuk's voice was almost a whisper. "Don't punish yourself for what happened."

Small paws tapped at my arm. "It I, Inbikh." Another set of paws. "It me, Radjek," his tinny voice said. They both made chittering noises and climbed on my shoulders, winding their tails along my back.

More gwynbees swarmed around me. Normally all their chatter was funny, but right now it was too much. I needed to be able to hear, to orient myself.

"Quiet," I said to them.

They hushed.

"I need to help the injured. Can you help me, Inbikh, Radjek, and the rest of you?" I asked.

They chittered in acknowledgement, and I turned toward where Selchuk had last been. "Put us to work," I said.

His hand was on my arm. "If you feel up to it, we have a lot of supplies that need refilling and sorting. When Bejah and Mikosh arrive, you all can help them with that."

"Good. Something simple." I grinned. "That won't take too much out of me."

He laughed. "Yes. But remember you can still call the water back into your body when you're ready."

"When I'm ready," I said. All the liquid still felt like it had been drained out of me. I inhabited a lone island of sadness. However, I couldn't let it consume me. Self-destruction wasn't an option. I did not want to become like Gulnaz. There had to be a better way.

Were all the memories she deposited in me weighing on me as well? A stirring at the back of the healing center distracted me. When I heard Mikosh and Bejah's voices, arguing amongst themselves, I called out to them.

"Bejah, Mikosh!" I said, hoping I was facing them.

"Oh, Leanora," Mikosh said.

"We were looking for you!" Bejah said.

I joined them in sorting the vials.

"Are you and Neelan...um...together?" Mikosh asked Bejah.

"Of course!" Bejah's voice was so happy.

"Good, good." I heard the sense of loss in Mikosh about how to navigate these things. "He is a good pilot...and builder."

"We get you someone too," Bejah offered.

This I had to hear. Mikosh had never mentioned any romantic interests. If anything, she'd acted awkward discussing anything that involved love.

"Get me someone?" Her accent was really thick, dragging on the consonants. "What kind of *someone*?"

"A lover?" I offered, my face heating up. It was frustrating to not see how she responded. "Say something—I can't see your face," I said.

"Right. Well...umm...a lover. Maybe I just need to get used to things here. Good food, nice animals. And then, maybe I see an Eloian who looks nice. We talk...I don't know." There was a long awkward silence, no one moving. "I feel so strange," Mikosh said.

"You look strange too. Need to loosen you up. Get you to dance with a Hagothian." Bejah was cackling. I hated not seeing their faces.

"Absolutely not. Those warriors are scary," Mikosh said. "They remind me of Yarats."

We laughed for a while, because Mikosh being afraid of anyone was news to all of us. She'd been through so many battles, it was inconceivable. It was just like Bejah to bring out this other side of her.

MY BACK ACHED after hours of sorting, pouring, often misgauging where something had to go and needing help cleaning up broken vials and powders. At least I'd done something and not moped about.

"Bye, Leanora. I see you tomorrow?" Erena asked me at the door. I couldn't keep avoiding Tarrok the rest of the day.

"Yes," I agreed, and she kissed me on the forehead before departing.

The door creaked, and Vali barked, but no one approached us, so I helped Selchuk carry storage vials out.

"You could be fit for travel in a week," Selchuk said. He leaned in closer to me. "What do you say?"

"I'm not ready to go back to Lepidaia," I said.

"They'll need a healer in Lepidaia. I'm going too." He was hiding something from me. "I think you should..." His voice trailed off.

The scent of citrus was strong in the air. Vali bolted toward Tarrok.

"It's Tarrok," his voice boomed.

"I know," I said, figuring he was again asserting himself in front of Selchuk.

"You ready to go home?" Tarrok asked.

"It depends," I said. I wanted to go home with him as my old, seeing self. Not who I was now.

"See you tomorrow," Selchuk called out to me and shuffled off.

There was a weighty silence now that the healing center was empty.

"I'm not going to leave without you, Leanora." Tarrok took my hand in his and brought me close to him, cradling my head against his chest, his heartbeat steady in my ear. It was his steadiness that I loved. Vali hummed, and some of the pinpricks came back to me, giving variance and dimension to the light in the room. When Vali stopped, the light faded.

"Let's go back to your old house," I said. "Can I help you cook?"

There was a lift in his voice. "Of course. Just lay off chopping vegetables for a bit." We both chuckled. It felt good to smile, to feel that something normal like dinner was happening.

When we ate the soup we'd made together, the gwynbees flitted about to help me. Every time a replay of the battle came back to me, or a failure from my training, I reminded myself: *The war is over. You can let go.*

Our respite was broken by the arrival of my father and brother.

"We still have food, I think?" I turned to where I thought Tarrok was.

"We already ate," my father said. "We just came to check and see how you are. And to share some news." Dad's voice wobbled a little. He took a deep breath and moved to where I could feel him within inches of me. We had never spoken about difficult things without Mom. He came closer and started to say something, cleared his throat, then inhaled deeply again. Whatever he had to say it wasn't good.

"She knew...your mother, that is...that she...didn't have very long with us," Dad finally said, his voice cracking.

The words crept in slowly, spreading like a slow burn through me, licking flames at my stomach and then settling like a rock in my intestines. I let go of him. "What do you mean?"

The entire room was full of static as he exhaled deeply, his breath catching. The silence was worse than whatever he had to say.

"You cannot stay silent, because there is nothing coming from you," I yelled. "What did she know?" I hit the cushion next to us. "Say something."

It was her foreboding of the future. The ability that had kept her from rescuing me on my journey from Asanis to Lepidaia. "It's why she sent me away," I said finally. "And kept Alaric with Tarrok."

His voice was thick with sorrow. "She didn't know when or how. She just had a sense it was coming and that you needed to be ready to fight. And that Alaric should keep to a separate ship, in case Zer knew about him."

I smacked the couch. "She told you, and not me or Alaric? This might have been useful information."

"Leonora, please. Try to understand that she had to tell me. She knew it would destroy me if I didn't know it was coming. You and Alaric are young. If you knew, you would concentrate only on protecting her. At least she died for the right reasons." He sniffed and put his arm around me.

He sounded so at peace. I did not understand it.

I was yelling again, my voice operating almost independently from my body. "You don't know how it was on Hirana, how hard I worked and for what? For her to die...to lose her twice...all those years with Zer and not ever knowing about you or Alaric." I walked away from him, Vali immediately at my side, guiding me across the room and away from Dad.

My voice caught, my nostrils filled, but no tears came. My insides were stone. "You need to go."

"Leanora, this wasn't—"

"Go!" I yelled.

I was silent until he left. I wanted to break things, but if I did I'd only hurt myself.

"Why didn't he tell me earlier?" I asked Tarrok. I sunk to the floor, my head on my knees. He sat beside me, a hand gingerly on my shoulder.

"He isn't thinking clearly. None of us are." Tarrok put his arm around me, his warmth comforting. "This is what war does. It tries to tear us all apart. We have to fight to keep going, to move on and believe that things will be better." He sounded like my mom.

I put my head in my hands and willed myself to cry. But no tears came. Outside, the chimes of women walking by echoed as ulsos barked and everyone went on like the war had never happened.

34

TARROK

I had watched her struggle for a week. Refusing to go back to the healing center. I knew it could take months before she was herself, but everything was compounded by her being a hero. Everyone knew who she was. She was the girl who helped us take down the Yarats. To go from hero to...emotionally crippled, blinded again...I wanted to mend it, but I didn't know how. I couldn't keep watching her staring blankly past me, petting Vali, refusing to eat more than a few mouthfuls.

To me, she was the same person I'd always known and loved, though deeply wounded. How did I get her to see that she was still beloved?

She leaned against Vali who hummed while she was silent, her dark, limp hair hanging to her waist. At least her sun burns had faded, the natural red patterns dancing across her bronze skin. I sat next to her, and she didn't move.

"What?" she asked.

"It will get better, Leanora," I said.

"I want to feel that," she replied.

Once again, my words weren't enough. They were stale in

my mouth, and my actions were all too late. Or wrong. Or not what she needed.

I slid the slate door open and checked on the ulsos running around with Vali. Carki stayed beside me like glue. Only her sister, Dona, was content to go running about with Alaric and Possum. I searched the golden dunes, always different from day to day. I loved Hagoth, but coming back proved it wasn't my home anymore. I missed the ocean, the green in the hillsides.

At some point we had to go back to Lepidaia. I was useless in Hagoth. In Lepidaia we could rebuild. Start our lives again.

I took in the cacti gardens and stream running behind the crops. It had been so long since I'd been able to enjoy the sparse landscape. As people milled about, asking how I was, my sign language was rusty. I never thought that coming back would feel so disorienting. But I had chosen to leave for a reason. I held onto the reins of four ulsos and ran the circuit of my neighborhood, keeping us clear of the cacti gardens. It was good for our skies to be ours again. I just wished Leanora felt some relief now that the war was over.

Would it ever be over for her?

I clicked my tongue, guiding the ulsos back to the stables. I needed to bring Leanora outside or persuade her to do something other than vegetating inside.

Leanora

TARROK CLEARED his throat and stood in front of me, the scent of lemons mixed with sweat. I put my hands out, and he took both of them.

"Methriel told me a group is going to Lepidaia tomorrow...." He exhaled. "I didn't expect that he would say this to you now, not when..." His voice trailed off. "...And make things worse."

"I needed to know," I said, squeezing his rough palms. "I can't go back to Lepidaia."

"We have to wait for the crossing-over ceremony here anyway." Tarrok kissed my hand. "When do you want to go back to Lepidaia?"

"I don't know. Everything in me feels wrong and upside down." I reached for his face and felt air. "I don't even know where you are." I exhaled and felt like I would cry, but something was stopping me again. I tried to release all the tension into the air, call the water to me, restore something inside me, but I couldn't do it. I exhaled and tried again, sipping in my breath slowly. Nothing.

"Do you want me to bring Selchuk?" he asked.

"He already checked me yesterday. Plus, there are much worse cases."

"You may not be bleeding, but you can't see. You barely eat." He put his arms gently around me, his large palms on my back holding me closer than I could recall him doing before. "You're disappearing, and I am afraid I'm going to lose you." A horrible silence sat between us. His worry palpable.

My breath caught, a lump forming in my throat. I couldn't stop the swell of emotion as I leaned over, gasping sobs wracking my body. All the sorrow leaked out of me with him. It was terrible to feel this and not see him, to not know with my eyes what he was feeling. I reached for him, and he was there so quickly, his arms around me. I clung to him, my tears quickly wetting his shoulder.

Such love coursed through him as he kissed my cheeks.

"Keep crying, Leanora, let it all out."

We stayed like that for a while, both of us eventually weeping for what we had lost, finally on the same plane of emotional existence. I could have reached into his mind then, to give him my memory, to let him hold it for me. But I didn't have the strength. I stood up, wiping the tears off my face. He took my hand, and I let him lead me back into the bedroom where I'd refused to sleep since arriving at his house. A woman sang faintly outside, and for once the song felt like it reached me on a deeper level, like music had before the war.

"Can we stay longer?" I asked.

"Of course."

"I'm afraid to see Lepidaia again." He brought his arms around me from behind and kissed my cheek. "But it's stupid to worry about it, because I can't see!" I raised my arms to the air and accidentally smacked him in the face. "Sorry."

He leaned down, gently approaching my face to kiss my cheek. "Maybe you will see again."

"Will it change how you feel about me if I don't?" I asked.

He groaned and rolled away from me. "Leanora, why would you think that?" He took my hands again, clearing his throat, the ensuing silence comfortable and familiar. His voice was lower, softer than usual. "I could never leave you. Whether or not you see me is not who we are. I love you for this." He put his hand on my collarbone. "And this." He put his fingers to my mouth. "All of the things inside of you, that is what I love." He let go of me. "I just hope that you feel the same, that the time on Hirana didn't change your feelings about us."

I thought back to Selchuk, the moment he pushed me off the bridge. Turning in the air to witness that he wasn't worried or even concerned. Selchuk's face was completely calm as I fell, too calm in fact. Like he knew that the war was more important than what he felt for me. The mist rose up to obscure his face as I'd sung myself to the ground before the velocity of my fall killed me.

I reached for Tarrok, and he took me in his arms, the warmth of him more than temperature, more than just a feeling. He was a strong oak in the middle of winter, a deep reservoir of constancy. He was joy and home and security all in one feeling that I could sing better than I could say. But I had to tell him what was inside of me, or he'd never know.

"My feelings for you could never change, Tarrok," I said. "I want to be with you. I have always known that since we made our way through Nedara and I thought I was going to die there. You are what kept me fighting to come home." I wiped tears off my cheeks, my voice catching, my affection deeper than I'd ever experienced before. "You're the reason I want to keep going."

He came closer, and I folded myself around him, pressing all of me against him. His long fingers caressed my bare arms. We said very little, only humming tunes back and forth, until we fell asleep in each other's arms.

THE NIGHT AIR the next evening was punctuated by the mozab drums that vibrated in my chest. I stood in a large procession between Tarrok and Alaric. Pipes and string instruments followed the mozab's beat, pounding the sadness out of our souls. Tarrok and I had our arms entwined around each other's waists. The names of all the dead were read aloud, followed by the drums beating their names into the wind.

"Melzi Fugata," a male voice spoke.

Another chorus of deep drums.

"Drash Ugiz," a woman's voice called out.

"Dextor Markor," the Hagothian man said. I saw my childhood friend that last day when I brought him back to Hagoth, so hopeful and eager to rescue Asanis from Zer's tyranny.

Then a woman's voice sang a low and mournful song, followed by members of the chorii and the hearing Hagothians and Nedarans. We all sang with the woman, harmonizing the melody she had begun. The drums softly accompanied the procession of voices. The music died down. One last name remained. I had been waiting for it, and the release that hearing her name might bring. The bass drums started first, followed by the hand drums, then a series of four more Hagothian drums, each incrementally higher in pitch. Then they stopped.

"Saren Tela."

The music began again, the drums harmonizing. This time I heard my voice, almost outside of my body, calling her soul to a place of peace. My song wove in with Mikosh's alto voice. Bejah and Neelan joined in, followed by Tarrok and Selchuk, all our voices melding into one. The rest of the crowd around us hummed in unison with the ulsos and gwynbees as the song came to a climax, the crescendo of instruments resonating through our bodies.

Then the song stopped, and my father and Alaric were behind me, hugging me, all of our faces wet with tears. The night wind blew past us, and we stood there for a while, acknowledging how much we'd lost to drive the Yarats out.

IT TOOK us a while to get back to Tarrok's house, where we ate mooncakes and drank too much plum wine. All the sugar made my stomach acidic. I sat there with Tarrok after everyone left and wondered what it would be like to hear the sea again. The draw of my home didn't feel painful anymore.

"We can go back," I said.

Tarrok shifted behind me, like he wasn't certain I was serious. "Really?" he asked.

"Don't act so shocked. There's work to do."

He stood up, shooing Vali away. "We can take the next Marwatha trip with Neelan."

"I wish I felt comfortable transporting all of us there," I said.

He folded me in his arms. "There's time. At some point you'll feel comfortable traveling again. It doesn't have to be today. Or this year." He held me in his arms, and we rocked back and forth in the oversized terraform chair. It felt good to know that I had him through everything.

The front door slid open, and our peace was shattered. Gwynbees rushed in with the ulsos carrying food from Erena's house.

"Sweet foods, sweet, foods. Yum, yum, yum," the gwynbees sang.

"Gwynbees," Tarrok groaned, and I slipped out of his arms, moving toward the savory smell of delicacies they'd brought in.

WET-AL-WIRTH

TAKING ON THE LIGHT

I want to love you, but I can't.
I need to touch you, but we won't.
I have to hold you, but I stop.

Until your eyes shine, so bright.
when our fingers touch I'll know.
I have to leave you when you say...
I'm going far away.

I need to hold you, even now.
that look killing me more.
Moons appear, crested and broken,
too much ocean and not enough you.

Light rises over crystal waters,
I cling to what I have left of you:
even if it's only the memory of this song.

—Selchuk's Song for Leanora (translated from Hiranian)

35

LEANORA

After the war, we expected our lives to settle neatly back into place. I would often stop in the middle of the day at Pakopaikka, listening to a patient's heartbeat, and wonder what my mother would think. I would turn to ask her or even tell one of the Kardush healers to send for her. They would stand there, hushed voices stopping their healing music. In the silence, I remembered she wasn't there. I had to consciously remind myself that there were others to ask and that somewhere, if only in memory, she still existed. I owed it to myself to keep loving the people around me.

TWO MONTHS after our arrival back in Lepidaia, Tarrok and I stood under a tree with golden leaves and white blossoms. It was a young brightan tree, the last one standing that had blooms. The rest of the Lepidaian forest around us was charred; only saplings survived. The guitars started first, followed by reed flutes and hand drums. I relished the sound of instruments after coming back from Hirana. The voices of the hundreds around us soared

336

with the music. It was the song of two planets that had become united as one.

Mikosh and Bejah broke in, joined by Neelan as their voices crooned my mother's song.

Come meet me there,
under the brightan tree
I'm afraid you've been
gone too long at sea.
You'll forget why
you did love me

Come meet me there
away from the salt night air
we'll entwine under starry night...

The faint outlines of figures came into view as the song crescendoed. The figures morphed from dark grays to smudges of color that changed into a grainy view of the crowd that had gathered for our ceremony. Their faces shone under the tree, everyone's clothes becoming a muted array of blues, yellows and reds before me in the dusk light. It had been months since I'd been able to see anything. Selchuk smiled, his blue eyes glowing. I looked at him. *How can I see in this moment?* He smiled wider, his teeth flashing and kept singing, turning his attention to Mikosh who stood beside him. I let him have his miraculous moment and gazed back at Tarrok.

The music died down to a gentle hum as my father raised his arms. He stood between us, saying the words of the promise we were to echo back to each other.

Step by step, mile by mile.
I will follow thee with soul, heart and body.

My words are thine, my heart is thine.
Forever bound, forever free in loving thee.

We repeated the words together, and my father smiled through tears. I felt a glow behind him. A woman with dark hair and white robes floated above him. She stood out clearly compared to the hazy figures before me, so beautiful and young. At first, I did not recognize her until she joined in the song, her voice like tinkling bells.

It was my mother. She floated forward to me, her hands outstretched before kissing my forehead. It felt like a wet mist on my face, her touch so light, the lavender scent of her on the breeze. Her spirit had come to join us. Then she faded away, her voice singing on around us.

I looked down at my billowing white skirt and the yellow tunic Bejah had found in a burned-out house. Tarrok adjusted the wreath of sea flowers adorning our heads, took my hand, and guided us down the hill. Alaric held a torch that lit our way, a wide grin on his young face. Everyone followed us in a singing procession of torches as we walked the hillside back into Lepidaia proper, the city looking almost normal from this distance.

My eyesight faded the further we got from the brightan tree. I could see occasional flashes of light, but mostly a dull gray that modulated with the nearness of light. Tarrok patiently helped me step over boulders and paving stones.

We danced and ate with our guests, many who were new arrivals from Asanis and Nedara. Hope surged within us that we had not felt since coming back. Tarrok lifted me into the air, and a new lightness spread across my chest as I felt such deep affection for him. I didn't think I could love him more than I already did. But my heart swelled every time he kissed me. Rings of people danced in the square, which was cracked in places. We were all a little grimy, but we kept dancing. At the point in the night when the bride and groom are meant to leave, I took Tarrok's hand. "We really need to bathe in the sea."

"Is that all we're doing?" he teased me.

I couldn't help giggling. Yes, there was still some of the teenager left in me.

He led me to where the northern promenade had been. All five moons glowed in the sky. I followed them out to the water, leaving my clothes in the sand. All the worry of the past months receded in the warm tide. Was I ready for this?

"Wait for me!" Tarrok splashed after me.

"We're just bathing, silly," I said, trembling with excitement and nerves.

He came close to me, all of him unclothed and ready.

I held him close to me, and we were slow coming to know each other in this way. We had all of our lives, after all.

THE END

WWW.BRITTAJENSEN.COM

DID YOU ENJOY HIRANA'S WAR?

A few sentences on Amazon or Goodreads help a lot!
E-mail us at murasakipress at gmail dot com with your published review and join our VIP list as thanks for your time!

PLEASE WRITE A BOOK REVIEW!

ACCESS BONUS CONTENT HERE

https://britta-jensen.com/2020/04/29/hiranas-war-bonuses

ACKNOWLEDGMENTS

First thanks go to my editor, Brad Wilson, for staying with me through the Eloia Born series. I couldn't think of a better person to help me extricate the experience of having been surrounded by war. Danke Brad, for your patience, guidance and friendship!

I'm thankful to my Heavenly Father for inspiration and blessing me with incredible family+friends. *Domo arigatou goza-imasu* to: Jodie and Mark Jensen, editors Rachel Carter and Dave Aretha, cover-design wizard Stuart Bache; Fatima Humphreys, Alexis Clukey, *Super-frauen-power-freunde*-Sarah Jobst, *manga takk* to Devin Mattson; Yalonda Willhoite, Amanda Bennett, Stephanie Macias Gibson, Dwayne Goetzel, Flor Salcedo, Charlie Reed, Chris Kerns, Catherine Castoro, Amelie Corner, Gogi Hale, Gina Springer Shirley, Rebekah Bushey, Milo Jens and many more friends. This book would not have been possible without the generous support of: William Summitt, Jan Hansen, Audrey Reader, Cynthia Pierron, Vince & Connie Hazen, Andy Bailey; wonderful book blogger, MJ Vaughn, my students and readers like you. Thank you!

ABOUT THE AUTHOR

Britta Jensen's debut novel, *Eloia Born* was long-listed for the Exeter Novel Prize. Her short stories were short-listed for the *Henshaw Press* and *Fiction Factory* prizes. After living overseas in Japan, South Korea and Germany for twenty-two years, her multi-lingual, cross-cultural heritage influences her writing in myriad ways.

She now lives in Austin, TX where she is working on her next novel, *Orphan Pods*, beside her two (almost) real-life gwynbees. Britta has taught writing to adults & teens for the past fifteen years, edits books and essays with the Writing Consultancy, and entertains teens and adults in her writing classes and on her book tours.

Get free stories, writing advice, and access bonus content on her website www.brittajensen.com.

   goodreads.com/7731330.Britta_Jensen

   amazon.com/author/britta.jensen

   instagram.com/britta.murasakipress

   twitter.com/Britta_Murasaki

   facebook.com/Britta.murasakipress

CPSIA information can be obtained
at www.ICGtesting.com
Printed in the USA
JSHW030853231220
10436JS00003B/22

9 781732 899544